A] FROM HELL

The Angel Chronicles

Mick Norman

ANGELS FROM HELL
The Angel Chronicles
by
Mick Norman
ISBN 1 871592 43 7

First published 1973/4 in 4 volumes by
New English Library
This edition published 1994
by
CREATION BOOKS
83, Clerkenwell Road
London EC1
Tel: 071-430-9878
Fax: 071-242-5527

*This is for James and Stewart,
whose enthusiasm has enabled the Phoenix
to rise once more from the ashes.*

CONTENTS

INTRODUCTION

"They both thought there had been something in the ideals of the old Angry Brigade, but that was long over. Now there really wasn't that much left."   **– Mick Norman.**

Looking back, I'd say '74 was a frustrating year. I was stuck at Sheerwater Secondary School, geared up in Oxford bags and tank tops. The really hip kids wore cherry red DMs but all I had was a pair of army boots and some wedges. Glam rock was on the wane and there was a 50-50 chance of being turned away from the cinnema when I lied about my age as I attempted to get into Bruce Lee flicks.

At school, various paperbacks were passed around beneath the desks. The *Confessions* books were popular, but I got bored with those and took to reading youth cult stuff by Richard Allen and Peter Cave. One day I wandered into Woolworths and left with a copy of *Guardian Angels* by Mick Norman. At the time, I thought it was the strangest novel I'd ever read. Set in the near future, it was both apocalyptic and politically progressive.

Today, Mick Norman's biker books appear prophetic, imbued as they are with the atmosphere of a country reeling under the blows of unemployment and economic decline. Re-reading these novels makes the boom years of the '80s seem like a mirage, an unrealisable dream. It's as if the imminent threat of political violence and social breakdown has been hanging over us for the past twenty years.

Mick Norman is a pen-name of Laurence James, who was an editor at New English Library in the early '70s. *Angels From Hell* was his first book. Back in the '70s, New English Library was a creative hot-house. The legendary Peter Haining was in charge of the operation. Under his direction, a handful of talented authors, such as James Moffat, hacked out endless youthsploitation novels using dozens of different pseudonynms.

As an editor, Laurence James cleaned up innumerable manuscripts prior to publication, including such million-sellers as *Skinhead* and *Suedehead*. However, with the success of his Hell's Angels books, he swapped his editorial duties for the life of a professional writer. Soon he was churning out a slew of cowboy novels under a string of pen-names. More recently, Laurence has been hard at work as James Axler, authoring the excellent *Deathlands* survivalist series. But that's another story. Right now, all you need to do is sit back and enjoy the best biker books ever written...

– Stewart Home.

Book One:

ANGELS FROM HELL

1. SEE HOW THEY RUN

Jerry Richardson was blind.

He was sitting on the dusty plush seat of the last train on the Dartford Loop Line. It was Thursday night, drizzling slightly, as his carriage eased out of the heights of Lewisham Station.

Jerry swayed in his seat when the train rocked, first gently to the right, then more sharply to the left, picking up speed towards the next station – Hither Green. He heard the slight change of tone as they passed over the High Street. Another couple of minutes and he'd be home.

Tonight's meeting of the London Buddhist Society had been an unusually noisy one. A vocal minority had tried to push through a motion to send a message of support to the Home Secretary in his stand against the Permissive Socialists and all their fringe elements. Although he was opposed to all the violence in the country, Jerry had voted against the motion, saying he felt that it was contrary to the ideals of the Society to take part in active involvement in politics.

Gravity tugged him softly forwards in his seat as the driver started to apply his brakes just outside the station. Jerry picked up his briefcase and stood up.

'I say.' A hesitant voice – eager to do good, but afraid of giving offence. This is Hither Green. Is this the station you wanted?'

Jerry nodded his thanks briefly to his would-be Samaritan and felt for the door handle as the train edged to a stop.

He hardly needed his stick to help him find his way along the platform. It was familiar territory. It was nearly four years since he had moved into his digs in Longhurst Road and the whole area was now familiar to him. He could almost visualise the platform stretching ahead of him and then the long slope down to where the ticket-collector would be waiting.

Suddenly his stick brushed against something that shouldn't have been there. Over-confidence had robbed him of that edge of reflex speed that might have saved him. Before he could check his forward momentum, his knee had caught whatever it was and he fell helplessly forwards, dropping his case as he flung out his hands to try and save his face. He stumbled onwards and down, jarring his wrist and scraping his chin on the platform concrete. As his body rolled over there was a splintering crack and then he was still.

Strong hands pulled him to his feet and dusted him down, while someone else handed him his case. He heard a woman's voice, thick with anger. 'Those damn hooligans, tipping over the bench. The boy's blind you know. Blind. That's why he tripped. He couldn't see the bench so he fell over it. Bastards! He's blind, you know. And he's broken his stick, poor boy. Picking on someone who can't see. If only Hayes would do something instead of just bloody talking. Here [to Jerry], do you want me to see you home; with your stick gone and you being...'

'Blind!' interrupted Jerry, recovering himself, but still shaken by his fall. 'Look, I'm all right now and I can get home without a stick. Would you please now leave me alone?' The subdued mutterings of outrage faded down the platform and Jerry was left alone. He wiped the thread of blood that he could feel running down his chin, adjusted his suit, feeling a tear at the knee, and stood still for a moment, getting his bearings before he continued home.

It probably had been a gang of young thugs. Maybe he should have voted to support George Hayes and his policy of harsh reaction against the suedeheads, the terrace boys, the motor-bike gangs and the long-hairs. The violence and killings by young hoodlums had reached its anarchistic peak in the eighty-six deaths at the Salisbury Festival of Heavy Rock. The massive slaughter had been caused, according to the television, by rival gangs of Hell's Angels fighting and by the death on stage of two members of an Afro group, shot, so left-wing troublemakers insisted, by army units sent in by worried politicians. Whoever started it, the blood of the gentle people had been liberally spilt in an unprecedented tribute to political paranoia.

His thoughts had carried him halfway down the steep slope. He stopped walking for a moment, his hand brushing against the chalky brickwork. The echo of his footsteps died away slowly and there was silence; or as near silence as one could get in that part of London. There was the steady hum of arterial traffic on both Lee High Road and Lewisham High Road. A crackle of voices somewhere on his left and a girl giggling. High at the edge of his hearing there was the rumble of several high-powered motor-cycles. The absence of whistling meant that the ticket-collector hadn't bothered to wait for him and had taken his bicycle and rushed off home.

Jerry moved on.

Hither Green is effectively split into two by the Southern Region railway lines. The station stands high and tunnels connect the platforms to a gloomy subterranean passage which runs under the tracks and joins Staplehurst Road to Nightingale Grove. This constricting, narrow tunnel is the only way to get from one side of the area to the other. During the day it is a busy, echoing thoroughfare. At night it is a gloomy, noisesome catacomb. Late at night it is best avoided; it is then that the somewhat drunk use it to hide the emptying of their bladders. It is then that the very drunk retch up their overloads of bile and stale alcohol.

Jerry reached the bottom of the incline and stopped before turning to his right. His hand held the angle of the brickwork; if he had put out his left hand he would have touched the other side of the passage. It is barely five feet wide, seven feet high and is about two hundred feet long. He suddenly realised that the sound of the bikes was much louder.

Louder and nearer.

Jerry started to move as quickly as he could along the tunnel, nearly falling as his hand missed the wall and found only space. It was the slope up to the next platform. He was nearly halfway along.

The air around him began to vibrate with the thunder of machines and he heard the screeching of tyres on asphalt as a corner was taken too fast. He could also hear the sirens of police patrols.

Another platform entrance passed. Jerry was panicking now. If he could have thought more clearly he would have turned into one of those tunnels and he would have been safe from the impending noise.

The leading bike was right at the opening of the passage and Jerry's breath sobbed raggedly in his throat. He knew what was licking at his heels. He had been told of the tabloid pictures; he had heard enough T.V. pundits fulminating about the social evil; he had heard the strained tones of George Hayes talking of stamping out the useless pariahs. Normal people didn't ride unsilenced motorbikes in a pack.

Although they were supposed to be outlawed, Jerry knew what the noise meant. The sweat of fear ran into his blind eyes as he turned to face the Angels.

The rider of the first bike twisted savagely at his ape-hanger, high-rise handlebars and just missed Jerry, pressed flat against the wall – paralysed like a mouse in front of a weaving cobra. The second Angel had his view blocked by the first bike and had no chance. His elbow smashed into Jerry's shoulder and spun him into the centre of the passage. The next machine skidded wildly and a corner of the yellow teardrop tank hit Jerry high on his left thigh, cracking the femur and thrusting the screaming boy to the filthy floor. Before his head could hit the ground he had been hit by three more bikes. One crushed his right wrist and pulped the fingers of that hand. Another drove into his rib cage and caved the splintered bones into the lungs. The back wheel of that same bike gouged through the wreckage of Jerry's chest and forced other pieces of broken rib into his straining heart. Jerry was medically dying even before the last bike made things finite by hitting the thrown-back head just under the chin with its front wheel. The vertebrae parted easily under the strain and his head bounced twice against the concrete, flopping loosely on the neck.

Amazingly, none of the riders had come off their bikes. The scream of their machines faded away in the direction of Burnt Ash Road. The body of Jerry Richardson was still and crumpled, apart from a slight residual twitching of his right leg. Soon, even that stopped.

It was nearly three minutes before anyone came to see what had happened. By then it was all over, apart from tomorrow's headline.

Jerry Richardson had been blind. Now he was dead.

2. NEWS AT NINE

'There is still no news of the missing round-the-world yachts-man, Mike Cornelius, who set off nine weeks ago in his ketch, "Elric", to sail round the world and through the North-West Passage along the north coast of Canada. Radio contact was lost eleven days ago. It is believed that his boat may have suffered rudder damage during the severe storms in the South Atlantic a fortnight ago.

'Finally, we go to South London, where Neville Dempsey brings us this report from the scene of the latest in the current series of Hell's Angels atrocities.'

The usual crowd of whey-faced onlookers, features crudely etched by the harsh arc-lights of the colour television cameras. In front of them is the sharp-dressed, sharp-voiced Neville Dempsey. His delivery is the traditional, clipped, portentous style beloved of all second-rate interviewers.

'Late last night, a blind young teacher, Jerry Richardson, caught the 23.36 train from Charing Cross Station. He had been to a meeting of the pacifist London Buddhist Society. He was only a hundred yards from his flat in nearby Longhurst Road, when his journey ended.'

The camera zooms with an unwholesome relish onto the angle of the wall and floor, where an ineffectual attempt has been made to cover up a large pool of blood with sand.

'It was here that blind Jerry Richardson ended his journey [long pause] and his life. He is the most recent innocent victim of the new wave of violence instigated by the self-styled "Last Heroes" motorcycle gang and their messianic leader, Vincent. Jerry Richardson was not the first person to die [pause] savagely and brutally [pause] at the hands of these thugs. Unless we heed the words and implement the policies of Home Secretary, George Hayes, he will not be that last.

'Where are they now, these animals with their obscene oaths, their vile practices and their illegal machines? A police spokesman told me earlier today that they believed that Vincent and his dangerous outlaws have a hide-out somewhere in Essex. Road-blocks set up only minutes after the Richardson killing were unsuccessful. However, extensive inquiries are, at this moment, going on in areas known to be popular haunts of the Hell's Angels.

'If these gangs are not stamped out, this [cut again to the spot where Jerry died] could be your blood, or the blood of your daughter. This is Neville Dempsey. News at Ten. Hither Green.'

Back to the studio where a complacent news-reader is putting on his best conscience-of-the-people face.

'Well, that's the way it looks tonight. Goodnight.'

3. MINE EYES HAVE SEEN THE GLORY OF THE COMING

For once, the police spokesman hadn't been too far out. It was actually in Hertfordshire not Essex, but the 'hide-out' was only about four miles from the Essex border. It was the ruin of what had once been a training college for missionaries, in the days when the emergent nations had not yet emerged and the word of God was still a viable commodity to usher in the merchants and exploiters. Now, it stood in its own grounds, surrounded by trees, a couple of miles from the A414. It was here that the "Last Heroes" had gathered after the run that had reached its unexpected but exciting climax in the death of the young teacher.

It was only a few years ago that they would have been on a run at least once a week raising a fair amount of hell. Now, life for an Angel was very different. Authority had come down on them in the biggest way possible and any gang member caught wearing his colours or riding a chopped bike was likely to draw a punitive jail sentence. There was another hazard if you fell into the sticky hands of the fuzz. An unlikely percentage of bikers appearing before the new local magistrate's court were either carried into the dock on a stretcher, or walked in with broken ribs, teeth missing or other facial injuries. The magistrates had stopped asking questions and the Angels had never complained anyway. There wasn't any point. 'Resisting arrest', 'he had a fit in the cell and it took seven of us to restrain him. He broke one of our staves with his elbow'. Some of the coppers could still say with a straight face: 'He must have fallen down some stairs and banged himself'. What the fuck did it all matter anyway? The only thing you did was be bleeding careful that they didn't catch you in the first place. If you got caught you knew what was going to happen.

At first it was real class to wear your colours anyway and blow the minds of the citizens with your hair wild and long, your Harley or your Norton screaming at the world and your mama clinging to the back of your levis like she was a second skin. That was O.K. to begin with, but too many of the classy brothers were getting busted. So, slowly, things had changed. But, for many of the Angels, things had changed too little and too late. Towards the end of the sixties there were well over a hundred motor-cycle gangs with membership running up towards eight thousand – with nomadic organizations like the gangs it was difficult to make any sort of accurate estimate.

Now, as far as the authorities knew, there were only about five gangs left, with a total membership of less than four hundred.

In the south-east there were the Last Heroes with their leader, Vincent. In the Birmingham area there were the Jokers; the Martyrs came from Manchester; Glasgow had the Blues. The fifth gang was a more nebulous entity and was reputed to roam the whole of Wales from the Rhondda to the isolated cwms of the Lleyn. The gang's name was doubtful but was popularly supposed to be the Wolves.

The Angels had become the first true Underground in Britain for centuries. For the dilettante scribblers of the early seventies the name had been a collective affectation – for the bikers it was a necessity of existence. Either they hid their true colours or they were busted or they were run down by posses of paranoiac motorists and the self-styled social protection groups, or vigilantes, as they preferred to be called.

Although the right-wing tabloids and the less responsible T.V. programmes screamed otherwise, the run had now become a rare and treasured occasion. Once every couple of months, the Last Heroes came together at the old missionary college, driving grey, undistinguishable vans and trucks with enclosed side panels. Often they got their mamas to sit behind the wheel, while they lurked in the back, guarding their precious machines; the polished, revered hogs.

For a couple of days after each run they went to ground like the killing animals they had become, until the spoor was cold and pigs were occupied elsewhere, maybe with one of the increasing number of race riots. So late on that Friday evening, nearly twenty-four hours after the slaughter of Jerry Richardson, the Last Heroes relaxed with their drugs, their drink and their old ladies and talked about good days gone and the great times that were still to come.

When the diversion came, it was welcome.

Tiny Terry had been sitting near the end of the long, over-grown drive, his back against a tree. Officially, he was supposed to be on guard. Unofficially, he had his right hand clasped round the remains of a cheap bottle of Graves, while two fingers of his right hand were busy inside his mama. She had unzipped the fly of his filthy jeans and was gently rolling his semi-erect penis between her finger and thumb.

Terry suddenly pulled her hand away and simultaneously extracted his own fingers. Hissing at her to keep quiet, he stood up and edged behind a tree. Di, his mama, was used to the unexpected – like the time Terry had temporarily swopped her for two gallons of petrol. At least he had come back for her, although he had left it a bit late. The garage-hand was actually inside her before Terry reappeared like an apocalyptic angel. Di smiled when she remembered the amazed look on the guy's face as the chain made its first cut into his white, thrusting buttocks. Now, she stood close behind her man and waited for him to make the next move.

'Go and tell Vincent. Somebody's coming. Sounds like two of them. Tell him to send Mealy and Dylan – if the fuckers are sober.'

Di sneaked away without another word. Behind her, Terry started to move quietly from tree to tree. The three joints that he had finished in the last couple of hours and the best part of a bottle of wine had hardly touched him. He was a big man, over two hundred pounds, but he made virtually no noise as he crept through the trees. The evening wind had begun to move the leaves on the trees and any sound he made was swallowed up by that.

He paused for a moment and listened. Somewhere close, probably just the other side of the drive, there were two people moving. One of them was doing his best to move in approved boy-scout fashion but his companion was making it difficult. By the querulous squeakings it was obviously a girl, and a dissatisfied one. Terry moved across the drive and began to close in behind the rash couple.

Gerald Vincent had been thinking for some time now that his idea, which had seemed so good and idealistic in the warmth of his bedroom, might not be quite so good after all. And he wished he hadn't brought Brenda. She had been keener than he had to begin with. She had talked about the Angels as 'the last hope for the left' and 'the ultimate apostles of freedom'. Now she moaned that it was getting dark, that she was cold, that her new boots were pinching her feet, and how could they be sure that the Last Heroes were going to be there anyway?

'You saw the news last night.' hissed Gerald. 'We know that this is their centre and we know that they always come here before and after a run. It must have been them killed that blind guy last night down in London. So, they must be here.' Even he realised that he didn't sound all that convincing.

Gerald was twenty-eight years old and, like nearly three million of his fellow countrymen, he was without a job. He was an arts graduate who had found that his degree was totally useless. There was a glut of teachers, the result of the saturation induction to the profession during the nineteen-seventies. Although he was short and sturdily-built, Gerry had been able to get into the army and had done particularly well in unarmed combat and general weapons handling. He had signed on for five years and had seen a lot of service against both the Irish Republican Army and against the Protestant Defence Force – known as the Paisleyites, after the first great Protestant martyr of the twentieth century.

Gerry had seen atrocities on both sides; women mutilated when a public house burst into fragments around them; a child's head explode into shreds of bone from a bullet meant for the soldier seeing it across the road; whole streets of houses burnt down by their owners rather than see them fall into the hands of people of a different religion; factories wrecked, mindlessly, in a country whose unemployment figures were the highest in the whole western world. When his five years were up, Gerald would not be persuaded to sign on again. He preferred to go with all the others and endure the petty humiliations of clerks whose sole virtue to themselves was that they had a job. He found life difficult, but he could sleep again at nights.

He had met Brenda at the Young Anarchists and had been impressed with her enthusiasm and idealism. Like her, he felt that the country was being run down by the old and reactionary. Like her, he felt that personal freedom had gradually been eroded. It had reached the stage where people had forgotten what it meant to do something on one's own – to take an individual decision – to spit in the eye of conformist society. They both thought that there had been something in the ideals of the old Angry Brigade, but that was long over. Now, there really wasn't that much left. She had convinced him, rather against his inherent prejudice, that the country badly needed a force like the Angels that would help to purge it of its complacency and would raze the shibboleths of conformity.

Now they were in a wood above a small village in east Hertfordshire, it was nearly dark and their idealism was about to be put to the test.

From a previous visit, Gerry knew that they must be getting near to the house. He turned to help Brenda over a muddy bit of ground and saw her face change from irritation to horror. He let go of her arm and swung back to face the house. In front of him, appearing from the ground like a pantomime demon, was Tiny Terry.

In an age of smart suits and short hair, the Angel looked literally unbelievable. He stood a couple of inches over six feet and was big-built. His hair was shoulder length, matted and oily. He had a full beard, partly tufted, with short lengths of greasy ribbon tied in it. His teeth were mostly broken or missing; those that still remained whole were blackened. He wore scuffed flying-boots, torn levis, and his colours over a bare and filthy chest. In the centre of his chest was a red-winged skull tattooed with the words: *Hell's Angels – North London Chapter*. Down the outside of his right arm Gerry could just read the roughly marked words: *Yea, though we walk through the valley of the shadow of death, we fear no evil, because we are the evillest mother-fuckers that ever walked in the valley.*

As he looked up at this monstrous apparition, Gerry was conscious of two things. One was the almost physical aura of fear and crude power that emanated from the Angel. The other was the stench from the colours – the sleeveless jacket worn by all Angels. It was the smell of ground-in machine oil, urine, stale vomit, spilt drink and simple sweat.

'Who the fuck are you? And what the fuck are you doing?'

Heavy silence hung in the air. Gerry could hear leaves rustling in the wind. Far off he could hear crashing in the undergrowth as someone came their way in a hurry.

'We've came to see Vincent and the Last Heroes,' said Brenda, recovering some of her former courage. 'Will you take us to him?'

Terry ignored her and looked at Gerry. 'You want to see Vincent?' he asked, disbelief in his voice. 'Are you a fucking reporter?'

Brenda pushed past Gerald. 'We want to see him because we want to join him.'

The crashing grew nearer but Terry took no notice. Still ignoring Brenda he said: 'Do you always let this big-mouthed cunt do your talking for you?' He laughed, 'You really want to join us?'

For the first time Gerald spoke. 'Yes. If you'll have us. If not we'll just go away.'

A bush on their right disintegrated as two more Angels hurtled through it, pulling themselves to a stop when they saw that Terry had the situation in hand. They were both a little shorter than Tiny Terry, but their general appearances were similar.

'What's going on, Terry? Who are these two?'

'We haven't got round to names but they say that they want to join us – if we'll have them.'

'What if we don't want them? Or him anyway.'

'He says' – here Terry affected the rather more refined speech of Gerald – 'that they'll just go away.'

The three Angels fell about laughing at this ridiculous idea.

Mealy pointed at Brenda, continuing the send-up of Gerald's speech. 'Oh, won't you first stay for some tea and a bite to eat I've got something to fill your mouth with.' He bellowed with delight at his own humour.

'Are you going to take us to Vincent or not?' snapped Brenda.

Terry, Mealy and Dylan just watched her. She turned to Gerald. 'Come on Gerry, it's pointless. They aren't like I thought. They're just animals.'

All three men moved but it was Dylan whose fist got there first, catching Brenda at the corner of her mouth, chipping a front tooth, and throwing her on her back. Her head hit the base of a tree and she lay there for a moment, stunned, her lips bleeding. She put her hand to her face and tried to get up but Dylan stood over her and stamped his foot down onto her breasts, knocking her back.

'Watch your fucking mouth! You do what you're told and keep quiet. Cows like you think you know it all. You know fucking nothing. Now get up and shut up.'

Brenda pulled herself to her feet and leaned against the tree, crying quietly to herself.

During the sudden spasm of violence Gerry hadn't moved. He had enough experience of brawling to know that he couldn't have done much to help her, unless he had been very lucky. Anyway, he reckoned that she had really deserved it. He stood there and waited for the Angels to make the next move. He didn't wait long.

Terry grabbed him by the arm, while Mealy pushed Brenda in front of him.

'Let's all go and see Vincent.'

Di had prepared the other Angels for their visitors and all of them who could still stand were waiting in the grand hall. Sitting in an old chair he had found in one of the cellars, was Vincent.

In the early days of the seventies an American Angel had been interviewed for an English magazine. He had been asked about the then-embryonic British chapters. He had said: 'They're just a bunch of kids with big names and no class. I guess most of them are jumped-up kids in grey suits. I hear that their mothers wash their colours for them every Saturday morning.' The average age of the American Angel was then about thirty while that of the English equivalents was ten years less.

Things had changed. The Wallace-Nixon coalition had created a new post – Secretary of State with Special Responsibilities for Social Hygiene. What that really meant was someone who would rid the Land of the Free of the free-loaders, the hippies, peaceniks, deviants, long-haired students, black militants, communists and – Hell's Angels. There was only one obvious contender for this position as the Government's knight in shining armour. And Reagan did the job in just fifteen months.

Techniques that would not have shamed the police in Montevideo or Southern gentlemen in their pillow-case hoods were employed. Ralph 'Sonny' Barger, probably the greatest and most archetypal of all Angels, suddenly found that his beloved Harley had no brakes. Sadly, he didn't discover that fact until he was gunning into a sharp curve on the Sacramento Freeway at over ninety miles an hour. When they buried what was left of Sonny, the police arrested every one of the many hundreds of Angels who showed up to pay their last respects to the late President. That one single day broke the back of the Angels in the United States. Chapters folded everywhere and it was believed that there were less than one hundred Angels left in the whole North American Continent. Even that tiny handful lived in total secrecy and may, possibly, have been apocryphal in a land of law and order.

In Britain there had been a parallel decline but there had not been the equivalent total fall. The numerous gangs of soft young boys had been replaced by the small number of hard-core men. The age had crept up to an average of over thirty and those that were left were very tough indeed. They had to be.

Vincent was the archetypal new Angel. Physically hard, he also had an intelligence that put him into the top one percent.

He had dropped out of his university when he saw that graduation wouldn't give him any priority in the dole queue. Like Gerald, he had tried the army but had deserted when it became obvious that his particular talents did not include tolerance of discipline from people who thought themselves his superiors.

He had risen slowly through the ranks of the North London Chapter of the Angels. As the police pressure increased he found his progress easier. His predecessors as President had all suffered from the one failing of stupid, needless pride. They had all gone the same way.

Vincent had been able to convince the other Heroes that discretion actually was the better part of showing class. He instigated the plain vans and encouraged as many members of the chapter as possible to cultivate a straight appearance. He developed their highly-sophisticated security systems which had, so far, kept them a lucky jump ahead of the pigs. Vincent was very tough indeed. He had to be.

Vincent sat back and looked silently at Gerald and Brenda. He waved Terry, Mealy and Dylan away from them.

'All right. Nice and short. Just tell me who you are and what you want here.'

Brenda stepped forward but was pulled roughly back by Gerry. 'For Christ's sake let me talk. Unless you want to get beaten up again.'

He pushed past her and stood directly in front of Vincent. For the first time he felt a shifting of the tightness in his stomach. This was a wildly different sort of animal from the big thug who had brought them here. Vincent had none of the crude power, none of the physical revulsion. He was just on six feet tall and only weighed about one-eighty pounds. Like most of the others he wore his colours over a bare chest, with denims and motor-cycle boots. But he was considerably cleaner than virtually any of them. His hair was long by contemporary standards, but it wasn't likely to attract more than a second glance. He had no beard but wore a moustache of the type favoured by the trendies several years ago, turned down at the edges, below his mouth. The sort that Marlon Brando had when he played Emiliano Zapata. His eyes were veiled by heavy lids and he looked older than his thirty-two years. The only odd thing about him, Gerry noted with a start of surprise, was that the papers, for once, had got something right. Vincent's left ear had been cut, or ripped, from the side of his head. All that was left was a small hole and a scrap of gristle.

Gerry tore his eyes away from the bizarre sight and replied to the question.

'All right. We both want to join you.' He paused. 'Is that short enough and simple enough for you?'

There was a brief silence, then laughter. Vincent didn't laugh. Nor did his eyes change. The laughter and the movement stopped.

Behind Gerry there was the noise of a scuffle and he turned to face it, ready for whatever trouble there might be. His body relaxed and he couldn't resist joining in the new outbreak of laughter.

One of the smallest Angels, Rat, had knocked against one of the old-fashioned hurricane lamps that flickered windily under the arched roof. It had fallen off its packing-case pedestal and, to save it from exploding, Rat had been forced to catch it. The lamp was almost red-hot, and the rest of the Angels cheered at the sight of the little, wizened figure capering and cursing like some bedemoned juggler.

Finally, he put it down safely and attention drifted back to Vincent.

'Why?' Vincent believed in economy.

'Because we think society's fucked up. And, we don't want any of it any more.'

A boot pointed at Brenda. 'Is that tart your mama?'

Her reaction was sadly predictable. 'I am not...'

Slightly to his own surprise, it was Gerry's hand that hit her across the side of the head, sending her staggering.

'For the last time. Keep your bloody mouth closed.' Then, to Vincent: 'Yes, she's my girl.'

'All right. You think society's fucked up, so you come to us. I don't get it. You think we're some kind of alternative salvation or something? It's us who are trying our best to fuck it up even more. You know what, mate? I reckon you're a liar. I reckon that you're just another fucking creepy reporter. You know what happened to the last fucking journalist who tried to sneak in here. He kept talking about going on a "burn-up, man". So we gave him a special burn-up. We got him pissed out of his tiny little mind then we poured a can of petrol over him and...'

'Lit his bleeding touch-paper and retired immediately,' bellowed Dylan, to everyone's delight.

'Yeah. He kept running round in circles, screaming and pulling at his clothes. His hair went first, all over his head. He got most of the flames out and then he sort of fainted and fell over. He wasn't dead so I got a funnel and put it in his mouth and poured some more petrol down it and then dropped a match into his mouth. It was fucking great. His whole chest sort of exploded.' Vincent licked his mouth at the thought of how good it had been. 'That was the last one. I think you're one as well and [pointing at Brenda] I reckon that that lippy cock-sucker is another. But I'll be fair. We'll take a democratic chapter vote on it.' He stood up. 'Members of the Last Heroes Motor-cycle Chapter, affiliated to the late and great Angels Chapter of Oakland in California, I ask you what you think of these two. Do we let them join?'

The tone of the replies left Gerald and Brenda in no doubt as to their future

– or lack of it.

Right from the very start of their enterprise, Gerald had suspected that this moment would come. He took one step forward and shouted over the jeering and the obscenities.

'Listen. Fucking listen. What have you got to lose? I'd be a right fucking imbecile if I expected you to believe us. But think – just stop shouting and fucking listen – just think for a minute. Think what you can all gain by having us in.'

For the first time, Vincent smiled a little. 'All right. Tell us exactly what we can gain by not killing you, or, at the best, just throwing both of you out.'

Gerry put his arm round Brenda's shoulders. 'First, there's her. A girl's always useful, right? Well, I don't hear any of you actually disagreeing with that. *And*, she looks like a straight. So, she has at least two important uses. Then me. If you wanted to throw me out or kill me, you'd almost certainly be able to do it, because there's so many of you. But, you wouldn't find it that easy, and some of you would die first.' He ignored the catcalls that rose around him. 'I shouldn't laugh. First, most of you are drunk, stoned or hopelessly out of condition. I'm none of those. Second; I know more about death than any of you, and I've killed more people than all of you put together. And they were mostly aware that I was trying to kill them. Not like some poor blind bastard trying to get home late at night.'

The shouting had died down, but Terry's voice rasped into the quiet. 'It's all fucking talk, Vincent. Make that little bastard prove what he's saying. Let me kick the crap out of him, then see if he still wants to join us.'

Vincent moved until he was nearly touching Gerry, who could smell rancid wine on his breath. He grinned at him.

'He's right, mate. Tiny Terry here is so right. Before we can even think about giving you the great honour of being asked to join the Last Heroes, you are going to have to prove yourself. And your girl. Our test's easy for her. All she has to do is pull a train for anyone who wants her.'

Gerry felt Brenda shiver beside him. The popular press had left no detail unstated in the gory facts about the Angels and they both knew only too well what it meant to pull an Angel train. The only miniscular shred of comfort that Gerry could find in him for Brenda was that most of the Heroes were too drunk or spaced out to be able to perform.

Vincent continued: 'As for you, I think Terry's got a good idea. If you really reckon yourself that much, you can take him on. If, and I mean if, you can beat him, then we might even be prepared to have you in.'

This last was delivered with such heavy sarcasm that Gerald realised what he had suspected about Tiny Terry from their first meeting, that the big man must be good. Must be very good.

'Do I just have to beat him, or do I have to knock him out or what?'

Tiny Terry came forward and put one large hand on Gerald's shoulder. 'If you beat me mate, then you'll know that you've beaten me. Because you'll still be alive.'

Gerry studiedly ignored him and spoke again to Vincent. 'I thought you ran this mob. Do you make the decisions or does this fat, smelly poof?'

Terry's hand dropped swiftly from his shoulder.

'This thick thug thinks he can beat me. He probably reckons that the smell from his breath will be enough to knock me over. I asked you a question, Vincent, and I haven't heard an answer from you. How far do I have to go to beat him?'

Vincent looked at Terry. 'Well. You heard him. How far does he have to go to prove that he's beaten you?'

'All the fucking way. You won't have to worry about throwing him out afterwards, 'cos there isn't going to be anything to fucking well throw. And [poking Gerry between the shoulder-blades] I'm going to have second go at your tart and I'm going to screw the bleeding backside off her.'

Gerald finally turned to face the big Angel. 'You stupid mother; you won't be in any condition to screw yourself. Anyway; I reckon it's all talk with a big queer like you.'

Terry grabbed him but Vincent intervened. 'Wait. Let's do it properly. Everyone clear back and give them some room. You aren't the only one with a bit of learning, mate. This is like a duel, so we do it under proper duel rules. Tiny Terry here is what the call the challenged party. Right?'

'Right,' grinned Terry.

'So, he has the choice of weapons. Right?'

'O.K.,' agreed Gerald, wondering why Vincent found all this so amusing.

'Terry. What weapons are you going to use?'

The ever-erudite Dylan interrupted him. 'It ought to be pistols for two and breakfast for one.'

'I don't care about that, you silly fucker. We haven't got any bleeding pistols.'

'I'll take him with what I've got. Just me belt and me knife.'

Gerald looked at the big man's belt. It was the highly-polished drive chain from a motor-cycle. The knife that Terry produced from the back of his levis was an ex-officer's Nazi bayonet. It had a black bone handle, hooked at the end like a polished eagle's beak. The blade was about ten inches long, sharply pointed but with a cutting edge on just one side.

He turned back to face Vincent. 'Who's going to lend me a chain and a knife then?'

'Oh dear. Haven't you got one of your own, then?'

'No, I fucking haven't.'

'Well, that's your hard fucking luck then, isn't it?'

Brenda had been pulled to one side by Dylan but she pushed him away and tried to get to Vincent. 'But, it's not fair.'

'It's not supposed to be fucking fair, love,' said Dylan. 'If he's as good as he says he is it shouldn't make all that much difference. If he's not then it's going to teach him to keep his fucking mouth shut, innit?'

'It seems perfectly fair to me,' said Vincent. 'It's up to Terry to choose what weapons he wants and our friend here, I didn't catch your name?'

'Gerald, and that's Brenda.'

'Our friend, Gerald, should abide by his choice. Terry said that he would "take him with what he'd got". So Gerald here must also fight with what he's got. Right, enough of the chat. Let's get on with it. You ready, Terry? Good. Gerald?

Off you go then lads. I want a clean fight, no hitting on the break, no mauling.'
Vincent was still talking when Terry made his first swipe with the chain.
Luckily, Gerald had been expecting it.

He'd had a lot of training in unarmed combat, and the moves instantly started
coming without any conscious prompting.

*Pivot off the right foot sideways and back. Quick look round the room. Nothing
on the floor. In he comes again. Don't watch his eyes. Load of balls. Sergeant
Newman right as usual. If he's good his eyes don't give him away. Watch the
whole body. Shoulders. His arm's going back. Inside!*

As Terry's arm swept back for another swing with the chain, Gerald jumped
inside the blow, parried the knife with his right hand and jabbed his left hand,
stiff-fingered, for the Angel's groin. But he had been right in his guess. Terry
was good. He half-turned his body so that his hip took most of the force of the
bruising blow. As they broke apart again the whipping chain caught Gerald a
glancing knock across the shoulders. Despite his success in avoiding Gerald's fast
attack, there was a hint of concern in the eyes of the big man as they circled each
other again. Around them, Gerald was very conscious of the screaming and
yelling of the other Heroes.

*Christ! He's fast. Moving in again. Chain swinging like a figure eight both
sides now. Knife held low. Point up. Waving it fast across his body. Trying to
back me away from him into that corner. Too big for me. Can't take someone
like him close in on those terms. Slow him down a bit. Have a go at his legs. The
knee joint is the most delicate piece of muscular engineering in the whole body.*

A fight, a real fight, isn't John Wayne crisp rights to the jaw knock them
through the bar-room window come up best of friends with a small bruise on the
left cheek. It's being that vital half-second ahead in the thinking, which makes
you that vital half-second ahead in acting. It's letting your reflexes carry you
through what you are doing now and then having the time to calculate what you
are going to do next.

Gerry feinted left and then dived forwards and sideways. His hands hit the
cement floor first, and he used them as levers to whip out his feet under the
dropping knife. As Terry stumbled sideways away from him, Gerald's striking
foot hit him with enormous power just on the knee-cap. The steel heel on his
boot smashed the delicate joint, splintering the bottom of the femur, rupturing
cartilage and displacing the patella – the tiny, crucial bone at the very centre of
the knee. The big man toppled away screaming high and thin, like a gelded
stallion.

*Up. Quick. Move away and watch him. Felt right. Good solid crack. Like when
you crush an apple. Should slow him down or even stop him. Watch the big sod.
Thank Christ he's stopped screaming. Looks like a bloody great stinking crab,
scuttling around trying to get up. He's not going to make it on that leg. Can
almost see his knee dribbling apart. Please God! Don't let him get up. That
wouldn't work twice. Thanks God!*

Tiny Terry had abandoned his attempts to get back onto his feet and had pulled
himself to the middle of the floor. He just sat there. A carnivore. Stricken.
Waiting for what could be death. Still dangerous. In those few seconds, the Angel
achieved – for the only time in his life – a moment of true nobility.

Gerald walked slowly round him, keeping about eight feet away. The Last Heroes were silent now, seeing their giant champion struck down by the smaller, quicker man. Only Brenda shouted now. 'Kick his head in, Gerry! For me. Please.' This time, no-one tried to shut her up.

Terry swivelled round painfully, clutching his ruined knee, trying to face Gerald. The chain in his right hand scraped harshly on the floor. The knife was still steady in his left. The only other sound in the large room was the mumbled string of curses. 'Come on. You fucker. You little bastard fucker. Oh bleeding Christ. You bastard cunt. Just come here. You fucker. Come on.'

The chain first. The wrist holding the chain. Faster. Round him. Indians round a wagon train. Keep circling. Make him dizzy. Faster. He can't keep up. When he tries to swing that chain again he'll fall. Watch his hand. Faster. Now!

As before, Gerry's speed was too much for the Angel. Crippled, he had no chance of avoiding Gerry's rush. He was in on the right foot. He pivoted and swung his left toe into Terry's wrist. The radius and ulna both cracked with the force of the blow and the chain snaked away across the floor, to finish near Vincent's feet. Now, even Brenda was silent.

Only the knife now. Keep moving round him. Never take anything for granted, son. Once had a Nip with no arms try to tear out me jugular with his bleeding teeth. Watch them all the way. Must know he's had it. Keep an eye on his hand with the knife. He's only got one choice.

The last gamble was almost pathetic in its predictability. The big man desperately threw the knife at his tormentor's face. He was so badly injured that he could not balance and Gerry didn't even have to move. The knife sparked off one of the roof pillars and fell to the floor. Slipping sideways, the Angel could only just hold himself upright with his uninjured hand. Sweat streamed through his beribboned beard as he looked up at Gerald.

'Well, Terry. You still reckon you can kick the shit out of me. Do you?'

It was Vincent who replied. 'You've proved your point. You don't need to kill him.'

'I know I don't need to. But I'm still fucking going to. You really think he wouldn't have done me if I'd given him a chance?'

Terry looked mutely at his President.

'Like he said, Terry. You'd have done him. It's the rules, innit? Anyway; I don't really reckon that you're all that much use to the Last Heroes now.'

Although callousness and indifference to suffering were a fundamental part of the Angel's philosophy, such a bitter rejection caused a murmur round the still, vaulted room.

'O.K. If you reckon you can kill him, do it. I still don't reckon you're going to find it all that easy. Go ahead.'

'I was going to anyway. Not you or anyone would have stopped me.'

Without giving the least warning he spun round and kicked out for the third time. His toe caught Terry full under the base of his nose. His head started to snap back from the impact, but the boot was still moving faster. The gristle and bone near the top of the nose was crushed first and the splinters were forced back deep between the eyes until some of them reached the brain. Before the back of his head pulped into the floor, Terry was dying. The carnage to his central nervous system caused his body to thrash and jerk for some seconds, his fingers and feet moving convulsively. Then he lay still. His breath continued to rasp in his throat and blood gouted from his smashed nose while a darker thread inched from the corner of his mouth.

One last kick, aimed unhurriedly, got home just under and behind the left ear. There was a startlingly loud crack, the head rolled sideways, the eyes flicked open and stayed that way. The harsh breathing finally ceased.

The room was still. In the corner Di sobbed. The fight had relegated her from being the most secure of the gang's mamas to just another old lady – collective property to be used and rejected at will.

Vincent clapped Gerald on the shoulder with a grudging admiration. 'I never thought you could take him. Terry was always the second best of all of us in a rumble. It was him who killed those two coppers at the festival last year. If you can take someone like Terry then you can take pretty well anybody.' The grip on the shoulder tightened. 'With one or two exceptions. Get me?'

Gerald nodded and turned to look for Brenda. His part had gone more or less as he had thought it might. He had guessed that he would be able to provoke one of the Angels into a fight, and win it as ruthlessly as he had done. He had also imagined that the initiation exercise for Brenda might have some kind of sexual nature to it. They had talked about it and he had tried to point out to her the sort of thing she would be expected to do. At the time, she had been so enthusiastic about joining Vincent and his gang that she had made very light of the possibility. Now, that possibility had become reality.

Before he could reach her to try and give her some kind of encouragement, he was pulled back by Vincent. 'You did fucking well, mate. When we next go on a run we'll arrange for an initiation for you. You know what it involves don't you? Good. Now it's her turn. I go first and then you and then anyone else who want to. Then me again and so on.'

Gerald looked at Brenda. She pushed the hair back off her forehead and gave him a defiant, if rather trembly, smile. He figured that she would probably be all right. If she wasn't, there wasn't very much he could do about it. The least he could do for her forthcoming ordeal was to leave her alone. She had said before, when they had been discussing the sexual side of Angel's life, that she didn't mind what they did to her as long as Gerry wasn't there to see it. And, as long as he came back to her and she could still be his girl when the unthinkable initiation was over.

'Listen, Vincent and all of you. Once you've all had a go for this initiation, no-one touches her again, except me. She's my mama. Anyone else tries anything and he'll get what that fat bastard got.'

Vincent ignored this oblique challenge to his authority with a smile that made up in breadth what it lacked in sincerity. 'If that's the way you want it...? I just realised. We don't know your full name.'

'It's Gerry. Nothing else. Just Gerry. She's Brenda.'

'Right, Gerry. I'm not going to introduce everyone. You get to know them quite – intimately – when you get your colours. Official. Time's getting on. We better get started.'

He began to move towards Brenda, when Gerry's voice stopped him. 'I'm going out for a bit of a walk round. See what sort of defence this place could put up. I'll be back in about an hour. I hope you'll be finished by then. If anyone still wants to go on after that I might have a bit of a word with them and try and persuade them to change their minds.'

Without waiting to see what effect his speech might have on the Angels in general and on Vincent in particular, he walked through the door of what used to be the great hall. He pushed past the Angel on the main door and out into the cool of the early Saturday morning. Behind him he heard the tearing of clothes and a short scream, quickly muffled.

The smear of blood on the right toe of his boots was soon brushed off as he walked through the thick carpet of dead leaves that covered the gravel drive. Then he was in amongst the trees and all noise from the house had faded. The dominant sound was the morning chorus of blackbirds, starlings and pigeons, reacting to the sun that was crawling painfully over the edge of the world. It was quite idyllic.

Her hands had been tied behind her with a leather belt. To stop her screaming, her torn blouse had been forced into her mouth and held there with her tights. Terry's body had been dragged away and she was the centre of attraction. Mealy and Dylan held her legs, fingers digging into her ankle-bones. She was completely naked.

Gerry broke through the last of the fringe of trees and stood looking across the Lee Valley. The sun was not yet up properly and he could see the lights of a station, peering through the white mist down in the water-meadows. He sat down with his back against a tree and waited.

She wanted to shut her eyes, pretend it was all a dreadful fantasy, but morbid fascination kept her eyes open. Vincent towered over her, his eyes on her body. His levis were round his knees and then he had knelt between her legs and rammed himself into her. His teeth gouged at her neck and his fingers twisted her breasts and clawed at her nipples. His body began to drive into her as he neared the straining speed of his climax. Her body arched away from him as he shuddered into her, his hands tearing red furrows down her stomach.

From up the valley, in the direction of Hertford, Gerry could just hear one of the early trains, worrying through the mist, snarling at crossings and fussing through half-awake stations. The birds were quietening down a little and he could see some traffic building up on the arterial by-pass round the village.

By the third one, Brenda was past screaming and the gag had been torn out of her mouth.

To pass the time more quickly, Gerry had smoked a joint. It had helped him to relax a little and the adrenalin flowed more slowly. He looked at his watch and stood up. It was time to go back. If Brenda had performed all right, and hadn't cracked, they were in. Even if she had fucked up completely, he reckoned that he had done enough to ensure his acceptance. He started back to the house, his heels dragging in the leaf-mould.

For Brenda it was over. All of the Angels who could still raise an erection after the weekend's drinking, and some who couldn't, had panted and spent their animal lusts between her thighs, or in her mouth. In one nightmare coupling, a tall, saturnine Angel, known simply as The Priest, had explored other avenues of her body. All told, and allowing for those who had come back for a second and even third try at her, Brenda had been used by a total of thirty-one men in just over the hour. The count did not come from her, for she had soon been unable to tell how many men were having her at any one time, never mind what the running total was.

It had not all been as she had imagined. She would never have dared to think that the sixth Hero would make her aware that she was enjoying it, or the ninth bring her to screaming orgasm.

Then Gerald was back and he took her home and it was over for that weekend.

4. MIDNIGHT REVIEW (TWO YEARS AGO)

Judith Parsons: But, can you not put in more simple terms, just why you found it necessary to wreck the festival and cause so much disappointment and unhappiness to the young people?

Vincent: Nobody's going to kick my bike and get away with it. Nobody.

Judith Parsons: Did that really justify the killing of three people and the injuring of many more?

Vincent: I'm not here to ... justify anything. I told you what ... happened, and I don't care whether you like that or not.

Judith Parsons: Well, let's change the subject to something a little less provocative. Your name. I understand that you have taken the nickname 'Vincent' because you are a great admirer of the French painter Van Gogh. I also can't help noting that you have suffered an injury to your left ear. Would you like to tell us about that?

Vincent: No.

Judith Parsons: Oh! I see we are running out of time, but I did want to ask you for your opinions on the subject of the Female Liberationalists. They are now becoming a force to be reckoned with, but I believe that your gang do not subscribe to any concepts of female equality.

Vincent: I suppose that's one way of looking at it.

Judith Parsons: Have you no message at all for the ladies who might aspire to join your group on equal terms?

Vincent: Yes.

Judith Parsons: If you could keep it as brief as possible, Vincent. We are over-running a bit.

Vincent: My message to the lovely creatures is dead brief.

Judith Parsons: Well; what is it?

Vincent: Let them eat cock.

Fade-out

5. IN THE COURSE OF A ROBBERY

A smooth, pale, delicately-manicured finger reached across the green leather top of the executive desk and depressed one of the keys of the "Inter-Office Communication Device".

'Yes, Mister Pinner.'

'Miss Nolan; would you ask Mister Vinson to step in?'

'Oh, Mister Pinner?' Hesitatingly.

'Yes. Miss Nolan?'

'Mister Vinson has someone with him. His accountant. A Mister Priest.'

'Very well. Ask both gentlemen to step in.'

Depressing another key on his mahogany intercom, Reginald Pinner sat back in his Norwegian chrome and leather chair. He placed his fingertips together and assumed his best bank manager's face. Expression eight – getting ready to greet a new customer who didn't sound as though he was going to be all that important. Although he was generally a good manager of the United Merchant Bank, Holloway Road Branch, Reginald Pinner had just made the worst miscalculation of his long ('Twenty-two years and never a day off') commercial life. He assumed that Gerald Vinson wasn't important.

There was a brisk knock on the office door. Reginald always made people wait for the psychological couple of seconds until he fluted a 'Come in'. It had been in the U.M.B. executive training manual, that he had played such a large part in drafting. 'Always keep customers and subordinate staff waiting before admitting them to your office. It creates the correct atmosphere of their being "one-down" and will make any dealings that much easier.'

To that end he had a large notice on his door that said tersely *Knock and Wait*.

Mister Vinson having knocked, he expected Mister Vinson to wait. Poor Reginald! Right from the start it wasn't his day.

Straight on the heels of the knock, the door crashed back, chipping the mimosa emulsion that he had chosen with such care. In walked two young men of the type he didn't usually meet. The first one, who introduced himself as 'Vinson' and sat down across from the desk without any invitation, was not tall and not particularly ill-dressed. But he had an air of not being prepared to take any nonsense from anyone. His hair was a little longer than Reginald would have approved. Compared to his companion, Mister Vinson was a paragon of neatness.

Crammed into a suit that seemed to have done service in a meat market, Priest was a sight to blow the mind of any straight, never mind Reginald Pinner – bank manager. His hair was thick and long, with heavy grease clinging to his scalp. His face was angular, and scarred across the temples from a collision with the gravel of the North Circular Road some years back. The same collision had damaged his left eye, leaving it with a milky-white iris and a bloody white. His hands were large, accentuated by his black silk gloves.

'Oh. Please, er, please sit down Mister ... Mister...?'

'I'm sorry Mister Pinner. I should have introduced you. This is Mister Priest, my financial adviser.'

'How do you do. Mister Priest. Could I ask which firm of accountants you work for?'

'He works as a sort of a free-lance, Mister Pinner. He doesn't actually work for anyone. Not officially. Just as a free-lance.'

'Really. Well, do sit down, Mister Priest and we'll get on. I'm afraid I have a lot to get through this morning and we haven't got all that much time.'

Reginald was beginning to recover a little of his self-possession., He could handle a couple of jumped-up lads without any trouble. Probably in the popular music or film business. That would account for their informal appearance. Still; mustn't give away how much I dislike lads like them. Never have them in my bank! They may have a lot of money, though.

'Mister Priest. Won't you sit down? Over there.' Pointing to a low and rather uncomfortable chair against the wall.

'I think Mister Priest would rather stand, if you don't mind, sir. He's had a lot of trouble with an old rugger injury and he finds it more comfortable to stand.'

'Rugger! Who on earth did he used to play for?'

'Harrodians. That's the team of people who work for Harrods. You know, the big store.'

'Of course I know Harrods. My late wife had an account there for many years. I intend to give my daughter one as a coming-of-age present next year. But, well, quite frankly, Mister Priest doesn't quite look the sort of person who I have always associated with Harrods.'

'Yeah, well, he was a porter wasn't he? Not one of your creepy toadies that poof around in the shop.'

That wasn't how Reginald would have described the assistants in that noble Knightsbridge edifice. 'Perfect gentlemen' is how he would have described them. Only the other day he had been talking to his wife's sister about them. 'The thing I really enjoy about shopping at Harrods, Clarys, is that the assistants there still know how to cringe.'

Gerry sensed that the conversation was slipping away from him a little.

'A daughter, Mister Pinner. Is that her picture there? May I say that she is a most strikingly attractive young lady, Mister Pinner. Is she still at school?'

'Yes. She takes her Advanced Examinations later this year. If she does well enough, and I can say with all due modesty that I'm sure she will, then she will go on to read Modern Languages at Saint Hilda's.'

'Where's that?'

'Oxford. It's a ladies' college. Anyway. Enough about Angela. What can...'

'Fond of her, are you?' The first words that Priest had said since they arrived.

Reginald turned round at the unexpected interruption and forced a rather thin smile for the figure, leaning casually against his afromosia teak veneer book-case.

'I'm sorry. Fond of her? Yes, of course I'm fond of her.'

Before he could go on again, Gerry interrupted him. The slightly formal tone was gone from his voice and the change penetrated even through Reginald Pinner's wall of smug self-assurance.

'Of course he's fond of her, Priest. Any father would be fond of his only daughter. I would be. So would you – well, I don't know about you. A pretty, tall, dark-haired like Miss Angela Pinner, who's in Form Six Alpha at the Roseberry Convent.'

'What the bloody hell?'

'Shut up, Pinner. I haven't finished. The question I would like you to answer, *Mister* Pinner, is this. Just how fond are you of your daughter?'

'Look here. It's perfectly clear that you two thugs have come here for some despicable reason to try and frighten me. Well, I can tell both of you that I don't frighten easily. My daughter is perfectly safe at school at this very moment. I will give you just ten seconds to get out of my office and out of my bank before I call the police.'

His hands pressed at the green leather desk-top, starting to rise self-righteously to his neat little feet.

'Don't fucking bluster at me you fat bastard. Now you've made me bloody angry and you're going to be bloody sorry about that. Sit still and answer my question. How fond are you of your simpering daughter? I'll make it easier. Is she worth twenty thousand pounds?'

Pinner sat suddenly quiet. As though someone had miraculously slotted all the pieces of a difficult jig-saw together in front of his eyes. He was in the picture. He now knew the name of the game they were all playing and he knew the price. The room seemed large to him. Larger than he remembered.

'Come on. I hope you think she's worth that much. Because we think that's what she's worth.'

Conditioned by society to believe that all policemen were his friends. Men of super-human ingenuity and brain, able to outwit even the most cunning criminal. Always ask them for help as soon as possible. That's what the films said on television. They were infallible. Under George Hayes, all films and plays that showed the police in an adverse light had been 'suspended'.

Of course. Call the police! They would arrest these animals and his money would be safe. Oh, and his daughter as well, of course. His soft hands relaxed. One tugged at the edge of his virgin executive blotting-pad. The other spidered off the side of the desk toward the small plastic alarm button.

'Priest!'

The tall figure moved smoothly from the wall, until he was right behind Pinner, and slightly to one side of him. A black-gloved hand was laid on the manager's shoulder – oh, so gently – and he shuddered uncontrollably. For the first time in his sheltered life he tasted real gut fear. He felt the wings of the Angel of Death flutter the air around him and he sat very still and quiet.

'He's sweating like a fucking pig.'

'That's good. Show's he's going to listen carefully and quietly. Aren't you,

Reggie?'

'Yes. Yes, I am. But...'

'Gently. No questions. Not till I've finished. And wipe some of that sweat off your face. No need for the manager of the Holloway Road Branch of the United Merchant Bank to sweat like that, just because he's had a visit from a couple of reporters from the *Highbury Advertiser* is there? No! I said no questions. What time do you make it, Reggie? Reggie!!'

'It's twenty past ten.'

'Wrong. Wrong and sloppy. And inaccurate. It's twenty-two minutes past ten. That's one of the few good things I learned in the army, Reggie. Always be accurate. And always plan ahead.'

'Look, just what the hell do you want? And what the hell is the connection between twenty thousand pounds and Angela?'

Gerry sighed, soft as a razor-cut, and leaned back in the chair, looking worriedly at the bank manager. He shook his head and spoke to Priest. 'It's what I said, isn't it? These white-collar bastards are as thick as shit. You have to keep on telling them. Keep our Mister Pinner nice and quiet and we'll explain it to him in nice simple phrases even his semi-detached suburban brain can comprehend.'

One silk-gloved hand went blackly round his mouth, crushing his soft, gentle lips against his porcelain-capped teeth. The grip was so hard that Pinner actually heard his teeth creak protestingly in his jaw-bone. He tasted his own blood inside his mouth. Priest's other hand clutched him, surprisingly in his left arm-pit, the knuckles forcing up under the socket of the joint.

'Christ, Gerry!' cursed Priest. 'He's sweated all the way through his bleeding jacket.'

'Yeah. That means he's frightened and that means he'll listen. Reggie, him and me, we're members of the Last Heroes – that's a chapter of what's called "Hell's Angels". Don't wriggle like that, mate! He's only got to push his knuckles up a bit harder and your shoulder-joint'll pop apart like a rotten walnut. Just keep fucking still.'

'Now, I joined them about five months ago, and they were really close to the end of the road. Right, Priest?'

'Right, Gerry.'

'All you middle-class vigilantes and that reactionary sod, George Hayes! Nearly snuffed us all. Well, I used to have a sergeant in the army, Newman his name was. Middle-aged bloke but tough as a year-old-turd. He used to say: "A man what hasn't got any discipline when the going's easy – he won't have any chance of discipline when the going gets harder." So, I helped out. Gave the boys that bit of discipline. Toughened them up in the right way. This, today, is by way of an exercise. It'll show that my way's right and that Vincent's way ... rather, that anyone else's wrong. A guerrilla army, fast and mobile.'

'Now, it's just twenty-five minutes past ten. In exactly five minutes that phone'll ring. And you'll take the call, and you'll be careful. You dig me, Reggie. If you aren't very careful, then things will start to happen and the first will be that Priest will waste you. Then the second thing will be that your living doll of a virgin daughter will cease to be a virgin and will probably cease to be living any more.'

'Let him go, Priest. But, stay with him. All right Reggie?'

Reginald Pinner touched his hand to his cut lip and stared blankly at the smear of blood that marked his fingers. It was the first time since ... Oh, longer than he could remember, since he'd seen his own blood. Yes, he remembered the last time. It was when he had been trying to replace a broken string on Angela's cello and it had snapped and cut the back of his hand. When he spoke, his voice hardly rose above a whisper.

'Angela. Have you hurt her? Please, have you?'

'Not yet. Now sit quiet for three minutes and just think about how you can help her. We'll all sit quiet.'

Time passed. Listen inside your heads and hear it moving away from you. Think back. Three minutes isn't long. But it's long enough to think. Each man in the room, alone with his thoughts.

Creep into the black cave inside Priest's head. Listen at the corners of his mind to the dark, unspeakable thoughts that lurk there. Thoughts of blood, rending flesh and cutting. Bodies, open to his hands. Girls, begging for him to take them. Orgasms, fire-crackering across the skies. The soft neck of Reginald Pinner, cartilage cracking between his fingers. The artery pumping blood to Pinner's brain. Slowly cutting off that flow. Death. Death. Death. Death.

There is no need to enter the mind of poor Mister Pinner. His thoughts are there, writ large across his perspiring face. Fear. Lack of comprehension. These monsters have got his baby. Will hurt her. Unless he helps them. But, twenty thousand pounds! There is that much in the bank. How? How? Can he stop them? Angela! Poor Reggie! *Maybe they'll kill us anyway. Oh, God. Holy Mary, blessed are thou among women. Please. Just don't let them hurt me.* To see them hanging. Eyes protruding and tongues swelling from their tortured mouths. Or whipping them. The lash drawing neat strips of flesh from their bloody backs. *Maybe they'd even let me do it.*

Reginald Pinner is only a short step away from total breakdown. Something Gerry hasn't reckoned on, for all his clever planning. Just one step. Near to both the cradle of insanity and the grave of violent action.

Gerry sits and waits. Calm. Certain that his careful planning and training are bearing fruit. It will be a triumph that will establish him beyond all doubt as the pretender to the throne of Vincent. It will make he and Brenda secure. It will give him the step up ready to challenge Vincent as soon as he shows any sign of weakness.

Only five months, and already he was nearly the leader. The Last Heroes were now strong and unified. They'd cut away the dead wood and dropped some of the superfluous girls. Di had done her own bit to reducing the numbers by killing herself only two days after Gerry had snuffed out her old man, Tiny Terry. Gerry remembered how revolted he had been when he had seen the corpse. Di had been on heroin for too long and had chosen a massive overdose as her way out. She had retched up most of her last meal and choked on her own rancid vomit, fouling herself as she died. To Gerry's surprise, it had been Brenda who had volunteered to clean up the pathetic corpse. They had buried her in the woods, alongside the huge grave of Terry.

Gerry grimaced as he remembered the smell of the body. The odour brought back the memory of his own initiation into the Last Heroes.

He'd turned up for the meeting wearing a new levi jacket and jeans. On his back was embroidered the spotless emblem of the chapter. Everybody had got drunk on cheap white wine and beer. Several of the men had been dropping acid and joints were being freely handed round.

Vincent calling above the shouting and the songs, bellowing for everyone to gather round. Then lying on the filthy floor while the men of the chapter gathered round him. The mamas and old ladies standing round the walls, giggling excitedly at what everyone knew was going to happen. The baptism of an Angel was a carefully cherished ritual. The new member had to prove he was prepared to subjugate himself to the needs and desires of the majority.

'Quiet! Quiet everybody! Shut your bleeding gobs! We are all here to welcome and initiate a new member to the chapter of the Hell's Angels, known as the "Last Heroes", affiliated by special charter dated 1971 to the great chapter of the West Coast of America, Oakland, California. Our new member has the given citizen's name of Gerry. Henceforth he shall be known by his brotherly name of "Wolf". Because he's always alone.'

'Not always!' That was Brenda interrupting from the back. Gerry watched her face as the climax of the initiation grew nearer. It was alight with a strange, almost sexual heat, as though she was savouring the humiliation to come. Relishing the fact that Gerry was going to suffer just a little of the sort of embarrassment that she had undergone only a week or so ago.

Since the gang-bang at her expense, Gerry had noticed the way she had changed. Hardened.

Ignoring the interruption, Vincent went on, fingering the place on his head where he had once had an ear, and now had only a red piece of gristle. 'Come on Wolf. Lie down and take your medicine like a man.'

Trying to take it all in good part and show some class, Gerry flopped to the floor and lay spread-eagled on the dirt. Vincent leaned down over him and whispered in his ear: 'You know something? I'm really going to enjoy this. It might just show you who the President is. Don't try with me what you did with poor old Terry. I'm not stupid like he was. Try anything with me and I'll kill you. Just like that. Play your cards right and you'll be a good number two.' In the act of standing up, Vincent dropped his knee for a moment on to Gerry's face, cracking a hard blow to his nose.

No point in retaliating. Not here and not now. But, one day!

The only good thing was that it hadn't taken very long. Vincent had exercised his privilege as President and had begun the initiation of the colours himself. Standing to one side he had unzipped himself and directed a jet of urine all over the new jacket and jeans. With whoops of glee, the other Angels had followed his lead. Gerry was soon soaked in it. Vincent had been none too careful with his aim and had 'accidentally' sprayed him in the face. Then there was shouting at the back and Rat staggered in to the circle with a large plastic bucket.

With a cheer from the other Angels, Rat lifted the bucket high over his head and emptied its noxious contents all over the prostrate Gerry. The stench made him retch and he came close to mixing his own vomit with the sickening mixture of dung and urine that soaked him.

Amidst more cheering, Dylan managed to show a deal of class by lumbering over to the mob and pushing his finger down his throat to flash all over him. It added the odour of stale drink and puke to the other smells. Two Angels grabbed him by the feet and rolled him in the mess, making sure that his originals were well and truly sodden. It was over and he hadn't thrown up himself. He had managed to show real class.

He was about to get up and take the congratulations of the others when he saw another pair of black leather boots push into the circle. A voice said: 'Well, what about us old ladies. Why shouldn't we get a go as well?' Christ, it was Brenda!

There was a sudden hush, broken by Vincent's sneer. 'Yes, why not? It'll make a change and it's only fair. Give them a go too. You can start, Brenda.'

She's been waiting for this. To get back at me for leaving her to pull a train on that first night. Memories rushed in. Brenda looking down on him with a strange smile on her lips. Legs astride him. Hands reaching for her zip. Smiling down. Then. No!

The harsh sound of the intercom broke into the thoughts of all three. Gerry looked at his watch. It was exactly half-past ten. Dylan had learned well.

It buzzed again.

'Come on. Answer the damned thing, Reggie. We don't want Miss Nolan getting her knickers in a tangle do we?'

Pinner picked up the intercom phone and nervously cleared his throat before answering. 'Yes, Miss Nolan. What is it?'

'I'm sorry to interrupt, Mister Pinner. But it's your daughter, Angela.'

'Very well. Put her on.'

'Yes Mister Pinner. Er, one thing sir. She ... well, she sounds a bit troubled. Sort of hysterical.'

'Miss Nolan, the state of my daughter's health is really no concern of yours. Kindly put her through.'

The intercom went dead and the ivory Trimphone on the other corner of the desk gave a muted chirp. Looking first to Gerry for approval, Pinner picked up the phone.

'Hello, Angela. This is Daddy, darling. What's wrong? Where are you? ... Darling. Darling ... Please don't cry, dear ... Angela...'

The phone was taken from his hand by Gerry and the receiver rest depressed. Reginald put his head in his hands and sat silent. Waiting for whatever these animals might have to say or do next.

'Now, Reggie. Now you believe us. Don't you? I said, "Don't you?" Come on Reggie, don't just nod. I want to hear you admit to me that you know what's going on and what's going to happen. Now. You do believe we have your daughter, Angela?'

'Yes,' brokenly. 'Yes I do. But, I don't know what you want from me. It must be money. But, how? Just tell me, and then let my little girl go.'

'One more little word, Reggie. What do you say when you want someone to do something for you? There's a little word that polite people use. I'd like to hear you say it.'

'Please.'

'Louder.'

'Please.'

'Mister Vinson.'

'Please, Mister Vinson.'

'Good boy.'

Reginald Pinner did something that he hadn't done since he left his expensive public school some thirty years ago. He put his hands over his eyes and he cried.

'Bloody hell, Gerry. Look at him. You said that you'd make him cry and you bloody well have. Vincent said you wouldn't be able to pull it off. And, and you're going to.'

'Enough self-indulgence Mister Pinner. You may take out your Irish linen handkerchief and blow your little nose and wipe your little eyes. There now, isn't that better? Mister Priest here is now going to take his camera out of his coat pocket and I will produce my notebook and pencil. Now you see before you two representatives of the marvellous local paper – the *Highbury Advertiser* – who have come to do a feature on "Money, what does it buy you?" To help us, you, as the manager of a large local bank have agreed to let us take a few photographs of you seated behind a pile of cash – about twenty thousand pounds. Let's just say that figure for the sake of argument.

'Mister Priest and I will then place the aforesaid money into large canvas sacks which we are wearing concealed about our persons and heave them through your nice window. A couple of our friends will, I trust, be outside with their motorbikes at the ready at precisely eleven-thirty. You will remain here. Priest will render you temporarily quiet until we are safely away. You can then ring the police or the vigilantes or any bugger you care to. Round about mid-day, and don't move too far from this phone, we'll ring you and tell you where you can pick up Angela. Yes, Reggie. Unharmed. Just as long as you play ball with us and don't try and get clever and mess us about. Now, two final things. Don't bother telling us that we won't get away with it. We've all seen the tele-pix when right is triumphant. This is a chance for you to learn a bit of how the world really is. Because, we will, almost certainly, get away with it. Secondly. Don't raise any half-arsed, fucking stupid objections like there isn't that much money in the bank or any crap like that. Understand?'

'Yes. Yes I understand. I'll do anything you want but please don't harm my little girl. How should I get the money in here without any suspicion?'

'Buzz frustrated Miss Nolan on your executive toy intercom and get her in here. Tell her who we are and why we're here. Then get a couple of your clerks to bring the cash up here – in tens and twenties, nothing smaller. Then, when it's all in here you tell them all to get out. Simple. Any problems?'

'No. No, I don't think so.'

'Don't think, Reggie. Unless you think about your Angela with the Angels. That Vincent, out of sight. He's a bit of a nutter, actually. Isn't he, Priest? Bound to take a fancy to your little girl. Very impatient. Didn't even believe that this would work. Thought I'd fuck it up. If you want to prove him right and me wrong, Reggie. Just pick up your phone and get straight through to the police. They'll catch us; and beat us up and put us away for a long, long time. You could do all of society a big favour, Reggie. Be a hero. Get a medal. Wear your medal every time you put flowers on your little girl's grave. Get on with the call to Miss Nolan. Hurry up. Unless ... unless you fancy being a hero ... Good. Angela should be grateful. Not every little girl has a Daddy who turns down the chance of a medal from nice George Hayes and a pat on the back from the Prime Minister. God bless him and his flat vowels.'

Gerry sat back in the chair and mentally crossed his fingers. It was on! His plan was right and he was going to pull it off and that would make him even stronger and it would weaken Vincent that crucial bit more and make his leadership a little more suspect. He had mocked the plan long and loudly. And now. It was going to work. Reginald was going to do as he was told. Miss Nolan had been bloody suspicious until Reggie had nearly bitten her head off. The two bespectacled lads in their neat, cheap suits had struggled in with the money and piled it on the desk. To keep them happy, Gerry had carefully taken their names down – 'to make sure it's spelled right in the paper' – and Priest had used up a couple of flashes on their beaming idiotic faces, grinning away behind the mound of cash.

Then they were out of the office and the door was shut. The little red light that meant "Do Not Disturb" was flashing. He and Priest quickly unwrapped the bags from under their jackets and started stuffing the money in. Reginald sat and watched them, stealing surreptitious glances at his watch. By the time they had finished, it was just after twenty-past eleven.

'What now?'

'We sit and wait. If you're very quiet, you might hear the bikes before we do. Listen. And, don't fidget.'

Ten minutes. Time for one short trip into the heads of the three men in that office. First, the dank cavern at the centre of Priest's mind. Thoughts so dark that the imagination recoils as from some primitive, blasphemous evil. The one black silk glove rubs gently at his damaged eye. The bloody white and the creamy-yellow iris are vacant, far away. His other hand lies in his lap and he touches himself, softly, through the stained trousers. His gaze brushes across the face of Pinner and on to the photo of Angela on the desk. His long, reptilian tongue trickles from his mouth and laps at his cracked lips.

Pinner watches him with the awful fascination of a mouse hypnotised by a boa-constrictor. When the tall, dark man smiles, suddenly and absently, Pinner is almost sick. If he could wriggle through the darkness in the Angel's mind, he would vomit with fear and loathing. All that fills his mind is fear. Dread of what these people will do to his daughter. What had the leader said? That he would get that tall animal to 'make him temporarily quiet'. That meant pain. For him. His daughter would be all right, though. While he got hurt. She probably wouldn't appreciate what sacrifice he was making for her. They would beat him up, hurt him. His bosses wouldn't care about family pressures. It meant his career was virtually over. But nobody would realise he had done it for his daughter. She would never thank him. Just like her damned mother. Never cared. None of them.

Alone, inside his own confused and self-pitying mind, Reginald Pinner began to cry again.

Gerry waited placidly, conserving his nervous energy. It had been a big job, long in the planning and tedious at times. Some of the Angels, notably those that were strongest members of Vincent's clique, had moaned and carped at the constant, military-style rehearsals. But, it was going to be so very beautiful. Soon, with the backing of some of them, like Priest, he could challenge the big man and then he was made. The Last Heroes would be his own guerilla army and the rest of society could go take a running fuck at itself. His mind slipped way back, before Ireland, before the Army, back to his Comprehensive School. Hot, summery afternoons, dozing at the back of the class. A bit from Shakespeare. Henry Four Part Two. Fat, corrupt Falstaff. He had a speech that was just how he felt when this was all over. Something like: 'Take any man's horse for the laws of England are now at our command. Happy are they who have been my friends. And woe unto my Lord Chief Justice.'

Never mind any Justices. Everyone had better look to themselves when he took over the chapter. And it was 'when', not 'if'. This job was going to help him on the way up there to the real power. And Brenda. She had been getting close to Vincent. He hoped she wasn't going to go so far in backing a loser. There was something about her. Despite the tenseness of the situation he felt himself swell at the thought of her. *Not long now!*

Far and high, the muted roar of powerful motor-cycles. Straight, citizen's machines, stolen just for this to play the part of honest hogs. After the job they would be chopped or discarded. Riding righteous through the heavy morning traffic clogging North London's arteries. Careful hand signals, into the car-park at the rear of the United Merchant Bank. Stop by the third window along on the ground floor. The one that "Wolf" Vinson had showed them on the plan.

Gerry stood up and waved a hand through the window to the two Angels straddling their machines outside. He opened the window ready. 'Chuck us the bags, Priest.'

In that flush of success, he had forgotten yet another of Sergeant Newman's pet sayings: 'People who take chances when they don't have to, lad, will end up either as heroes or as corpses. Generally as corpses.' Reginald Pinner could have done with a benevolent deity to whisper that in his ear as well – only, of course, there isn't one.

Gerry took an unnecessary chance because he thought that Pinner was completely beaten and cowed, so he temporarily forgot about him. He thought that common-sense and the awareness of the danger to his daughter would check him from the obvious stupidity of having a go. What Gerry had failed to take into account was the truly inspirational effects that money can sometimes have on people.

When Reginald saw all his bank's money, no! his money – twenty thousand pounds of it – about to vanish in the arms of a couple of sub-human monsters through his very own back window, then a door opened at the back of his mind and it revealed a room that he had never even suspected existed.

Mewing softly, a shocking, unreal, unlikely sound, he rose to his feet and ran clumsily at Gerry, striking out at his back with his green onyx paper-knife. Although he was cut on the neck by the attack, Gerry didn't even turn round. He simply lashed back with his free hand, hard-edged cutting into the bank manager's unprotected groin. Pinner fell, dropping the knife as his hands scrabbled at the more urgent need, to attempt to relieve the agony in his balls. He retched and moaned, feet kicking out ineffectually, mouth straining for air.

Only when he had finished helping Priest out with the bags of money did Gerry bother to look at the prostrate figure.

'Shall I waste him, Gerry?' asked Priest eagerly.

'No. Just lay the silly bastard out for a bit. Give him a fair bit of boot to remind him how bloody stupid he was.' He thought privately to himself that he should also try and remember about estimating how people behaved when there was nowhere left for them to run to – not even inside their own heads.

He dabbed at the splash of blood on the back of his neck with a grubby handkerchief. As the boots started to swing, he perched himself on the edge of the desk and whistled softly to himself, counterpointing the thuds with the theme song from an old Gene Kelly musical.

Priest neared the end of his rites. The steel toe-caps probed and sank in here and there, wanderingly almost lovingly about the body of Reginald Pinner. The crying and the moaning had stopped and the only sounds in the plush office were Gerry's whistling and Priest's heavy breathing, interrupted by the occasional crack of bone or cartilage.

'Enough. I don't want him wiped out all the way. Right then, my brother. Let's go.' He tipped an imaginary sombrero to Reggie – or what was left of him. 'Adios amigo. You lost, you always lose.'

One on the back of each bike they rode sedately across the car-park, through Holloway, Finsbury Park and away to the north.

The room they had left behind them was quiet at last. The wind from the open window fluttered the leaves of the memo pad on the desk. A thread of bright blood crept silently across the olive-green carpet – a rather pleasing colour combination for those with an eye for it. Follow the blood back along its slow-flowing course, and you came to Reginald Pinner's mouth. Not quite what it used to be. In fact, the whole face has taken on a different appearance.

The nose is pulped and pushed sideways towards the right eye. Both eyes have vanished behind mounds of puffy, purpled flesh. The skin across the forehead is scuffed and swollen. The lips are cut and there are less teeth in the mouth than there were first thing this morning. His cracked dental plate lies on the carpet under the desk. Only a fluttering of the vein under the left ear reveals that he is still alive. He groans and coughs. once. More blood come from his mouth and ears.

Startling in the silence. The buzz of the intercom. Repeated twice. A click. Miss Nolan's voice. Nervous. Worried at having to interrupt her boss. 'Mister Pinner. Mister Pinner. I'm sorry to interrupt, sir, but your eleven-thirty customer is waiting ... Mister Pinner ... Excuse me, sir. Can you hear me ... Mister Pinner ... Mister Pinner...'

A fly alights on the carpet and dips a foot elegantly into the pool of darkening blood.

'Mister Pinner.'

6. BIKE GANG THUGS MUG BANK MANAGER – RAPE DAUGHTER!

The condition of Bank Manager, Reginald Pinner, mugged and brutally beaten by a gang of thugs calling themselves "The Last Heroes", is still grave in the Royal Northern Hospital, Holloway tonight. He has severe facial injuries and extensive bruising to the body and lower abdomen. Doctors suspect he has broken ribs and possible breaks to arm and fingers. A statement will be issued later tonight.

In the same hospital, in an adjoining ward, is Mister Pinner's daughter, sixteen-year-old Angela. She is known to be in a state of severe shock after being found wandering in Epping Forest, naked except for jumper and shoes. It is believed that she had been sexually assaulted by other members of the same gang who attacked her father and stole forty-five thousand pounds from his bank – The United Merchant Bank in Holloway Road.

No trace has yet been found of the animals who carried out this carefully-planned and skilfully-executed raid. Police believe they may be members of an illegal motor-cycle gang hiding out somewhere in East Hertfordshire. If so, they are the mob led by Vincent – that's all the name anyone knows him by – the one-eared king of the pack of human rats.

The *Leader* has always prided itself on its civic awareness and responsibilities to Society. We do not shirk to condemn this latest outrage by the motor-cycle hoodlums who have made our streets dangerous for decent folk. The *Leader* backs Home Secretary, George Hayes, in his drive on these scum and we are proud to publicise – exclusively – his latest comments on the Holloway Bank Raid.

'I have been told by the police officers heading the investigation the full terrifying story of gang brutality. The whole tale raises the question of whether our society will allow gangs of well-trained thugs to take over our country so that decent people are frightened to go out of their front doors. So that an honest man cannot do his job without risk to life and limb. So that a young and innocent girl cannot go to and from school without being vilely assaulted.

'There can only be one answer. An emphatic "No". This decision on my part will, I promise, be reflected in the sentences that will be passed on those guilty of these crimes when they are apprehended. And, have no doubt, they will be caught. We will teach them a lesson, so that those who are minded to follow the examples of these thugs will know the risks they run.'

Fine words from a fine politician. Let us all take them to heart and help, through our local vigilante groups, to stamp out this foul cancer at the heart of our society.

Tony Pitt – The *Leader*.
April 7th, 1997

7. THE ORDER IS RAPIDLY FADING

'I don't care if you are the fucking President. That was my run on the bank and you agreed to play it my way. My way didn't mean you and half the chapter screwing the kid,'

'Watch it Wolf.'

'Watch it Wolf,' mimicked Gerry. 'It's no bloody good. You're still living in the past when it was all colours and runs and tangling with the law or the skinheads. The days of Little Larry and Chopper are gone, Vincent. I know it. You ought to know it.'

'You want to drop everything and turn us into a bleeding army unit.' That was Dylan.

'No. I want to keep the old customs but they've got to be brought up to date. We're Underground Angels now. Really out of sight. No crap about being the "One Percent". We're a lot less than that now and we've got to alter our methods or we'll go to the wall. You,' pointing to one of the oldest of the Angels standing round, 'Atlas. You've been an Angel longer than any of us. How many chapters when you started blowing minds?'

The tall figure of Atlas thought long. A chance meeting between his head and a policeman's stave three years ago had slowed what little wits he'd ever had.

'Well, there was The Wanderers, The Vagrants, The Nomads, The Iron Crosses, The Coffin Cheaters...'

'O.K., Atlas. I don't want you to name them all. But I can tell you. Five years ago there were still around sixty chapters in this country. Now, how many?'

'Four.' said Vincent.

'Wrong. Five. Us. The Jokers in Birmingham, The Martyrs in Manchester and The Blues from Glasgow. The fifth one is the mob from North Wales. The Wolves.'

'The Wolves! They don't even exist. They're some old folk story. Hell's Angels riding down from the mountains, wrapped in a handful of mist and a tattered sheepskin. You ought to be at home with a bunch of loonies like that. You ought to sod off and join them, if you think they really exist. You're pushing me to try and make President of this chapter – don't look like that. I know it and everyone here knows it. If you really want to be a President, go and lead the Welsh mob. You've got the right name for it. You could be "Wolf" of the Wolves.'

'Don't laugh, mate. I know they exist.'

'How?' spat back Vincent, suspicious that some kind of political manoeuvre was going on behind his back.

'I just know. That's all. One day, in a week or so I'd like to take a few of the brothers up in the vans to have a scout round up there and renew, or rather, make contact with the Wolves.'

'No. I give the orders. Wait a minute. You know, Wolf, apart from that bank raid, that could be the best idea you've had yet. We'll go up to Wales all right. But we go up mob-handed. All of us. Mamas, old ladies, colours flying. Blowing the minds of all the straights.'

'A run.' That was a gasp of almost holy wonder from Dylan, eyes open wide in amazement at the thought. 'We haven't had a real run, oh since ... I can't remember. But not for bleeding months.'

There was a silence in the vaulted room for a couple of heartbeats as the Angels gave various thoughts to the magic ritual that was being contemplated. A run.

Bursting over a city hillside like a ripple of thunder. Throttles revving hard, hair streaming in the wind, booted old ladies clinging to the shoulders of stinking denims, screeching abuse at the citizens, hands easy on the ape-hanger bars, chrome gleaming in a summer sun that beat through your hair. Coursing through your veins, lifting your mind. Laughter just because it was damned good to be alive and with the brothers. Jesus Christ, but on that kind of day a man could really feel like a king. Like a fucking king!

Against that kind of romanticism, that emotional thrill, Gerry didn't have much chance. It was Brenda's voice that broke into the spell.

'I remember the last time there was a full run. I saw it on television. Down in South London. Don't you remember, Vincent? A blind boy. You killed him. Just because he got in your way. Blind!'

Brenda's cold voice had blotted out the dream for many of the Angels, more effectively than any argument of Gerry's could ever have done. Gerry saw the moment was there for a challenge, and he took it.

'It'd be crazy to even think of going on a run now. The whole country'll be crawling with coppers and those bastard vigilantes backed by the Hayes Code. I say we ought to wait for a bit, then it might just be possible. But, it would really need a fantastic amount of planning to make it safe.'

'Jesus. Not more of your boring bloody planning!'

'You talk too much, Dylan. Planning brought us that twenty thousand pounds, didn't it? If I were you – thank Christ I'm not – but if I were, I'd keep my mouth shut. Dig?'

'Thanks, Priest. It's O.K. People like you, Dylan. You make me want to push your teeth right out the back of your neck. Better still. I could let Priest have you. Shut up. It's always the men with biggest mouths that have the smallest minds. Listen. What we've got on our side are speed, mobility and fear.'

'And it is written that the greatest of those is fear.' The speaker was Kafka – one of the oldest of the Angels. A mild-faced brother, with thinning hair and round, plastic-rimmed spectacles. Anyone confusing mildness for weakness were corrected with the help of an open razor that nested in a leather pouch at the back of his collar. A trick he'd picked up from one of the classic western heroes of the seventies. He had a reputation for being something of a intellectual. He was. Then again, compared to most of the Last Heroes, Andy Pandy would have seemed a mental giant.

'True, Kafka. Once the bloke in the bank knew who we were, he was ready to do anything for us. That's what fear did.'

'Including trying to cut your throat.'

'Right, Vincent. That's exactly my point about planning. That's what makes it safe. Everything went well apart from that. And apart from you and half the chapter breaking our agreement by having it away with the daughter. But I got a bit careless and that's what happened. It was only a small operation aimed really at just one man – the manager. Just think – all of you – how many things could go wrong if we put on a run. Maybe it would work, but only if we planned it right.'

The silence was broken this time by Vincent. 'No. We're the Last Heroes and we don't take shit from anybody. We're strong enough to show some class whenever we like.'

His response brought a quick and angry retort from Gerry, almost a straight challenge. 'In that case. Take any stupid bastard who agrees with you and go and have a fucking run. See how many of you manage to get back here.'

It wasn't almost a straight challenge. It was a direct confrontation, and it was Vincent who had to find a way of backing down. He tugged at what remained of his left ear and thought fast. 'One thing, and only one thing stops me. It's true what you say about the fuzz being all over the place at the moment. So we will wait. But not for long.'

'How long?'

'That's my decision. Don't keep pushing. When I give the word, we'll go on a run. For real. Just like the old times. That's what we're here for, isn't it?'

'Death or glory. Is that it?'

'The runs used to be good. Once.' It was the slow quiet voice of Kafka. 'But that wasn't why I joined. I came to the Last Heroes because I was sick of society. I was sick of what life had become. I was sick of the standards that had come to be important. One thing made my mind up for me.'

'For Christ's sake. Not your mother again!'

'No. Wait a minute. I haven't heard this before. Go on brother.'

Kafka smiled at Gerry. 'Like Vincent says. It was my mother. She wrote a letter to a paper and that made me suddenly realise what a rotten state things were in. And I decided to opt out. All the way out.'

'What the hell was the letter about?'

'The Queen. Mainly about the Queen. It was her Silver Wedding, or something like that, and this paper asked all its readers to send in their memories of the twenty-five years of Royal love. This is what my Mum sent in. And they published it.'

Kafka reached into the top pocket of his colours and pulled out a faded newspaper cutting, sealed and protected by a clear plastic wallet.

'I keep it safe, so I can remember the sort of things my mother considered important. She died about a month after this was published. Listen.' He didn't look at the cutting once, simply holding it in his hand. 'I used to work as a house-maid at a big house in Norfolk during the nineteen-fifties. One weekend we were all in a flutter below stairs because we'd heard that Her Majesty the Queen and Prince Philip were coming to stay for two days. You can imagine how excited we all were. The Fairy Princess and her Sailor Prince! I saw them arrive from an upstairs window and, my, didn't she look radiant! The next morning, I'd got up early to clear out the living rooms and make them spick and span. I'd only just emptied out all the ash-trays and wiped them, when the Duke of Edinburgh walked in. I nearly jumped out of my skin. He was wearing an old dressing-gown and smoking. Ignoring me, he stubbed out his cigarette in one of the clean ash-trays. I wasn't going to have that so I said: "Here, Sir, I've only just cleaned that." He turned to me and said, straight-faced: "Well, you'll just have to clean it again. won't you?"'

He paused for a moment before finishing off the letter. The rest of the Angels were all poised ready, knowing the last sentence almost as well as he did. They all shouted it together. 'That was the most memorable moment of my entire life.'

The cheering and clapping subsided slowly after the well-known reading. Kafka looked up at both Gerry and Vincent. 'If that was the most memorable moment of my mother's entire life, and it really was, then something is wrong. I just don't want any part of that kind of life. We deserve something better. Maybe not "better". But at least something different. Both of you, remember that.'

The last sentence hung in the air, almost daring either man to pick up the threads of the argument again. It was Vincent who spoke first. 'I still think we should have a run. A real run. Like the old times. All of us. Like Kafka says, we're here to spit in the face of society. We can show them that their standards stink. How many of you agree?'

For the briefest second there was a hush – a moment that must have laid the first seeds of doubt, laid them lightly, in the mind of the President. Not everyone in the chapter was that confident in his leadership. Then Dylan raised his hand, followed by Rat and Mealy. Atlas shouted 'Yes' in his thick voice. Others followed – Moron, Riddler, Harlequin, Dick the Hat and Crasher. Soon, there were only a handful of Angels left with Gerry. There was Priest, Kafka, Cochise and Vinny, plus a couple of others. Vincent still had over two-thirds of the chapter on his side. Or, to look at it in another way, Vincent had lost the support of nearly one-third of the chapter. Before Gerry's arrival, his authority had never been questioned. It wasn't a good feeling. Maybe he could...

'Well, Wolf. You've been pushing all the time, all the way. This, brother, is where the pushing stops. We do things my way, or we don't do them at all. You stand out and say in front of all the chapter that you realise that I'm the leader here and that you'll do as I say. That includes going on a run when I say.'

The situation was tense. With the small number of Angels on his side, Gerry knew he had no chance. Equally, if he once backed down publicly he'd have less chance to make a bid for the leadership at a later – and easier – moment. He'd just decided that he had to take up the chance and go down fighting, hoping that Vincent would have enough appreciation of his talents to just have him badly beaten and not snuffed. His muscles tensed and he began to crouch. A voice from the back of the crowd shattered the moment. A girl's voice.

'You're crazy. Both of you. Vincent, you know that Gerry's ambitious. He wouldn't be any use to you if he wasn't.'

'Or to you,' came a bitchy voice from one of the mamas across the other side of the vaulted room.

'True. Nor to me. I don't want to go around with a dead-beat ex-greaser like some of the scrubbers around here. Know what I mean?' The laugh that followed turned the atmosphere a touch easier. Brenda went on: 'Gerry ... Wolf, is just as good an Angel as any of you. If he doesn't think it's a good idea to go on a run just yet, then he's got a bloody good reason. It's not that he's chicken.'

'No?' a mocking voice that sounded much like little Rat.

'Remember Terry? He thought he was a big man. And he was. Bigger than you'll ever be you pissquick little bastard. I could knock you clean through that window, never mind what Wolf could do to you.'

More laughter. Rat was not notable for his bravery or his fighting ability. His peculiar contribution to the Angels was his skill with underhand weapons – the booby-trap, or the knife in the back. He would not forget the insult. Gerry wondered why Brenda was taking so much on herself. She had come to stand by him and leaned close to whisper, her voice covered by shouting and joking at Rat's expense.

'Vincent wants to kill you. This is his chance. I've got to break the mood. Play along.'

Gerry squeezed her arm.

Vincent moved forward to face Brenda. His face was more like that of an animal, a creature thwarted of his prey, making one last effort to secure his kill 'Well, Wolf? Hiding behind this tart's skirts again. She reckons you're as good as any of us. Now you've got a great chance to try and prove it to all of us. Are you really that good?'

Again Gerry's body tensed ready for violent action. His back was against a wall, in every sense of the word. On either side of him he could sense Priest and Cochise moving into position to guard his flanks.

'All right Wolf. Show this crowd of freaks how good you are. Even with odds like these.'

'Get her out of the way, Wolf, so she doesn't get hurt. If anything happens to you, and I only want this to he a bit of a friendly rumble, like – but if anything should happen to you, then I'll take care of Brenda here myself. I promise you that I'll look upon that as a labour of love.'

'Come near me with that diseased body of yours, and I'll cut it off. Gerry's ten times the man you are. There isn't anything you've done that he hasn't done. Not a ... Oh. No, nothing.'

Vincent leaped like a panther on to her hesitation. 'Why did you stop then? What did you just think of?'

Gerry had got to know the new, harder Brenda quite well, and he guessed that the hesitation had been a deliberate move on her part to postpone the rumble. The only thing he couldn't figure was, what exactly had she thought of? He remembered the initiation and shuddered inside. He knew that she would never forgive him for her own nightmare initiation ceremony when she had been laid by every Angel in the chapter, more than once by some. Whatever she'd thought up to try and save his life, he guessed it wouldn't necessarily be pleasant for him. Still, he thought resignedly, life was life.

At Vincent's question, she had stood dumb, as though regretting what she had nearly said. She shook her head. 'Nothing. I wasn't going to say anything.'

'Yes she was. Come on tart, out with it. You just thought of something that Vincent has done that Gerry hasn't. What was it?'

Good old Dylan, thought Brenda. She had known she could rely on him to leap in. Ever since Gerry had snuffed out Tiny Terry, Dylan had been worrying at him, like a terrier at the heels of a bear, waiting for him to slip. He thought this was it.

'It's nothing. Honestly. It's just that Gerry ... Well, he's never had the chance to ... Sod it, I'm sorry, Gerry. I didn't mean...'

'What?!?' The cry came from half a dozen eager throats. Sensing something between Wolf and his old lady. Something more than between Wolf and Vincent.

'Come on, Brenda.' The quiet command came from Vincent. 'You've gone so far. You may as well go all the way. What hasn't he done?'

'It ... it's just his wings. He hasn't got any wings.'

'Yeah! She's right! Let him do it now!'

'Later.' That was Vincent, suddenly seeing his moment sliding from him. But, there was no holding the brothers when that kind of suggestion had been made. Gerry would have to show class straight away. He swallowed hard to try and hide his disappointment. He shouted to make himself heard. Might as well try and make the best of it. 'All right, brothers. Wolf here is going to show us some real class and earn himself his red wings.'

A great burst of cheering followed this. Drowned by it, Vincent spoke directly to Gerry and Brenda. 'Fucking clever. Both of you. This time the luck's with you. Don't try and ride it too far – or too fast'. Dylan had leaped to the middle of the room. 'Come on now, all of you lovely ladies. Which of you is going to oblige Wolf, here, and help him to his wings. Which of you've got the flags out?'

'I have.'

'You have? Hey, that'd be fine. Wouldn't It, Vincent? Brenda here's going to oblige Wolf herself.'

'Very nice too. As long as it's genuine.'

'Don't worry, Vincent, it is. In fact there's bound to be enough for you.'

'I've got my wings, sweetheart. I don't need to show that sort of class any more. Come on, then, Wolf, let's see you get at it.'

Gerry stood still, thunderstruck by the weird turn that events had taken. Brenda had saved him. That was true. But, he was going to have to pay a price.

As the remainder of the Angels and their women made themselves comfortable round the walls, his mind raced ahead to the ritual he was going to involve himself in. He shuddered, despite himself, and breathed in to try and clear his head. He spat on the dirty floor, relieving his mouth of the thin bile that had risen to it. He hoped to God that he didn't throw up. That would finish him.

Vincent ushered Brenda, with a superb send-up of a doddering old verger, to a battered arm-chair, and helped her to sit in it.

Looking back on it later, Gerry found that he could not remember it in any kind of sequence. Just a series of random and disconnected images.

He'd read about earning wings in several of the great Hell's Angels' novels and magazines. It was one of the ways that a brother could show class to the rest of his chapter. A way to blow the minds of the righteous citizens. There had been an interview with an American Angel in an old magazine. He'd talked about winning wings, but the magazine had taken the safe way out and described it as 'a singularly unpleasant sexual act, the details of which are too revolting to describe here'.

The Angel had gone on to describe one of the finest examples of class he'd ever seen. It had been a West Coast brother called "Smackey Jack". A waitress in a hamburger joint had been rude about his appearance so he'd simply vaulted over the counter and knocked her out. While she was still unconscious, he'd pulled out five of her teeth with a rusty pair of pliers he always carried with him. Then he'd screwed her. Now, that was real class!

But, he'd showed class, and he now wore his red wings proudly on the breast of his colours. They'd been hard earned!

Brenda's face, proud and arrogant ... the cheering ... his knees grating on the filthy floor ... her levis round her ankles, and her black pants ... nearer her ... noise muted as his ears were covered ... prickling at his mouth ... tongue ... salt ... sticky ... pressure on his head ... juddering ... over ... more cheering ... class ... Brenda satisfied with a double victory. Class!

After, before he'd even wiped his face, Vincent coming to him. Having to counter with greater class. That was what it was all about being President. Taking him by the shoulders and pulling him close. Kissing him, thrusting his tongue deep into his mouth. Both mouths slobbered. Horror piled on horror. The ritual, then the kiss.

Worse. Something that he would never ever admit to any person, as long as he lived. During the kiss, in the moment of closeness to Vincent, he had felt a stirring in his groin. A swelling of pleasure.

He had enjoyed it!

8. 'RIDING HIGH OVER CONCRETE SKYWAYS'
An extract from a sociological study by Mike Olsen, called:
Hell's Angels – A Key To Unlock The Head Of Uptight Society.
– Arkadin Press, 1996.

Mess around with the Angels and you mess around with the inside of your own nightmares. Tangle with the men in blue denim riding stinking keening high and few far across a lone Bergman skyline, death on their shoulders and dope burning up their veins, and you tangle only with your cave sabre-tooth past.

Side with Hayes, big Daddy security blanket Hayes, Leader of Light, watching over the small children. For him you can kill an Angel for God. For him you can band in your friendly neighbourhood ghettoes and stab and hunt and kill the animals that threaten your pure Anglo-Saxon wife and fair-headed, blue-eyed children. Vigilante. Vigilance. Keep a vigilant vigil on your plasterboard castle, walls thin and tumbling down down down into dark.

Underground Angels. Hiding from light and riding the night. Alone. Mrs Middle-Class's favourite rape fantasy nightmare. You wouldn't want your daughter to marry one, your son to become one, your wife to encounter one late at night, your husband to ... anything. Fill in the blank yourself.

Where did they come from, where do they go? Out of poverty and dissatisfaction in rural urban Amerika. Get stuffed white-collar Republican! Freedom-riding, easy-riding. Take the freeway down to Oakland and see how the Angels row. Black disaster at Altamont. Rock 'n' Roll murder. Just one of the days that the Music died.

Now they're here and gone in England. Look over your shoulders, people. Walk gentle into the good night, but watch the shadow that rustles unseen in the hedge-rows. Careful Mister. Don't turn your head! Because you know a fiend that you helped make doth close behind you tread. Waiting for you to make one mistake. Then it will be on you. Mighty, nails rending, teeth tearing at your throat.

Remember what Himmler said. Remember who Himmler was. Remember that this is a quote that the Angels like. Remember. "As you are, so I was. As I am, so you will be." Remember.

For the Angels ride up from the eighth circle of a new Renaissance Hell. There is only one way they can live. They must go on. On and up. Through blood to the stars!

9. 'SO FULL OF UGLY SIGHTS, OF GHASTLY DREAMS'
Richard III, Act One, Scene IV.

The bank raid in Holloway and the rape and kidnapping of the manager's daughter had brought the Hell's Angels back into the public gaze. There was no way that Home Secretary Hayes could pretend that they didn't exist. There was the plain evidence for all to see, blazoned across the headlines of all the daily papers and blaring out of the video and television sets. Everyone knew what these hooligans had done. People even knew exactly which window of the hospital where Reginald Pinner had been recuperating from his beating had been left open. An 'X' marked the window, and thick white dots down the side of the building (in the picture) showed the path followed by the falling body, while another 'X' indicated the place where the manager's corpse had come to rest. Colour news film had gloated in close-up on the pool of blood and lighter brains that still stained the concrete after the cadaver had been removed.

The verdict of the Coroner's Jury was, of course, 'Suicide while the balance of the mind was disturbed'. But the police had made a public statement that any Hell's Angels caught anywhere in the South of England would be arrested and charged with murder. Quite right too, mouthed the leaders of the local vigilante groups and they sharpened their sickles or loaded their shotguns. Housewives took to carrying keen-edged carving knives in their shopping baskets. Just in case!

Apart from the magazines, papers and television people, other forms of the media were interested in the revival of the violent cult. Repression had long made any glorification of violence illegal, but here was an opportunity for someone to cash in. They could make a block-busting film about the Hell's Angels and, by tacking on a moral epilogue, justify it as a moral film about immoral people. Calvinist film critics would loathe it but the public would queue three times round the block to lap up the mayhem. And there was only one director who could make such a film and get away with it.

Donn Simon! Leading film critic turned film-maker. Advocate of the "auteur" theory of directing. Donn had been the only major critic to knock the key film of the sixties, *Easy Rider*, claiming it was facile and catered to the worst elements in the youth cult. What he meant was that he was highly pissed-off that he hadn't thought of it first!

Now he was looking at the Hell's Angels. Not since that darling of *Cahiers du Cinema*, the once-great Roger Corman, had made *Wild Angels* had there been a film of any distinction about the cycle outlaws.

'Now has to be the time. Incest is now as dead as can be and the public are going to be looking for some new kicky experience at the movies. Right?'

'Right, Donn.' The yes-man was the gay figure of Rupert Colt, assistant director of Donn Simon on most of his best films, and sometimes bed-fellow when the director happened to be swinging in that direction.

'O.K. Rupert, baby. I'm glad you dig the idea of something new. Just exactly what do you suggest we do that will really blow people's minds at the box-office?'

'Well, how about some Black Magic? Or, maybe some more of the Poe flicks?' Sensing a chilling in his master's eyes, Rupert staggered on. 'Or, yes, I've got it.'

'Well, don't give it me sweetie, whatever it is.'

'No, listen, Donn. It could be great. Nothing like it. There can't be an idea to match this. We make a big violent Western with the Mormon Brothers as the white hats and the Thompson Six as the black hats. Lots of love interest for the weenie-boppers. Bags of violence and a whole double album of great new songs. What do you think? Eh, Donn?'

'Rupert. I want to ask a little favour of you.'

'Anything, Donn. Just name it.'

'I want you to have that idea typed up for me, with three copies. Right?'

'Yes, sure. Then what?'

Then my little fairy friend, I would like you to roll all three copies up into a cylinder, tie it up with red ribbon and seal it with your favourite purple sealing-wax. Are you still with me?'

'Right on, D.S. Then?'

'Then stuff the whole thing up your flabby arse.'

The conference collapsed into helpless laughter at the speed with which Rupert's face dropped. But, Donn was still talking so the laughter stopped like someone threw a switch.

'Hell's Angels. That's what we're going to do. They seem big here in England. Killings, rape and robbery. The last rebels. Guerilla fighters on chopped hogs. Raiding the highways. Them against us. It's a cert to catch the imagination of the kids.'

'Wonderful, Donn. But...'

'Rupert, I like the "wonderful" but I'm not so hot on that quavering little "but" stuck on the end. It'd better be a good but, or you'll be out on your big butt.'

'It's this censor guy, Hayes. He's got a tight ruling about subjects for movies. They have to be real moral and lay down a clean line.'

'So we play a straight line. We use Tarquin Wells as the hero – wipe that leer off your face Rupert. Tarquin may be a little gay. He's also very careful about the company he keeps. He can be a straight who joins up with a chapter of the Angels and becomes their leader. Then we can have Nancy Thompson for the leading lady. She's the original dyke that the little Dutch boy had his finger stuck into. She and Tarquin should be great together. They won't be able to decide who does what to who.'

'Who to get to play the Angels? How about the "Wreck" stunt team? They've got some lovely leather clothes and some big powerful motor-cycles.'

'No. I'm going to use real Angels. Just like Roger did with *Wild Angels*. That way we get a barrel-load of free publicity and we don't have to pay the bastards much. A few bottles of beer, and they'll pull anything that we ask them to.'

'Great. Just great! I figure you may have to pay them something though. I don't think you'd get them for a few bottles of beer any more. But Donn, where are you going to find some real Angels? They've all gone underground. If this politician Hayes can't find them, then how are you going to get to them?'

'I'm not.'

'Great! Really great, Donn! You've got a plan to get them to come to you?'

'No. You, Rupert, are going to get them for me.'

'But. But. Donn. Hey, you're joking. You are. I can always tell, Donn. You are joking? Come on.'

'O.K. everybody. That wraps it up. We meet again in seven days' time when Rupert here will have made contact with the great unwashed battalions from the maw of Hell. At next week's meeting Rupert, you'll have a feasibility study made for me of costs for the film. Budget for ninety per cent location with a minimum team and no names apart from Tarquin and Nancy. Right. Any questions? Rupert, you got any questions? No? Good. Don't let me down, Rupert baby. You do well for me, I might get you a new lollipop to suck on. Right?'

'Right. Right, Donn. Seven days.'

Although Donn Simon treated his assistant as something less than human, it was partly a pose. He had learned from bitter experience that Rupert didn't work well if treated with kindness and consideration. Therefore he pushed him and leaned on him as hard as possible. That way he got superb work from the best assistant in the film business. Rupert also got what he wanted, which was to be ill-treated and dominated by a good-looking man. Every now and again, as reward for a particularly fine piece of work, Donn would go to bed with Rupert and let the little man service him in the way he liked best. In some ways, Donn actually looked forward to the times when Rupert would have done something outstanding for him. If he got to the Angels, he would have earned, maybe, two nights.

Rupert had one advantage that George Hayes didn't have, for all his resources and man-power. Rupert had money. Access to lots of money.

All he needed to do was put a full-page advert in both the daily newspapers printed saying that a film was to be made dealing with the activities of the motor-cycle outlaw gangs and that large sums of money would be paid to anyone coming forward offering any information that might help the makers of the film.

Rupert gave a phone number and a box number so that anyone who mistrusted the universally-tapped phones could try writing. He struck mountains of dross, most of it abusive or obscene. The tiny specks of gold that filtered through to him gave him a blurred and indistinct picture of a hide-out somewhere in Hertfordshire, or, maybe Essex. Three days had passed and he wasn't even close.

Like in all the best stories, Rupert finally got his break. It came on the sixth day of his labours. It was a typed note, in a plain envelope, delivered by hand, during the night. It was brief and very much to the point. It simply said: *We've checked and you may be straight. If you aren't then we'll kill you. If you are, leave your office NOW and walk into Soho. Go into Berwick Street. There's a specialist bookshop there. Sells nothing but Science Fiction. Run by a bird called Mary Shelley – you know Shelley, like in "Frankenstein". It's called "Light She Was And Fleet Of Foot" – it's a quote. Be there in ten minutes. We'll be watching. Someone will approach you there.*

No point in hanging around. Rupert left his office in Wardour Street and cut through into Berwick Street. The market traders were just beginning to set up their stalls. There were fewer than in the old days, since all retailing of foodstuffs had come under Government control. Most of them were either licensed to sell food at four per cent less than the approved prices or they sold oddments of household goods and clothes at a big discount. Inflation had meant the pound in people's pockets was worth about seventeen per cent less each year. This had hit the old age pensioners particularly hard, and in an hour or so the street would be full of elderly people queuing and pushing to get a bit of scrag-end meat at that pitiful four per cent discount. Four per cent! It was hardly worth bothering with.

The other difference that Rupert noticed – it was years since he'd been down Berwick Street – was the lack of cosmopolitan faces and accents that had made Soho a good place. Once. The Prime Minister's repatriation policy had changed all that, It had also changed the country's medical system. At a stroke he had depleted the medical staff of every hospital by fifty per cent. England really wasn't a good place for anyone to get sick in any more.

Rupert pushed along the pavement, past the frontage of what he remembered used to be a porny book shop. Since Longford and Mary Whitehouse both entered politics, their joint lobby had been almost totally effective in clearing literary filth from the streets. Sadly, sex crimes had rocketed. If one now wanted to purchase "adult" reading, one had to write for a catalogue to one of the few firms that were allowed to advertise – discreetly – in the papers. The danger was that everyone knew that police intercepted mail and that put you on a list of known sex deviates. You couldn't win.

Nearly there. That was the front now. "Light She Was And Fleet Of Foot". He put his hand on the doorknob and paused. The seedy, balding figure peering in through the shop window. It was – the face turned to him and rheumy, vacant eyes looked through him – it wasn't. Just for a moment Rupert thought he had recognised a leading screenplay writer of a five years ago. An author who'd produced a classic anti-police novel. A year or so after, he'd been busted – the whisper was that he'd been fitted by a jilted girlfriend – and his head had collided with a stone bannister as he was being led away for questioning. He'd never written again.

No, it couldn't have been old 'D'. He'd gone back to live in Ireland. In fact, Rupert was sure that someone had told him a month or so ago that he'd died. Jesus, thought Rupert, they were hard times. Like Ray Charles used to sing.

He wandered around the small shop, glancing at the ranks of paperbacks, picking up a book here and there, then putting it back. He guessed he was being watched. His eye was caught by a Frazetta poster on the wall. A hero, mighty of arm and keen of eye, fighting overwhelming odds against a horde of barbarians. Beautiful thigh muscles.

Rupert jumped as someone tapped him on the shoulder. 'Excuse me.'

He moved aside to let the man pass. Gradually the shop filled up. Still no approach from the Angels. As it neared lunchtime, Rupert reluctantly began to think that the letter had been a con. 'You're Colt.' It was a statement not a question. 'You're still interested in getting in touch with some people to help make a film? You've got money to spare. Get the tube ticket to Epping. Walk along the road towards the Forest. You'll be watched all the way. Someone'll pick you up there. O.K.?'

Rupert nodded, feeling words to be somewhat superfluous. As he left the shop and forced his way towards Tottenham Court Road Tube Station, he felt nothing so much as relief. Although he knew the reputation of the Angels, he also knew that they rarely hurt people out of simple malice. Stupidity, lust or ignorance, yes. But not often sheer vindictiveness. If he played his cards right, he'd get that two nights with Donn. He licked his soft, pink lips with expectation.

On the way to Epping he hadn't actually seen anyone watching him. If he had been observed, then it was bloody well-organised. Almost with military thoroughness. He'd just begun to enter the fringes of the Forest when a plain van pulled up alongside him and he climbed in through the open door. A black-gloved hand round his neck pulled him into the back and he was expertly and silently searched.

'He's clean, Gerry. Not even a spotter bug.'

Rupert blessed his intuition that had made him neglect his usual precaution of having a radio bug in the collar of his jacket. "Gerry" – that was the name of the Angel who had led the attack on the Bank. The one with the black gloves must be the one called "Priest". Unbeckoned and unexpected, a tiny serpent of fear crept out of a corridor at the back of Rupert's mind and hissed a warning. It was noted. Rupert actually felt fear. It wasn't just a game ending with a kiss-and-make-up with Donn. These men weren't playing.

He was forced to lie face-down in the back of the van while it twisted and turned through country lanes. After what he estimated as around forty minutes the van bumped over a very rough piece of land and stopped. A rag was tied round his head and he was led into a building. The rag was pulled roughly off his eyes.

'Welcome Mister Colt, to the headquarters of the Last Heroes Chapter of the Hell's Angels, affiliated by special charter to the Chapter of Hell's Angels of Oakland, California. We know why you're here. I'm Vincent, President of this Chapter. That's Wolf, the one who planned getting you here and who favours helping you. I don't. And it's what I say that goes. So, try and convince me. If you don't, I'll have both your knees broken and have you dumped back in Epping Forest.'

'Thank you, Vincent. I must say I was beginning to doubt that you even existed. Anyway, my company want to make a film based on a young man, played by Tarquin Wells.' Someone interrupted with the cry of 'Poof', delivered in a high falsetto.

'Don't knock it dear, if you haven't tried it,' retorted Rupert in his best camp voice, getting something of a laugh. 'Where was I? Yes. Tarquin joins the Hell's

Angels and tries to take them over. He falls in love with one of the women, what do you call them? Mamas? She's the girl-friend of the leader of the ... chapter. She's played by Nancy Thompson. They all take off into the hills for a run and there's a battle between Tarquin and the leader. Tarquin wins and leads the chapter back to ... well, off on a run.' Rupert felt it better not to mention at this stage that the whitewash ending would have Tarquin queening it back to London to lead his men to accept an amnesty offered by a kind Government.

'Where do we come in?' The question came from Gerry, leaning against a wall, with his arm round Brenda.

'We, that is the Director, Donn Simon – you've probably heard of him...' he paused waiting for some sign of recognition that didn't come. 'We thought it would be rather nice if we had real motor-cycle outlaws to play the parts of the Hell's Angels. And you lads, er, men, seem to be about the only Hell's Angels around. We'd pay you and feed you on location, of course.'

'Where's location?'

'Mainly in the Midlands. Round Birmingham. Donn wants a concrete setting to give it a kind of inherent plasticity. We'd pay each man and woman ten pounds a day plus food.'

'Make it twenty, and I reckon you might have a deal.'

'Just a fucking minute, Wolf. I don't care if he makes it fifty pounds a day, I still don't like it and I'm not prepared to agree to it.'

'With the greatest of respect,' said Gerry, sarcastically, 'the very first time we met you told me that all decisions were taken democratically. How about putting this to the vote. Apart from anything else, it'll give you and your men a chance to show how fucking brave you are by going up to Birmingham on a run. Unless you're all fucking chicken.'

Gerry hugged himself inside with glee. 'I've got him,' he whispered to Brenda. 'Like he got me. Up against it. Back to the wall. Look at them all, licking their lips at the thought of all the money they can make. They want bread they can spend now. That hot bank money's untouchable. Vincent knows that. We've got him.'

Vincent saw the tunnel he had driven himself into and tried to find a way out of it. 'I wouldn't mind so much if it *was* twenty pounds, but he only said ten.'

Gerry turned to the film-man, standing fascinated by this blatant and naked power struggle. 'I *thought* I heard you say twenty pounds each person *plus* free food and drink. Wasn't that what I heard?'

'Yes, that's right. Twenty pounds. And free drink. I can probably lay on some pot, speed, coke, acid, dust, whatever you like.'

'There you are, Mister President. I move officially that we put to the vote of all brothers here present that we accept the offer of this film-man and co-operate with him on the making of his movie. When would you want us to start?'

'We're doing preliminary location searches this week. We should have the package ready to move in about six weeks.'

'All right, brothers. Time for preparation for all those old-timers who want to join Vincent on his run in full colours. Time for those who want to come with me in the vans to make their own plans. Vincent, will you please put it to the vote?'

'Yeah. Of course.' Vincent tried to put a brave face on it, but he sensed defeat. Those who want to take up this deal with the film company and work for them, raise your hands.'

Up went the hands of Gerry, Priest, Kafka, Cochise ... a moment more and up went the hands of Atlas, Moron, Dick the Hat, Riddler, Vinny and Harlequin. The hands continued to go up until there were only Vincent and Dylan, with a couple of other Angels, so stoned that they didn't realise what was going on, unmoving.

'Passed by a fair majority,' admitted Vincent graciously.

'Can we put it to the vote to see how many brothers will go on the run with you? That is, unless you've had second sensible thoughts about it and prefer to travel safely with me and my mates? If you do, we won't mind. We won't think you've chickened out'

Rupert Colt was forgotten. This was the real one. Vincent put the question as Gerry had asked him, as he was bound to by their own set of rules. Dylan raised his hand at once, as did Rat and Mealy. They were followed by Crasher and Moron. Then a pause. Then up went the hand of Atlas. 'Sorry, Wolf. But I really used to dig the old days when we all had good times on a run. It might be nice to do it again.'

A longer wait. Then one last hand. Priest! He looked sideways at Gerry, his one good eye meeting Gerry's with a hint of defiance. 'It's been a long time. It's a bit like Atlas said. I used to like it on a run. My younger brother got snuffed on a run up in Birmingham. My eye got done on a run years back. We don't get many chances now, so I figure, like, I might as well take this chance. You understand, don't you? I mean it's not personal. It won't make things different. You know what I mean?'

'Yeah. That's all right, Priest. You go, mate. Well see you in Brum.'

That was it then. Vincent lost the face-down, but he had the chance to make it up. If the run went well, and nearly half the chapter elected to go on it, his position would be strengthened. If the run went badly, Gerry would be able to face him with over half the brothers on his side.

Over the next few weeks, Gerry laid his plans with his mates for their trip to Birmingham in vans and cars. Hogs had to be stripped and serviced. Clothes cleaned to maintain their appearances as straights. Plans made and people trained. Gerry did it well. Brenda pulled the old ladies and mamas into line.

Vincent also made his plans. Part of them involved Dylan and the object of part of them involved - although he didn't know it - Gerry's own lieutenant, Priest.

On that sixth day, Rupert had laboured, so on the seventh and eighth he rested. Donn had set up the backing for the movie and secured agreement from Tarquin and Nancy. As he and Rupert lay together in his Fulham flat, Donn was content. So was Rupert.

'Donn,' came the muffled voice from under the bedclothes.

'Hey. Don't you know it's rude to talk when you've got your mouth full? What is it?'

'Those Hell's Angels. I quite like one or two of them. There's one thing I didn't like though.'

'What was that my pearl without price? Whisper it unto me love of my life, O fire of my loins.'

'Promise you won't laugh?'

'Of course my little chickadee. My darling brood mare. My own Queen of the May.'

'Ooh. You're awful sometimes, Donn.'

'Come on, for Christ's sake. Part of me's getting cold. What the fuck is it you don't like about the Hell's Angels?'

'They all smell of poo-poo!'

10. INTER-DEPARTMENTAL MEMO FROM CUTTINGS AND RESEARCH TO SPECIAL BRANCH

Heading: Motorcycle Gangs.
Source: Cinema Trade Press.
Date: May 15th 1997.
Reference: C/R 15/5/7X-SEJ

Comments:

We feel this cutting should be of interest to you in the Special Branch because of the reference to the fact that the maker of the film alleges that he has employed, or has it as his intention to take into his employ, members of a group purporting to be outlaw motor-cyclists. This claim, if substantiated, is contrary to the Home Secretary's Act on the subject, subsection 18. The cutting mentions a possible location for the making – or 'shooting' of the film. This is alleged to be in the vicinity of North Birmingham. We respectfully suggest that Number Six Patrol Force could liaise with any recognised Vigilante Group in the area. We also believe that it is not totally beyond the realms of possibility that Number Six Patrol Force may have located a member of the self-styled "Jokers" outlaw motor-cycle gang in that area who would be prepared to inform police of any local activity. Surveillance and tapping are, as a matter of course, being carried out on the offices of the director of the film, Mister Donn Simon, and the home of his closest associate, Mister Rupert Colt. It is worth bearing in mind that Colt has a criminal record for offences against young male persons and is frequently on the Deviates' List of the Social Offences Branch. Simon has several convictions for drugs.

It is obvious from the references in the attached cutting that the group of outlaws is certainly the "Last Heroes" under their self-styled leader, "Vincent" (no real name known). They probably include "Wolf" (a.k.a. Gerry a.k.a. Gerald Vinson) and his associate "Priest" (a.k.a. Mister Priest a.k.a. One Eye a.k.a. Christopher Harrington).

cc. S.B./N.P.F.6/S.O.B./I.R.

Cinema Trade Press. May 14th 1997.
DONN PREPS BIKE QUICK FLICK.

Go-ahead director Donn Simon – remember his drag version of *The Long, The Short And The Tall* – leaps aboard a dangerous carousel with his scheduled quickie. Starring Tarquin Wells and Nancy Thompson he has asst. dir. Rupert Colt sussing out locs. in the North Midlands right now. Big pub. gimmick to hype the youth audience is that Donn has lined up some real – count the scars – Hell's Angels to give some real action to this exploitation film. Filming will be in secret to keep the heavy hand of the fuzz off some collars that ought to be felt. Donn claims members from killer club "Last Heroes" helping out on cast list. It'll probably rake in loot but it can't help the movie industry. Whatever happened to the family film?

11. A BEGINNING – A MIDDLE – AN END – IN THAT ORDER

"One has no great hopes from Birmingham. I always say there is something direful in the sound."

EMMA – Jane Austen

During the weeks that they were preparing for the big run North to Birmingham, Gerry was busy. He had managed to get in touch with brothers of the exiled Jokers, the chapter that still existed in the Birmingham area. Whittled down by the fuzz to a mere handful, they held on by the skin of their teeth. Their kicks came from burning out a coloured family now and again and a quick rumble with the local skinheads.

What the Jokers didn't know, and what Gerry didn't know, and what you have to remember, is that there was an informer in the ranks of the Jokers. A spy for the fuzz. He was called "Les the Ruin" – "Ruin" for short. The local police chief was that rarest of animals, an intelligent copper. He had deliberately not hassled the Jokers, knowing he could pull them all in at any time he wished. They were more useful to him as a threat to the citizenry, a bogey-man to point out the dangers of a society without police. Also, he felt that one day he would be able to use his informer for a larger purpose.

Ruin had already left him messages to tell him that the London chapter was considering a run up to Birmingham. This was getting uncomfortably close to the constituency of the Prime Minister. 'No mistakes, Mister Sanders,' that was what that bastard Hayes had said to him. He knew roughly where they were going to run, he knew roughly when. He didn't yet know how many. Time was beginning to run out for the Jokers, for Mister Sanders, and for others.

July 1st. A notice appeared in the Personal Column of the top people's paper. *Henry VIII, Act Two, Scene One. Rupert says.* It had been a suggestion from Kafka. In that scene from Shakespeare's play, Buckingham makes the traditional speech just before his execution. During it he says: 'Go with me, like good Angels, to my end'. Even the usually withdrawn Vincent had found that amusing.

So, the race was to be run.

During that long, hot, hazy, summer day, final plans were made. While the mamas and old ladies lazed around on the soft turf, Vincent, Gerry, and the top brothers held their last meeting before the run the next day.

Sides had been drawn up. Gerry had the easiest of it. He was to take most of the Angels up with him in the vans and cars. They would travel openly, mainly driven by the women. No bunching, leaving by different roads, some to go up the M1, some on the old A5, driving off at irregular periods. There shouldn't be any problems. They would rendezvous at their agreed meeting-point during the evening of the Second July.

'Now, you're sure yon can find the meeting place?' The question came from Gerry, the planner and strategist. He'd questioned the brother from the Jokers at great length. He'd wanted somewhere that they could all get to, somewhere quiet.

He'd even travelled up to the concrete, soul-less Midlands, scouting out the land. Finally, he'd found exactly what he'd been looking for; a deserted sand quarry, north of the city itself. Close to the M6 where it ran round near to Great Barr. The quarry had been a haunt of kids years ago, but had gradually become more dangerous and had finally been wired off by a local council. They had only taken action after a young brother and sister had drowned there. Now it was deserted. A place of stagnant pools and shells of an iron works. There was even the bones of an old air-raid shelter. It was perfect.

Gerry had been careful not to let on to anyone exactly where he planned to hole up for that night. He had told Rupert and had taken him up to see it. Strangely enough, he had developed a liking for the little film-man, and trusted him more than anyone in the chapter. Rupert had been ecstatic and had raved over the old iron works. 'So menacing, don't you think, love?'

The rest of the Angels had been told earlier that afternoon, and most of them had found his instructions easy to follow. But, there were always exceptions.

Vincent had used his old power to lift the numbers of those going on the run. It was almost exactly half and half, with many of the older Angels taking the chance of a run. Those who were going with Gerry, called by Vincent the "Ladies' Outing", included all of the women of the chapter. It was one of the men who were going to drive that was his biggest problem. Cochise, for all his name, was hopeless at reading a map and just couldn't remember the instructions. When they ran through the details, he was still vague.

'Look. Don't worry, Wolf. A tracker like me could find his way in a snow-storm. I'll be there. Me and my old lady.'

Cochise's old lady lived up to the name. She was nearly forty and had the biggest breasts of any old lady. Or mama, come to that. She, her name was "Forty", had a strange relationship with Cochise. In a world where odd relationships are the rule rather than the exception, theirs really *was* odd. They had never been seen having if off with each other. While other couples screwed all round them, they would simply lie quietly in each other's arms. He would open the zip at the front of her leather jacket, tear down her stained tee-shirt and tug out her breasts. Despite their size, Forty never wore a bra. Then, for hours on end he would simply apply his mouth to one of the nipples and suck happily on it while she ran her fingers through his long hair.

The only clue that anyone ever got to Cochise and Forty was when he once got spaced out of his head on acid and began to mumble about her. 'Best old lady in the whole fucking chapter.' The he laughed, almost choking, 'I'm the luckiest Angel in the whole bleeding world. My old lady really is my old lady. In fact she's a real mean mother.'

Other brothers put two and two together and made only three. But, what if she was ... It was their business.

Gerry shook his head at Cochise. 'Listen. Here's a piece of paper. That's where to go and that's how to get there. Right?'

'Don't worry about us, Wolf, baby. We've got more chance of being there than Vincent and his nutters.'

The basic plan was simple. Vincent and his brothers would leave together at about four in the morning, before it was light. They would rely purely on speed and surprise to get them through. The police on previous runs had tried to hassle them but their superior speed and mobility had always got them through. Now, though, there was a depth of feeling in the country that there had never been before. The straights were out against them as never before. Since the brutal, casual killing of the blind boy down in South London, hatred was high. The bank robbery had brought the briefest of changes, with the Englishman's traditional love of the clever and slightly romantic criminal. When details of the brutality used came out, coupled with news of the girl's rape and her father's subsequent suicide, opinion hardened still further.

So, speed. Speed and discipline. Common sense said that they should make the run completely at night. Pride, prompted by the nagging tongue of Gerry had resulted in an uneasy compromise. A night start with a dawn finish.

While girls dozed in corners, all the men had been up all night making last-minute adjustments to the bikes and to the vans. Almost without anyone noticing, it was suddenly four o'clock. Departure time.

Vincent swaggered out, his colours making a due splash of blue in the shadowy room. His good ear sported a gold ring, and his hair was tied back with a silk band. The rest of the Angels who were going on the run all wore their colours. Priest had a patch over his damaged eye to protect it from the night wind. Atlas had ribbons knotted in his beard.

Gerry stood watching with Brenda as they straddled their polished machines. At the last minute, Vincent walked over to him. 'O.K. Wolf. This is, like, it. Sorry you didn't have the guts to come with us, but someone has to look after the women. See you in Brum. Bye.'

Gerry said nothing. There wasn't any point. Not now. The dice were down. He looked across at Priest, studiously rubbing at a mark on his shiny ape-hanger bars. 'See you, mate.'

Priest looked up at the shout and half-smiled, his eye glinting in the light. 'See you. Hey, Gerry. This is great. Honest. Like old times.'

A gloved hand lifted high in salute. Engines revving deafeningly under the arched roof. Screaming of tyres and they were gone. No lights. Not till they were through the village and well round the 414. Single file.

The big room, smoke from the engines lingering, the roaring hanging in the air. An air of unease and anti-climax.

Gerry broke the silence. 'All right brothers. Let's start getting things into the vans.'

Brakenham Parva was sleeping as the convoy of Angels rolled through at a sedate forty miles an hour. Few citizens did more than turn in their sleep and roll back into dreams, strangely coloured now with shadows and night-shapes. Only one man saw them at this stage. A night-worker, strolling home from his shift, heard the crackle of their exhausts, snarling from the other side of Brakenham. He stopped still in the shadow of some elms at the side of the road and watched. When he saw the Angels from Hell ride past him, faces turned forwards, arms draped on the bars, lying back at rest, he felt a choking mixture of fear, drowned by anger.

The first telephone that he ran to was shattered, the black plastic scorched and twisted. It took him nearly ten minutes to reach the next phone. It wasn't wrecked.

By the time he got through to the police to give them the warning that the Angels were loose and riding free, the run was near to the motorway. Through Hertford, Cole Green and Hatfield. The still, warm air trembled at their passing and was still. An occasional lorry driver saw them ghost past him, a raggle-taggle band of outlaw riders.

Then they were rolling on the motorway, heading for the M1. Speed building up, hair streaming, eyes squinting against the pressure of the summer slipstream. Far behind them and far ahead of them, the police cars were beginning to roll. Straps tightening under firm, law-abiding chins and fingers ramming shotgun shells into the breeches of 'Law Officer' sawn-off, pump-action guns. Stroking the polished walnut stocks with a sick kind of near-sexuality. The police were ready. And waiting. It would soon be time for outlaw bride and police groom to consumate their union. Far-fetched? Think of all the hate that lies in love. Think of all the love that underlies hate. Without Hell's Angels, the police would have no super-enemy. If the police and their civilian bastard offshoot, the Vigilantes, did not exist, who would the Angels have to hate and fear?

So they travel through the ending night.

The run is on. Well on. Twenty or so mind-blowing monsters, double lining at ninety-plus up and onto the biggest of the motorways. Number One. If you'd had a helicopter that July night, you could have ridden low over them and seen all.

Leading, Vincent, slightly ahead of Dylan. Both riding the Angel's elite hogs – Harley-Davidsons. Since the clamp-down in the early nineties, motor-bikes had almost gone out of production, even for legal citizens. This meant that all the chopped bikes ridden by the Angels dated from about 1972.

Vincent straddled an Electra Glide, a six hundred-weight monster with 1200cc. thrusting it on. All the trim that made it a Rolls-Royce bike had been cut off, and more chrome added. When pushed it could carry Vincent along at over one hundred miles per hour. Dylan rode the slightly smaller and lighter Super Glide, painted in day-glow colours with a flake-finish. The frame and seat had been lowered and the front forks raked and extended by about twelve inches. The mudguards had been peeled back to the minimum, with foot-rests and control pedals pushed right forward. High-rise ape-hanger bars had been added, gleaming in polished chrome. The exhaust pipes had also been chromed and dragged up high on either side of Dylan's broad shoulders. It was a thing of supreme beauty and a joy to Dylan's dark soul.

He and his President talked – or, rather, screamed, at each other as they tore along. Confirming plans for the imminent departure of one of their brothers.

For Priest it was an up-trip. His head cleared to bursting with a charge of coke, he was reliving all the good days. Rolling along with the boys 'neath blue suburban skies. Head high, girls waiting, miles to go before sleep. His black-gloved knuckles clenched round the throttle, forcing a mile or two more out of his rare Dunstall 750 Mark 2. The headlight reflected off the shining back of Vincent's machine. A tear caught at the corner of Priest's one good eye. Nothing else mattered to him but the run and his brothers. He muttered to himself, the gospel of Freewheelin' Frank, Angel hero: 'All on one and one on all. Our scene is forever. We know it. We don't need to believe, we know.' He was going all the way home.

Others behind him and around him. Crasher and Moron, Rat and Mealy, Atlas on his beaten-up Norton from the early sixties, Riddler and Harlequin, Dick the Hat. An assortment of faces, beards, long hair streaming. Shouting and cursing each other. Drinking and stoned to the wide world of night wonder. Bikes, an assortment from the past – a Bultaco-Metralla Mark II, a 650 Yamaha, a big MV Augusta, a B.M.W. and Triumphs and Nortons. All big powerful bikes. Nothing under a "ton".

No incident till Junction 13, the B557 Woburn Sands turn-off. Then a heavy lorry, lumbering along at sixty-five in the slow lane. The first streaks of morning light peering over the trees to the right. A driver, more stupid than brave, seeing the Angel convoy unbelievably in his mirror. A chance to kill an Angel for Christ, swinging the wheel, snaking into the middle lane, the trailer missing Atlas by less than a foot. A huge juggernaut of death. Crushing out the dying past with forty tons of glazed sanitary ware, and steel tubing.

The driver chuckled to himself as he saw the pack scatter. High and secure in his heated cab, he watched with amusement when he saw them drop back. He confused withdrawal with defeat. They had dropped back, slowed down to take off chain belts, and ease tyre spanners from brackets under the frames. Then they accelerated, led by Atlas.

The driver saw them coming, smiled. Drifted to the right to block them, whipping the trailer to the right, hoping to flick at least one of them into the centre railing. It had been so long since the Angels rode like this, so long since people saw bikes out in force. Everyone, and that includes the driver, had forgotten just how quick and easy to handle a hog is.

Atlas eased back a little, behind the trailer, waiting for the driver to make another move. Harlequin came forward at his wave and feinted with Dick the Hat on the left. The driver responded and Atlas and the rest were past him on the outside, chains swinging. The first blow clanged on the panel of the driver's door, then the second Angel was alongside. A bottle broke on the side window, starring the thick safety glass.

He hung to the right, trying again to wipe them off. No smile now. Just fear and rage. As he moved, foot hard down on the accelerator, a back-hand chain blow from the skinny figure of Dick the Hat broke the windscreen. His fist pushed through the splintered glass, cutting him high up on the wrist. Blood splattered onto his overalls and he knew that they were going to try and kill him.

Just before a blow with a tyre lever took off his near-side mirror, he caught a flash of headlights, double-beam, coming over the crest of the hill, about two miles behind him. Light – and hope.

Blinking blood from his eyes, where fragments of the windscreen had cut his face open, he started to snake the long lorry, making it as difficult as possible for the Angels to get at him. Then, as they fell back and ranged either side, ready for the last run at him, he hit the vacuum brakes as hard as he could. The force of gravity dragged him forward out of the bucket seat, and the tyres shrieked in protest at the violent deceleration.

The move threw the Angels into temporary confusion. Half screamed past on one side, while the other half got tangled up near the central crash barrier. The trailer snaked off to the right, delicate and lethal, with a load of polished steel tube. One batch of the tube protruded out beyond the end of the lorry by just six feet. Harlequin had been about to move up on that side and was further forward than any of the brothers. When the brakes went on, he was winding his chain around his wrist, ready for another attack at the bastard in the high cab. For a second or so he wasn't concentrating. The very last thing he saw was the gleaming tube scything at his head. The last thing he felt was that tube tearing open his skull and driving into his dying brain. His last thought was a small one. He was glad he was wearing his colours. That was all.

Harlequin's hands relaxed on the bars and the weight of the steel tube, embedded in his head, swung him off his Triumph, high and wide into the air, then flinging him far over the other side of the motorway, into bushes and trees.

It was three days before his body was found. Rats had taken what was left of his brains. His eyes were also eaten. His precious chopper was wrapped round the heavy girders that made up the central barrier. He was the first Hell's Angel to die in a road accident for nearly three years.

The driver had no idea of the success of his trick, for his mirror was smashed. He was too busy to look back. The rest of the Angels were rapidly regrouping only fifty yards ahead on the motorway, waiting to see what his next move might be. He reached down to the floor of the cab, his hand closing warmly over the walnut butt of a sawn-off shotgun. With that in his hand he risked a glance back up the motorway, and saw salvation. The Seventh Cavalry of the Highways – the Motorway Patrol Police, barrelling along at eighty with headlights full on.

Safe and secure, he leaned forward and blasted off both cartridges at the Angel band, ignoring the fact that they were too far off to be at any hazard. It made him feel better. The Angels had also seen the police and turned, ready to make their move. As the gang revved up, ready to move, one small figure detached itself and ran – an odd, slinking, crippled, sideways shuffle – on foot towards the lorry. Behind it, the patrol car was slowing down, ready to squeeze past the monster that blocked almost the whole highway.

Suddenly scared again, the driver grabbed for the spare cartridges he kept in the glove compartment. Fumbled to try and break the gun and slide them into the breeches. The little, rat-like figure was only about twenty feet away. Had stopped. Thought better of it? No. Was holding a ball? Something like a large cricket ball. Pulled something from it. Stood there. Frozen. Hands lifting the gun. Too slowly.

Like a petrified nightmare. The police car, right alongside. The ball bouncing heavily under the cab. The Angel scrabbling back to his hog. Away.

When the hand-grenade exploded directly under the driver, reflex tightened his fingers and the shotgun blasted high into the sky. The burst of flame tore through the cab and ripped him apart The cab was flung into the air and smashed down onto the police car alongside. The tank of the car caught fire and all four policemen perished within seconds. Their patrol radio was live at the moment of their deaths so the whole police force was alerted within minutes of the outrage perpetrated by the outlaws. The net began to close!

Back at the headquarters, most of the loading of the vans was completed and everyone was resting. Cochise was sucking peacefully on a breast and Gerry and Brenda lay together. Half dozing, barely moving to keep the rhythm of love intact, they hugged each other and waited. Waited for news and waited for time to move.

The run neared the M45 turn-off. Vincent had intended to cut through the Coventry by-pass and run round Birmingham on quieter minor roads. Sanders, the brainy fuzz, had managed to second-guess him. The turn-off was completely blocked with cars and a couple of lorries, hastily commandeered. It had to be straight on.

Light! Dawn peering through the eastern mist like a leper through a church window. The road, dew shining in that first grey light. The run, together, tension high. Knowing that after the first death there would be others.

Vincent and Dylan. Together. Another heavy articulated way ahead. Dylan dropping back. Signalling Priest up in front of him. Smiling. Priest high and happy. Throttle round another notch. Inside Vincent. Being called up closer. Dylan very close just outside his rear wheel. A chain dangling loose in his left hand. Low and unseen.

Vincent pointing at the lorry in front. Priest shook his head, not clear what his President wanted of him. Willing to try anything. Then they were level with the back of the trailer. Vincent easing him in towards it, Priest, still not guessing what was to happen. A hand raised, a flick at his ape-hangers, skidding in towards the lorry. Still time to save it. The bite of a chain in his rear spokes. The Dunstall wheeling and pitching. One good eye open in horror. No last thoughts of beauty or repentance. Just naked, blind, red, bloody, rage. Priest died as he had lived for much of his life. With his lips pulled back from his teeth in a snarl of hate for all the world. Black.

It was an unwritten rule of a run that nobody stopped if anyone flaked off or got snuffed. There was enough light for everyone to see that Priest had no chance. To strike a bitumen road with your bare head from a height of about twenty feet and at a speed of something like ninety miles per hour means that you are dead. Instantly. Blackly.

One thing that Vincent and his lieutenant hadn't reckoned on was quite *how* light it was. It was just light enough for Kafka, riding at four in the phalanx, to see the winking of the chain in Dylan's hand. No way of involving Vincent. But Dylan ... Kafka edged up behind Dylan at number three and waited.

Waited till Junction 19. The turn-off for the Midlands. For Birmingham. It was there that Sanders had prepared his best trap. The whole of the M1 was closed off and nearly three hundred police were there or thereabouts. Not only was the M1 itself closed, but the turn onto the M6 was also barricaded by cars and lorries. Behind the Angels came a solid block of police vehicles, the leading ones only a few miles behind. Ahead roamed a helicopter, with a mixed crew of police and television reporters. The media had been very swift to the scene, with a little prompting from the lads in blue, anxious that the honest citizens shouldn't miss anything of this crucial confrontation with the riders of the night. So confident was Sanders of the success of his plan that he had persuaded George Hayes' department to allow the news reporting to go out live. An almost unique event in days of careful 'editing' of all news items. What he hadn't done was taken into account the careful planning that had characterised the Holloway job, and reckon that the mind that had planned that might also have a contingency plan of its own.

As they rocketed up to the turning, Vincent saw the trap, and realised that it was almost exactly how Gerry had said it would be. So, having no other alternative, he raised his right hand in the agreed signal. Apart from simple strategy, Gerry had a great gift for lateral thinking. What he had reckoned on, and what Sanders had forgotten, was that every road has two ways.

The pack swerved across the gap in the central reservation, up onto the feeder road from the north and round behind the police trap onto the M6 on the wrong side of the road.

Millions of early morning viewers saw the police stand frozen as the Last Heroes swept past them, passed their careful block, leaving behind a scene of total confusion as drivers ran for their vehicles, only to find them trapped in the web of lorries and cars. It was fully two minutes before reason re-established itself and the T.V. picture was blanked off with a bland apology about a 'technical hitch'. The Angels were through and riding free. The local police chief, for all his intelligence, was about to be replaced.

Full dawn now. Time for the first of the vans to begin moving. Driven by Brenda, with Gerry and a couple of mamas in the back, huddled round the shrouded, magical shape of Gerry's big Harley. Their route was to be the old, quiet A5, right up to near Shrewsbury. Round the town, then sneak back to their meeting-place from the north-west through Wolverhampton and Walsall.

'That was King Cliff with his new ragga-rock version of "Peace In The Valley". Well, brothers and sisters – seems there's not too much of the old peace in England's green and pleasant valleys this warm morning. The latest on the cycle drive currently being run by the Last Heroes Hell's Angels gang seems to show that the last may soon be the past. We'll all cross our fingers, brothers and sisters – I can see a couple of fingers uncrossed down in Bournemouth – and we'll all hope for the best. And, of course, for the endest of the worstest!

'Latest we have. Here it is. Off the shoulder and straight to you. The gang that has already been responsible for the deaths of several people – including eight policemen – narrowly and luckily avoided a trap set for them. That was at the junction of the M-for-Motorway One and the M-for-Motorway Six, so drivers, I should steer clear of that junction for the next hour or so. Four of the animals are already dead on the highway, and the remainder of the depleted mob are still heading for Birmingham.

'So, get ready Vigilante brothers and sisters. Arise and sharpen up those knives. While you're all doing just that, here's some good music for you. It's the best from the best. A rave from the grave. A zoom from the tomb. A blast from the past. It's the late and very great Eddie Cochran with the magic of "Dark Lonely Street". Suss you soon!'

Come on, up and away with the police helicopter. Ahead of the run. Up to what used to be called "Spaghetti Junction". There were so many slaughterhouse crashes there it got re-named "Intestine Corner". So it goes.

Scurrying through side streets, black dots of people, all heading for the motorway. Mainly women. Not young, hair swept up in curlers. A few men, drab clothes. Some women in dressing-gowns and lime-green, fluffy bedroom slippers. Occasionally a flash of weak sunlight off something metal held in the hand or tucked in the belt. Up and onto the road. Hundreds. Waiting.

Waiting for the Last Heroes. Winging nearer. Three minutes away. The distant early warning of the powerful engines. Police sirens whining at their heels. Containing them but not yet catching them. Closer.

'Jesus fucking Christ! Look at that!' Vincent, screaming high against the noise of their passing. Hands wrenching back on throttles, brakes biting, rear wheels wavering as they slow from one hundred, to fifty, to ten, to ... a stop.

'We've got to go through them. They'll cut us to bits if we wait!'

'Yeah. And the fuzz are coming!'

'Vincent! Fucking do something!'

Confrontation. The crowd of Vigilantes, waiting, moving, one, two, a few at a time, forwards. Nearer. Wanting blood. Angels' blood.

Vincent sat there, straddling his hog. Frozen. It was like nothing he had ever encountered. If it had been police, or other Angels, or blacks. But this was a crowd of honest citizens, mainly women. Holding fucking great knives and axes.

Vincent froze.

The police were nearly on them. The mob was nearly on them. All the Angels were looking at Vincent or at the slowly approaching Vigilantes. Nobody was watching Kafka. He was right behind Dylan. Just behind him. Close up. Nobody was watching. Dylan wasn't worried. He figured he'd get away, whatever happened. Like Bobby Zimmerman sang, about how everyone thinks they are going to be the only survivor after the war. The grey, slimy cogs inside Dylan's head hardly moved. He wasn't worried.

Kafka thought about Priest, snuffed out on the highway. Murdered by a chain. By Dylan. And he moved. Bent down, hooked his arm under Dylan's left leg and heaved him up and off his chopper, pushed the bike on top of him. Simultaneously screamed out: 'Let's go! Let's fucking go!'

Revved up, straight at the crowd, yelling and cursing. Vincent following him without looking back. The others seeing the gap, driving for it, not looking back.

The women opened out as the bikes roared at them, let them through. Closed up, encircled the bike lying on its side. Stood, ringing the fallen Angel. Dylan, struggling to his feet, leaving his hog. Looking round him. Police stopping, beyond the circle. Seeing, but not interfering. No way round, and others had held their chance. Got clean away, sneaking all into their meeting-place. And the vans. All made it. All but one.

Dylan.

He didn't try and run. He didn't try and fight. He just stood there as they tore him down. As the knives flashed and the nails tore, he died. Quickly. The pain was not long.

Although he died quickly, the mob were not easily satisfied. His head was hacked from his shoulders and passed gleefully from hand to hand. His clothes were ripped to shreds. Some women dipped pieces of his jacket in his blood and took them away. One elderly women, dressing-gown and hair still in tight curlers, got the biggest cheer when she went and sliced his genitals from the white flesh of his stomach, holding them high over her head.

Violence breeds violence.

All the Last Heroes made their rendezvous. All but one.

Dylan.

12. REPORT OF POLICE INFORMER LESLIE EUBIN, A.K.A LES THE RUIN, A.K.A RUIN

I wasn't able to get too close to them or find out much of their plans. But, I guessed roughly were they might be heading and I kept watch up there. I saw a lot of vans up in the North Birmingham area, close to the Great Barr turn-off from the Motorway. The base is an old quarry, off the A34. There are about forty of the Last Heroes there, including their Pres., Vincent, and the brother who seems to be the real leader, that's Gerry. I made contact with them, like you wanted, and got talking about their plans. They were all shaken up by the events of the run, with three of them killed. The names of the dead were Harlequin, Dylan (a big brother who was right-hand man of Vincent) and Priest. I think it was Priest who was a friend of Gerry's and might have been the one who did that bank job. It seemed to me that there was quite a lot of tension between the two top brothers. Some of the others said that they were blaming each other for the two deaths of their lieutenants. I don't know if that's true or not. When I left them tonight, there was a kind of truce there and they were all getting stoned together. If I was you, I'd keep an eye on that Gerry. He seems to have more cool than any of the others. His old lady, Brenda, is also quite dangerous. She seemed particularly suspicious of me.

The film company are due to move into the quarry early tomorrow morning, and they aim to start shooting the film more or less straight away. I asked if I could stay with them, but there is always a lot of hassle when a member of a rival chapter is around and I was told to leave.

I think that's all I can do to help you. They won't allow me back again. Can I have some bread for helping you out again? Let me know next time you want any help, though I am worried about them rumbling me as a snout.

Get the money to me at the usual place. I'll be there from three till four next Wednesday.

Les.

Note attached:

From Assistant Chief Constable Stout to Head of Special Branch.
This is a copy of a report from one of Sanders' informers. He won't have any use for him any more and it sounds to me as though the informer has outlived

his usefulness. Have him picked up at the usual place, I believe this is a record shop in Hunt Street, Birmingham. The report states when he'll be there. Charge him with being a member of an illegal organisation and possession of drugs. I leave it to your discretion to decide what drug is to be found on his person. I suggest cocaine, since the magistrates have instructions to be particularly hard on this drug.

Please send me your report as soon as possible. If you have any worries we can discuss them this afternoon at the meeting to organise our raid on the quarry.

13. LANDSCAPE WITH FIGURES

'Come on sweeties! Gerry, love, can you get your chums to go into their places. I really want to have things set up before God descends on us from his wee mountain.'

The Angels had set up their makeshift camp the night before with practised inefficiency. Tents were spotted all over the deserted quarry, and cooking fires smouldered. Most of the Last Heroes had finished their breakfast – egg, bacon, pot and Southern Comfort, the Angels' current favourite drink.

Gerry drank the remainder of his black coffee down, feeling it burn out the lingering peach flavour of the booze. He patted Brenda on the shoulder and got up, answering the call from Rupert Colt.

'It's going to be a gay morning,' he said, feeling the unexpected cut of his colours under his arms. He must have put on some spare weight. He'd have to watch it.

'O.K. Rupert. I'll get them moving. Do you want them to have any make-up or anything like that on, first?'

'No, sweetie,' squeaked Rupert. 'They all look perfectly lovely as they are. Donn'll just love them. So will Tarquin and Nancy.'

'Yeah. When do we get to see the big name stars?'

Rupert tapped Gerry playfully on the wrist with a small riding-crop he had taken to carrying. 'Patience, dear boy. Be patient. Donn said they'd get here some time around nine this morning. He'll be here. So, wait. Ooooh!'

The squeak at the end came after he had again flicked Gerry on the arm with his little whip. Gerry turned on him and pulled it away from him. 'Don't fucking piss about with me, Rupert. I can see through your soft exterior and I can see what's underneath. So, watch it. Right?'

Rupert took back the crop with a small smile. 'Right, Gerry. We dig each other. Right I ... I thought, just for a moment there that you were going to take my whip and use it on me.'

'Sorry to disappoint you, baby. Another time, maybe.'

There was a shout from Rat who was acting as look-out.'Car coming. Big black Jaguar. Chauffeur. Two fellows, I think, and one bird. Must be the film mob.'

It was.

So they began. And, while the Angels and the film crew worked away in the quarry north of Birmingham, things were happening elsewhere. That day can be best seen as a series of short scenes with different players.

EXTERIOR. QUARRY. MORNING.

One of the black magic scenes was being shot, which involved a deal of nudity and a lot of alcohol being consumed. Nancy was spread-eagled on top of a makeshift altar while Tarquin played a priest, naked except for a long black robe, holding an enormous stiletto. The Last Heroes played themselves and lounged about in the background, indulging their sexual appetites.

Cochise was stoned out of his head, nibbling on the breast of his mama. Vincent lay on his back, being plated by one of the old ladies – "Split" – drinking Vodka from a bottle and watching Gerry.

Director Donn Simon stood on one side of the set, lining up the shot and talking to Rupert. Rupert was, in his turn, eagerly watching Tarquin, licking his pink lips as he caught odd glimpses of the star's much-vaunted equipment hardly concealed by the loose robe.

As the sun rose higher, the red, sandy walls of the pit began to reflect the heat. Gerry and Brenda found a little shaded area, behind the rusted ruins of one of the trucks that used to carry gravel. There, partly hidden from the others, away from the peeking lens of the camera, they made love.

He unzipped her faded jeans and tugged them off over her ankles. Brenda wore no pants and her red-gold pubic hair glinted in the sunlight. Gerry quickly freed himself from his own levis and pants and rolled close to her, his right hand caressing and rousing her. She took him in her hand and stroked and fondled him, until he was close to coming. He tried to roll on top of her, but she wasn't ready yet. She locked her fingers in his thick hair and pulled his head down. Normally, he would have no hesitation about pleasing her with his mouth, but the need was too urgent. He twisted her wrists making her let go of him, and drove himself on top of her and into her. She gasped at the strength of his penetration, and then moaned as their rhythm began to build up near to a climax.

Brenda's nails clawed at the back of his colours at the peak of sex. Then it was over and he rolled off her and lay panting beside her.

'You bastard! You know I like it best with your tongue. You bloody wait.'

'Every now and again, when it suits me, and only when it suits me, I'll do that for you. Otherwise, we do it the way I want and when I want. Remember, you may have more bloody brains than most of the other mamas, but the most useful part of your body is still that,' leaving his hand on her moist thighs.

During that long hot morning, the filming continued.

INTERIOR. ASSISTANT CHIEF CONSTABLE STOUT'S OFFICE. MIDDAY.

'Jean! Could you just ring round to everybody on the list for this afternoon's meeting. Make sure everyone's coming. Oh, and can you ask Henderson to check my revolver and ammunition belt? Then you and I might just stroll round the corner to the Bull Ring Bistro for a nibble of lunch.'

INTERIOR. DONN SIMON'S CAR. TWO P.M.

'Donn, I'm a bit worried about the way things are going. Tarquin spends all his time making eyes at the Angels. Nancy does nothing but prick-tease them and play the super-star. And...'

'Yes Rupert. What about me?'

'You know me sweetie. I hate to criticise. Especially when it's the guy who's paying my cheque each month.'

'But?'

'But, you're playing it wrong with these guys. You've let them have free access to the drink and to the dope. You try and push them around like they were nothings from Central Casting. Then you try and get them to show class and french kiss each other for the cameras. They know you can't stand them...'

'Fucking right, Rupert. But, please go on with your clever explanation of everything that I'm doing wrong. I shouldn't have interrupted you.'

The director's sarcasm didn't stop Rupert. He had heard some of the muttered comment from some of the outlaws and Gerry had taken him on one side to warn him that several of the Angels, led by Vincent, were already pissed-off with the ill-concealed contempt of some of the film people, combined with the cynical exploitation.

'For God's sake, Donn. Don't. I'm really serious. It's dangerous to push these guys. Something could snap as easily as that.'

'Rupert, my little love. The only thing that's in danger of snapping round here is your knicker elastic. Now, let's get on with it.'

INTERIOR. ARMOURY. CENTRAL POLICE STATION. BIRMINGHAM. FOUR P.M.

'Can we check that one more time. Two hundred standard issue revolvers. Two thousand rounds of ammunition. Forty pump-action shotguns with twelve rounds of ammunition per gun. Ten of the Belgian rifles with sniper-scopes. Don't forget those are only to be issued to men carrying an L.K.109. Teargas, twenty-four launchers with six grenades each. Walkie-talkie units as requested. And the Ordnance Maps, Twenty of sheet 131. That's all.'

EXTERIOR. QUARRY. FOUR-THIRTY P.M.

Brenda is reading a note that had been left with one of the look-outs for Gerry. It's from Ruin. She looks at Gerry. They don't speak.

EXTERIOR. QUARRY. FOUR-FORTY P.M.

Shooting has just finished on the black magic sequence. Donn stands with Tarquin and the rest of the film people.

'That was really super. A few more like that and we'll be finished here. You know Rupert is getting worried about us working with this mob of filth. I reckon he might just be right for once. I want to try and wrap up all the shots with this crowd and then fake the rest in London. It shouldn't take more than three days. Then Tarquin, my love, you and I might have a bit of a break. Maybe a very long weekend in Tangier. Remember those little Arab boys from the last time. The one in the hotel with the mouth like silk?'

Nancy Thompson had retreated to her tent for a flask of coffee. Dick the Hat had attached himself to her as a kind of guardian angel. She, in return, had turned all her charms on him. It helped to pass the time. He had carried her bag for her back to the tent and she had poured him out a cup of coffee. They sat close together in the small tent.

INTERIOR. ASSISTANT CHIEF CONSTABLE STOUT'S OFFICE. FIVE P.M.

'Any questions? No? Right, gentlemen. We'll all meet as arranged at four tomorrow morning. One final thing. Try and avoid using guns. The Home Secretary's getting just a little bit touchy about law and order. It's bound to be an issue in next year's Election, and there seems to be a move elsewhere towards more liberalism. But, if they show fight, then let them have it all the way. Good luck, gentlemen.'

EXTERIOR. QUARRY. FIVE-THIRTY P.M.

Vincent was sitting alone when Tarquin wandered or, rather, staggered – he'd been getting heavily into the supply of Southern Comfort – and stood by him.

'Vincent. Vinnie. You know, I really dig you Angels. You reckon it might be possible for me to join your group? I've got lots of leather gear and studded jackets and belts.'

He sat down next to the President and leaned back against a pile of rusting metal. His right hand held the remains of a bottle of liquor. As he talked, his left hand edged over until he was able to emphasise a point by putting it onto Vincent's thigh.

INTERIOR. NANCY'S TENT. FIVE-THIRTY P.M.

Nancy sits on her bed, smoking a joint, wearing a dressing-gown. Dick the Hat has been joined by Riddler, Moron and Atlas, sitting on the floor of the tent. All four of the Last Heroes are smashed out of their heads. Nancy is only slightly stoned and as she talks, she allows the dressing-gown to slowly fall apart. Feeling herself begin to get moist with the kick of exposing her sex to these masculine apes. Knowing that they won't have what she lets them glimpse. Saving it for when she gets to London and can get back to the flat and the slim, blonde little maid.

Thinking of it, she opens her thighs wider.

EXTERIOR. QUARRY. FIVE-THIRTY P.M.

Rupert and Gerry talking.

'It's worse than that, Rupert, mate. If I were you, I'd get your intellectual film-making friend, the dyke and the poof – no offence, of course – away from here as soon as possible. It hasn't worked out. They all take the piss out of us the whole time, and all the brothers are getting thoroughly choked off about them. Somehow it turned bad from the start.'

'I reckon you're right, Gerry. It was all Donn's idea. I thought it might have worked, but it hasn't had a chance. Still, it wasn't your fault.'

'The run went sour. Three killed. I don't give a fuck about Dylan. Kafka told me he killed Priest. But, three dead. That's a lot. We ought to get away. I've just got a feeling.'

'What about?'

The fuzz. Vincent did for some on the run, and they're not going to forget that easily. I didn't trust that Birmingham brother, Ruin. He stank of fear.'

'Donn was thinking of folding it in a few days anyway and matching the rest in the studio. You reckon we can hold out for, say, four days?'

'Maybe. But, I doubt it. Not with Donn's continual snide cracks about us. Or the dyke's cock-teasing. Honest, mate, we're on a barrel of gelignite. All it needs is someone to light the fuse.'

In fact, Gerry was both right and wrong. He was right about there being a fuse. But, as it turned out, there were three separate fuses and they all got lit round about the same time.

EXTERIOR. QUARRY. FIVE-THIRTY-FIVE P.M.

'Keep your fucking hands to yourself, you bastard! I'll fucking show you!'

INTERIOR. NANCY'S TENT. FIVE-THIRTY-FIVE P.M.

'Dick darling, roll me another joint. There's a dear. What are you staring at? Didn't anyone ever tell you it's rude to stare? What do you think...? No. No!'

EXTERIOR. QUARRY. DONN'S CAR. FIVE-THIRTY-FIVE P.M.

Donn has had more than enough for one day and is about to leave for the night, though there are still hours more of light. The rest of the crew are staying at a hotel in Walsall. One of the sound boys had seemed interested – and interesting. That was one way of working this filth out of one's artistic system.

. Donn got into his Jaguar and pressed his foot savagely down on the accelerator. The big car surged forwards, then slewed off to the left as the rear wheels skidded in a pool of greasy slurry. The front wing caught the high-rise bars of Riddler's bike and knocked it into the next chopper. The hogs went down like a pack of cards, and the big car drifted into the confusion.

There was agonised screeching of torn and crushed metal and then hush. From all around the quarry, Angels came running towards the carnage. Donn got out of the car and glanced at the mess he had caused. He spoke to the first Angels who arrived: 'You! Get these bloody motor-bikes out of my way! Bloody move them. Don't just stand there like a crowd of ruptured apes, move them!'

So, the three fuses were lit. Almost simultaneously, the three explosions went off. The first explosion was really not so much a bang as a whimper. Vincent had stood up and tried to push Tarquin away. The star whispered urgently up at him, promising him all kinds of pleasure. He pressed his face against the Angel's thighs, his mouth eagerly seeking the bulge at the front of the tight levis. He pushed the bottle into Vincent's hand, urging him to drink. His own fingers tugged impatiently at the zip on Vincent's jeans.

'Fuck off, you bastard!' Vincent slapped him open-handed. Tarquin crawled back to him, pulling himself up his legs, his hands working at his groin, his mouth drooling open. Almost without his realising it, the half-full bottle of Southern Comfort swung high in Vincent's hand, then arched down. It cracked across Tarquin's cheek, drawing blood. A second blow caught him across his expensively remodelled nose, wrecking several hundred pounds worth of plastic surgery. Moaning, Tarquin slumped at Vincent's feet.

With almost fanatical strength, he scrabbled at the Angel's boots, trying desperately to get to his feet. Vincent lifted one foot and stamped down, as one would on a revolting slug, cracking the skull and forcing the pulp of a nose into the gravel. Then, Tarquin screamed, once only. Vincent stamped twice more, then edged back and kicked accurately for the base of the skull. The toe of the boot seemed to dig in a dreadful distance, then cartilage and bone parted and Tarquin Wells was dead. His neck broken, his face bloodied and stained from the vomit that had stirred the sand into mud, Tarquin Wells, a million dollar investment, was dead.

He would rise no more.

Explosion two was more of a bang than anything else. Lovely lesbian, Nancy Thompson, sweet dream baby of a dozen films. Masturbatory fantasy become flesh for tens of thousands of adolescent boys – and some girls – had pushed her luck a little too much with the wrong people. Like her co-star, she was used to playing games with rich and beautiful people. Like Tarquin, she discovered that there are some people who will simply not play your games. People who won't take that sort of shit from anybody.

Prick-teasing is not a game to play with the Hell's Angels.

Nancy had played it in her little tent, snug with four of the Angels. There is no point in giving the details of precisely what happened. She was raped by all four, then by others who were attracted by the noise. Her dressing-gown was torn from her shoulders by Atlas, but it was Dick the Hat who penetrated her first. Then more, singly, and in pairs. When she tied to scream she was brutally silenced by one of the brothers punching her in the mouth, breaking teeth, destroying the beautiful and expensive caps and crowns.

Oddly, after it was all over, and she was safe – for the Angels let her go when they had finished their sport – she found herself little touched by the nightmare. As a star actress, she had forced herself to sleep with men, and women, that she found totally repulsive. She had done things and been places that few dream of. The experience didn't alter her at all, unless it strengthened her lesbian tendencies.

Nancy Thompson sold her story to a nauseatingly popular Sunday paper, had her teeth fixed again, and found she was a very hot property. She stayed a star for many years. But she never made that one mistake again. However much good came incidentally out of it, she never again played the game of prick-teasing with Hell's Angels.

But she lived.

Finally, to the last and greatest of the explosions.

EXTERIOR. QUARRY. BY DONN'S CAR. FIVE-THIRTY-SIX P.M.

'You! Get these bloody motor-bikes out of my way! Bloody move them. Don't just stand there like a crowd of ruptured apes, move them!'

'Ain't nobody gonna kick my motor-cycle!! You bastard, you hear me? Everything in this stinking world that I've got is invested in that thing.'

'Listen to me sonny-boy. Fiddler, or whatever they call you. Shift that mess or I'm going to get back in my car and drive right clean over the top of everything and you can whistle for your money. It's over. Dig. It's over!'

Riddler, the foremost of the Angels to reach the chaos where Donn had knocked over a pile of their bikes into the dirt, grabbed him by the sleeve of his trendy Madras cotton jacket. 'You prick! I love that hog better than I love anything else and you want to drive over it. Man, I know what you are.'

Donn shrugged the hand off his sleeve, as though he had just discovered a particularly repugnant insect. 'All right. What am I?'

The voice that answered was quiet. It came from the back of the group. It was the voice of Gerry.

'You are dead, Mister Simon. You get down now and pick up each one of those bikes and polish them off and you say how sorry you are to the brothers. Then, you will live.'

'Come off it. You don't frighten me, Wolf. If I want to I can get the police to hound you to the end of the country. It's over. Right now. And you, leave that camera alone! Come on Rupert. Or stay with your butch friends if that's what you want.'

'Mister Simon. I mean what I say. You won't tell the police, because you will be dead. One last chance. Take my advice and take that chance.'

'Up your arse. You wouldn't dare hurt me. I'm a big man. Tell them Rupert.'

'Yes, Rupert, mate. Tell him.'

The confrontation was interrupted by a scream, quickly choked, from the other side of the quarry. Almost simultaneously, Nancy's small tent began to thrash and billow. Again there was just one scream. Again, it was quickly muffled.

Gerry turned to Rupert. 'I reckon it's too late my little mate. That first yell sounded like Tarquin and that [pointing to the heaving remnants of Nancy's tent] is the end of our Nancy. And those bikes are going to be the end of Donn Simon.' He pulled the little man to one side. 'Listen. All the film crew are gone. He's as good as dead. When the brothers get going they might get a bit indiscriminate and I don't see why you should buy it as well as that bastard. So, push off, Rupert. I'll see you one day.'

Rupert looked up at the taller Angel. He touched him quickly on the arm. 'Thanks, Wolf. See you. Sorry it ... well, you know.' He slipped through the ring of Angels and was gone.

Donn Simon opened his mouth as though he was about to say something, and then closed it again. With the disappearance of his right-hand man, and the screams, realisation had come to him with the chill sudden horror of the Angel of Death.

The group parted again to let Vincent through. He walked slowly to stand by Gerry. The blood on his boots had picked up sand. He held the broken neck of the bottle in his right hand. Gerry turned to him. 'Tarquin?'

'Snuffed.'

'What the hell does he mean, "snuffed"? Where's Tarquin?'

'He just told you, Mister Simon. He's dead.'

'Oh, God!! God Almighty!! Why? For Christ's sake. Why?'

'Because he tried to fucking blow me. And I just didn't want to be blown. Not by that bastard narcissistic queer. I told him to pack it in, but he wouldn't. He just kept on and on. So, I hit him. With this bottle. He still tried to keep on with his filth. So, I kicked him a couple of times. And he died.'

That was more or less that. The gang-bang continued for another hour or so, until everyone had had enough. And they let Nancy go. They even let her wash herself. Then they let her go.

But Donn Simon was different. He was the boss man. It was his fault. It had all gone wrong, and it was entirely his fault. Worst of all, he had messed with their bikes and he had dared them to do something about it. *And*, he had even had the bleeding nerve to threaten them with the fuzz. Any one of those three crimes could have got him killed by a Hell's Angels chapter. All three meant that he didn't have a ghost of a chance. The Last Heroes unanimously passed sentence of death on him, and they kept their word.

While Kafka operated the camera, and while the krieg-light blared, Donn Simon took part in his last film. It was a unique movie. For a man who made his reputation as a director, he ended his career as the star. Sadly for Donn, there weren't any stand-ins available for him, so he had to do all the action stunts himself.

First of all there was the grand race. Donn, on foot, had to try and beat Riddler, on his scratched but still functional hog, in a race round the gravel and sand floor of the quarry. It was Brenda who pointed out, with her usual thoughtfulness, that it was hardly a fair race. So, Vincent offered to help him out.

He gave Donn a tow. An offer which didn't seem much appreciated, as far as one could gather, for Donn was having trouble communicating. It could have been the piece of cotton waste that was wired into his mouth. Vincent gave him a length of rope to hang onto, tying the other end to the highly-polished cissy bar. Just to make absolutely sure that Donn didn't accidentally let go of the rope, Vincent tied the end securely round both his wrists.

Then, both Angels revved up their engines, let in the clutches, and the race was on. Vincent's big Harley lagged behind at the start, but he soon picked up. Donn couldn't run fast enough, so he got towed round behind the bike, his clothes being torn from his body by the gravel.

Kafka discovered that the camera had nearly run out of film, so there didn't seem that much point in going on with it.

A little later, Vincent decided that Donn had become totally superfluous.

So, he killed him.

14. THE LAW IS FOR THE PROTECTION OF THE PEOPLE

Phil Kennedy (Reporter for B.B.C. News team): The time is three in the morning. The place is a police station, a few miles north of Birmingham. The day is July 3rd. Here around me, in the early morning half-light, are several hundred policemen, gathering for one of the biggest raids in Great Britain, since the second of the so-called "Angry Brigade" assaults in 1994. Here with me I have Assistant Chief Constable Stout, who is heading the operation. An operation that could spell the end for the gang of motor-cycle outlaws reportedly hiding out a few miles from here. Chief Constable, could you tell me a little about this gang?
Assistant Chief Constable Stout: Well, as far as we know, they seem to be the gang that call themselves the "Last Heroes". You'll probably remember that this was the gang that we suspect may be able to help us with our investigations into the Holloway Bank job.
Phil Kennedy: Do you know any of their names?
Stout: Well, I believe that the leader is still a man named Vincent – after the famous horror-film actor – but we have reason to believe that there is some kind of power struggle going on within the Angels, and that a man named "Wolf" is trying to take over the presidency.
Phil Kennedy: How many do you think there are? And, could you tell us about rumours that film stars Tarquin Wells and Nancy Thompson are in the quarry with director Donn Simon, making a film about the Hell's Angels?
Stout: I would prefer not to comment on who else may be involved, as this might prejudice any trial that may result from our investigations. I would only say that it has come to my attention that rumours, such as you have just mentioned, are going the rounds. To answer the first part of your question, we believe that there could be as many as fifty outlaws up there. We aim to find out precisely.
Phil Kennedy: What are your instructions to your men if the Hell's Angels attempt to resist?
Stout: I'm sorry. I really can't divulge that to you. All I can say is that we hope that there will be no violence. We are certainly not going to go in there looking for it. Although, just in case of trouble, I have ordered that certain selected officers may carry arms. I will not expose them to any unnecessary danger from these hooligans. The sooner they are all behind bars the better.
Phil Kennedy: Of course, they will have to be tried first, won't they?

Stout: Oh, yes. Of course. That's what I meant. But, we think that these are the same group that went on that run up the motorways, killing and raping as they went. We also suspect that their numbers have been swelled by local hoodlums. If they are in uniforms or have any sort of para-military organisation we'll have them ... I mean we will be forced to take action against them under sub-section seventeen, sorry, as you were, eighteen, of Home Secretary Hayes' Act on the subject.

Phil Kennedy: The operation is scheduled to begin just before dawn. Squads of police will shortly be moving into their planned positions. Mister Stout; I'm sure that all the viewers will join with me in wishing you the very best of luck in stamping out this gang.

Stout: Thank you, Phil. As long as everyone remembers that the law is for the protection of the people. We only do our job.

Phil Kennedy: Assistant Chief Constable Stout, thank you.

15. A DARK AND LONELY PLACE

Rat was dozing about a quarter of a mile away from the main band of Angels in the quarry, near to the concealed turning off the road. He had enjoyed the violence, and found the killing of Donn Simon as the real high-spot of the run, so far. Though the blowing-up of the truck driver and his load of lavatories had also been fairly kicksie.

He thought back with a satisfied smile to the events of the previous evening. His hand crept inside his jeans and grasped his shrunk organ, stroking it as he remembered the fun of cutting at the body of Tarquin. The fun of threatening the petrol-soaked director with a box of matches. The hot blood drying and cracking on his knuckles, staining his arms rusty-brown. His hand moved more violently as he thought back to the fun with Nancy. Fun that he had been a little too late to share, but he had, at least, been able to watch the ending and gloat over the exposed thighs of the woman he had often desired from the thinly-populated stalls of his local cinema. Faster!

Suddenly, Rat woke back to full alert. Where he lay in thick bushes, he could see the main entrance to the quarry. And someone was there. He had heard a stone shift. He rose quietly to his feet and peered through the darkness. Yes, someone was there. He scuttled off silently to tell Vincent.

The first member of the invading police contingent to realise that they had been spotted far, far earlier than they had ever thought was Police Constable Simon Glazer. Ironically, he had fought with Gerry in Ireland, but had opted for the Military Police as a safe line for his hobby. (His hobby was beating other men into unconsciousness with a large truncheon.) Now, he was in civvy street, but still able to practice. He was the first of the police to encounter the Angels, because he was in the lead.

Before describing this encounter, and everything that followed, it should be noted, gentle reader, that Gerry was not taken by surprise. In fact, he rarely ever was. You may recall that Brenda showed him a note from Ruin. The fallen Angel had changed his mind and had been driven by a conscience to warn his ex-brothers of his treachery. In any case, Gerry had known that the fuzz would not take their defeat, in the eyes of all Britain, during the run, without making every effort to come out on top. That meant a lot of killing. So Gerry had sussed out all the angles as to where and when they might strike.

He figured that they still wouldn't expect to be expected, so they would take the easy path from the road. Just in case, he had set sentries at other points in a circle round the quarry. But, it was the onanistic Rat, never one to let pleasure interfere with business, who had spotted them. Things moved so fast and in so many areas after that, that any attempt to give a coherent account is impossible. So, we'll go back to Simon Glazer and then dart around for some random impressions, Right?

Simon Glazer was a married ran with three children, one more than the socially-accepted norm. He liked the police force, but was terrified of guns. That fear was the result of facing an armed boy of thirteen in the Springfield Road when the Vanguard movement took to the streets. The boy had pointed a snub-nose automatic at him from a range of about twelve feet. Three times the boy had pulled the trigger, and three times the pistol had misfired. Glazer had stopped shaking just long enough to realise that he wasn't necessarily going to die on that wet street. He had leapt at the boy and beaten his head into a bloody pulp. On a day when three hundred and forty-seven people were known to have died, the death of one boy went generally unnoticed. But, ever since that day, he had not liked guns.

So, when he was given a sawn-off shotgun and told that he might well have to use it that morning, you can understand that he wasn't happy. In fact, as he paused for a brief rest, before crawling on, he laid the gun at his side and leaned his back against a hawthorn bush.

Gerry, his colours and his face and arms smeared with mud to help him in the near-dark, was just the other side of the bush. The drive-chain of an old Norton, heavily greased, was in his hand. He whipped it round the bush, digging into Police Constable Glazer's throat, caught the other end, and pulled. Simon Glazer was too shocked by the gross suddenness of the attack to even try to scream. He made one desperate effort to get his fingers between the bite of the chain and his torn neck, but he was too late. The cold wood of the hawthorn pressed into the back of his head as Gerry threw his weight back on the chain. It dug deeper and deeper into skin, into flesh and into bloody muscle. It crushed the larynx and the windpipe. In a very few seconds, Glazer could not even breathe, let alone try and cry. His feet scrabbled in the leaf mould, his hands tore at the steel chain, then his wife became a widow. She was already deep in an affair with a driving instructor and didn't really regret his passing. But, he didn't know that.

Gerry picked up the shotgun and eased a shell into the breech, thumbing off the safety catch as he did so. About a dozen feet to his left, one of the other police had been disturbed by the brief scuffle and whispered urgently to Glazer. Since his mouth was full of his engorged tongue, and blocked with blood, there was no reply.

Knowing that whoever it was in the bushes would soon become suspicious enough to want to move over and see what the hell was going on, Gerry didn't waste time. He took the dead policeman's hand-gun, and all the ammunition he could cram into the pockets of his colours. A quick glance at his luminous watch – six minutes to four, everyone who was sober enough should be more-or-less ready in position – then he swung to his left and fired into the darkness.

The flash from the shotgun lit up the area for a second, the heavy charge tearing through the bushes and smashing into the body of the next policeman in line. Simultaneously, Gerry screamed at the top of his voice: 'Now! Let the fuckers have it!!'

Riddler dropped from a sycamore onto the back of a sergeant, his Finnish flensing knife hacking at the man's jugular. Before the blood had finished spouting high, he had a gun and ammunition.

Rat used his favourite length of piano wire, with wooden toggles at each end. Looped round a man's neck, it could come close to cutting off the head. His first trophy was a Belgian rifle, with a special night sniper-scope. He soon began to employ it usefully.

Cochise jumped from a tree onto the back of a police superintendent. His weight snapped ribs and caved the man's chest in. Broken bone penetrated the heart and the man died, conscious only of a great weight and a faint feeling of surprise.

Brenda fought alongside her man, the only one of the old ladies to do this. The rest huddled by the bikes and waited. All they could hear was screaming and the occasional shot. While Gerry fought silently and viciously, for the first time in his life at peak efficiency, Brenda was just behind him. None of the policemen had a chance against his explosive violence. In the dark, there was no chance to see your enemy, and by the time Gerry was close enough to reach you, he was too close for you to have any chance at all of stopping him. There was no wasted energy. Every blow told. As he moved on, never bothering to look behind at the men he had put down, Brenda tidied up. If the copper fell on his face she would kick hard and accurately for the base of the skull. If he lay on his back she would simply jump high, landing with her heels on the unprotected groin. Either technique generally proved fatal.

Of course, it wasn't all one way. One of the younger brothers, Crasher, was wrestling with a sergeant for possession of one of the shotguns. Sadly, he didn't have the brain to keep his stomach out of the way of the barrel. So, as he tugged, the sergeant simply placed his finger on the trigger. Crasher's own muscles did the rest. The charge of shot ripped through his colours and tore his guts apart. As he fell to the soft, green earth, his fingers clawing at his bloody intestines, vainly trying to push them back, he looked up at the horrified face of the policeman, seeing death for the first time. 'You know, I always wanted to look through my uncle's microscope,' he said conversationally, and then died.

During the first five minutes, the Last Heroes had much the better of the exchanges. Surprise was on their side, and they had the tremendous advantage of being trained by Gerry for several months. He had taught them the terrible waste of killing unnecessarily. Even more important, he had taught them the value of total aggression when the chips were down. Then, it ceased to be a game and was, literally, a matter of life and death.

In those first five minutes, nearly fifty policemen were killed or critically injured. Vincent had got possession of a grenade launcher and wreaked dreadful havoc. From his position near the main road, Stout quickly received reports of the reception his men had got from the Angels. But, it wasn't till after that he believed the reports of the massive injuries and killings. Over his walkie-talkie he ordered his first wave back. Masks were put on and the gas went in.

Seeing the police pull back, Gerry shouted for the Angels to begin their withdrawal. But Vincent stood against him. With tear-gas already ghosting through the trees, they shouted their arguments. Realising that this was futile, Gerry led a number of the brothers back to where the mamas and old ladies had the choppers ready to roll. Vincent led a charge against the withdrawing police, only to run into the gas and the second wave of attackers.

Now there were two fronts to the battle. Attacked by only a handful of police, Gerry was ready to make a run for it. Straddling his hog, Brenda hanging on tight, he took one look through the lightening gloom at the scene around him. With him were about eight of the Angels, including Kafka, Cochise, Riddler and Dick the Hat. Each with an old lady perched, Valkyrie-like, behind him. Two of the mamas had commandeered a chopper and were also ready for the off.

Back in the bushes, the Angels were losing both the fight and their lives. Legs and Moron died early in that abortive charge. Police reinforcements poured through the wood, firing indiscriminately at anything that moved in front of them. Suddenly, the high throaty note of bike engines tore through the air above the battle. The fuzz, hampered now by their greatly superior numbers, rushed around, shouting and countermanding orders at each other. Vincent, seeing the day was lost, deserted what was left of his chapter and ran. With him came only one of the Angels, slinking along at the heels of his President, twisting rat-like among the shadowy bushes.

Screaming like demons from the seventh circle of Hell, the surviving Angels, led by Gerry, hurtled out of the quarry into the confused ranks of the police. Any attempt to check them was futile, though several shots were fired at them.

Assistant Chief Constable Stout stood cursing futilely as they sped past him. His walkie-talkie squawked and chewed at him as several of his senior officers all tried to communicate with him at once. Seconds leaped by, then two more Angels – one a large man and one very small – also made a successful bid for the open road and tore along after the main band.

It was some hours before the full story was discovered. It was a story that Home Secretary Hayes himself pushed under a Double-D Notice. Apart from the terrifying casualties the police had suffered, there was also the mutilated body of film-star Tarquin Wells, a charred body that was subsequently identified by his dentist as being cult director Donn Simon, and a screaming and naked lady who claimed to be the beautiful Nancy Thompson – and was.

Worse, far worse, was the fact that both leaders of the Last Heroes had been in the group that had escaped and had been last seen beyond Shrewsbury. Many of the brothers lay dead or dying – surprisingly, not one Angel lived through that morning to appear in any courts, though some were alive when Stout made his rounds of the disaster area.

Apart from the dead, the quarry also held many injured.

Even before these could be treated, Stout ordered a check into all guns and ammunition missing. There were five shotguns, two of the rifles, fourteen revolvers and three hand-grenades. Plus a quantity of ammunition.

Despite his fear, the Angels vanished. All the efforts of the police were futile.

It was as though they had never been. From Shrewsbury, the trail appeared to lead towards Wales. But there it ended.

The Angels had gone underground.

For the time.

16. THE SURPRISE ELECTION
– A FIRST APPRAISAL
by Keith Styles (– *Ortyga Press, 1997*)

It seems likely that the "Quarry Slaughter" – as it swiftly became known – had a cathartic effect upon the moral attitudes of the British people. An unprecedented expenditure of police life – killings on a scale unique since the last troubles in Ireland – and all for a few young men on motor-cycles. Although that is a gross simplification, that is, nonetheless, the way that it seemed to the majority of folk.

The real story of the Hell's Angels, and particularly of the gang – or chapter – involved is, of course, far from being untarnished. They were certainly responsible for deaths and for crimes of violence. But, as Mister John Citizen and his wife saw, that over *fifty* policemen had died, that not one single outlaw survived to face the majesty of the legal system, that shotguns and, even hand-grenades were employed, then they began to question the wisdom of their leaders. Words such as "overkill" and "credibility-gap" began to be bandied about.

Questions were asked on street-corners, in factories, shops, offices and homes. Most of all, in homes. Newspapers asked questions, radio and television asked questions. In both Houses of Parliament, in open meeting and in secret cabal, and even on the very floor of the House of Commons, questions were asked. The only trouble was – there was no single person in authority who was able to answer them.

Attempts were made to track down the survivors of the raid. George Hayes appeared personally on television and said publicly that the animals would be brought to justice. Bus they were not. So he offered to resign. And his offer was accepted. But, people were still not satisfied. The Number One record that month was called "An eagle flying free, above a land of crows". Everyone understood!

The Prime Minister decided finally to go to the country over the moral issue that had been raised. Most Opinion Polls indicated that he would succeed. But they discounted one thing. A factor that one pundit – with the glib phraseology that can often come from hindsight – called the "Robin Hood Syndrome". Meaning that a certain amount of public sympathy had been aroused for what seemed to them to be the underdogs. Wolf and his small band of brothers had vanished into the mountain fastness of Snowdonia. The whole forces of law and order, with all their most sophisticated equipment, could not find them.

Sympathy snowballed and the folk-heroes remained hidden. The victims were all buried (or cremated). In the grave (or up the chimney) with them plunged the British Labour Party, rending itself to the last. Socialism and Repression both died in that sandy quarry in the early hours of that July morning.

17. IN MY END IS MY BEGINNING

In that early morning quiet, the remaining Last Heroes sped along the road westwards. Racing the sun. They left behind them a scene of confusion and death. The police forces were in total shambles. Firstly they had never expected to find themselves expected, nor greeted with such anarchistic savagery. Secondly, it had never entered their heads that, with such overwhelming numerical advantage, any of the Hell's Angels might be able to make their escape. They were wrong, wrong, wrong. Wrong at every point. Although they had decimated the chapter, they had not destroyed it. Nor were they in any position to try and pursue the fleeing Angels. Their own vehicles were tangled together in hopeless confusion. No attempt had been made to put neighbouring forces on standby. So, that July morning, the Last Heroes had a clear road for their desperate run for freedom.

As soon as they hit the road, Gerry leading, they turned north, avoiding the feeder road to the Motorway, where any police might lie. Heading instead for the old A5. The traditional holiday road to Wales for the industrial Midlands. Vincent and Rat caught up with them quickly, and the tiny convoy of twelve bikes roared through the pink dawn. Away!

They made good time through to Shrewsbury, where one lone policeman made his bid for a Queen's Medal. Riddler leading the run at that point had his old lady holding a shotgun trophy. Quick-thinking, she rested it on his shoulder and blasted the constable. His face literally exploded with the impact of the shot, and his body was thrown into the gutter, his blood streaming down a storm drain. They were seen leaving the outskirts of Shrewsbury and a double block was arranged for Oswestry and Whittington. But, they never got there.

Children cried out in their sleep in the village of Tudor houses, Knockin. Throughout the Welsh Marches, early rising farmers spoke later of the raggletaggle convoy. Blue denims, long hair, and naked power.

Gerry now took the lead. Belting over the Berwyn Mountains, sweeping down through Bala. Angling round the end of the huge, dirty lake. Back again into the hills. Gerry slowed down just beyond the Llyn. Raised his hand. Shouted back: 'We'd better stop'.

'Why?' Predictably it was Vincent.

'Because it's nearly light. Full light. Anyone could see us, even up here.'

'So?'

'So, we hide up for the day. Move again late tonight. Down there, other side of the Tryweryn. See that old railway track. We can get down to it and hide up under it. Come on.'

'Wait a minute. I think we should push on.'

'Well, I don't. But, if you want to go on, Vincent; then don't let me stop you. Me and these others are going down there and we're hiding up. But, you go on.'

'Fucking bastard. You know fucking well that I don't know where to go. All you ever told us was that it was a ruined village. Wait! Wait!!'

As the wide valley got lighter, the group huddled closer together. A couple of the old ladies had some chocolate in their jeans. Melted and stinking, but welcome during that long hot summer day.

While some slept, Vincent and Gerry talked long and bitterly. Argued aside from the others. Swore at each other. And reached agreement. Agreed. That when they reached the village that was their destination, then they would fight. And they would fight to kill.

'No weapons, Vincent.'

'All right, Wolf. No weapons. Just hands and chains and boots.'

The day dribbled on towards evening and dusk became dark. Later, he never knew when, and he never even knew if it was Vincent, or the dark-loving Rat, but Gerry knew that one of them loosened a nut that was better left tight. He knew about it at around three the next morning when they had begun to move again. They were coasting over the Carnedds, close to Pont Nant-y-lladron, with Vincent pushing for more speed and nobody even bothering to listen any more.

A slight bump in the gravel road, invisible at night, and Gerry's steering was gone! Even at thirty it could have been fatal. As Brenda and Gerry rolled off the careering machine, he blessed the soft, springy Welsh turf. Brenda had less to bless for she was saved from serious injury by a large, yellow-topped gorse bush.

'That was really lucky, Wolf.'

'That depends on how you look a it, Vincent. I tell you one thing.'

'What's that?'

'It's fucking lucky we didn't go fast over this road. Like you wanted. You creepy cowardly bastard.'

'Any time. Any time.'

'No. Kafka, help me fix this "accident" and we'll get on. I don't want to kill you here and find I've wasted so much time that the police see us ride through some little Welsh town. When we get to the village.'

They quickly repaired the loose nut and went on. Through misty villages, empty, waiting only for their absentee tenants to drive down from Manchester and Cheshire for a super weekend. The second-home middle-class from England that had depopulated a whole area.

Gerry led them a long way round to avoid the toll-road into Portmadoc. Through back-ways and unmade roads, away from the sea, but never too far. Twelve bikes. Finally, they saw twin peaks looming black against the slightly lighter sky. Yr Eifl – The Rivals. Mountains that saw the Romans hunting the Celtic fox, old Vortigern himself. That had seen a town of a thousand folk spring up and die on their flanks, long before Christianity reached Britain, the Ultima Thule.

Threading quietly past Llanaelhaearn, engines hardly ticking over, round the steep right-angle at Llithfaen post office. Winding up the steep hill past silent white cottages, into a wraith of sea-mist, then off the road.

Years back there was a path down to Nant Gwrtheyrn. Then it was a flourishing little village. An L-shaped block of cottages, a church/school and the master's house, bigger and alone. Ships came to the pier and took off slate and gravel chippings, brought food and ale. Then the demand dropped off and the village died. That was over twenty years ago now.

Gradually, time eroded the paint, children broke windows, teenagers saw the chance for kicks and started fires that destroyed doors and ceilings. Holiday-makers still came. Then, there was an attempt to sell the whole village in the early seventies. This had aroused the justifiable wrath of the Welsh Language Society and they had taken steps to make the path down to the village quite impassable.

So, gulls and sheep, curlews and cormorants, took over what was left of Nant Gwrtheyrn. The only sound in the steep-sided valley was the falling of white water and the shrill cry of birds. But, there was still a way down. Only a stout walker could find it, or determined people on powerful motor-cycles. The Last Heroes, what was left of them, were very determined, and they had very powerful hogs. So, led by Gerry, they straggled into the ruined village. Sheep stirred at the invasion, then went promptly back to sleep as the engines were cut, and quiet returned.

Everyone got off their bikes and stretched – it had been a hard ride. Gradually, they formed a sort of circle around Gerry and Vincent.

'Now?'

'Now!'

It was quickly agreed the terms for the fight. It was a duel to the death in the best Angel tradition. The man who is at the top, the President, facing a challenge from the man who thinks he's better. Rat announced he would be Vincent's second, and Gerry pushed Brenda back and chose Kafka. Near the sea, there was a huge tower of toppling concrete, with forty-foot high mounds of loose dusty gravel stacked against it.

Gerry was to ride a hundred yards back up the hill from it, while Vincent rode the same distance the other way. They were to ride together and fight – to the end. No weapons. Vincent kept on his belt, the highly-oiled drive chain, while Gerry chose to depend on his hands alone.

Rat and Vincent conferred long together in the still darkness. Scuttling bent over, Rat disappeared up to the tower, just 'to pick out the best ground for my man', as he explained.

Brenda went up after him and returned a couple of minutes later, brushing dust from her hands and smiling at Gerry.

A touch of the hand, then Gerry rode up to his starting point. Peering through the half-light – dawn wasn't all that far away now – he saw Vincent do the same. Rat had appointed himself honourary umpire and looked up at Vincent.

'Are you ready?' Then a glance at Gerry: 'You ready, Wolf?' Without a pause to find out the answer, he dropped his hand. 'Go!' he screamed, his voice cracking with the excitement.

Not taken at all by surprise, Gerry and Vincent hit their throttles together. Aided by the gradient, it was Gerry who reached the bottom of the tall tower first. He skidded to a halt and began to dismount. Vincent drew first blood by riding straight at him, only veering at the last moment, his bucking rear wheel throwing up a cloud of bitter dust and knocking Gerry's chopper away from under him.

As he got to his feet, Gerry was surprised to see the President backing away from him, towards an angle of the cracked concrete. The remainder of the chapter gathered round on the hillside above, shouting and cheering. All but Rat shouted for Gerry. For Vincent, it was the end of a long and bloody road. He had seen Gerry fight and suspected, though he had never admitted it to anyone but himself, that Gerry's training in unarmed combat would give him the edge. He could still hear the cracking of cartilage and bone as Tiny Terry had been easily and neatly defeated and killed.

But, there was one trick left.

As Gerry closed in on him, moving easily on the balls of his feet, hands out and weaving in front of him, Vincent reached behind him into the grey dust. And found – one of the shotguns.

The shouting stopped, as though someone had lifted the arm off a record. Suddenly, all you could hear was the sullen whisper of the sea, hundreds of feet below them, the heavy panting of the two men, the scuffling of their boots as they shifted in the gravel chippings.

One voice.

Vincent stood there, clicked off the safety, smiled, levelled the gun at Gerry's stomach. Gerry saw death in his eyes, and smiled back.

One voice.

The voice of Brenda.

'Gerry!!! Trust me. Go for him. He daren't fire!'

Vincent smiled more broadly. 'Yes, come on, love. Come closer.'

Again Brenda. 'Move!!'

So Gerry twisted and dived, praying for a misfire, that he might get at Vincent's feet. But he was too late. As he knew he would be.

The big gun blasted the Welsh morning, and there was a high scream. Gerry lay still in the dust, feeling the shock of the charge. But, feeling no impact of slugs. He had missed!

He hadn't. Gerry rolled over and looked up, and Vincent wasn't there any more. The seamed concrete wall where he had been was slobbered with gouts of blood, streaked and already running down.

He stood up and walked to the edge of the slope. Vincent had been standing near the edge, and the force of the shotgun exploding in his hands and face had thrown him back to fall sixty feet down into the heap of dust, where he rolled and screamed and cried.

The shotgun had exploded. Any shotgun would if it had been crammed full of gravel and dirt, clogging the barrel. The charge can't escape so it bursts the gun. Gerry turned to Brenda on the hill opposite. She smiled back at him and held up her hands, still smeared with mud and dust. That was another debt he would owe her.

Below him, Vincent had made it to his feet. His right hand was completely gone and jetted blood in a slowing arc. The left was mangled and torn, hanging from what was left of his wrist by a thread of gristle. He was bleeding to death. But there was more. The gun had been at his shoulder, and he had been sighting it, making sure that he would hit Gerry full in the guts. The burst had also ripped his face open and slashed at the jelly of his eyes. He staggered and nearly fell. Vincent was blind. Totally blind.

Concrete dust clung to his wounds, soaking up the blood. The dust about him was spotted and rivered from the bursts of blood. Finally he fell and did not get up. In the quiet, as gulfs circled overhead, they could hear him crying.

'My eyes! Oh, Lord God. My eyes! Help me! Mother! Help me! Please! Help me! I can't see! Gerry, help me! Please help me, Gerry! Mother help me! Mom! Mom, it's me. Can't you hear. Help me, Mum. Please. Mummy. It's me. I can't see you. Mummy. It's Vincent. Vincent. And I can't see. Help me.'

The cries died away. There was one last plea: 'Mummy, come and help Vinnie. Please! It's so dark.'

The rest was silence.

Gerry wearily walked over to where the rest of the Angels stood waiting for him. He put his arm round Brenda and they stumbled together towards the sea. All that was left of the Last Heroes lay down on the shingle. Quietly.

High, very high, above them, on the top of the cliffs, stood four men. Unseen. Watching. Seeing all. They wore jeans and faded blue levis. Behind them, the weak sun was just pushing over the crest of Yr Eifl, shining on their backs. Brightening the backs of their levis. Reflecting off the design picking out the white head of a wolf on each jacket.

The four men began to walk down towards the sea.

18. AN EXCERPT FROM AN ESSAY ON THE SUBJECT OF HELL'S ANGELS
by A London Boy (14 years of age), August 1st 1997.

It seems to me that too many of the people at the top enjoy persecuting young people. Look at all those policemen that were killed last month in Birmingham. All that because the Last Heroes Hell's Angels motor-cycle chapter were making a film and the authorities didn't approve of that.

I, and a lot of my friends, think that it's all terribly unfair the way the people in power have a down on us. We know that people like Gerry and the Last Heroes did a lot of rotten things – stealing and killing – but they never had a chance. And they never dropped thousands of bombs on innocent peasant people. If you don't give people any freedom at all and jump on them if they try and show that they want to be free, that they're individuals – however they try and show it – then you're bound to make them worse. It's like when America banned drink but everyone still got it and lawlessness flourished. It's the same with any kind of restriction.

Although my friends and I are still too young to be able to vote at this Election that's coming, I know that a lot of my older friends feel the same. We wait and it'll be our turn. We want a little more freedom, and more of a chance to make our own mistakes and then learn by them. That's why I hope there'll be a change at this Election. So that there can be more freedom.

Finally, this is a poem I wrote about the Hell's Angels that sums up the way we feel. One day, if they're still alive up in the mountains, I'd like to go and join them. One day.

Everywhere I look I see
Faces grey with misery.
Everybody looks the same,
I just don't know who to blame.
I don't want to grow up grey,
With a boring job and rotten pay,
Spend it all on birds and booze,
Nothing to win, so there's nothing to lose.
I'd like to leave it all behind,
Ride my hog, see what I'd find,

With my old lady behind me,
We'd ride with Gerry and all be free.
Brothers running high we'd see
What we wanted when we're free.
Really, that's what I'd like to be.
Out of it all and free, free, free!

Book Two:

ANGEL CHALLENGE

1. AFTERNOON ALL

'Haven't you finished that bleeding bottle yet?'

'Nearly. Anyway, I'm buggered if you're getting any more of it. You had well over half of the last bottle. I reckon you've had about five pints to my three. That's what I reckon. So, no bleeding more.'

'That's just the bleeding trouble, Arthur. I need the empty bottle to slash in.'

Arthur Samuels drained the bottle, adding a touch more colour to his veined face. He passed it to Morry Gannon, who unbuttoned his long grey raincoat, unzipped his flies and carefully positioned the bottle. He cursed as he under-estimated his need and wiped his wet hands on the front of his coat. He carefully put the bottle down on the step by his feet. Grinning, Arthur leaned across and nudged it with his foot, sending it rolling down through the crowd, spraying trousers and shoes and chinking along until it hit a metal barrier stanchion and shattered. What was left of the liquid soaked into the dusty concrete.

Nobody saw it happen.

Well, in fact, one person saw it happen. He was about sixteen years old and was standing directly behind Morry and Arthur. He wore tight faded jeans, white shirt with a ruffled front, an elegant embroidered waistcoat and black ankle boots with platform soles nearly four inches thick. His hair was cropped almost painfully short, his skull gleaming bone-white through the stubble. He had long curling side-boards. He saw Morry Gannon pee into a bottle and he saw Arthur Samuels roll the full bottle into the crowd. He had half a dozen mates with him. He told them about it.

There were about eight minutes to go. First Division Arsenal, bidding for the Cup and League double, were leading three-one against Third Division Manchester United. Once at the very top, the northern club had slumped badly during the mid-nineties having, at one time, to struggle to avoid relegation from the Third Division. The appointment three years ago of Bobby Charlton as manager had signalled the beginning of a revival. Now top of their Division with promotion a mere formality, they had fought through to the quarter-final of the F.A. Cup.

There were six minutes to go and Manchester were on the attack. In the manager's box Charlton leaped to his feet, sparse hair waving in the wind, and urged his young team forward again.

Happy now the pressure on his bladder had been relieved, Morry sportingly encouraged his team: 'Kick the fucking poofs off the park!' Then, as the veteran striker, Ian Wright, slipped on the damp turf: 'Jesus Christ all bleeding mighty!'

A man could choose better words to have on his lips as he leaves this world for the doubtful values of the next.

The long, thin blade of an eight inch flick-knife had whispered out, slicing through his old raincoat (which let him down) and probing up between the fourth and fifth ribs on the left side. The youth behind him – whose name was Charlie Marvell – stepped in closer and supported the corpse (for that's what Morry had become so suddenly), pulling out the knife and passing it quickly back to one of his mates who immediately left with it.

On the field, Manchester were mounting a last attack and the Arsenal defence was forced to give away a corner. Arthur spoke to Morry without turning his head: 'Last chance, eh, Morry? Get this one clear and we've done it. I said, nearly there. Morry. Hey!'

'I think your mate's come over all queer.' That was Charlie, who coincided his words with letting go of Morry's arm and letting the deceased slump to the floor. The body dropped to the terracing with the gentle ease that comes only to the very drunk or the dead.

Unfortunately for Charlie, the late and not-yet-lamented fell on his face revealing the torn and bloody back of his coat. When people "come over all queer" in a football crowd they don't usually have a gash in their back that's poured out their life.

Arthur was no fool and he knew a knifing when he saw one. Killings were too much of a feature of football matches for it to be a total shock, but you always thought it would happen to someone else. He saw the bizarre figure behind him and grabbed at him, shouting at the top of his voice.

'You bastard. You've chivved my mate.'

Charlie was two steps higher up the terracing and that, combined with the platform soles to his boots put him at just the right height to swing at Arthur's groin. But, as he lifted his foot his head exploded and he dropped to the steps. Unable to believe his luck, Arthur kicked him hard, three times, in the face, before a hand on his shoulder stopped him.

'That's enough, mate. We don't want you in court as well as him.'

At that moment, a couple of uniformed policemen, one in his late thirties, the other about sixteen, burst in through the ring of goggling spectators.

'All right. What's going ... Oh, sorry sergeant. Didn't know it was you. Saw the ripple in the crowd and came a'running. He dead?' Pointing at Morry.

'Unless he's got an extra gallon of blood tucked away somewhere in his pocket, then he is.'

Arthur found it all a bit much. He guessed the man who had saved him was one of the many plain-clothes detectives who patrolled football grounds in large numbers in the generally futile effort to stop crowd violence.

'Er. Excuse me. But, what'll happen to him?' indicating the unmoving figure of Charlie Marvell.

'That's Charlie Marvell. He's been arrested three times, not counting today, and charged with murder on each occasion. Every time, he gets off. I would bet anything you like that he hasn't got a knife on him. It'll be out of the ground by now in the pocket of one of his mates or in the bag of one of his scrubbers.' He kicked the recumbent youth casually in the groin. 'There's fuck all we can do about it. Once upon a time we could have got him down the station and given him the treatment. Now, with these bleeding-heart liberals running things, he'll get off. Is the stretcher coming?'

'Yes, sergeant. I radioed for it.'

'Well done lad. I don't think I know this one, do I Tom?'

'No sergeant. First time out for young Andrews here. Andrews, this is detective-sergeant Warren.'

'Pleased to meet you, sir. Excuse me, sir.' He sidled nearer to the detective, away from the ashen figure of Arthur who had now sat down and was just beginning to think how he could possibly break the news to Morry's wife. Widow.

'Yes.'

'Well, I was just wondering.'

'Come on lad. Don't stand there like that. You look as though you're trying to make your mind up whether or not to risk a fart.'

'Sorry, sergeant. It's just that I wondered if there might not be a knife down at the nick that we could fit to this "skull". If he's as bad as you say.'

'Once, maybe. Now, I'm not saying "Yes". I'm just saying "Maybe". Not now; not even for a murdering bastard like this skull here. Not even for Charlie Marvell. In the days of good old George Hayes we could have done it. Not now. Things have changed, son. The law's for the protection of thugs and killers. Look at that poor old sod, down there. Crying because he won't have anyone to go to Highbury with any more. Marvell'll get off without blinking. The only thing is, oh, here's the stretcher, the only thing is, that one day he'll come up against a bigger animal. And you know what? When they push him up the crematorium chimney I'll be there taking big deep breaths of the smoke and laughing. Yes, laughing.'

Police-constable Andrews walked away from the station that night with the older policeman, Tom Mayhew. Andrews had been unable to eat much of his soya-sausage and chips and Mayhew had finished it off for him. As they walked together through the grey streets, Mayhew answered the young man's questions about George Hayes, about the skulls and about the radical change in public thinking.

How, about a year ago, there had been a General Election, when the reactionary Home Secretary, George Hayes, and the Government he typified, had been narrowly ousted from office by a Labour/Union coalition. Throughout the country there had been a new spirit of freedom and some of the fringe youth movements that had previously been outlawed were now reasonably acceptable. The Hell's Angels motor-cycle gangs had spawned afresh and the working class, football-crazy youths had gone back to their roots and formed a counter movement.

'And that's the skulls?'

'Yes. Mix in the old skinheads of the late seventies and add a dash of "Clockwork Orange". Work in a bizarre dress sense, odd rules and season well with incredible viciousness. That's your skulls.'

'But, Mister Mayhew...'

'I keep telling you. Tom!'

'Yeah, sorry, Tom. But, I still don't see what really made things change. I read history for my special entrance to the force and our teacher said that all great movements had one tiny root. What was the root that made the whole country sweep in favour of freedom?'

'Remember Gerry and the Last Heroes? Course you do. Every kid must remember them. Well, I suppose it must be about a year ago now. When we tried to finally wipe them out and a hell of a lot of people got killed, Angels and coppers. Well, people had had about enough. It was too much. Too brutal. Too savage. So, like the pendulum swept the other way. And this is what we've got. Murder on a Saturday afternoon and a maniac killer who's got away with it before and will get away with it this time. Makes me want to bloody throw up. Makes me want to get out of the force.'

They walked in silence for a block.

'Tom? What happened to the Last Heroes? A lot of papers said they were all killed. Were they?'

'No. Most of them were. But the rest rode through the night and joined up with a group of Welsh Angels. They never found Vincent, the bloke who used to lead them, but our Special Branch know that Gerry and his tart are still up there somewhere. Every now and again a gang of bike outlaws pull some caper and it's always got his finger-prints on the job. No. He's still alive. I reckon that one day he'll move back South. Maybe soon. Then you'd better duck.'

Charles Edwyn Marvell was charged with the wilful murder of Maurice Solomon Gannon. He was formally acquitted without the police offering any evidence.

Arthur Samuels stopped going to football matches. He stayed at home instead, and watched the wrestling.

Thomas Mayhew resigned from the Metropolitan Police Force about a month later and opened a small newsagents.

Rachel Gannon, the evening of the cremation of her husband, went quietly from her flat, walked quietly to a nearby canal and quietly drowned herself.

In the third minute of injury time, Manchester United scored again. The final score was three-two.

2. ANOTHER HAPPY VALLEY SUNDAY

'Its mild winter climate and warm summers make Llandudno one of the most favoured of North Wales' resorts. Much loved by the labouring and middle classes of the Midlands and the North of England, it has something to offer for everyone. No matter how unusual your tastes, Llandudno will have something to offer you.'

In the hills behind Conway, a raggle-taggle band of men and women were preparing to spend half an hour in Llandudno. About twenty men and three young women lay around on the springy turf, listening to some last words from a slim-built man of average height. In a crowd, wearing straight clothes, you would probably not have given him a second glance. Unless you got up close and looked into his eyes. His name was Gerald Vinson and he was thirty years old. He was known either as "Gerry" or as "Wolf" to his brothers and sisters.

More than any other person, he had probably been responsible for the change of Government at the last General Election. He was the leader of one of the most powerful chapters of Hell's Angels in Britain. After the massacre in a quarry north of Birmingham a year or so ago, he had fought and beaten the then leader of the Last Heroes, Vincent, assuming the Presidency of the chapter (or, what was left of it) and uniting it with the shadowy Welsh chapter, the Wolves.

Now, they were legal again and could go on runs more or less when they liked. The police still bore bitter grudges against them and looked for any chance to get back at them. But, with Gerry's cunning and leadership, the Last Heroes and Wolves had kept out of trouble. Every now and again they would ride out from their secret hide-out and blow the minds of any straight citizens they encountered. But, money was always short. So, they were going to try and get some to keep them going for a while.

Of the old Last Heroes chapter, Gerry had only five brothers left. Kafka, one of the oldest of the Angels; Cochise, with his mysterious old lady, Forty; Riddler and Dick the Hat, and the tiny Rat. Rat had been the right-hand man of Vincent and had played a part in at least two attempts on Gerry's life. But he was a virtuous brother with peculiar skills that Gerry found useful at times. Rat knew when to step carefully. He was particularly hated by Brenda.

In an intensely male-dominated society of motor-cycle outlaws, Brenda was unique. A year or so younger than Gerry, she had unusual physical strength and agility. On top of that she was completely ruthless when it came to getting what she wanted. These qualities made her feared even among the hardest men. In every way, she was closer to Gerry than anyone else.

Apart from Forty, there were only two of the old ladies left from a year ago. They were the couple who had taken a bike between them after the slaughter – Lady and Holly. When the Heroes had incorporated with the Wolves, there had been attempts to take them over as old ladies by brothers of the Welsh chapter. The take-overs had all failed and the Dyke Duo, as they were called (but never to their faces), had an unusual position. They were no man's old ladies but they had no intention of ever being dropped to the insultingly low position of mamas.

One of the brothers had tried to force Holly to plate him after a heavy drinking session, but he had not succeeded. His failure had been a dramatic object lesson to the others that, at least as far as Holly and Lady were concerned, female liberation was a force not to be ignored.

By punching her repeatedly in the face he had succeeded in knocking her into semi-unconsciousness. He locked his fingers in her hair and pulled her to her knees in front of him. With his other hand he unzipped himself ready. Blood trickling from her nose, Holly allowed him to force her mouth open and begin the bestial act.

He tugged her head backwards and forwards, trying to make her participate. In the dungeon-dark cavern of her mouth, Holly simply closed her teeth. Hard. Bit hard. Although he screamed and wrenched at her hair, Holly held on like a steel trap. Blood filled her mouth but still she bit until he fainted from the pain. Then she let go, got up, and walked away from him without even looking back. The ring of Angels who had watched the horrific incident let her pass.

The brother died from loss of blood. Gerry tried to stop the bleeding, but there wasn't enough left to tourniquet.

Apart from the remnants of the Last Heroes, there were several members of the Wolves chapter, led by their own vice-President, Draig. No old ladies along on this run, so Mochyn, Buwch and Geneth stayed with the other women in the village of Nant Gwrtheyrn. But Bardd was there, his harmonica tucked in the pocket of his denim coat. So was Cyllell, Mynydd, Ogof and the terrifying berserk albino, Gwyn.

Their bikes were the usual mixture of Nortons and Triumphs, with an old 650 Yamaha, a B.M.W. and Gerry's own Harley. Their clothes were the usual Angels' gear. The men with generally long hair – Cochise had plaited ribbons in his – and some with beards. Stinking levis, rank with vomit, sweat and urine, colours flaring on the back. The skull of the Last Heroes and the snarling head of a wolf for the Welsh brothers.

The old ladies uniformly in leather jackets and stained jeans. Long hair, tied loosely back. All of them wore boots, zipped motor-bike boots for the men, ordinary leather for the old ladies.

'All right, brothers and sisters. That's it. Anybody got any last minute questions or anything they aren't sure about? No? Right then. Ladies and gentlemen of the combined Last Heroes and Wolves Motor-cycle Chapter, affiliated to the Oakland Chapter in California, I propose that we move. Let's go!'

Springs heaved, boots kicked at starts, engines coughed into life, throttles were savagely twisted. Tyres gouged up mighty divots of turf and they were gone. A long time after they had gone, the air smelled heavy with petrol. And evil.

'Thank you. Thank you. That was "Elsinore Blues" – a little song that just goes to prove that you can never make an 'amlet without breaking a few eggs. Ouch! Did you, listen, did you hear about the Hell's Angel who decided he was fed up of riding motor-bikes all day – yes, missus, and all night. Very tender on the testimonials! So he thought he'd be converted into a skull. Went up to Oldham, round to the football ground. It was getting on for Spring. He could tell that easily. People were leaving their clogs off! No, listen. He went up to Oldham. Found the local gang of skulls and said to their leader: "I want to be converted." So they kicked him over the crossbar! Thank you. Thank you. Now, would you welcome please the entire company in a song that has stopped many a show – "Where In Hades Is The Ladies In The Lords?" Thank you again!'

The Happy Valley Concert Party were in full swing. In the mild, early June weather the banks around the small theatre were well covered with happy holiday-makers. Lounging either on the grass or in the striped deck-chairs, hundreds of contented families lay back enjoying the fun.

'Happy Valley is situated on the side of the picturesque Great Orme, Llandudno's most distinctive beauty feature. The pleasant sea breezes blowing from the bay make it a popular spot for relaxing after your luncheon. Convenient for public transport it is easily accessible for even the less adventurous walker. Holiday-makers of all ages will enjoy the highly-professional band of entertainers who perform there daily throughout the season. The well-tended grass and beds of flowering shrubs make this one of the most attractive theatre sites anywhere in the Principality. Happy Valley is full of hidden surprises. It's a place where the unexpected is always just around the next corner.'

'I do like it here, Madge. I really feel, you know, that I can relax up here. Fresh air, good entertainment, a nice hotel to go back to. The only thing I really regret is that I'm going to have to go back to work next Monday.'

'Still, Harold, you've got another week in October to look forward to. I think ... what on earth is that noise? It's like some motor-bikes. Very loud and ... Oh! Harold!!'

'My God!'

Bursting into that sylvan scene of serene serendipity, came the Angels. Gerry and Gwyn appeared first, engines revving as they tore off the Marine Drive and up the slope into the big, natural amphitheatre. Gwyn, stark white hair pouring over his shoulders, blood-red eyes gleaming from his pale face, bulging with the effort of wrestling the big Norton round the flower-beds.

Deck-chairs fell and overturned, trapping fingers. Picnic baskets toppled and feet trampled fish-paste and soya sandwiches into a mess with sodden coffee and cheap orange squash. Children quivered with a mixture of fear and excitement and were snatched up by fathers. Aged grandmas discovered a new lease of life as they fled for the exits.

On stage, the Happy Valley songsters faltered in their jokey ditty; the pianist, deafened by his own fortissimo, plunged on alone for eight bars. It's all very well for old troupers to say that the show must always go on. They never had to deal with concentrated interference from a chapter of the Hell's Angels.

The bikes reared and snarled through the crowd. Three of the Welsh brothers trapped a teenage girl in a whirling circle of bikes, riding like Indians around a beleaguered waggon train, cutting ever closer until the girl collapsed in a sobbing lump on the grass. All the trivia of a holiday, clothes and food and paperback books were gouged into the dirt by the spinning wheels. Kafka ploughed straight for the bandstand, where the frightened stage-manager was making an attempt – inexorably doomed to failure – to calm the crowd. Since he was holding the microphone with fear-whitened fingers and screaming in a panicky falsetto: 'Don't panic! Don't panic! Don't panic!' it's not surprising that people panicked all the more.

Kafka broadsided to a halt in a shower of grass and dirt and, even before his rear wheel had stopped spinning, had thrown the man from the stage and ripped the microphone from his hands. The amplifiers boomed in protest as Kafka bellowed obscenities and curses at the fleeing mob.

Within a couple of minutes, the area was almost completely clear. Two of the Wolves were busily engaged in kicking the writhing body of a middle-aged Manchester grocer who had thought he could use his experience as warden of a boys' club to quieten them. In the middle of a bed of "Sweet Williams", Madge had been caught by Rat and three of the Wolves. She was screaming hysterically and trying to beat them off with a torn sun-shade. They were almost crying with laughter at her efforts. Every now and then, Rat would sidle in and cut a bit more of her dress away with his knife. Already she resembled a hula dancer, her skirt ribboning out as she turned. Her stockings were in shreds and there were trickles of blood on her heavy, veined thighs, where Rat had been accidentally careless with his chiv. Although nobody could have ever have convinced her of the fact, Madge was less unlucky that she might have been. Although Harold had fled the field in considerable disarray, she was in no immediate danger. The Angels had other things to do and there wasn't time for any kind of gang-bang.

A couple of children, eleven-year-olds, were about the only people not to go into a frenzy of fear at the appearance of the Angels. With one astride the tank, and the other hanging on behind, Ogof was riding them round the Valley, spinning through the shattered flower-beds. Apart from the sound of the powerful engines, the only noise was blaring over the sound system. Accompanied by the wailing harmonica of Bardd, Kafka was pouring his soul into one of the latest pop/folk hits. Composed by a teenage boy, it had been an underground hit a year ago. Now it had become respectable.

'Blood on the road,
And a white heron flying.
Blood on the road,
And the grey mist rising.
All alone
All alone
All alone.'

Kafka was giving it all the soul he could and was winding his voice up to spring into the second verse when Gerry held up his hand and shouted for quiet. The bikes slithered to a halt and the engines softened. The brothers kicking casually at super-hero stopped and wiped blood from their toe-caps on a torn paper table-cloth. The man lay still, hands grabbing at his savaged groin. Madge was allowed the dignity of a slow faint. The children were put gently down by Ogof. The song stopped and the chapter waited for its President.

'Listen. Pigs!'

Sure enough, over the bike noise, riding above the endless whispering of the sullen Welsh sea, they could hear the whining of the switchback police sirens, somewhere in the town below, coming their way.

'Gwyn, get them moving. Kafka wait with me. We've got to let them get close enough to think they have a chance of getting to us. Move.' The last word had a crack of command behind it.

While the big albino led most of the Angels away, round the Great Orme's Head, Gerry and Kafka wheeled slowly down the hill from the Happy Valley area until they had passed the pier. Nobody tried to stop them. It was too nice a day for suicide. Only when they heard the sirens nearly on top of them did they make their move.

Up on the steep Ty-Gwyn Road, then along the tramway and up towards the exclusive Great Orme Hotel with its unequalled views over the headland.

Behind them, the police cars screamed in pursuit. Seeing that their quarries were escaping them, they stopped. Seeing this, Gerry and Kafka stopped and turned back, cutting across and sharply down, through to the Invalids Walk, through Tyn Y Coed Road. Then, waving casually to the police cars which were jammed together as they tried to turn, they were back on the Marine Drive and heading steeply up and round the Great Orme. Behind them, they watched the cars take up the pursuit again.

'Not too fast,' screamed Gerry to Kafka. 'Keep them thinking they've got a chance. The longer they think that, the better for Brenda and the girls.'

Not very far from Llandudno station are quite a few shops. Among them is a jeweller's and antique shop run by Lemuel Stacey. Not a very big shop, but with a surprisingly high turnover. None of your cheap tat; Lemuel is very choosy about what he buys and what he pays. Generally speaking, he paid as little as possible and sold as dear as he could. Good business, did I hear someone say? Is it good business to pay a retainer to girls working on most of the North Wales papers to keep him informed the moment some bereaved person rang in to place a "Death" announcement in the personal columns?

Lemuel would leap into his sports car – a flashy model but painted in a discreet black – and speed round to the house of mourning. He would assume his most unctuous air and flash his expensively crowned teeth as he oozed compassion from every sweaty pore. He would tender his deepest sympathy to the widow, or widower, or children, and lead the conversation easily round to the touchy subject of funeral costs. From there it's only one short step to a delicate enquiry as to whether he might be allowed to help out at this difficult time by relieving their financial worries by the charitable disposal of any odd bits of furniture or bric-a-brac.

When one is still in the shock of feeling death's wings flutter in the rooms of one's house, then one is not prepared to deal with someone as cunning and vile as Lemuel Stacey. Those who knew of his activities hated him, but the visitors loved his little shop and his worldly air of knowledge. It was very rare for anyone to buy anything from Lemuel without coming away feeling he had a real bargain. It was even rarer for anyone actually to get such a bargain.

Because he paid his way into the right circles, Lemuel had been accepted into various organisations. He had even recently been proposed for the pending vacancy at the local citizens magistrates' court. Two or three other things that you should know about him. He was a usurious money-lender who specialised in married women who had fallen behind with the rent or had squandered their house-keeping at streamline Bingo (Stingo). This leads to item two. He had a great fancy for watching little girls dance for him, without any clothes on. Naturally, it's not that easy to find acquiescent little girls, but, if their mums are in debt to you and you threaten to reveal all to a husband. Well ... Lemuel had built up a truly remarkable collection of amazing pictures – that he took and developed himself. The third fact, that he once revealed to an especially nubile young maiden, was that he didn't trust banks and kept a great deal of money on his premises.

Now you know more-or-less everything of any relevance about Lemuel Stacey. Physically he was rather fat with a face so plump and pale and moist, that you automatically had to take a second look to make sure you hadn't actually seen traces of mould in the wrinkles.

Even in the quiet street where he kept his shop, Lemuel had heard the noise of sirens. He had been about to walk out to see what was happening when his shop door sprang open with a savage tinkling of its glass chimes. In walked three girls. Too old, was the instant assessment from Lemuel. And, too dirty! Filthy leather jackets, muddy boots and greasy hair. The biggest of the three came straight to the counter and straight to the point.

'Money, Lemuel. Now, in these bags.'

The bags were canvas, with long leather handles. Not that it mattered to Lemuel, but they were nearly identical to those used by Gerry and Priest in the Holloway Bank job.

Lemuel was the wrong end of the counter to his police alarm button, but he wasn't in the least worried. Three girls. They might look tough, but he reckoned he could handle them. Lady had slipped the catch on the door behind them and pulled down the blind. Holly moved alongside Brenda, the end of the counter where that button was neatly inset under the walnut trim.

'Money, dear lady? I'm afraid you are under some kind of false impression of my purpose in life. You pick out some item from my shop and I will tell you how much it costs and you give me that amount of money and I give you the item. Now money. No, I don't think that I will give you any money. Even if I had any to give. Which I don't.'

'Because you are a fool, Mister Stacey, I will explain it very briefly. I know you have a great deal of money in this building. It's in a large, brass-bound trunk, locked up under your bed. The double keys are on a chain round your neck. Either you give us those keys and you will only be hurt a little, or you choose not to give us those keys and you will be hurt a lot. Please don't think you have any chance of defeating us in a fight, Lemuel. If you try you will have cause to regret it. We can do things to you that will cause you to cry if you catch a glimpse of yourself in a mirror. Children will throw stones at you in the street and dogs will creep away from your shadow. The money please.'

Gerry's old fighting instructor, Sergeant Newman, had impressed the value of clever talk in a tight situation. 'Tell the gook what you plan to do to him. Particularly if he's not used to violence. It'll make him start thinking about it and he'll lose his stomach for it. Just tellin' him you'll hurt 'im 'orrible's no good. Tell 'im exactly how and where.'

That was good advice and Gerry had given it on to his chapter. But, when you're a girl and you're faced by a middle-aged man, he just will not believe it. Even the teeny riots of the early nineties, when security guards were burned alive or literally torn apart by little girls panting to see their idols, even those hadn't changed centuries of conditioning. Whatever Brenda said to Stacey, he wasn't capable of believing her. So...

Hanging a grin loosely in the middle of his mouth, Stacey reached across the counter and grabbed at Brenda. He hadn't got much idea what he was going to do after that, but it seemed a good start. The only thing it was a good start to was a bad ending!

Brenda brushed his hands away contemptuously and countered his feeble attack by taking firm hold of his ears, digging her nails cruelly into the back of them. Holly slipped round behind him. Her right hand knotted in Lemuel's hair and tugged his head back. Brenda released his ears and smashed her right elbow viciously into his throat. The scream that had been on its way out of his mouth was still-born and his hands went to his crushed neck. He had sagged at the knees with the speed and violence of the attack. Holly, perfectly positioned behind him, reached with her left hand between his legs, grabbed and twisted with all her strength.

A whisper of a scream barely bruised the air and Stacey fainted. Holly casually let him drop to the floor behind the counter.

'Tie him up and gag him.' Brenda didn't look to see if Lady and Holly were doing what she had told them. She knew they would. Leaving them to their fun she went through the shop and up into Lemuel's bedroom. Under the bed was the trunk, exactly as the little girl had described it. 'Holly, get the keys and bring them here!'

The money was in the trunk, a lot of it. After they'd filled the bags, Brenda went through the rest of the contents. Literally hundreds of pictures of Lemuel's little hobby, plus a carefully filed selection of promissory notes, mainly from women, with neat notes on each, giving details of the daughters of each family. Brenda piled all of them into the bottom of one of the sacks. 'The dirty perverted bastard! The rotten little queer! You know, Holly, I think we ought to teach the fat swine a lesson before we go. Teach him about not touching little girls and blackmailing stupid women.'

When they had staggered back into the shop with the money, only a couple of minutes had passed, and Stacey was just beginning to come round. His chest heaved as he fought for breath and his eyes rolled as he tried to look up at the girls. Sweat dripped down his white face onto the dusty floor. Lady had been taught the art of tying people up by Gerry, who had learned it from the good Sergeant Newman. She was good at it. Like most experts, she really enjoyed doing it.

Lemuel's ankles were crushed together with a length of thick cord. It ran up, pulling his feet behind him, and was tied in a slip knot round his pudgy neck. A last piece of rope was pulled tight round his upper arms, bringing his elbows back so that they actually touched. A length of filthy cotton waste was shoved in his mouth and tied in place. Any sudden movement and Lemuel was likely to strangle himself. Which was the idea.

'Comfy, Mister Stacey? How rude, not to answer a lady when she asks you a question. I think a boot in the ear might remind him of his manners. In fact, a boot in each ear. Together now! Good. Don't wriggle too much, you'll throttle yourself.

Now, listen. We must be going, but I want you to know that we've got your money and your pictures. And all those nasty promissory notes. We'll arrange that the word gets around that it's all gone. Without the threat of your unpleasantness hanging over them, I wouldn't be surprised if a few ladies of Llandudno took it into their heads to pay you a visit. So, I wouldn't hang around here – if you'll pardon the expression.'

Lady moved forwards and stood over the choking Stacey, pressing down with her foot on the taut rope. 'I think he's getting off too light. I know we've not got much time, but I reckon he needs a lasting lesson. Otherwise he'll just go of somewhere and start it all over again.'

Less than five minutes had passed since the three girls had entered the small shop. Brenda went upstairs to the flat and listened out of the window. In the distance, she could still hear the rumble of powerful motor-bikes and the high-pitched sound of the police sirens, as Gerry and Kafka led the fuzz around the houses and stopped them worrying about a closed antique shop in the middle of the afternoon.

'All right. But two minutes only. You can have one go each at him. Then we go.'

Holly hadn't a lot of imagination. She took her knife and carved a word of four letters deep on Lemuel's pale forehead. Most of the letters were easy, but the curve on the first one gave her some difficulty. Blood mixed in streaks with the sweat that ran in the dust. Stacey rolled sideways trying to avoid the knife, but the choking rope round his neck held him helpless.

Lady had found what she wanted on a table in the shop, priced at a reasonable seven pounds. 'Brenda, keep him still. I don't want him rolling around.'

She knelt alongside the man and held his hands in her left hand. With her right hand, she delicately adjusted the heavy brass Victorian nut-crackers over the first joint of the little finger of his left hand. Then she began to squeeze.

The police lost Gerry and Kafka in the hills overlooking the River Conway, near the village of Eglwysbach. They met up with the other brothers at a hideout in the mountains above the quarries of Bethesda. About ten minutes after they got there, the crackle of two exhausts announced the arrival of the three girls.

Gerry and Brenda made love that night in the cave, expending their passion on top of over five thousand pounds. The rest of the chapter slept near them. What enthusiasm the local police had been able to raise would have evaporated by the next day and they would be able to complete their run back to their base in reasonable safety.

When the first police detachment arrived at the Happy Valley area, they were appalled by the scene of devastation that met their eyes. The immaculate green turf was scarred and torn, while most of the flower-beds were totally demolished. The whole area was littered with overturned deck-chairs and scattered bottles, clothes, bags and enough food to feed a regiment. The stage was scarcely touched but the microphone was still switched on after the duet of Kafka and Bardd. It whistled and hummed to itself, occasionally giving a roar of rage that echoed around the Great Orme.

'Duw! Look at that, man! In that deck-chair. There's a body in it. Those sodding Angels! It's an old man.'

At that moment, the body stirred. It was indeed an old man. With not a mark of violence on him anywhere. As his eyes opened, he gave a visible jump at the carnage around him. The police ran forward as he stood shakily upright and began to shout in a quavering voice: 'What the 'ell's been goin' on here then? I just drop off to sleep for a couple of minutes and look what 'appens. Like the bloody war. What was it, an earthquake?'

'No, dad. It was a gang of Hell's Angels. But, don't you worry, we'll soon...'

The old man held up his hand to stop him. 'Wait a minute, son. Wait on. I can't hear you. I have a bit of trouble with me ears.' Having plugged in his hearing-aid, he waited for the policeman to go on. 'Come on, son. Tell me what I been missing having a bit of a kip. Eh? Eh?'

At about ten-thirty the next morning, the Angels resumed their run back to Nant Gwrtheyrn. Convoying along the winding mountain roads, they roared defiance at any motorist they met. Gwyn, spaced out on mescalin, led the Wolves in a complex arabesque, weaving their bikes in and out of each other, taking it in turns to lead.

In a village, high in the hills, a small school was at play. Hearing the noise of the run nearing them, the children ran to the railings and hung there, shouting and screaming at the circus of riders. Their middle-aged teacher came running from the corner of the playground, trying to bustle her tiny brood back into the school, but she was too late.

Many of the Angels played up to the obvious adulation, riding hands high on the ape-hanger bars, or sitting way back on the raked seats, laughing and waving.

Dick the Hat, less zonked than most of the others, spotted the lorry backing out of the turning with its load of sheet metal, and shouted a frantic warning. A warning that all but one of the brothers heard and noted. Gafr, the goat, rode alone in a mandrax dream and the cry of warning was no more than the cry of the east wind off the mountains where he ran.

Goronwy Williams, licensed haulier, hardly heard the bike roar over the struggling whine of his old Foden truck. He had backed right across the road and was hacking round on full lock with a narrow gap at the rear of the lorry, made even smaller by the protruding edges of sheet metal – his load for the extension to the Ogwen Rescue Hut. Some of the brothers, including Dick the Hat, Gerry, Gwyn and – even – Brenda, put their hogs at the gap and squeezed through. Some, less stoned, throttled back and waited for the lorry to complete the manoeuvre.

Not Gafr; a folk song on his lips: 'Ffarwel fy annwyl garaid.' Fatalistically appropriate. 'Fare thee well, my own true love.' He saw the gap, ever narrowing as Goronwy edged back again. Didn't see the edge-on steel plate – narrow-gauge – as it flicked at the corner of his eyes. Aimed for the shrinking gap. Like a hawk between the clashing peaks of a glass mountain.

The Angels were past the lorry before Goronwy even saw them. He clamped on the aged brakes and leaned out of his cab to watch. Not to spit or curse. He'd been there too long and knew too much. He just watched. As Gafr went past there wasn't even a judder. Too clean and too sharp. Just one last motor-cycle and one last rider. Speeding crazily from hedge to hedge. 'Duw!!' From Goronwy. For Gafr's Norton still had a rider that held it to its path. Legs that clamped tight round the frame. Hands that gripped the throttle open. But no head!

Gafr's head bounded into the ditch on the right of the road. Blood jetted high from the severed neck, fountaining as the heart still beat. Forced it out, gradually slowing.

Pumping less. The bright spout speckling the dusty road. Until the motors all failed and the hands relaxed and the bike crashed. The strings were all cut.

The teacher fainted. The children laughed, without any understanding of the suddenness of death. Goronwy sat very, very still, only his lips moving as he muttered over and over again: 'No head. He had no bloody head. No bloody head!'

Those Angels who had gone past stopped and looked back. Those Angels who had waited pulled slowly round the back of the lorry, carefully avoiding the dripping edge of the razor-steel.

Then on. No point in stopping. No miracle of modern surgery could help Gafr. Lady stopped their bike and Holly picked up the blood-splashed Norton and mounted it. The engine was still ticking over and she had no trouble. Well, there was no point in wasting a perfectly good bike.

As they ran on towards the sea and Nant Gwrtheyrn, Gwyn eased alongside Gerry and shouted over the machine roar: 'Shame about poor old Gafr, eh? Still. Real fine way to go. Like that. Showing real class, eh?'

Gerry turned his head and looked across at the grinning albino. 'It's always a toss-up, Gwyn. Heads he lost!'

An old woman, squatting behind a hedge heard the high, wild laughter and, peering through the leaves, saw the white face and red eyes, gaping red mouth. She heard the laugh again. And crossed herself. And crossed herself again. It pays not to take any chances, when one sees the Devil riding free.

3. GHOULS RUSH IN

Yes, my friends. There's only room at the top for one. And that one just has to be the best. The toughest. The biggest. Every one else better step aside. A lot of folks didn't and we all know what happened to them. Room at the top for just one. For the best.

That's why the Ghouls rush in where all the other Angels fear to tread. And that includes the mythical Gerry and his equally non-existent band of Last Heroes. Or, should that be "Last Zeroes"? Looking like the inside of one of your worst nightmares, the Ghouls are the end. The ultimate. The very scariest.

Unique among outlaw gangs, they emphasise their top-ness by not messing around with women. At all. No mamas. No old ladies. Just each other and their hogs. And their President. No grey little nobody like Gerry Vinson. No dwarf on an ego-trip like Man Ritt of the Bloody Dead. But a big, big man like Evel Winter.

Shiny satin instead of blue denim. Eye-shadow and sequins instead of beards and filth. A soft voice that turneth on fear. A few years ago, brave men or fools would have called the Ghouls a camp of queers. Now, here and now, there isn't anyone left who's that brave – or that stupid.

Watch it you Angels. Evel Winters says that he's the best and that the Ghouls are the best. He's been saying that for weeks now and no-one seems ready to contradict him. A few skulls tried to beat them down, a few skulls got broken. At least no ordinary citizens got hurt. And that's always been the concern of the *Leader*. Protect the ordinary, strengthen the faint-hearted, aid the afflicted.

Are you reading this, Gerry Vinson? If you can read! Evel says that you and your gang are yellow. Why don't you come creeping out of those Welsh hills and let us know what you've got to say. Come on. Come on.

Melvyn Molineux – *Daily Leader*, June 5th, 1998.

Lawyer's Comments:
Valentine:
I think that your M.M. has really gone a bit far this time. He seems to be inciting warfare between two gangs of Hell's Angels as well as libelling two of them. I must admit that I would doubt if either of them is likely to begin an action against the *Leader*, but do remember that the *Daily Leader* is in the business of selling newspapers, and not winning law suits.

I only hope that this character Gerry doesn't take M.M. at his word and come riding down to London breathing fire and vengeance. I suppose it might help to sell a few more copies, though. I just hope M.M. has some hefty life-insurance.

I'd let it go through with some reservations. In any future articles on this subject I'd try and tone down the hectoring note of sensationalism a bit.

– Krepy, Shirer, Durst, Kyle and Moorehead.

4. SILHOUETTED BY THE SEA

'What are you going to do, Gerry? I mean, it's a straight challenge, really. That creepy reporter is just being a mouth-piece for the Ghouls. Isn't he? What do you reckon?'

A hundred and fifty feet below the ruined village of Nant Gwrtheyrn, where the Last Heroes and Wolves had their permanent headquarters, in the north-west extremity of North Wales, is a long shingle beach, where seals sometimes come and cormorants wheel and dip. The village is more or less inaccessible to any but the fit and nerveless, so few walk that beach. That warm June evening, there were only two pairs of boots stirring the pebbles. Gerry and Brenda.

'Yeah. But, what you've got to remember is that he's a journalist. What he's got to do is help to sell his shitty paper. So, what's news? Youth cults. Like skulls. Like Hell's Angels. Every now and again, a paper will decide it's time it took a high moral tone and it'll have a go at something. It might be porn or rents or books or vacuum cleaners. At the moment slimy Molineux is making capital out of Evel Winter and his poofs. What he wants is for us to go down to London and have a massive run with killing and class all over the place. Then he can purse his chubby lips and "Tut, tut" all day long about how shocking it all was. And, you see Brenda, it'll all be his fault. Bastard!'

Gerry punctuated his words by picking up smooth, sea-polished stones and shying them at a boulder, lazing half in the rolling water. He turned away from the beach and walked up to where there had once been a plant for breaking rock down into gravel fragments. There was still a huge waste tip of gravel, pouring down nearly to the shore. He kicked out a hollow and sat down, lying back and closing his eyes.

Pushing the hair off her forehead, Brenda lay down beside him. They were a good half mile from the rest of the chapter. Long miles from anyone else. The air was very warm. Gerry was pleasantly high on hash and was happy to lie still and listen to the murmuring sea. Brenda was also high, but had a more pressing need. Her fingers rustled through the gravel, climbed up the side of Gerry's denim jacket, and edged down, across his flat stomach.

It was only when he realised that she was intent on tugging down the zip on his jeans that Gerry came to life. He put his hand over hers to help her. Once the zip was down, there was only the copper button that held the trousers together. With a bit of struggling, that soon gave way. Arching his back, Gerry let Brenda pull the jeans off, his pants coming with them. He groaned as the gravel pricked at his naked flesh and got quickly up to move on to patch of soft sand at the top of the beach. Brenda scrambled down near him, taking of her own jeans and pants before lying down. Gerry lazily reached out and caressed her breasts, smiling as he felt the nipples harden beneath his fingers. He rolled on top of her, his other hand probing lower down her body. She moaned softly and nuzzled her mouth into his neck as his fingers moved and vibrated inside her.

'Come on,' she whispered. 'Come on. Now.'

The sand shifted about them and the sea crept slowly closer. Their coupling was soft and gentle. For two such tough animals, Gerry and Brenda were capable of surprising gentleness towards each other. But, they were both also capable of dreadful violence against any person who threatened either of them.

Satiated, Gerry lapsed again into a quiet calm, eyes closed, the lower part of his body covered with a fine coating of golden sand. Brenda idly eased her hand over his chest, stroking down towards his thighs. Just at the top of his genitals, where the dark tendrils of hair curled up towards his stomach, she felt the puckered skin of an old scar. Not so old. He stirred as she touched him, and her mind went back a year to the moment when Gerry had finally made his move to challenge for the presidency of what was still just the Wolves.

After the quarry massacre, the whole country had been searching for them, and the Wolves had been happy to shelter their brothers from the South. Just as long as they toed the line and didn't try to cross it. But, Gerry was never one to follow anybody's rules. He waited. Planned. He only had a small handful of brothers and sisters and the Wolves were a hard and well-organised chapter. In those days all chapters had to be well-organised, with the police harassing them whenever and wherever possible. Tudor, their ex-President, had been a tough leader.

The rules that govern the lives of Hell's Angels are simple. There is no Boy Scout concept of honour. No Marquess of Queensberry to oversee their brawls and make sure they fight fair. If any citizen, or outsider, started any trouble with an Angel he would be promptly stomped by any or all of the chapter within yelling distance. There was loyalty to each other and to the chapter. An outsider who wanted to join any chapter became a prospect and would have to show a deal of class – blow the minds of the straights – to be accepted. Once in, there was no reason why he shouldn't try and challenge for the top man's job. This system generally meant that the top man was the toughest. He had to be.

When Gerry had joined the Last Heroes, he had first to make himself accepted by the majority of the chapter; then he could challenge the President – the legendary Vincent – for the presidency. He had fought and killed him, thanks to Brenda's help and despite an attempt by Rat to ensure that Vincent won. But, he was the President of a chapter that scarcely existed.

From the moment that the Wolves first accepted them into their chapter, Gerry had been waiting and watching. He had waited for the right moment, and it hadn't been that long in coming. Tudor was tough and tricky, but he lacked the depths of cunning that had made Vincent such a dangerous opponent. After only a couple of months, Gerry had been able to persuade a number of the Wolves – including the paranoid albino, Gwyn – that he might make a better President than Tudor. After that, it was just a matter of picking the moment.

Beside her, Gerry had just dropped off to sleep and snored quietly. Brenda sat up and pulled on her pants. The sun had nearly vanished behind Anglesey and the air was growing a little chill. She leaned forward and rested her chin on her knees, looking at the dull sea. She tracked her finger idly through the circus sand and thought back to the moment when Gerry had challenged Tudor.

It had been a clear day, and one of the old ladies – Mochyn it was – suggested that they take a few of the straight bikes and go have a picnic. The straight bikes, unchopped, were for this kind of occasion and it was a nice day, so a few of them rolled along. About half of them were Wolves, including Tudor and Gwyn, and the rest were Last Heroes, including Gerry, Rat and Brenda. Rather than run, they had just tooled along back roads, heading westwards, until they were in the most desolate part of the Lelyn Peninsula, near Aberdaron. Just before they reached the village, Tudor turned off to the right and they speeded up along perilous, narrow, twisting lanes that led in on themselves and then doubled back again. Every now and then, Gerry could see the sea below them on the left and he shouted across to Gwyn to find out where they were going.

'Mynydd Mawr – the end of the world. Right up on the cliffs. Take care Wolf. It can be, you know, very dangerous up there.'

Brenda remembered that Gerry had nodded his understanding and thanks at the albino. Had seen the red flash from his hooded eyes. Through tiny villages and large churches. Down and then up again. Through a gate and up a strange concrete road to a lookout hut. Whitewashed and locked. They had all dismounted and the men had stood in a line, sheltered from the strong wind and pissed, far down into brown heather. The mamas and old ladies had been a little more discreet and gone behind the rocks.

At that time of the day and season of the year there was nobody else up there. Across the choppy sound they could see the scattered buildings of Bardsey Island itself. 'Twenty thousand saints buried over there, boyo,' was what Bardd had bellowed at Rat. He'd looked unimpressed and had got a laugh by shouting back: 'All I hope mate, is that they were all fucking dead!'

It had been almost like a proper picnic. Just for a few minutes! They'd all sat around and eaten chocolate cake and drunk coffee from vacuum flasks. Several of the brothers lit joints and relaxed on the supremely springy turf. The cliff sheltered them from the worst of the wind and they could lie back and watch gulls wheeling and screaming against the clouds.

Kafka shouted across to Bardd, without even turning his head: 'Hey, would you like to be able to swirl around up there? Free as birds? Eh?'

Bardd inhaled deeply, and let the smoke trickle out from the corner of his mouth. 'Remember what Bobby said, Kafka? Do you reckon those birds are free from the chains of the skyways?'

'Fuck you and your bloody Celtic mysticism, Bardd. One blast from a scatter-gun and you'd be picking your free birds off the granite there. Not even Jonathan Livingstone Seagull himself would fly away from me. Anyway, Wolf, come for a talk over there. I've got a few things to talk about.'

Tudor walked away from the group without even looking back, certain that Gerry would follow him. As Gerry got up and followed him, he caught the whisper from Gwyn: 'Step lightly.'

The two men, Tudor taller and thinner, hair prematurely grey and Gerry shorter and stocky. Heavily-muscled. Both had their hair on to their shoulders, Tudor's curling and Gerry's straighter. They had originally worn ordinary denim jackets for the ride out to the headland, but these had been discarded and both wore their originals. Tudor's colours were the distinctive white wolf's head, while Gerry's were the death's head that had been the emblem of the Last Heroes.

Tudor stopped at the highest point of the cliff and waited for Gerry to come alongside him. Gerry felt his stomach muscles flutter with anticipation. This wasn't any casual chat. This could be the big one. It was a perfect place. Tudor pointed down over the edge. 'You know, there used to be a little church down there. Right by the sea. There's supposed to be a spring of fresh water down there. It's covered up at high tide, like now. But, if you look, you can just see where it comes out. Look! Down there, by that big jagged rock with the white splash.'

Most people in that situation, suspecting a threat to their lives, would have been watching for the push over the towering crags. And, they would have been dead. Gerry had been enormously influenced by his old unarmed combat instructor in the Army, at the time of the Irish troubles. Sergeant Newman was as tough and inflexible as the parade ground at Aldershot. Middle-aged, well under average height, and with a stomach that preceded him into a room by several inches, his only concession to personal vanity was a wig of quite unique awfulness that covered an egg-shell pate. The troops referred to it as 'the dead rat' – but only behind his back. One trooper who was overheard jesting about the wig suffered greatly for a couple of days, taking some nasty upsets on the obstacle course and finally losing most of his teeth when the butt of the sergeant's rifle caught him in the mouth during a demonstration of bayonet fighting.

Newman urged his pupils, of whom Gerry was one of the best, never to bother with that crap about 'watching his eyes'. Nobody who's worth a monkey's as a fighting man will give away anything by movement of his eyes. And, Tudor, like most Presidents of a Hell's Angels chapter, was far from inadequate when it came to a rough-house.

Gerry had spotted the glint of steel in Tudor's right hand and was ready for it. What he wasn't ready for was the tiny knife in the left hand. Tudor feinted with the long blade in the right arm and, as Gerry countered it, he lunged in with the small knife. The blade wasn't more than two inches long and it had been concealed totally in the palm of the Welshman's hand. Hilt gripped firmly between thumb and fingers, it made a deadly weapon.

Seeing it at the last second, Gerry turned sideways to try and parry it, knowing before he began to move that he was going to be too late. Even so, the speed of his reflex was enough to save the femoral artery in the thigh that had been Tudor's target. Ducking slightly as he pivoted, he felt the knife cut into his lower stomach, just above his groin. The pain made him gasp, and he felt the blood oozing, held back by his tight jeans. He wrenched free and broke away, back to the cliff edge. Tudor faced him, about ten feet away and watched. A knife in each hand, he smiled confidently at the unarmed and wounded Gerry. 'Come on, boyo. Just one step back and we'll get you all in the picture.' Without even glancing behind him, Gerry was sickeningly aware of the void that waited behind him. It seemed very still. Far, far below there was the sea, smashing itself into spume on the rocks. He could hear gulls screaming all around. He was even able to hear the buzz of laughter from the party of Angels, just the other side of the headland. Despite the warmth of the blood, Gerry felt cold. The sun lacked warmth. Once before he had miscalculated, and a bank manager had attacked him to try and save his money, though he risked the life of his daughter. But that had been nothing. This was different. Tudor was better than he'd reckoned. And he had two blades. And Gerry had nowhere to move.

One other sound. Slight. Like the rustle of a small lizard as it moves comfortably on a sun-warmed rock. Behind Tudor. To the left. *Don't!! Don't look at it! Whatever it is.* 'Well, Wolf. The Wolves will miss you. But, I won't. I'll have the friendly Brenda to keep me happy. She'll soon forget you. They all do. Fucking scrubbers. All the same. Now. Goodbye Wolf.'

Gerry tensed himself ready for the last desperate try. A try he knew wouldn't work, but a try he had to make. Then, a quiet voice. Close. From the left. 'Afternoon, all.' It was Rat. Unable to believe the evidence of his eyes and his ears, Tudor turned and gaped at the gnome-like apparition, sprung from the rocks like one of the old Pictish folk. Something out of a fairy story – or a nightmare.

Brenda had picked up the details from Gerry up to his moment, but she had walked over herself, worried by his absence. Climbing near the top she had come upon the tableau, frozen for ever in crystal. Facing her, back to the drop, Gerry. Also facing her, jaw gaping, a knife held loose in each hand, Tudor. Back to her, a tiny, filthy figure who could only be Rat. It was obvious that Rat had only just made his presence felt, his sneaking approach covered by the sea noise and the crying gulls. Rat wasn't armed in any way. He was just standing there, with his arms folded across his shrunken chest.

She had watched Gerry take two quick steps that brought him right up behind the paralysed Tudor. He grabbed him by the collar of his colours with both hands and then dropped backwards, tugging the leader of the Wolves over with him. Brenda's hands twisted nervously as she saw both men, apparently, about to plummet to their doom. But, as Gerry fell, he tucked his knees up so that he was able to push his feet into the small of Tudor's back. One violent shove and the President spent the last four seconds of his reign accelerating at a speed of approximately thirty-two feet per second per second.

If he hadn't been moving so fast, the fact that he hit the rocks feet first might have been a good thing. But, he was going so fast that it really made no difference at all. Carpals and both tibias and fibulas were compressed and smashed. The knee joints collapsed and the long bone of the thigh, the femur, was impacted into the pelvic girdle. The leg bones were shattered so drastically, that they were actually forced up into the rib-cage. Bones devastated the intestines and the heart burst. Any other damage – and there were awful injuries to the head – was irrelevant as Tudor was clinically dead before the impact was even over. In less than one half of one second the presidency passed from him to Gerry Vinson, sometimes known as "Wolf".

The sea disposed quickly of the human wreckage and Gerry went back to the others to tell them some of what had happened. But Rat's part in the affair wasn't mentioned. It would have been downright bad class to have needed help in winning. Gerry thanked Rat. But, Rat had his own motives. Rather a President he knew than a Welshman he could barely understand.

Back on the quiet beach night was moving in. Gerry woke up to find Brenda's hands still wandering over his body. He smiled vaguely up at her. 'Another?'

She nodded and rolled on top of him, taking the initiative. As she guided him into her, she was about to ask him again about the newspaper article. But, Gerry spoke first: 'You know love. I reckon it's time we went back down to London. Sort out the Ghouls and the clever Mr Molineux. Show them the Wolves and Last Heroes are the top. Always were. Always will ... Ouch! Watch what you're doing with your nails!'

Three days later, they all set off for London. On a full run.

5. RIDE A BLACK EAGLE
Lyrics copyright © Ortyx Press, 1997.

All alone, all alone, all alone.
Blood on the road,
And a white heron flying.
Blood on the road,
And a grey mist rising.
All alone,
All alone,
All alone.

Angels running, riding free.
Blood in the eyes.
And a grey goose winging.
Blood in the eyes,
And a red sun rising.
All alone,
All alone,
All alone.

I'm going to run and ride and die.
Blood in my brain.
And a black eagle stooping,
Blood in my brain,
And a dark river rising.
All alone,
All alone,
All alone.

Not alone, not alone, not alone.
Blood in my mind.
And a white hawk rising.
Blood in my mind,
And a free road waiting.
Not alone,
Not alone,
Not alone.

6. JUST BECAUSE WE GET AROUND!

Charlie Marvell and his gang of skulls had also read Melvyn Molineux's article about the Ghouls. Like Gerry, Charlie wasn't happy about any suggestion that his mob weren't the best. He even wrote to the offices of the *Daily Leader* to try and prove his point. But he got no reply. Melvyn wasn't interested in an ordinary crowd of skulls. They ceased being copy a year ago – like the skinheads of twenty years before. It was the Last Heroes that he wanted to provoke into an appearance.

So, Charlie and his mates never heard any more. So, they went looking for Evel Winter. The Ghouls had their turf in Camden Town, so that was where the skulls went. They piled into three old Transit vans they'd bought cheap, armed them-selves with chains and pick-axe handles and cruised about. They had to stop for petrol and Charlie got a couple of gallons put in a can. 'Never know when you might want to burn something...'

It was trad jazz night up at the Flag and Night Land. Over the last year and a half, the music of the late fifties had made a fantastic revival among the youth cults. Its heavy driving beat and repetitive rhythms made it good music to do the lay or the mad or the frout. The Flag, as it was known locally, was a small pub that had suddenly made it big when the landlord discovered that his dusty and scratched record collection would pull in young people and pack his pub. His wife had always been on at him to chuck out the old forty-fives. Now, booming through the biggest amplifier he had been able to find, the very best of Ball, Barber and Bilk lived again.

Five of the Ghouls had gone along that evening and had parked their precious hogs outside. Wearing their bright satins and stack-heeled boots, with heavy facial make-up on, including lipstick and mascara – long, waved hair and no beards. All big men. No old ladies or mamas with them. That wasn't their scene. At first, the Ghouls had been called queer. They had replied to that charge with such terrifying and single-minded savagery that people turned quietly away from them if they ever saw them, and prayed that their eyes wouldn't meet.

Apart from the absence of sexual activity, the Ghouls were a very traditional Angels chapter. Evel Winter had actually known the great Terry the Tramp. He'd even ridden with him only a few days before he'd o.d.'d. They wore colours in the form of sequin patterns on the back of their satin and silk jackets. Wings were carefully embroidered and were won for rather different achievements than those of more orthodox brothers. If possible, they were even more appalling. Unless public fellation is to your tastes.

They concentrated on big hogs and looked after them with fanatical care. Anyone who touched their bikes was as good as dead. You only had to move near them to get stomped. Where most brothers favoured a lot of chrome, the Ghouls went in for bright enamels and teardrop finishes.

It was five of those tangerine-coloured, streamline babies that Charlie Marvell and his skull mates saw outside the pub. 'I knew that petrol would come in fucking useful. Come on lads. They always reckon their fucking bikes are red hot. Let's make 'em even hotter.'

Motor-bikes are strangely vulnerable to fire. All the skulls had to do was quickly unscrew the filler caps of the hogs, tip them over, pour over their own two gallons of petrol and throw on one lighted match.

The bang! and the sheet of white flame brought half the pub running out, while the voice of Mister Acker Bilk (with his Paramount Jazz Band) blared out 'The White Cliffs Of Dover' and nobody paid any attention.

The five Ghouls were the first out of the door and brought up short at the sight of the carnage that had been their pride and joy. Across the car-park the gang of skulls watched and jeered. They had safety in numbers. With the crowd of straights around and police obviously going to be on the scene in a minute or two, this was no place for a direct confrontation. Cool being something of importance to the Ghouls, their leader showed no emotion as he walked towards the skulls. His name was Rohan. 'You're Charlie Marvell. Aren't you?'

'Yeah. And you're the big fairy off the top of the fucking Christmas tree.' Bellowings of laughter from the other skulls, Rohan showed no emotion at all. 'They say you know how to kill people. That you specialise in old men and cripples.' One of the skulls made a move but Charlie grabbed him. 'No! Not here and not now. You just better watch your mouth. Or I'll shut it for you. Oh; I forgot. The only thing you like to shut your mouth is one of your mate's...'

Rohan interrupted him. 'If you know how to kill. I hope you also know how to die. When Evel hears about this, he'll hunt you down and kill you. And any diseased rat that runs with you. There won't be anywhere to hide. We'll find you.'

'Yeah. When you do, then let me know. Can we give you queens a lift anywhere, now your bikes aren't exactly road-worthy?'

The question hung unanswered as the revolving blue light of a patrol car appeared at the far side of the car park. Charlie and his mates piled into their vans and drove off. Although it had been a successful operation for the skulls, Charlie wasn't totally happy. The Ghoul had been altogether too self-assured. As though he felt he had God on his side. Charlie had expected threats. But, angry threats. Not that calm, vicious threat. It had been too much like a promise. A mate passed him a bottle of Southern Comfort, a drink common to most of the young, and he tried to laugh it all off. But, he had never tangled with the Ghouls before and he had an odd feeling. One he didn't recognise. It's called 'fear'.

The skulls believed that cleanliness was next to trendiness. Their jeans were always spotless and their ruffled shirts would have made a soap-powder manufacturer laugh all the way to the biochemical bank. The platform-soled boots were always highly-polished and their faces clean-shaven. They bathed as frequently as possible. An off-shoot of this was that most skulls went swimming several nights a week. It was almost a hobby, like.

With the Highbury skulls, you've got to realise that they weren't all that bright. Charlie reckoned that the Ghouls might make some effort to get back at them for wrecking their hogs but he hadn't carried that a logical step further and tried to guess where they would strike. He and his mates just carried on with the same routine – a routine that included Thursday night swimming at the new Bounds Green Baths. They'd drive up there, a half a dozen or so in their vans, have a few jars and then go along to the baths.

Evel hadn't been pleased when he had heard from Rohan about the attack. So Rohan and four or five other Ghouls went straight by changing their bright clothes for some ordinary citizen's gear and hung around watching for the skulls. It only took a fortnight for the pattern to be clearly exposed.

'Yes, dear, but which is the time he's nearest to being alone?'

'Thursday night, Evel. Some of the skulls play billiards then, so there's not more than six with Marvell when he goes up Bounds Green Baths.'

'All right, then. Next Thursday night will be teaching night for smart Charlie. We'll all put on our nicest clothes and teach the bastard a lesson he won't even live to remember.'

Charlie and his mates got to the baths at about seven. There were never many people there on nights that the skulls took over a baths, and tonight was no exception. There was a young mother teaching her two kids to swim, a couple of middle-aged men plodding through what they obviously considered a keep-fit exercise, and four or five girls. As soon as the skulls came whooping out of the changing room the girls made for the side, followed by shrieked obscenities and coarse gestures.

Charlie and his best mate, Wayne, started bombing the others off the top board, ignoring the shouts from the elderly bath attendant. 'Fuck off you one-armed bastard.' The skulls didn't let anything spoil their simple pleasures. Recognising that discretion was a lot better than getting his other arm broken, the attendant mumbled off to his own cubicle to have a quiet cup of tea.

The mother soon left with her crying children and the two men realised that there wasn't much point in continuing their exercise with the skulls splashing and yelling around. Once they had gone, the baths grew quieter. Light was fading outside and the shadows were spreading in from the corners of the roof until Charlie went and rousted out the attendant to switch on the lights.

They were in the middle of a relay race when all the lights suddenly went out. Outside it was dark, and the baths suddenly became an echoing cavern of blackness. 'Put those bleeding lights on!'

Stuck out in the middle of the pool, Charlie and his mates were suddenly quiet. All the way round the baths they heard footsteps. Not the soft rubber shuffle of the attendant, but harsh staccato steps. The sort of noise that a gang of men would make if they were wearing high-heeled boots. Someone, for instance, like about thirty of the odd Hell's Angels chapter better known as the Ghouls. Led by ... 'Right, Strider. Put on the twinklies and let's have a look and see how many fishes we've caught.' ... Evel Winter.

The overhead light flickered on again. Looking round the pool, Charlie was chilled to see just how many of the Ghouls there were. Far too many to even think of starting anything. The lights bounced off the still water, causing strange highlights to whisper in the fold of the silk and satin jackets. Turquoise, blue, pink, orange, green and black. With Evel himself looking the weirdest in pure white satin trousers and top.

'Rohan! Were these the ones?'

'Yeah, Evel. And that tall one is the great Charlie Marvell himself. He led it. The others were all with him.'

'You wouldn't dare try anything here. There's the lady on the desk and the attendant and anyone else might come in for a swim.'

'No. The lady goes home at eight-thirty when they stop admitting any new swimmers. It's now eight-forty. And the poor crippled old attendant has met with a nasty accident. Must have fallen down, slipped in a patch of water probably. Don't you worry about him, though. I've left a couple of the brothers to keep a careful and considerate eye on the poor old sod. Don't worry about him, Charlie my little skull amigo. Worry about yourself and your friends.'

'Blimey. I thought you could take a joke.'

'Charlie. We all know that you're nearly shitting yourself you're so scared. But, don't upset me by saying such fucking stupid things. Five top hogs wrecked. In public. That's not a joke, duckie. That's a declaration of open war. So here we are. Now shut up and listen. Which of you is the youngest?'

The skulls looked at each other. Were they going to begin the beatings with the youngest, or were they going to let the youngest go? One of the black skulls, Mayhew Sykes, was the youngest of them; he had only just left school and was only fourteen and a half. 'I am. Why?'

'Cool it my ginchy friend. I want you to swim to the side and then go and get dressed. Two of my brothers will come with you to keep an eye on that lovely body of yours. Then, you can go. Weeeell. After they've had a wee private talkie with you about how naughty it is to tamper with big people's bikes. Then you can go and tell all your other crop-head mates about how the Ghouls are the greatest. You dig?'

Mayhew nodded silently. At least they were going to let him go. Watched by the other skulls, he turned away from them and swam slowly to the side, making ripples that licked at the edge of the pool, muttering and chuckling to themselves.

When he'd got out and been escorted down to the changing-rooms, Evel Winter spoke again to the rest of the skulls. But, not to Charlie. 'Unless something goes radically wrong, all of you will still be alive after you leave here. One at a time, beginning with the eldest, you will swim to the side and you will be taken to the changing-rooms. There you will each be severely beaten. Each of you will have a broken nose, both wrists shattered with a sledge-hammer and the right ankle smashed. After that, you will be taken individually out of London and dropped of at some distance from civilisation. There is no reason why you should not all live. You should be up and about in a week or so. There is no argument and no appeal. You were all fucking stupid and you now get to pay the price. And, all of you, remember not to mess around with the Angels again. Like that paper said, we're the tops. Now, one at a time, beginning with the eldest. The rest of you stand quite still and quite quiet. Where are you going, my flash Marvell?'

'I'm the eldest. I just wanted to get it over with.'

'No poppet. You wait till last.'

So it went. One after another the skulls swam to the side of the baths, where they were met by a number of Ghouls. In the recesses of the building, deep in the concrete bunkers of the changing-rooms, bones were splintered with heavy hammers. From in the pool you could only hear the muffled screams and shouts. The rest was very quiet. Evel had sent Rohan to switch off most of the lights in case a wandering pair of policemen came in to see who the late-night swimmers were.

Time passed. The Ghouls were good at their work and all but Charlie were efficiently dealt with in under twenty minutes and packed off to heal and ponder on their sins. In the black pool, Charlie got colder and colder. None of the Ghouls talked at all. Every now and then one of them would click his way up the tiled side and mutter something to another. Finally, they were all gone and just Charlie was left.

Unnoticed in the darkness, Charlie had been edging slowly towards the deep end and now, knowing that there wasn't anything else he could do, he made a dash for the diving board. He just made it ahead of Rohan and scuttled up to the haven of the top board. Twelve metres high. The Ghouls started up after him, but hesitated when it became obvious that Charlie was in a strong position. He could kick anyone off who came up first.

'Now what?'

'Now I have to come up and get you down myself. It'll be quite exciting. Have you read "Treasure Island"? No, I don't suppose you have. Well, this naughty little cabin boy is being chased by this great beefy sailor called Israel Hands. Now Hands is on deck when he sees the boy climbing up the mast. So he climbs up after him. Just like I'm climbing up after you now. The boy gets to the top and finds there's nowhere else left to run. Like you've just found. Then Israel Hands gets just below him, like this and he pulls out a knife, like this and he throws the knife...'

Charlie didn't wait for the rest of the rattling yarn. He ran along the board and dived – or, half-fell – into the pool with a scream of fear that bounced around the girders of the roof and echoed and splintered in the hollow prison. As soon as he surfaced he swam desperately to the side. At the moment he jumped, the other remaining lights went off and the pool was totally dark. He reached the side and swarmed out. He stood up.

A hand touched his shivering arm. 'Marvel. You're a real comic.'

It was nearly ten when the one-armed attendant came round and found himself alone. He staggered out and put on the lights that blazed around the pool. The Ghouls had gone. He didn't even know who had hit him – he'd been clubbed down from behind – but he had heard snatches of talk and could still smell the heavy perfume they all affected. But, he wasn't a fool. When the police came, he said he heard and saw nothing.

The fuzz dragged what was left of Charlie Marvell out of the pool and threw a piece of tarpaulin over it. The green, chlorine-heavy water was blotched and clouded with blood. It billowed out from where the corpse had been thrown. The pool had to be drained and refilled twice before all the taint of death was gone. Apart from immediate family and a few skull friends – some of them still on crutches – there were only two or three outsiders at Charlie's state-subsidised cremation. It was a Saturday afternoon, but Arthur Samuels gave up his afternoon's television wrestling to come along. Thomas Mayhew closed his newsagents shop for the afternoon and also came along. As the greasy smoke billowed out of the chimney, a sign that it was all over, ex-Sergeant Mayhew stood out by the ornamental gold-fish pond and took deep breaths of the air. He coughed once as some of the smoke crept into his lungs, but it didn't bother him at all. In fact, as he walked out of the crematorium gates into the afternoon sun, Mayhew was actually laughing.

Laughing.

7. I'M TALKING, YES INDEED!
An Interview With Evel Winter - From The British Rock Magazine
Telescopic Knife – June 1998.

TELESCOPIC KNIFE: Over the last year or so, Evel, you and your chapter of Hell's Angels – the Ghouls – have been getting a great deal of publicity from the media. That more or less dates from the change of government at the last Election and the legalisation of youth movements, such as skulls and bikers. What we'd like to know is, where were the Ghouls before then?

EVEL WINTER: Well, sweetie. We were around all right, but remember how tough the laws and the police were. It would have been like cutting our own throats to wear our colours.

T.K: You use the word 'colours'. Do you really think that you can claim to be real Hell's Angels when you wear these bright clothes and wear make-up? The original bikers wore filthy levis and denim jackets soaked in excrement, urine and vomit. They rejoiced in being dirtier than anyone else and they used their clothes as one way of blowing the minds of ordinary people.

E.W: Yeah. But the point is that straights are really outraged the moment someone does something that is different. Some brothers like pukey gear, but we go the other way. We like sharp, clean threads. Lovely soft, caressing silks and satins. Smartness, love.

T.K: And the make-up?

E.W: Remember some of the pop bands a few years ago. All camping around with snakes and weird gear. It was just a cult for a bit. But, we reckon, why not?

T.K: One thing that surprises a lot of people is that you never seem to have anything to do with girls. No women ride with you. You're never accused of gang-bangs.

E.W: So fucking what! Listen duckie, we get right pissed off when smart trendies try to make out we're queer. A lot of people have had breakies in their legs for that kind of thing. Be careful or one night you won't make it back to your Beacon Road flat.

T.K: How did you know where I live?

E.W: Because we're careful. When you asked for this talkie, I got a few brothers to check you out. That walk back from Caledonian Road is quite lonely, isn't it?

T.K: All right, Evel, you've made your point. Incidentally, can you tell us about your name. Where's it come from?

E.W: There was a great wheelie man ten years back who actually jumped a hog right across the fucking Grand Canyon. Jet-propelled with a parachute. His name was Evel

Knievel. Bloody maniac but the biggest class you've ever seen. Snuffed it finally trying to fly his Harley off the bridge at San Francisco. He made it O.K. but a police launch hit him when he came up and took his arm off. They tried to sew it back on but he died in the hospital. Shame. He used to wear the most lovely white leather suits. My old man took me to see him once. Super!

T.K: How about your clothes, Evel. Where do you get them from?

E.W: We all go to the same place. The satin comes from a gorgeous little man in Ladbroke Grove – "Fireclown" his shop is called. The boots come from "A Load Of Cobblers" in Camden Town. I get my make-up from the "Quaint Fairy" range.

T.K: I must say that you certainly look a lot nicer than another Angel I interviewed a few years ago. His name was Vincent and he ran a chapter called the Last Heroes.

E.W: Yes, dear, and look what happened to him. The chapter hardly exists now. They've got a new Pres. called Gerry and they spend all their time chasing sheep up mountains in Scotland or somewhere equally silly. Like my friend Melvyn Molineux said; there's only room at the top for one, and that's us. We're the top. Number One. Cream of the crop.

T.K: Thinking about Number One; what sort of music do you like? I understand that Traditional Jazz is quite popular with the Ghouls.

E.W: Yeah. Chris, Acker and Kenny. Lovely sounds. Drop out to that any time.

T.K: Any modern bands?

E.W: It's all too noisy for my shellies. Makes the brain do the whirlies. I don't mind Mealy Plum or Consumer Society. And Oldham Apollo. Nobody else.

T.K: One last question. If the Last Heroes...

E.W: I'd prefer it if you called them by their right name.

T.K: What's that?

E.W: The Last Zeroes.

T.K: All right. What will you do if they come down to London and challenge you to prove who's the top?

E.W: Don't worry about that. Put me and Gerry in a room together and you wouldn't even need to open the door afterwards to let him out. The creepy little bastard would be able to crawl out under it.

T.K: Thanks a lot.

E.W: Peace and love. Sweetheart.

8. THE HAPPENING

'Plastic Life' – the new multi-media exhibition is due to open to the public tomorrow at the Gallery for Visual, Audial and Spatial Arts. A mixture of films, paintings, sculpture (kinetic and static) and happenings, it's bound to excite a lot of interest among all of those with lively minds. It's for anyone who has ever wondered how up is when and where is now.

'What I don't understand is what that gang of pansy thugs are here for?'

'Well; the *Leader* is backing this, right? And Melvyn Molineux is currently pushing them as new cult figures, right? And the police think that the other gang of thugs, from up in Wales, are back in the South. The *Leader* has been deliberately building up this event and stressing that there will be this living slice of pop culture here at certain times. The Ghouls are high art now.'

'So?'

'So the *Leader* reckons that the Last Heroes won't be able to resist this chance to have a public go at the Ghouls. I mean, just look around. The place is absolutely crawling with pigs.'

'Either of you two seen Allen Ginsberg? He's supposed to be chanting a mantra at four. I only want to know so that I can walk about somewhere else. A mantra chanter is high on my list of people I'd rather not spend a wet afternoon with. Whoops, pardon my syntax. Anyone seen Germaine?'

'Over by the Rauschenberg, Clive. Talking to Joe D'Allesandro. Just beyond that purple pimple.'

'Thanks sport. What is that excrescence in mood indigo?'

'George's new hat.'

'I'm going to talk to Evel Winter, if I can drag him away from Alan.'

'For God's sake; when is that man going to give it up? At the moment he's ahead of Mrs Dale and only a couple of years behind Samuel Pepys. He's after old Parson Woodforde's record. Saints preserve us.'

'I bet he's trained his son to carry on.

Most of the Ghouls were huddled together in a corner, unused to the lionising they were getting. Melvyn Molineux kept glancing at the door in a mixture of anticipation and worry. If the Last Heroes did show up, he didn't know how things would pan out; and, if they didn't, then he was going to be left with a damp squib of a non-story.

Although there was a real risk of mass slaughter if there was a confrontation, that was a lot better than nothing at all. Bodies sold papers. The bloodier the better.

His editor caught his eye and waved an impatient hand at him. Molineux sidled briskly across to him, his campari swishing pinkly in his glass.

'Mel, we're spending a lot of money backing this arty-farty crap and I just hope that we get something to bloody show for it.'

'Don't worry about a thing, V.B; there are loads of other reporters from other papers covering this and that should help build up our story.'

'Mel, I'm trying to be patient with you, but just tell me in nine short sentences exactly what the fuck this story is going to be if this other mob don't show?'

'I've got a friend in the police force, and they say that their informers are certain that the Last Heroes have moved to London. If they're in London, then they're bound to come along here. I've made sure ... listen!'

'What is it?'

'Bike engines, V.B; bike engines! A lot of them. Jesus, they've come. Thank Christ.'

The editor looked at him coolly. 'I thought you were sure they were coming anyway. Why are you so relieved?'

'Well, they might ... I wasn't absolutely ... that is ... Look, they're here aren't they?'

Clapping his hands, Molineux ran into the middle of the large room. Gradually, the talk died away. One last, lone voice quacked on for half a sentence: '...so she used the Alsatian *and* the melon.'

'Thank you. You can probably hear from the noise outside that our uninvited but not unexpected guests are about to arrive. Evel, I'm relying on you to keep your men under control. If there's any sign of trouble, then Chief Superintendent Penn has enough men here and outside to check any aggro.'

The critics, hangers-on, freeloaders, reporters and other uninvolved persons, were hastily shepherded to the end of the saloon furthest away from the door. Just by the table bearing the exhibits from the Los Angeles casters in plaster.

The police, in a heliotrope variety of unlikely disguises, ranged themselves in a loose circle round the main entrance. Inside the circle were all the Ghouls – about thirty, with a few more outside watching the hogs. Standing next to Evel Winter, and hugging himself with a mixture of pleasure and simple fear, was Melvyn Molineux.

The roaring of bike engines outside died away and there was a moment of silence. Chief Superintendent Penn used that moment to hiss a warning to the Ghouls: 'Just one wrong move out of anybody and I'll see you all away. Remember this isn't my idea. If I can bust all of you then it'll have been worth while. So, if you want to keep clean, keep in line. Otherwise I'll have you.'

Even as he was speaking, there was the sound of boots on the staircase and the door was thrown back. Even some of the more cynical journalists gasped at the spectre that strode in. Tall, over six feet, with flowing, fine, shoulder-length hair that was as white as Arctic snow. Flesh as pale as a rain-washed bone and eyes that stared and flamed with a fearsome red intensity.

'I'm Gwyn. Let's see. You're Evel Winter and these pretty people must be the Ghouls. You lot...' a contemptuous wave of his gloved hand '...are obviously sworn officers of the law. And you, must be Mr Molineux. The reporter who says that the

Ghouls are the top chapter of Hell's Angels and that the Last Heroes and Wolves are scared to come down to London to say anything different.'

'Those are all reasonable assumptions, er, Gwyn. But, surely you haven't come down here from your caves just on your own? We heard several other bikes. Where are all the rest of you?'

Evel Winter brushed past the journalist. 'What's more to the point, whitey, where is Gerry? Is he hiding behind clowns now?'

Gwyn smiled gently at the insults. 'Now, now. Chief Superintendent Israel Pitman Penn there, lurking behind that strange mummer's beard, won't be pleased if he hears naughty provocative words. Right, sir?'

Molineux was getting a touch concerned. His unctuous smile started to slip away from one corner of his mouth as he felt control edging from him. He'd wanted a grand violent entrance with instant slaughter. All he'd got was a shatteringly self-possessed albino in stinking blue denim, with a white wolf's head blazing on the back. A man who brought an aura of bizarre death into that effete atmosphere. A man under control.

What Melvyn didn't know was that this scene had been very carefully rehearsed. Gerry had guessed that the art exhibition had been set up as the scene for a confrontation between the Ghouls and his own chapter. A few quiet words and a couple of pounds spent in the right pubs had revealed the plans laid by the police and the name of the senior officer involved. Gwyn had been chosen as the brother most likely to freeze the minds of some of the straight trendies there – a man who would not blow his cool under pressure or provocation. Gerry knew that Gwyn would say what he'd been told to, and that he could also trust him to play the chat by ear.

Gerry had a suspicion – unfounded as it happened – that Molineux, and, even, the Ghouls, were all part of a police plan to trap the Last Heroes and Wolves. So, they waited while Gwyn sussed things out.

While Molineux sweated, Gwyn suddenly turned and walked out, down to where the other brothers waited. He was followed by whispered insults from the Ghouls, and a mutter of 'fucking cowards' from Evel Winter.

It only took a minute for Gwyn to convince Gerry that things seemed to be on the level. Leaving a similar number of brothers to the Ghouls attending to the hogs, Gerry led his chapter up the baroque staircase and in to the 'Plastic Life' rooms.

'Ah. You must be the elusive Gerry Vinson?'

Gerry didn't reply to the reporter. His brothers fanned out around him, Kafka, Riddler, Cochise and Dick the Hat stood in a half-circle while Brenda and Gwyn stood together, just behind him. Rat also came in the room with them and he was ... actually, nobody really noticed his slinking, tiny figure and he melted somewhere round the back.

Finally, Gerry let his eyes settle on Evel Winter. He looked up and down the satin figure of the President, taking in the heavy make-up, the sequins on each cheek-bone. Seeing behind the trivia that made up the public image. Detecting the ruthless streak that made him the power he was. Seeing even beyond that to a psychosis that created a figure of quite unpredictable danger. At last, he smiled.

'You wear soft clothes. You call yourself an Angel and yet you dress like a ponce. Like a queer. Like a girl. What sort of a brother are you?'

One of the Ghouls stepped forward angrily, but Evel was just as much in control as Gerry and reached out and squeezed the cheek of his errant brother between finger and thumb. The Ghoul yelped at the pain. Evel held him steadily, until he suddenly let go, leaving a white, pinched weal across the man's face.

'Careful Evel. You might make the poor wee fellow's mascara run.' That was Kafka.

'Quiet. We won't do anything to upset these silken folk or our steadfast defenders of public safety. We're not here for that.'

'In that case, Vinson. What are you here for?'

Yet again, Gerry ignored the querulous interruptions of Melvyn Molineux. 'Evel. I read in that little man's paper that you reckon that the Ghouls are the top chapter.'

'Yeah. I always believe what I read in the papers. Especially when it happens to be the truth.'

'I would venture that a statement like that could be called ... what was it old Churchill said?'

Kafka answered: 'He called a man a liar by saying he'd used a terminological inexactitude.'

'Thanks, Kafka. Yes, Evel. I reckon that Molineux is a liar. And that anyone who believes him is either stupid or a liar as well. That's what we've come all the way down here for. Nobody likes liars.'

'Now just a fucking...'

'Shut up Melvyn. This is between him and me. All right, big bad wolf. What are you and your gang of smellies going to do to prove that you're the best? You want one big crash-bang brawl, or would you dig something a bit more subtle?'

'Subtle from you means tricky. What have you and your creepy mate got arranged?'

"We haven't got anything arranged. The *Daily Leader* would never lend its name to anything that wasn't absolutely clean and above-board.'

'Clean! You couldn't even guess at what the word means. What do you suggest, then, Winter?'

The police had relaxed as the talk went on. While people were talking there wasn't that much danger that violence would suddenly spew out. Although the chat was insulting and somewhat provocative, it wasn't anything that they could move on. Not by a long way. So, they relaxed and waited.

The ladies and gentlemen of the press were also relaxing after the burst of tension caused by the appearance of Gwyn. Led by one or two of the braver ones – with a bravery that owed much to the alcohol laid on by the exhibition sponsors – they began to push forward to hear the exchanges.

All this movement meant that there were gaps in the room, areas where a small man might creep and brew up evil and mischief. A small man, like – for instance – Rat. Barely five feet tall in his stinking socks, Rat was one of the longest established of Hell's Angels in Britain. He had been a member of the Last Heroes during all their dark underground days, long before Gerry even appeared on the scene. At least twice he had attempted to help the ex-President, the late and little-lamented Vincent, to kill Gerry. Distrusted by many of the Wolves and hated by Brenda, Rat was still a useful weapon in the armoury of the chapter.

However, because of his satanic sense of unpleasant humour and his anarchic love of violence, there were times when he was something of a liability. Like now.

Sneaking gently through the fringes of the crush, Rat was barely noticeable. Only the smell of his colours gave warning of his presence. By the time your nose had registered the miasma of his passing, and your eyes had sought the source of the odour, he had moved on.

As the journalists gathered round, forcing the police into a useless, huddled mass, the two leaders of the Hell's Angels chapters were pushed almost eye-ball to eye-ball. At the rear of the Ghouls, hidden by the Palladian column, a hand came round a corner, spidered softly towards the back pocket of one of the beautiful satin jackets and poured some liquid in to the pocket, splashing more over the side and back. The hand disappeared and then eased round again, holding a small cigarette lighter. A flick of the thumb and the high octane fuel burst into flame. A scuttling dash and Rat was well over the other side of the room before the unfortunate Ghoul even noticed that he was well ablaze.

In fact it was a blonde lady journalist from a popular daily who first saw the fire and screamed a warning. Instant panic! The Last Heroes and Wolves gathered round Gerry to face the unknown threat. The reporters fled for the doors and balcony. The police milled uselessly around and the Ghouls tried to help their stricken brother. He ripped off the blazing coat and heaved it across the room. It knocked over an early Warhol silk-screen, which flamed down on to the table of plaster casts, breaking many of the most famous phalluses in show-biz history.

Fortunately, Penn of the Yard was a man of action and he proved his reputation by leaping at the spreading fire and beating it into submission with a leather and brass mobile. A quick-thinking constable, hampered by a flowing cotton kaftan, earned himself a commendation by slashing open a vermilion plastic water-bed that had been waiting for the group-grope on a small platform. A couple of hundred gallons of water soon extinguished the flames and reduced the danger to a smoking heap of rubble.

Wheeling quickly round, Penn spotted a more immediate danger. The two chapters of Angels were facing each other, ready for one more spark to set off a battle.

Banging his truncheon on a ringing Hepworth sculpture, he bellowed for attention. 'Hold it! Everybody stay exactly where they are. One movement and my men will move in and all my men will come running from outside. I warn you. One word in the wrong place and I ... I will personally guarantee that every single one of your prize motor-bikes will be pounded into scrap metal. The Council of Civil bleeding Liberties can protest all they like afterwards. It'll be too late then. Right?'

It was the threat to their hogs that really kept the Ghouls and Last Heroes and Wolves apart. But, it was a tenuous and desperately uneasy peace. Fragile as a spun-crystal ball. Aching in a void that shrieks to be violently filled. They stood and faced each other, stiff-legged and bristling.

'Not here, then?'

'Right.'

'Where, and when? Somewhere away from this army of fucking piggie-wiggies.'

'Wait a minute. Wait. Listen. Wait. Listen to me. I've got an idea. Wait.'

Evel Winter turned to look stonily at the capering figure of Melvyn Molineux. He had promised the Ghouls that he would set it up for them so that they would have the chance to grind the Last Heroes into the shit. He'd said that they wouldn't dare start any kind of fight with the place packed with police. But, the Ghouls had lost face. The incident of the burning jacket would be splashed over most of the daily papers the next morning. Since Molineux hadn't delivered what he promised, it would have to be settled with knives and chains and fists and hogs. In the grand old manner.

Molineux gabbled his plan. His careful plan. 'A sort of duel. That's it. The losers agree to disband and publicly burn their colours and their jackets with the badges and things.'

Gerry turned from the door, interested. 'What sort of duel? You mean pistols at dawn? Or lances on our Harleys?'

'He means a sort of trial by combat. That way he'll get rid of all of us. Or have us busted for disturbing the peace.'

'No. No. No. Not like that. More a sort of competition rather than a duel. I'll draw up a list of clues giving places that you have to go to and things you have to find there. The team from each chapter that does it fastest and gets them all right will be the winners.'

Cochise made one of his rare public utterances: 'When I was a kid I used to go on car rally things like that with my brother, Nigel. He'd put on his deer-stalker hat, his super suede jacket and we'd roar off in his M.G. sports car. We never won though 'cos he was so frigging thick.'

'I think it might be funsie and save you Heroes from getting badly hurt.'

'Good. Well, Gerry. What do you think. Evel has agreed on behalf of the Ghouls. Are you going to come in or are you too scared to risk it? Maybe you lot are only good at stealing and grandma-bashing.'

'Why you dirty...'

'Cool it, Dick. He's just trying to get us rattled. I'll tell you what. We'll talk it over and I'll ring you at your of office tonight at nine o'clock. If we agree, then I'll want a proper meeting to get the rules straightened out. Just so that nobody has any doubts what's happening. OK?'

'Yes, that's very fair, Gerry. What do you think, Evel? Will you agree to that?'

The sound of sirens drawing nearer heralded the arrival of the Fire Brigade and drowned the answer from the President of the Ghouls. But, everyone saw the nod. Brenda saw more, and pushed forward to whisper in Gerry's ear.

'Watch it, lover. I smell a rat, or, two rats. One little reporter who wants a scoop for his paper and another who's the President of a crowd of sodding queers and who might go along with any plan that gave him the chance to carry on with his boasting about being the number one. I reckon they intend fixing it between them.'

Gerry turned to whisper back. 'Maybe you're right, but we haven't got a lot of choice. His paper will blow this up into a big thing. Just think about the fucking class if we can pull it off. I reckon we could. With a bit of luck and a lot of planning. I'll get us plenty of time for the planning and then we'll go ahead. But, we'll have a full chapter meeting out in Hertfordshire tonight. Relax.'

He turned back to Molineux and confirmed his agreement that he would ring later that night. Molineux could hardly hide his pleasure and the two groups of Angels started snarling threats at each other. Penn moved his men in between and asked the Last Heroes and Wolves to leave first.

They filed out, Gwyn remaining facing the room and leaving last. They pushed past the huddle of reporters hiding on the landing and were gone.

All but one. Rat sneaked back along the landing and stuck his head round the door, whistling to attract the attention of the Ghouls. When he saw that they were looking, he held up his cigarette lighter and flicked it on. Penn was hard put to hold back the angry Ghouls but, in a flash, Rat was gone. With a jaunty two-fingered salute.

Chief Superintendent Penn turned away towards Melvyn Molineux and mopped his brow. With a totally unconscious humour he said: 'You know, Mister Molineux. For a few moments it got quite warm there.'

9. PROBLEMS ALL DAY LONG

A highly confidential memorandum from Melvyn Molineux to his editor – Valentine Bergen – concerning the happenings of the afternoon and his plans for the competition. June 9th, 1998.

Dear V.B,

As I told you last night, the leader of the Last Heroes rang me to confirm that he had persuaded the other members of his gang that it would be wise to accept my challenge. So, the day after tomorrow they (not all, but a few selected senior members of the group) will meet in our offices with Evel Winter and a few of his gang to discuss the rules. These will be broadly as you and I discussed them the other day – subject to any minor amendment that Vinson may ask for.

I have just left Evel and I think I can say with some confidence that it is unlikely that his chapter will not win. I kept to our arrangement that we would not offer any help to them unless they were obviously losing. Evel Winter is quite happy with this arrangement as he has come to believe our publicity on his behalf and thinks that they really are the top gang in England. Perhaps they are. But having met Vinson, I am not now so confident as I once was about the outcome of this challenge.

However, if things look like going against our investment, I can arrange for a little 'help' for the Ghouls. Apart from anything else; I have no doubt that the last of the five clues that I have prepared is insoluble without help. I attach a list of these clues – we discussed them after our first meeting with Evel Winter, just after we arranged the contractual details of the Ghouls' story.

If you have any recommendations to make about these clues, I will arrange a talk with you for the 12th and we can polish up the details. I think, V.B, that we are going to be on to one of the biggest winners in journalistic history. I have already had several inquiries from the commercial television networks for rights to the challenge. Plus a couple from the States and one from France. It has to be a big winner for the *Daily Leader*.

Melvyn Molineux - Senior Features Editor.

NO COPIES – FILE IMMEDIATELY AFTER READING UNDER SECURITY LOCK. FOR V.B.'S EYES ONLY.

FIVE SUGGESTED CLUES

1. George Yard Buildings saw my death,
   A whore was I, till my last breath.

Thirty-nine cuts bled me fast,
I was the first, but not the last.

2. Philip and Herbert shared a flat here. Though neither had any reason to expect great things, they never found themselves out of pocket.

3. First the Marsh in 1882. Then Northumberland Park in 1885. Now at the corner of Park and Worcester.

4. One thousand yards between the wicked ladies and the wicked men. In that order.

5. Rossetti on one wall, Turner on another and Constable on the third.

Melvyn:
I suggest making four into one as it is the easiest and we want the TV boys to have a spectacular race to start with. Then one becomes two and so on. I must make sure I don't change any of the prints in my office before the final day. Apart from that – it's all OK. We can appear as socially conscious and still sell on the sensation aspect. Let's hope that there are lots of clashes between the two mobs. Frankly, I wouldn't be averse to a killing or two. If a few innocent people get hurt as well it'll generate more interest and make us look even better as saviours of the public.

Once it's over and the Last Heroes have packed up, how do you feel about us having a go at this other crowd? Maybe we can try and rig something up with the police to fix a bust on them for drugs or blackmail or something. Bear it in mind.

– Valentine Bergen.

10. ACROSS A CROWDED ROOM

'All right. Those are the rules. Nice and simple. Seven days to pick your teams of six and get ready. So, on Tuesday next, the cameras roll and away you all go at mid-day sharp. Remember to come here first at eleven to get the first clue. Then, one a day till the big last one on Saturday. Each chase starts on the forecourt outside apart from the last one. That runs from Marble Arch. Just to be different. Have any of you got any questions?'

Brenda spoke first. 'Each clue will lead us to a specific place. At each place there will be a man with a copy of the *Leader* for each chapter and all we have to do each day is find the place and the man, collect the copy of the paper and bring it back to the main doors here.'

'Right. Absolutely right.'

'Thanks. I wanted to be sure. And, each time we get the clue just one hour before the off at twelve.'

'Yes. Evel, have your team any questions?'

'Melvyn, about the money from the television...'

'Shut up, Vanya. We've spent bloody hours arguing about that this morning. Drop it. It's settled.'

Kafka disturbed his bulk from one of the Danish tubular steel and mustard canvas executive chairs that had been brought into the conference room at the *Leaders'* offices near Fleet Street. He peered through the clouds of pot smoke and asked his question. 'Can you tell us anything at all about these clues? What sort of subjects they'll be – that sort of thing?'

'Well now. I don't think it would be at all fair to give too much away. They'll be single clues to each place – not a great string of them. The first one is quite easy, the next two are a bit literary, the third one is ... well, let's just say it's not literary, and the last one is a bit tricky.'

The room was edgy with tension. Security guards stood round the back of the room, but there had been no actual trouble. The Ghouls had a smug air of superiority but the Last Heroes and Wolves were far from happy. Though Gerry, backed by Brenda, Gwyn and Kafka, had finally convinced them that they had to go through with the challenge, there was a strong feeling that the whole thing might be a fix and that they were going to get crapped on from a great height. As Melvyn ran quickly through the rules, suspicion had been swelling nearer the surface. Gerry was relieved when

Melvyn gathered up his papers and Evel led the Ghouls out the room. It had been agreed beforehand that the Ghouls would arrive first and leave first. Just to avoid jostling in the hallowed corridors of the paper.

As the Last Heroes filed out in turn, Gerry felt a hand gently on his arm. It was Gwyn who winked encouragingly at him. 'Don't look so glum, Wolf. We can beat those queer bastards without raising a sweat.'

Gerry turned to face the albino. 'I think we can. Otherwise I'd never have agreed to it. But, I'm sure that fly little cunt Molineux has arranged some kind of fix with the Ghouls. It's not just that we can win; it's that we've got to.'

During the week before the challenge began, the *Daily Leader* gave it saturation coverage. Pictures of nubile, clean young ladies wearing unlikely combinations of leather and denim filled the centre pages. Articles on how to chop bikes, on the lore and language of Hell's Angels, plans for the start, interviews with concerned sociologists and psychiatrists – the whole show.

One or two other chapters claimed they should be included in the challenge but they were cold-shouldered. One set of brothers from Windsor even ran up to London and roared round the paper's offices carrying picket cards. Mynydd, Cochise, Draig and Rat happened to be riding round the area, trying to familiarise themselves with the roads, when they came across the demo.

Bearing in mind Gerry's instructions to keep out of trouble until the challenge was over, they made their attack carefully. Since it had to be sneaky, it was a happy chance that Rat was along. He 'arranged' a couple of pints of oil, punctured the can and rode sedately through the other outlaws, muttering the most gross insults under his breath. Watching police saw only the small figure of a solitary Hell's Angel ride gently past. Then the Windsor chapter seemed to go crazy. They dropped their placards, revved up their engines and roared off after the single rider. Then, the craziness increased. They'd only gone a hundred yards, and were catching up on Rat, when they all skidded wildly across the road and fell in a tangled heap of cursing men and screaming machines.

The police dashed towards the scene of carnage – the lone rider had proceeded gently along – when there was the roar of more bikes and three other Angels sped round the corner, keeping within the legal speed limit, and rode into the wreckage. The Windsor brothers hadn't even got to their feet when they found themselves the targets for three heavy bikes ridden by three expert riders. Skidding round the oil on the road, the Last Heroes and Wolves chopped their way through, breaking arms and fingers and smashing bikes beyond salvation.

The only thing the police could do was charge what was left of the Windsor chapter with dangerous riding, without due care etc etc. The others got off since they obviously couldn't have expected to see a load of men and bikes sprawled across a busy road. They never traced the first motor-cyclist. The one who must have had a leaky tank, or something. Or something.

Nobody else challenged the Ghouls or the Last Heroes after that. It wasn't worth it.

One of the most surprising side-effects of the paper's coverage of the coming challenge was a vast increase in the numbers of people who suddenly wanted to join the Hell's Angels. An idea of the difference between the two chapters involved comes from the way they treated applicants.

The Ghouls attracted girls more than boys, which was rather a shame. And a waste. Many of the girls were only just in their teens and they were sent screaming away. Evel Winter liked his amusement, but he didn't like jail-bait. When a group of school-girls refused to leave them alone, Evel broke one of the cardinal laws of Hell's Angels – he called the fuzz to collect them. And, he insisted that they were charged.

Prompted by Rohan, Evel agreed to let twenty or so of the best-looking women into their club-house in Camden Town. There they were doped up until their minds were wobbling free. Then, Evel announced a contest to find the most lovely mama. Miss Ghoul. But, it had to be done nude. So, the hopefuls, spaced out of sight, stripped off their blouses, tore off skirts or trousers, pulled down tights. Posed and preened themselves all along one wall, while the made-up Ghouls admired them from the other side of the room.

Shelob, fattest of all Angels, unusual among the Ghouls in that he had a beard, collected up the girls' clothes and took them out of the room. To be kept safe? No. To be burned!

Evel lined the girls up and kept them waiting for nearly half an hour in the freezing cold while they 'added up the marks'. Then he announced that they had reached a decision. He called Rohan over to him. 'Now my brother. Let us show these little breasties what we think of them.'

All the Ghouls immediately burst into howls of laughter and derision, throwing food and drink over the frightened girls. The vicious joke continued with Evel grabbing Vanya and kissing and fondling him. Before the horrified gaze of the prospects, Vanya dropped to his knees in front of his President and began to unzip his trousers. All round the room, other Ghouls began to make love to each other.

Their laughter rose even higher as the crying girls ran into the other room and found only a smouldering heap of rags where they expected to find clothes. As they clawed their way out into the night, Evel himself came to the studded door and shouted: 'Come back when you've got something more to offer us. Like another eight inches!'

That was one story that Melvyn Molineux didn't use in the *Leader*. He did use a feature about the number of men and boys who'd tried to join the Ghouls but had finished up coolly saying that not a single applicant had measured up to the strict tests imposed by the Angels. Well, that was true. In a way.

Evel had warned Melvyn that the Ghouls never accepted prospects in the usual way. 'Sorry, sweetie. Nobody asks to join the Ghouls. Sometimes we ask somebody. But, not very often.'

To humour the journalist, Evel Winter agreed to lay on a test for anyone who wanted to become a Ghoul. A time and a place was announced in the *Leader* and over a hundred turned up. First off those who came without a chopper were immediately sent away. Then those who came along wearing either normal gear or a parody of the silk and satin jackets were dismissed. This left nine, with ages ranging from fifteen to thirty-eight.

Evel picked out the oldest and the youngest and told them that selection would be run on knockout lines – Molineux couldn't understand why the word "knockout" provoked such mirth from the assembled Ghouls.

The test was simple. The two prospects had to ride out into the back yard where a course had been prepared. It was a bit like the old tournaments that knights in armour had to ride. Two paths, about four feet wide, with walls eight feet high. In the centre of the course was quite a sharp bend, taking each rider to the left. The walls were made of heavy board partitions, in sections. Imagine that you are in one of the upper windows of the old warehouse, near the canal, which was the club-house of the Ghouls. Looking down you would see that the course was really like a big figure 'X', with the centre partitions moved so that it formed two runs, more or less at right-angles, but totally separate. No danger of the riders hitting each other. No. Unless...

Unless the centre partitions were moved; only if they were shifted around a bit. Then you might get an arrangement with one straight diagonal route through with a vision-obscuring chicane in the middle. See what might happen. Right!

Both riders thought they would come round the high partition in the middle, facing a turn to the left. What a surprise when they got there! Oh, how the Ghouls laughed! Since the gap was only one handlebar's width, and since both prospects had wound their machines up to peak revs, they hit each other, head-on, at an aggregate speed of nearly one hundred and twenty miles per hour.

When the screeching, crashing and ripping had died away, before they dragged out the fused mass of chrome, flesh, steel, bone, oil, muscle, water, brains and mud, Evel turned to the other prospects and whispered softly: 'Ride with care my doves. See how much better it is to travel hopefully than to arrive.'

Once the remaining contenders saw the carnage, and realised that they would each be expected to make that run with death, six of the seven split.

One tall young man, with immaculate gear and a finely-tuned Norton, insisted that he should have a chance to show his class.

'Rig up one of those screens, Vanya. In the middle. That's it. There we are, I'll ride through that first to show you how it should be done. Then we'll have a short break for some light refreshments and you can have a go.'

Evel turned his Harley and throttled hard forward, doing a wheelie for nearly twenty yards before he brought the front end down and powered up to the fibreboard partition. He hit it square on and ripped through, skidded on the patch of blood and oil in the centre of the natural arena, fought the bike round and rolled back to applause from his brothers.

'Great class, Evel!' shouted the prospect, whose name was Ingrams and who was a rather seedy outcast from Winchester School. Manners may have made him a man, but they had failed to cultivate his intelligence. Having seen what had happened to his two predecessors, you might have thought that his natural wit would have alerted him to the possibility ... probability, even, of treachery.

Not one fucking bit.

A few drinks under his belt, a new partition, in a different place, on his Norton, gleaming teeth for the cameraman from the *Leader*, gloved hands on the ape-hanger bars, foot kicking down on the starter, rear wheel gouging up turf and gravel, a half-hearted wheelie and up to full-bore to hit the partition well in the centre. What a pity!

The warehouse had once housed some gear for shredding and pulping soft bulk plastic. One of the huge units, now rusting, stood massive and immovable, directly behind where the roguish Shelob had placed the board. Though it was aged and corroded, it still had a functional effect when anything was projected at it hard. It was like, well, like a vast chipping machine.

His eyes still closed against flying bits of the fibre-board, Ingrams didn't know about it until he hit it. Then, it was obviously too late to do much. Though his mind may have been willing to stop, his flesh was weak.

Melvyn Molineux threw up on the spot, and even his hardened cameraman paled. Evel Winter found it all rather amusing. 'See that, Mel? They didn't know whether to push the rest of him through, or try and poke the bits of him back. Like I said, nobody asks to join the Ghouls. We're exclusive and we're going to stay that way.'

The Last Heroes and Wolves also had a number of applicants who wanted to join them. Though Melvyn played it down, they actually had far more than the Ghouls. Most young people who were interested in Hell's Angels preferred the traditional look of Gerry's chapter to the soft look of the Ghouls.

Gerry's attitude to prospects was much the same as Evel's. But, he played it differently. Any man without a hog was sent packing. Any girl who even looked as though she might be under the age of consent was also rejected automatically. The rest of the girls were taken on one side by Brenda, Lady, Holly and some of the other mamas and old ladies. They were told what their place would be – generally horizontal. That they would all have to pull a train as part of their initiation. If one of the brothers picked them out to be his old lady, then they would go through a marriage ceremony, over the tank of the brother's hog, using a service manual instead of any bible or prayer-book. Then they would be the exclusive property of that brother and no-one else would dare touch them. Some brothers insisted that their old ladies should be tattooed with their names, generally on the buttocks or on the stomach, just above the line of the pubic hair.

If they were accepted as mamas, then they were a lot less secure. Any brother who wanted them would be able to take them at any time he wanted. That was the rule. A mama didn't last very long with the Last Heroes and Wolves, unless she had some particular quality. Or, unless she happened to be very exceptional like Holly or Lady. The Last Heroes were not a typical chapter, any more than the Ghouls were. They had a far more careful attitude to authority, in that they would never deliberately damage property or beat anyone up for kicks. Nor would they indulge in the traditional gang-bangs of the seventies. It was O.K. at the time, one way of showing class. But, things had moved on.

But all that didn't mean that the Angels had gone soft. Most of them still had hair-trigger tempers and would brawl at the least provocation. And class still mattered. That was what this challenge was all about. The top chapter had to be the one that would never turn down a dare or a bet. Deintydd was living proof of that.

In a cafe in Caernarvon, he had been moaning about the state of his teeth. A girl had laughed at him and offered a pair of pliers from behind the counter and dared him to pull out his own teeth if he was so tough. Deintydd had grabbed the pliers and seated himself at the table and pulled out five of his rotting molars. The girl behind the counter had been rather surprised. She was even more surprised when he pulled her bodily over the counter and pulled out five of *her* teeth for good measure. Now called simply Geneth, she had joined the Wolves and had become Bardd's old lady.

The chat had its effect on the female prospects. No chapter likes a big surplus and the Last Heroes and Wolves were no exception. Only two of the girls were still prepared to go on with their initiation. But, they would have to wait to pull the train until after the men had been tested. Then, if any of them got through, there would be drinking and drugs. The girl prospects would present themselves to the assembled chapter and would be taken first by the President, then by any successful prospects – who would be initiated at a later date – then by the vice-President and then by any and all of the brothers. As many times and in as many ways as they wanted. It could last three or four hours. With two girls, it might last a little less.

The tests for the male applicants started with a check of their hogs. They had to be chopped and not custom-built by some garage that exploited youth cults. The prospects, all wearing plain denim jackets and jeans, with the sleeves cut out of the tops, had to show that they knew how to service their machines. Then a series of questions about the Angels' movement. How and when it began. The big names. How they died. What happened at the Altamont Festival. Who were the great writers – Cave and the mystic Stuart. About the Last Heroes and its history. What wings were and about other chapters. And, why did they want to join the Heroes?

A french-kiss from the aptly-named "Foulmouth", who suffered badly from halitosis, combined with ulcerous gingivitis, came next. After that – and failure here meant a crashing blow from a huge right hand – the numbers were down to eight. A simple test of riding ability brought the eight down to four. Of the four, one was outstanding. Still only a schoolboy, the curly hair of Mick Moore blossomed out over the neck of his denim jacket. Just seventeen, his parents' ambitions were for him to achieve a good degree and become a teacher at his old school in Wandsworth. So, at seventeen, he was still at school. Or, rather, he was supposed to be still at school. For the last three days he had been marked absent, devoting his time to preparing himself for his big chance. He had polished all the chrome on his hog and read up all the books and magazines on Angels in his library.

Gerry had pointed him out to Gwyn when the prospects were first paraded for him. 'Keep an eye on that one. He's got a streak of mean bastard in him. I reckon he might make it through.'

His time in the army, followed by his year and a half with the Angels had made Gerry a reasonable judge of men. Just as he had picked out Gwyn from all the Angels, so he had spotted Mick Moore as the likeliest prospect he had yet come across.

It was now time for the last four to take the test that would leave only one of them as a prospective Last Hero and Wolf. Mick had decided that it was going to be him. One of the other prospects was even more anxious to succeed in the last test as his girl friend was one of the two who were to take their own initiation later that day. Without him, she would run a grave risk of being a mama. Having gone as far she had, he was worried, he confided to Mick, that she might go ahead even if he failed to be accepted.

Mick felt sorry for him. Partly sorry. But not too sorry. The girl – her real name was Christine, but she said she wanted to be called "Modesty" – was very attractive and Mick even fancied his chances there. Play his cards right. But, first, the test.

All four would take part at the same time. It was to be a straight race round a country circuit near the ruined missionary college in East Hertfordshire which had been the headquarters of the Last Heroes before the apocalyptic happenings of the last couple of years. They had ridden a couple of times round the route and were to start together at ten the next morning.

After breakfast Gwyn took Gerry on one side. I arranged a few of the brothers on sentry rota last night, like you ordered. Bardd saw someone sneaking around. He followed him and saw him rigging up a thin wire, neck-high, on that shadowy part of our race-circuit, where it goes through all those overhanging trees.'

Brenda had joined them. 'Who was it? Those bastard Ghouls! I'd like to castrate them myself.'

Before Gwyn could reply, Gerry spoke. 'No! I'd take money it wasn't Evel's mob. My guess is Mick Moore.'

'That's right!' exclaimed Gwyn, surprised. 'How the hell did you fucking guess that?'

'I said, didn't I, Mick Moore's got a real bastard mean streak in him.'

'And he fancies that new prospect; the one who calls herself Modesty.'

'Right. Yet another motive. I hope that wire hasn't been touched, Gwyn.'

'No, Wolf. Right where he left it. I had a look at it myself. Nice job. Just neck-high.'

'O.K. Send them off then.'

The race began at one end of a bumpy, wide avenue of tall trees. Mick Moore waited discreetly at the back as they roared along, left at a sharp corner, where Modesty's boyfriend nearly came to grief, and then down the steepest and fastest part of the run, where the track grew narrower and more shadowed.

Brenda and Gerry chose that part as their vantage point and neither were surprised to see the two leaders plucked off their bikes by the wire, as though an invisible fist had struck them both under the chin. Their bikes skidded noisily into the deep ditch at the side of the track and both men lay still. From the angle of the neck of one of them, the wire had snapped his spinal cord.

The chasing pair managed to avoid the wire, the first by sheer luck as he broadsided under it trying to avoid the two bodies, the second by skill, aided by fore-knowledge. They both sped on, with Mick still not opening his hog full out.

'What the fuck is he waiting for? There's only about half a mile to go to the finish at the ford. He's going to leave it too late unless...'

Gerry's sentence remained unfinished as a crash and a scream, cut short by the thump of something striking hard into a tree trunk, interrupted him. 'Jesus. The cattle grid! He was busy last night.'

Very much later that night, most of the Angels were either pissed or stoned or, in most cases, both. But all the brothers were trying to keep a little soberness in reserve, for the double-headed train pull was due to start. Modesty was standing, shaking slightly, near to Brenda, when Mick Moore loped up, waving a half-full (or, half-empty if you happen to be a pessimistic person) bottle of the beautiful peach liqueur – Southern Comfort. He was grinning all over his face.

'Hey, there. Why not have a little sip to keep out the cold. Get you in the right mood. Gerry first, then me. That right, Brenda?' And he slapped her on her tight jeans.

'Yes, Mick. That's right. And if you slap my arse like that again, I'll cut your balls off.'

'Sorry. Anyway, must go and have a piss before it starts. Don't like working on a full stomach. See you later, Modesty.'

'Mick! What about after?'

'What do you mean? Like, if you get to be my old lady. We'll have to see.

Afterwards. See you.'

'Relax, Modesty. Your turn will come. When he has his initiation tomorrow. He lies down and has piss and puke and everything poured over him. Christening his colours. He has to just lie there and take everything. Like I say. That'll be your turn. Nobody can look cocky with a faceful of shit.'

When Gerry had exercised his presidential right over the two girl prospects, he stood and watched, his arm round Brenda. She nudged him to attract his attention from the orgiastic scenes. 'Gerry. You were right about Mick Moore. He really is a bit of a bastard.'

'Yeah. Good isn't it? Remember, God looks out for bastards.'

11. STAND UP, STAND UP, FOR ... WHO?

'Sit down. Now, before we have this morning's voluntary – a piece of Buxtehude – I have a serious matter to mention. Those of you unfortunate enough to read the popular paper called the *Daily Leader* will have seen the absurd amount of publicity they have been giving to these motor-cycle thugs who call themselves "Hell's Angels".

'You will also have seen that a number of boys and girls from all over London appear to have been so stupidly infatuated by these leather-clad layabouts on their powerful bikes, that they have been taking time off from their useful lessons to droop around these drop-outs and beatniks. I may say that I was disgusted, yes, I use the word "disgusted" and that is what I mean, when a parent of one of the senior boys at this school rang me up at my home last night to draw my attention to an item that she had been told was to appear in this morning's edition of that paper. I ordered my house-keeper to purchase a copy for me and I was revolted to recognise that what the lady had told me was true.

'Here, blazoned all over the front page, is indeed a picture of a boy from our fifth form. My only relief is that I cannot imagine that any person who was not personally acquainted with the boy in question would recognise him as a member of this school. But, that is not the point. The mere fact that the paper has not seen fit to go the whole hog and ... Stop that laughing! I'm not aware that this is a case for amusement. That the paper did not print his full name or address. That is not the point.

'It is my intention to punish this boy as severely as possible. He will learn at my hands a lesson that he will not quickly forget. I will not punish him so much for playing truant, as for dragging this school down into the gutter. By his foolish and inconsiderate action he has not only lowered himself in the eyes of the world; he has lowered me, he has lowered you, all of you, he has lowered this school and everyone who has, or has had, any connection with it.

'Let us look at this youth, this wretched individual, who was so stupid as to imagine that these hardened hooligans might consider taking him among their numbers. Michael Moore of Five Gamma Upper. It can be no surprise to many of you that this is the boy's name. Stand up Michael Moore and let us all look on the face of stupidity.

'Moore! Stand up! Come now, is it your intention to add cowardice to idiocy? Where is he? Can he be absent again?

'Moore! Stop talking! Balderstone; if you have anything relevant to contribute, I suggest you say it to me ... He has what? Nonsense! He cannot! They ... if you are not telling me the truth, I promise you that you will have occasion to regret it. Will you all stop shouting out. Who is Moore's housemaster? Very well, Mr Leeds. I will see you at my study, and you too, Balderstone, immediately after prayers. We will get to the bottom of all this.

'Now, Professor Grant, perhaps you would care to take us to a more real world with the Buxtehude Voluntary. Silence!!!'

12. YOU GET THE PICTURE? YES, WE SEE

The forecourt of the *Daily Leader* was crowded at eleven o'clock on Tuesday, 18th June. Most of both rival chapters were there, in their best colours. Choppers were parked under the gaze of armed security guards. Mamas and old ladies chattered together on one side, away from the Ghouls. Gerry and his principal lieutenants stood at the front, alongside Evel and the leading brothers. Television, radio and video reporters came to the edge of actual brawling for places with good viewpoints. Mike cables coiled everywhere, ready to pick up any word.

The Last Heroes and Wolves were silent, and, after a brief attempt to stir up some whispered aggro, so were the Ghouls. Neither chapter had picked their six riders for the challenge, each President waiting till the last minute, when they would have been given the first clue, and they would have some kind of idea as to what was likely to happen. At Gerry's request, they had each been allocated a room to which they could retire to discuss the first clue and select their teams. They had just one hour to go till the off.

Valentine Bergen, plump, South African-born owner and Editor of the *Leader* came down to the rostrum that had been specially built for the occasion. He tapped and huffed a few times into the array of microphones, before wallowing into his prepared speech.

It would be as boring to repeat the whole of that turgid piece of prose as it was to listen to it. Imagine a meal for the rest of your life that consisted of simply warm mashed potato, with lumps (like the best traditional school dinners) and warm semolina to follow – also with lumps. Nothing else ever to eat and only warm, flat water to drink. That was what Bergen's speech was like.

It was padded out with mouth-filling platitudes and tedious expressions like 'public good', 'pernicious violence', 'horrifying implications', 'disgust and dismay' and 'the *Leader* has always been the first to show how much it cares'. It was only when the slow hand-clap from the crowd, led by Kafka, became deafening and made it impossible for the recordists to pick out what he was saying, that Bergen finally gave up. He called Melvyn Molineux to the podium to give out the first clue.

'Thank you, sir, for that warming speech of introduction. Yes, we care, here at the good old *Leader* (the paper had only been going for a little over three years) – we care about all of you. And we care about these fine young men here. To avoid any violence that may cause harm to the innocent bystander, these boys have agreed to follow the sensible course suggested by the *Leader* and settle their differences by way of a sporting challenge. There will be five clues – one each day – that will take them to different spots in and around London. From each place they will have to bring back a marked copy of the *Daily Leader* to me or to Mr Bergen on these steps.

'There will be six from each team and they will start on their colourful motorcycles in just fifty minutes from now. And, quiet, and here is the first clue. A copy of it will be given to each team leader. The first clue is this: "One thousand yards between the wicked ladies and the wicked men. In that order". I'll repeat that once more: "One thousand yards between the wicked ladies and the wicked men. In that order". Right lads. Away you go to your rooms to pick your teams. See you back here in three-quarters of an hour.'

The meeting for the Ghouls took only a very brief time. Evel read out the copy of the clue and gave them the answer without any hesitation. Almost as though he had known the question beforehand. Which is absurd, because that would mean that Melvyn Molineux had cheated and given, the answers away to the Ghouls before they even started. Absurd! Actually, he'd only given them the first one, to get them off to a flying start.

The six from the Ghouls consisted of Evel Winter himself, with his number two, Rohan. The other four were Vanya, the fat Shelob, Alice and Howl. All were men. All were well into their twenties. All wore the silks and satins of the chapter, Winter in a new outfit of which half was white and half black. He had ordered it because he thought that it would look good for the television cameras.

When he won.

All was not so well or so smooth in the Last Heroes and Wolves' room.

'Shut your fucking mouth you stupid Welsh bastard!'

'I don't care if you are the fucking President. There are more of us Wolves and there should be at least four of us in the six.'

The argument between Gerry and a section of the Wolves, led by Ogof, had devoured ten of the precious fifty minutes. Gerry, feeling the time dribbling fast away, had to make a quick decision.

'Ogof. Come here a minute. Do you reckon you could climb out through that window over there, if you had to?'

The muscular Welsh Angel turned his head to look at the window that Gerry had pointed at, leaving his chin facing away from the shorter President. The punch that hit him on the angle of the jaw travelled not more than two feet but it had all the weight of Gerry's body behind it. Plus a lot of experience. Plus a roll of coins that Gerry had been fingering in his pocket. Ogof rose on to the tips of his toes and slumped straight to the floor, blood trickling from the corner of his mouth.

'Sorry, brother,' muttered Gerry. He turned to face the rest of the chapter, noting as he did that Kafka and Mick Moore had already moved in to cover his back. The only ones of the other brothers to do so. 'That was necessary. We just don't have the time to brawl and argue among ourselves. I'll tell you who I think should come, and then we'll hear if there are any major arguments. I'll lead. Gwyn comes along as my second-in-command, then Kafka, Bardd, Draig and ... [there was a long pause] ... and Mick Moore to make up the six.'

There was instant babel. Right from the start it was obvious that there was opposition from some of the older Angels to the selection of Mick Moore, but it was Brenda who first made herself heard.

'Me. Me instead of Draig. I'm quicker than him on a hog. I'm brighter than he is when it comes to solving the clues. And, if it comes to that, I'm reasonably sure that I could take him in a fight.'

'Silly cunt! You may have a bit more up top than me, but you haven't solved the first clue have you?'

'Yes.'

Gerry grabbed her by the arm. 'Are you pissing about, just to try and get in the six?'

'No. I know the answer to the first clue. Either I'm in or you can all take a flying fuck.'

'Right. If you know it, tell us, and you're in.'

'One thousand yards between the wicked ladies and the wicked men. When I was in the young anarchists I once went on a demo up in North London to help some comrades who'd been busted. There were some girls in Holloway Jail and down the road there were some fellows in...'

'...in Pentonville. I was there twice for G.B.H. in the early seventies. Before they really clamped down on us. Of course. They are about a thousand yards apart as well. Good girl.'

'Thanks Kafka. So I'm in.'

Gerry paused for a moment before answering. His relationship with Brenda had always been an odd one. Most of the time he was the dominant partner – in everything – and that was the way it ought to be. But there were disconcerting times when the roles became inverted. There was the initiation and the time he was forced to win his red wings by ... he felt the bile rise in his throat and skipped over that one. And she had helped to save his life on more than one occasion. But, would she stand up to what was going to be the toughest test the Angels had ever had to face? That one was answered for him when Draig, angered as he saw things going against him, lumbered forward and slapped Brenda hard across the face, making her nose bleed.

'Can't take real violence can you, you fucking bitch. Play around with your dyke friends, pretending you know how to fight. There's stupid!'

Brenda wiped her hand across her mouth, looking down at the streak of blood on it. Without saying a word she walked towards Draig, who backed away from her a little, despite his bravado. His knees banged against a desk and he stopped. She came closer to him, until she was only an arm's span away. Draig couldn't make his mind up whether to assume a defensive posture and then look silly if she turned away, or not and then look even more stupid if she attacked him.

Indecision. The worst handicap for a fighter. Draig was a good fighter of proven ability in brawls and aggro on lots of occasions. But, he was up against an unknown quantity. A girl – shorter and weaker than him. He'd seen her playing about at combat with Gerry and with Lady and Holly. But that was play. He'd heard about her in the quarry, killing, violently, secretly, efficiently and silently. But, he hadn't been there. So, he doubted what he hadn't seen. And he waited. Indecision.

Brenda again wiped her hand across her face, her left hand this time, and held it out wide of her body, in front of Draig. Unable to help himself, he looked down at the streak of blood. While he was looking at her left hand, she hit him with her right.

A back-hand chop, upwards with the outer edge of the palm striking unerringly at the base of the Welsh outlaw's nose. The crack of bone showed that her aim had been exactly right. Both the big man's hands flew up to hold his shattered nose, and Brenda kneed him hard, but not too hard, in the groin.

Draig doubled up with a gasp, air whistling in his lungs as he fought not to vomit. Blood starred the mustard-yellow carpet in the executive suite. His fists now clutching his damaged manhood, Draig could do nothing when Brenda grabbed him by his long, greasy hair, lifted his head and then brought it down sharply, to meet her knee which was coming up sharply. There was a dull thunk, a wheezing groan from Draig and then he slumped unconscious at her feet, his head lolling on the carpet, blood bubbling noisily from his nose.

'If I hadn't pulled some of those blows – any of them, in fact, he [she stirred the recumbent figure with her foot] would have died. Violence is only for those who know what they're doing. Now, anyone else think I shouldn't go?'

Gerry smiled to himself at the silence. It had amused him to hear the sage words of advice of Sergeant Newman coming from the lips of an attractive girl. The old instructor would have considered it sacrilege. Girls was for screwing, and nothing else. Though Newman had once, when drunk at an NCO's party, admitted that 'the best fuck I ever had was a young Arab boy. Lovely arse, Vinson. Lovely.' Then he'd passed out cold.

'Right, then. Me, Brenda, Gwyn, Kafka, Bardd and young Mick Moore.'

'Why that young punk? Why not one of the older brothers? The shit isn't even dry on his colours, and he hasn't even got a chapter name.' The voice was like its owner – sly, sidling, not very loud, the sort of voice that lonely spinsters dread in a late-night anonymous phone call.

'I can't do anything about the shit, Rat, but we can give him a name. Right here and now. We should have done this at his initiation, but things got a bit chaotic there.' He looked meaningfully at Modesty. 'What's the right sort of name for a bastard like you?'

Mick Moore looked a bit embarrassed. 'When I was a bit younger. I ... I fancied going into a monastery.'

'What? Be a fucking monk? Well, there's your name. We once had a brother called "Priest" but he ... well he snuffed on a run a year or so back. He got wiped out by a bastard who...'

'What happened to the killer?'

It was Brenda who answered: 'Kafka got him. Helped by a mob of housewives with carving-knives.'

'How about "Monk" then? Well, brothers. How about it? No objections, so meet our new brother of the Hell's Angels chapter of the Last Heroes, affiliated with the Wolves. Monk. Now for Christ's sake, let's get on with this challenge.'

For the next ten minutes the six, plus about eight of the more senior brothers, discussed their tactics. They agreed that it would be bad planning to all go off in the same direction, so a diversion was agreed. Gerry, Brenda, Bardd, and Kafka would head west and try and link up near Camden Town. Monk and Gwyn would blast out direct as fast as they could straight for Holloway Jail. Kafka said that he would ignore Holloway and try to make himself useful somewhere near Pentonville.

There was still twenty minutes to the off, and Rat surprised everyone by offering to go and keep an eye on the hogs. 'It'll give me something to do.' And he scuttled to the door, his right hand firmly inside his jeans pocket. He was actually opening the door when Monk threw, with fearsome savagery and accuracy, a glass decanter of water.

It struck Rat square on the back of the head, and exploded, showering everyone near with water and splinters of glass. The little Angel crashed to the floor, a deep cut in his matted scalp.

'Monk. You better have a fucking good reason for that. He was a little sod sometimes, but he was a classy brother. Real virtuous.'

Monk had gone over and rolled the still figure over. Avoiding the blood, he pushed his hand into the right-hand jeans' pocket. Grinning triumphantly, he pulled out three small packets of sugar, wrapped in white paper. 'I saw him take those and slip them in his pocket while we were having coffee at that caff this morning. But, he didn't put any in his drink and I asked if he took sugar in his coffee or tea. Kafka knew him best and said he didn't. Then he was suddenly all keen to keep an eye on our choppers. I wondered why, then I remembered the sugar. I don't think he was after all of us. Just me. He thought he should have gone. Sugar in my tank would have fucked me up and he would have had my place for the rest of the challenge. Cheeky little cunt.' He kicked him firmly in the ribs, just as an additional reminder, and walked out of the room.

'Where are you going, Monk?' shouted Gerry.

'Don't worry, Wolf. I'm going to have a quickie with Modesty. I always fancied having it away in a managing director's office, and everyone's out there waiting for the start. Don't worry, I won't be late.'

'Was I all right, Mick?'

Monk rolled off Modesty and pulled his jeans up over his thighs. He bent down and gave his old lady a friendly pat on the stomach, his fingers coming away moist with the evidence of their speedy but passionate love-making.

'Yeah. Not bad. For a beginner! No, I'm only kidding. You're great.'

While she wiped herself with a paper tissue from the box on the desk, Monk walked round the room, looking at things.

'Hey, the cunt does himself O.K. I nearly drowned in the fucking pile on this carpet. And look at those pictures. I know what that one is. It's called "The Fighting Temeraire", by Turner. We had that at school. And that's "The Hay-Cart" by Constable. I don't know what that one is behind his desk though. What is it?'

'It's a bird. I can't read the title. It's foreign. It says "A.s.t.a.r.t.e S.y.r.i.a.c.a." Funny title.'

'Who's it by?'

'I can't see ... oh, yes, in the bottom right corner, in little red letters. "D. G. Rossetti 1887".'

'I thought he was a poet. Rossetti. Never mind. Hurry up. We've got to get down. We're off in five minutes. Come on.' After they left the office, it was quiet. The only clue to their presence was a small, dark stain on the thick white carpet. The office was quiet.

With its heavy mahogany desk.

And its William Morris wall-paper.

And its disguised cocktail cabinet.
And its three paintings on the walls.
Three paintings.
By Rossetti.
By Turner.
By Constable.

13. DO NOT PASS JAIL – GO DIRECTLY TO JAIL

'Good afternoon, ladies, gentlemen, boys, girls and even babies. Welcome to this Afternoon Sport Special. Today, and for the next four days, we will be covering for you, and you only, the most astounding sporting challenge in history. Sponsored by the daily newspaper, the *Leader*, the two top gangs of Hell's Angels motor-cycle outlaws are clashing to discover who are the top dogs with the top hogs – as their highly-tuned and custom-altered bikes are called.

'The losers of this unusual challenge match have agreed to disband and never ride again as a mob. So, thanks to the *Leader* the streets will be a little bit safer for you and you and, yes, you. Tom Beck has explained the rules to you so all we have to do is wait and watch for the start.

'First a betting flash. The Ghouls are three to one against and the Last Heroes are five to two against. Now, I'll recap on the first clue – "One thousand yards between the wicked ladies and the wicked men. In that order". We've all been asked by the organiser, and there he is, in the yellow houndstooth jacket, Melvyn Molineux, not to speculate on the answer to any of these clues. I'll just say that I'll be a bit surprised if we don't see action in North London.

'They are all lining up now. From the left we've got the Ghouls, with their exotic leader, Evel Winter, in the black and white silk jacket. In the centre there is the leader of the Last Heroes, Gerry "Wolf" Vinson. Once suspected of playing a major part in a big bank robbery, he's here today to lead his chapter, as the gangs are called. Next to him is Gerry's young lady, Brenda, and next to her is the startling figure of Gwyn. He's Welsh, so there's something for you all to cheer down there in Cardiff and Swansea. A tough character this, who may be a contender for an early bath.

'Another betting flash. The Ghouls have shortened in to threes and the Last Heroes are out to five to two. In that small enclosure there are some of the reserves. Two of the Heroes' substitutes look a bit sickly. The big man with the beard has a badly swollen nose and the other little man has a lot of blood round his head and neck. That could bear out rumours of some pre-challenge tension in the planning room of the Last Heroes.

'And here's the starter. The popular figure of the owner of the *Daily Leader*, Mr Valentine Bergen. In his hand he's got the starting flag bearing the words, I can't quite make them out. They seem to ... yes, oh, sorry viewers. They are a rather naughty advertising slogan for his paper. He's up on the starting rostrum now. The engines are all started. No, one of the Ghouls has his hand up, it's the one called

"Vanya", but he's O.K. now. Just time for one last betting flash. The Ghouls have shortened still further to two to one and the Last Heroes are steady at five to two. Quite a lot of money going on the Ghouls in these last minutes.

'Valentine Bergen raises the flag. The engine notes reach a crescendo. The flag drops and, they're off!!

'My God!!!'

14. AS DARK AS A DUNGEON

All over Britain, and, indeed, Europe, millions of video and television viewers heard the astounded exclamation from ace commentator, Rick Austen. 'My God!' Not the sort of thing that good old John Snagge would ever have said. Not on the air anyway.

So, what amazing incident had prompted the outburst? The owner of the *Daily Leader*, Valentine Bergen, had dropped the starting flag for the beginning of the first of the five legs of the challenge between the Ghouls and the Last Heroes and Wolves.

Led by Evel Winter, the Ghouls roared out of the forecourt of the *Leader* office block. The draw had given them the slightly favoured outside place, and they were first into the road, through the narrow opening. Last of them was the fat Shelob, who skidded in the entrance and blocked it off for the following Heroes. There was instant chaos, and it was this mess of bikes and riders that had caused Rick Austen to lose his customary cool.

Cochise rushed from the crowd with his pendulous old lady, Forty, and quickly dragged the fallen Ghoul and his hog from the entrance, laying him out cold in the process. The rest of the Heroes also came running to help and all the six were soon off and rolling again. But, it had taken more than two minutes and the Ghouls had a lead that seemed almost unassailable. And, they knew that part of North London as their hunting-ground, so they had very much the advantage.

Leaving behind them a mass of police struggling to keep the two chapters apart after that incident, the Heroes sped up Chancery Lane. At the top they split, Gwyn and Monk turning right to head for Kings Cross and Caledonian Road. The others went left to go via Camden Town.

It would be dull to simply recount the chase that went on through North London. The Ghouls had the dual advantage of knowing the district and of having cheated a lead of a couple of minutes. Although the Last Heroes pushed their hogs to the limit, and a bit beyond it, they couldn't close the gap. When Evel rocketed into the small courtyard in front of the red-brick castle of Holloway Jail, they were still a full minute ahead. By cutting round through Middleton Grove and back on to the Caledonian Road, they were able to steal another couple of hundred yards.

The copy of the *Daily Leader* – marked with the large red letters *Last Heroes* – clenched between his teeth, Monk blazed after the Ghouls. At his elbow, sometimes screaming some fearful Welsh curse at an unwary passer-by, was the silver vampire of Gwyn. As they eased to a stop in the elevated yard at the front of Pentonville's dull façade, Gwyn reached out and snatched the marked copy of the second paper from the hands of the *Leader*'s man on the spot. Then, wheels kicking dust, it was full belt down the Caledonian Road back to the finish.

Realising that they were going to be too late, anyway, Gerry and the two Last Heroes had not bothered to go all the way to Holloway and had cut through, hoping to be able to do something to stop the Ghouls before they could get back. They could hear the sound of the Ghouls' choppers, whining away from them before they even got to Caledonian Road. Just as they burst out of a side road, they glimpsed Monk and Gwyn burning up the asphalt as they fled in pursuit.

Gerry waved Brenda alongside him. 'We've fucking had this one, love! Those two'll never close up on the Ghouls. From the noise, they're a good half mile ahead. And it's only about a mile to go. We'll have to do a bloody sight better on the next clue. What the...?'

Had you forgotten Kafka? Admit it. Be honest. You thought he was with Gerry? Look a bit back and you'll see Gerry and the *two* Last Heroes. That's Gerry, Brenda and Bardd. Not Kafka. After the shambles at the start he had not gone far with the main group. Seeing the futility of a stern chase with little hope of victory. Gerry, for once, had failed. He knew the latest brother, young Monk, was good and that the mad white-haired Gwyn would ride through Hell for his brothers. But, none of them could do the impossible. But, he might.

Kafka was one of the oldest of the Angels – and the one with the most tricks. Apart from Gerry himself, he was probably the only one with any grasp of what could be called strategy. As he rode slowly through the back streets off York Way, his mind was working furiously. Some kind of ambush seemed the only logical chance. But where? And he had to stop all five of the Ghouls. He didn't know who would have the precious papers, and he couldn't risk stopping the wrong one. Not far from the public baths, and on the opposite side of the road is Carnegie Street. The visibility is none too good down there, and that was where Kafka went.

Kafka breathed a quiet prayer to whatever gods he might have worshipped – possibly the blessed Harley Davidson, or the sainted Terry the Tramp – when he saw what was standing at the end of the street, just round the corner from Caledonian Road. A big barrow, loaded to the gunwales with fruit and vegetables. Surrounded by a small crowd of afternoon shoppers and with a big West Indian doing good trade.

Kafka rolled softly to a stop alongside the barrow, enjoying as he always did the confusion and panic his appearance created.

The crowd melted away like the morning dew and he was left magically alone with the owner of the barrow.

'Thanks a lot, man. You really did me a fucking good turn there. Springing out of the floor like a fucking pantomime demon. Do me another good turn and fuck off. Then I can sell some of me stock. Anyway, you're one of those Hell's Angels in the race, ain't you? Jesus! Sweet Jesus. What do you want?'

'Your barrow, mate. Sorry about this, but I don't have the time to do anything else. Hear those bikes? Yeah, well, they belong to a gang of bastards called the Ghouls, and I want to give them a surprise. Now piss off.'

The West Indian didn't move. 'That's O.K., man. But who pays for all this?'

'Don't worry. The *Daily Leader*'ll pay. If they don't, I'll pay for it. You got my word. Now, piss off.'

'Right on, man.'

Kafka dropped off his denim jacket with the deaths-head blazoned across the back and heaved at the heavy barrow to get it moving. To his surprise, the owner came and helped him.

'Know something? I know those bastard Ghouls. They ride around here like they was the Ku Klux Klan or something. You aiming to bust them up with my barrow? Then you are surely welcome. Let's go. They're nearly here.'

Packed and bunched together, the triumphant Ghouls tore up the road to get back to the finish and claim the first victory. Dim and far behind them they could hear the petulant whine of the leading Hero – Gwyn. Too far back to present any kind of threat. Evel, both copies of the paper stuffed down his harlequin jacket, raised both gloved hands from the ape-hanger bars on his bright Harley and screamed his joy at the amazed shoppers and spectators.

Timed to the most split of seconds, the heavy barrow lurched out of the side-road, angled round and overturned, just as the Ghouls came up to the corner at over forty miles an hour. The owner and Kafka leaped for their lives as Evel hit the barrow full-on, cart-wheeling over the bars to skid into a pile of oranges and aubergines. The fruit burst under his weight and carried him into the gutter on a tide of pulp and peel. His new jacket tore from shoulder to shoulder and the papers were shredded from his grasp. The rest of the chapter had no chance of avoiding his fate. Bunched as they were, they tried to find a way through the shambles of fruit, but there just wasn't the time for them. One hog slipped over a pile of hard nuts while another Angel was badly-bruised when he came down on a pile of very knobbly King Edwards.

The chapter was demolished in that moment and hogs and riders were scattered all round the road and pavement. The watching crowd, many of them local coloured people with no love for the perverted Ghouls, cheered their enemies' downfall.

Kafka gave his helper a quick pat on the back, then he was up on to his own hog and away round the loop at the top of Carnegie Street and gently back through Farringdon Road to the *Leader*.

He had seen enough in those cataclysmic moments to know that the first part of the challenge was theirs. Gunning down the hill, Gwyn and Monk had plenty of time to see the chaos at the function and steer a safe course through the fruit and vegetables on the road, round the fallen bikes and past the Ghouls who were just staggering to their feet. Those who could still stagger!

Gerry, Brenda and Bardd came down the hill seconds later and found it difficult to believe their eyes. Victory had been plucked by what appeared a miracle out of the very maw of defeat. They slowed down, as the other two had done and Gerry found time to shout at the torn and beslobbered Evel: 'You shouldn't be over-confident! Wasting time like that doing your shopping.'

A whoop from Bardd and the three rode off towards Gray's Inn Road singing away to Bardd's mouth-harp; 'Blood on the road and a white heron flying...'

The Last Heroes and Wolves won the first leg of the challenge by a full five minutes. That night they celebrated, but the cheers and the drinks and the offers from the mamas were all for the conquering hero, Kafka.

Evel had to reckon on wearing his second-best suit for the second leg the next day. He was very unhappy about the first result and he and his team spent a lot of time talking together. Planning together. Repairing their hogs together. Then, they all went to bed. Yes.

The bookmakers were unhappy and the overnight odds came down to evens on both chapters.

Melvyn Molineux was incredibly angry that night. He had a painful conference with V.B. that gave him a sleepless night. Alone.

The newspapers were full of the race and, though some queried the possible danger to the on-lookers, most entered the spirit of the competition and built up interest for the next day. They gave so much space to the first leg in the evening papers that there was scarcely any other news. The next morning, the papers were even worse. In fact, the death in a fire of nine people in a terraced house near Havelock Street, not far from Caledonian Road, gave nobody pause. Obviously those blacks with their paraffin heaters. One of the men who died – with his wife and two of his three children – was the owner of that famous fruit and vegetable barrow. It's a funny oil heater that starts a fire just inside the front door, right below the letter-box.

Evel Winter may have lost the race, but he wasn't prepared to be a good loser.

He had a long arm.

None of the Last Heroes – not even Kafka – ever heard about the fire.

'Go!'

'George Yard Buildings saw my death,
A whore was I, till my last breath.
Thirty-nine cuts bled me fast,
I was the first, but not the last.'

They were racing off on the second leg and this time the edge was with the Last Heroes. No interference at the beginning, and, though they didn't know it, no help for the Ghouls. That had been an absolute condition of the previous night's meeting with Valentine Bergen. Molineux knew his boss well enough to know just how far to push. And, he had pushed enough. He had leaked the answer to the first clue to the Ghouls, and they had still lost. He dared not leak the second answer. His big hope had been that neither chapter would solve it in the one hour that they were allowed before the clue became public and they were off to follow it up.

Had he been in the Ghouls' room he would have been happy, for they had little idea. 'Of course it's a murdered tart you silly bastards! Yes, Rohan; it probably is what you said. But, we still don't know fucking where. And old creepie-weepie smelly Melvyn ain't helping this time. We'll just to have to try and follow them. If they know. Let's hope they don't then this one will be cancelled. Fingers crossed chummies.'

The scene in the conference room of the Last Heroes was somewhat different. Only the six chosen plus the three nominated reserves were allowed to discuss the clue. And the reserves – despite a certain coolness in some quarters – included the ubiquitous and generally despicable Rat.

When Gerry read the clue out again to them, there was a long silence. Gwyn broke it: 'It's obviously some kind of murder.'

Brenda had little to offer this time but weighed in with the thought that it might be the nude murders that had baffled police in the sixties, down near the Thames.

Gerry suddenly got to his feet, waving the paper with the clue. 'Jack the Ripper. That's what it is. I bet it's about Jack the Ripper. The man who murdered all those tarts in Victorian England. Cut out their wombs and took away bits of their kidneys to eat.'

There was a murmur from Cochise, one of the other reserves at this information: 'Christ! That's real class! What a brother he'd have made.'

Gerry went on: 'But, where the sodding hell is George Yard Buildings? Wasn't it all done up the East End somewhere? God, if the Ghouls get this one they'll walk it. We haven't a chance.'

He looked round the circle of depressed faces. Brenda looking miserable. Gwyn and Bardd, gloomy in one corner. Cochise obviously missing his old lady. Kafka, poker-faced, but with nothing to contribute. Monk, looking puzzled and angry. Rat grinning away. Alongside him was ... Rat ... grinning!!

'What is so fucking funny, Rat? Share it with us.'

There was a pause before Rat spoke softly. 'When the lady there, [pointing maliciously at Brenda] got the first clue, everyone said "Good old Brenda" and she got a place in the six. Suppose I got this one. Just suppose. Now, if I did, then it would only be fair to let me come in as one of the reserves. The rules say that any reserve can be substituted at any time outside of the actual runs. If I came in, then I might insist that the lady drops out. And, I take her place.'

To his disappointment, Brenda concealed her true feelings and leaped into the vacuum left by his shock announcement. 'If you do know, Rat. And you're right. Then I will stand down and you can ride in my place. Because I haven't any idea this time. Don't grin too fast. Because, if you go and you're wrong, you'll learn to sleep lightly every night you stay with this chapter. My knife will make fucking sure of that.'

'It's agreed then, Rat. Tell us. If you know, then we might be on a real winner. And, you'll ride with us. Now. Come on.'

The trendy conference room was hushed as Rat hissed and whispered his tale. 'A few years ago I knew a bloke who used to run tours for kinky tourists. Not the regular ones that were in all the papers. These were a bit, unusual. He used to take them to all the murder spots in London, and he'd read bits out of contemporary papers and things. Really horrible. The Krauts loved it. More than anyone else. He gave them things that nobody else liked to touch. One of his big specialities was ... what you said, Wolf, Jack the Ripper.'

'Come on, Rat. You're making a fucking epic out of it.'

'Patience my young monastery friend, is one of the greatest virtues. Learn it. I'll go through it line by line. George Yard Buildings was the scene of one of the Ripper's killings. On Tuesday August 8th, 1888. It was in the early morning on the day after a Bank Holiday. The whore was a scrubber called, Martha ... Turner, I think it was. But there's a bit of doubt about the name. I remember that. Thirty-nine times. That's right. A two-handed attack they reckoned. With a bayonet and with a scalpel. Thirty-nine! Slashed her body to bits. She was the first, most people reckon. But, not the last. There were round about six more. That's it. There you are.'

'Rat. Where the fuck is George Yard Buildings? I know Whitechapel a bit, but I've never heard of it. It could be anywhere and had its name changed.'

'Sorry, Wolf. Forgot that bit. It's now called Gunthorpe Street. Just off Whitechapel

High Street.'

The Last Heroes lost that second leg. Though they knew the answer to the clue and the Ghouls didn't. Evel really justified his presidency by winning it for his chapter.

He noticed the change in the personnel at once and the greased tumblers in his mind quickly came up with the right answer. He called Rohan over to him. 'Look. They've dropped the tart. And they've brought in that tiny cunt what burned Alice. I wonder if that little bastard knew the clue and that's why he's in. Yeah! That's got to be it. Listen brother. You and I are going to follow that Rat, regardless of what the others will do. The rest can follow any of the other Heroes. They're bound to try a diversion.'

Obvious, isn't it? That's what Gerry thought as well, and had laid careful plans to cover exactly that happening. He would lead three of the chapter towards Hyde Park, Rat would deliberately act suspiciously and head east, but he would try and shake off any pursuers round Bank. Whatever happened, he wasn't to go anywhere near Gunthorpe Street. Bardd would ride slowly off and then fake a breakdown, so that he would be ignored. When everyone had left him behind, he was to ride slowly and carefully to Gunthorpe Street, pick up the marked copy of the paper and come back. Simple.

They all knew what they had to do, and Gerry knew, from past experience, that he could rely on them all to do their bit. He was only a bit doubtful about Rat, but he figured that his plan was foolproof.

But not Rat-proof!

In Evel's head, greased tumblers had meshed. In Rat's head, slimy cogs slowly engaged their gears. *I got that clue. Why should that Welsh git have all the glory? Once I shake off any tails, I can go straight there and quick back. No problems. No satin poof with lip-stick on'll have a chance of keeping up with me!*

So, Gerry, Kafka, Gwyn and Monk thrashed off westwards, followed by an equal number of Ghouls. Bardd had cunningly turned off the petrol tap on his hog so that it cut out at the very moment that the flag dropped. Cursing loudly and ostentatiously, he leaped off and poked angrily at his chromed engine. Apart from jeering at his ill-luck, none of the Ghouls took any notice at all of him.

Rat skulked around, looking suspicious – which was easier for him than for most people – and then set off eastward, off towards the shining dome of St Pauls. Trailing him were Evel and Rohan.

The eight members of the warring chapters who went westwards are of no further concern to us. They livened things up for the Thursday afternoon shoppers in Oxford Street and then came straight back to the offices of the *Leader*. Together with an anxious Melvyn Molineux, they waited for the return of Bardd with the paper.

Rat rode up past St Pauls, leaning back in the saddle, hands drooping over the bars. He could see Evel and Rohan clearly in his twin mirrors. Evel in dazzling white and Rohan in deep purple. They were only fifty yards or so behind as he reached Bank. Glancing quickly back over his stunted shoulders, Rat twisted the throttle right round. The powerful engine roared in protest at this mistreatment, but thrust forwards, rubber smoking off the roadway.

Without once looking back, he revved up Bishopsgate and then dived into the maze of small, narrow side streets between Liverpool Street and Aldgate. Middlesex Street led him into Wentworth Street, where he was held up for a moment by the traffic, and then across Commercial Street towards the end of Gunthorpe Street. He cunningly stopped in the gutter before he actually made the turn, looking round for any sign of pursuit.

The traffic was heavy, and he couldn't see that far back. There was the usual number of local delivery lorries and trucks, a few private cars and a handful of motor-bikes. None of the latter sported the dreaded Ghouls' colours. Feeling smug and safe, Rat turned into Gunthorpe Street and cruised down it towards Whitechapel Road. Exactly on the site of the old George Yard Buildings, he saw the representative of the *Daily Leader*, waving a copy of the paper at him.

He stopped and snatched it from him, and then, chuckling happily to himself, he set off on his triumphant return journey. As he reached Newgate Street, nearly there, he saw the crowds on the pavement, thick as fields of harvest wheat. Sexy little office girls, stretching their lunch hours in the hope of catching a glimpse of one of the dread Angels. He saw them waving to him and shouting. He couldn't hear what because of the roar of his Triumph and the noise of traffic. He waved a gloved fist at them – a gesture of victory. New Fetter Lane and he could free-wheel from there. He was home.

So, how could the Last Heroes have lost that second leg? Maybe Rat is being fractionally premature in claiming victory before he's handed the paper in to Valentine Bergen. But, he's so close that nothing could stop him. Could it? Yes, it could.

Go back about eight minutes to the moment when Rat paused at the opening of Gunthorpe Street and looked back. Looking for the distinctive jackets of the two Ghouls. Remember how he saw a couple of motor-bikes? And how he dismissed them?

Go back a little further and you'll recall how Rat was held up for a few moments in the traffic. During that briefest of stops, Evel and Rohan had ripped off their bright colours and ridden on, wearing plain shirts and dungaree trousers. Unseen by Rat, they had followed him down Gunthorpe Street at a discreet distance, then roared back to the *Leader* by using roads nearer the river.

Coming through the back of the crowd, nobody noticed them as the little Angel strode cockily through towards the editor, his marked copy already held out. Timing his move to absolute perfection, Evel stepped out in front of Rat, when he was only six feet from Bergen, and thrust his own copy of the paper into the astonished (and delighted) man's hands. 'I think this is what you've been waiting for, sweetie.' He turned round to the paralysed Rat. 'One all, tiny-weenie one. Thanks for taking us straight to it.'

The well-respected man, Penn of the Yard, had made it his business to be present at each start and finish and he grabbed Rat by the shoulders from behind. 'Bad luck lad,' he said with a ringing voice. 'Close that. Still, three more legs to go. I'm sure you're not going to be a bad loser, now, are you? Of course not.' In a quieter voice, designed only for the wriggling Angel, he whispered: 'Pull out whatever it is in your pocket, laddie, and I'll break both your wretched collarbones. No? Wise lad. Now push off.' Digging his knuckles hard into the little man's back, he propelled him into the arms of his glowering President. Penn added insult to injury by calling for, and getting, 'Three cheers for a very sporting little loser!' Nothing was said by any of the Last Heroes and Wolves until they reached their conference room. Kafka slammed the door shut with an ominous thump. Gerry opened his mouth when Rat spoke first. 'No. If it hadn't been for me we'd have had no chance at all, because none of you lot got the clue. And ... and...'

'Yes,' the menacing monosyllable from Brenda.

'And, I'm sorry brothers. I really fucked it up, didn't I?'

'Forget it, Rat. Let's all go back to base and start getting ready for Number Three.'

15. DON'T LET YOUR DAUGHTER ON A BIKE, MRS MIDDLE-CLASS!

An Extract From: *An Ogre For Society – An Investigation Of Incidences Of Delusional Psychoses Inspired By Youth Cults* **by Professor Norbert Offord, MA, M&E, MRN.**

The bikers! Not since the Viking reivers brought the sword, the brand and sudden death to English coasts has a term contained more emotive content. No Saxon peasant woman, seeing the dread longships ghosting in out of the sea-wraith, could have felt greater terror, than a solid middle-class mother who hears her daughter has been associating with the unspeakable Hell's Angels.

Why is this? Other movements – the Hitler Jügend and some junior branches of the Ku Klux Klan, that now extinct society of brave Knights of the Invisible Empire – were far more reprehensible than these one per cent motor-bike outlaws. Their ideologies were more abhorrent. The results of their passing more obvious and lethal.

Is it their growing responsive mobility? Is it the psychotic personality traumas that blossom in their wake? Or the systematised policy projection? It is almost impossible to determine the easy answers in a stress situation where there are, quite simply, no easy answers. Each man must pick the thing he loves and work out how much he values it. Because, when the chips are down and the Last Heroes or the Ghouls come riding into your small town; what do you do? Run to your house – house'll be a'burning. Run to your wife – wife'll be a'screaming. Run to the police – police'll be a'hiding. Run to the Angels – they'll just be a'laughing.

So, stay where you are and hope the hurricane's going to pass you by on the other side. Because Mister, hope is about all you have left to hang on to. That's why you or your wife or your children wake screaming in the night. That is, if you've managed to get to sleep at all. That's why sales of tranquillisers are higher than ever. That's why the number of doctors in practice is dropping year by year. And the number of psychiatrists has trebled since 1985.

More and more executives between the ages of twenty-eight and forty-five than ever before are just dropping out. They are saying, in effect, 'Fuck your job. It's not that important!' Each man has the right to work at what he wants.

But what about the children? Vandalism reaches towering new heights each year. Where are they to run to? Too often it is to youth cults like the skulls or the Angels.

Where they can feel secure and can be with their own kind. Until the do-gooders and moralisers can find a viable alternative for the young, then the problem can only grow worse. It is facile to lay it at the door of the under-staffed and over-worked teaching profession. More blame lies with parents. Career-conscious or of such limited education themselves that they can find no way to help their children when the door opens at the top of the slippery helter-skelter. Once they are sliding down, it's a hell of a lot harder to stop them.

All you've got to do is find some way of stopping them beginning the climb to the top of the slide. Make the earth seem more attractive.

How? Don't ask me. I only write this book. They're your children who run with the Angels. You find a way of stopping them.

16. GOING FASTER THAN A ROLLER-COASTER...

The third leg of the challenge beginneth here. Melvyn Molineux had read out the clue: 'Philip and Herbert shared a flat here. Though neither had any reason to expect great things, they never found themselves out of pocket.' The Ghouls had retreated to their room, and the Last Heroes and Wolves to theirs.

Despite his worries with Valentine Bergen, Molineux had again tipped off the Ghouls with the answer. He had so much riding on the outcome that he didn't even dare think what might happen if the Ghouls lost. After they were out-thought in the first leg, and lucky winners of the second, it seemed increasingly obvious that he could be backing a loser. Unless he added that little something. Like, cheating.

As soon as the Last Heroes assembled, it was agreed that the chosen six competitors should revert to those chosen for the first leg. That is; Gerry, Brenda, Gwyn, Bardd, Kafka and young Monk. As they, and their reserves sat round the afromosia teak veneer table, there was a note of optimism in the air. On the way up in the lift, Kafka had told them that he had a good idea of the answer. Leaning back in his chair, blowing hash smoke rings at the ceiling, Kafka assumed the air of an elderly professor.

He placed his chewed and stained fingers together, pursed his lips and began: 'It seems to me that the reference must be a literary one.'

Bardd interrupted him: 'Creepy Molineux told us that this clue was going to be a literary one weeks ago. Tell us something new you big lump of lard.'

'Quite, you hot-tempered Celt, you. First, who are Philip and Herbert, who shared a flat together? The clue to this lies in a couple of rather infantile inner references. The word "pocket" and the words "great things". Instead of "things", suppose we substitute the word "expectations". Great expectations.'

'Dickens' book. Well, wait a minute, Kafka, The hero, Pip, was Philip and Herbert was ... pocket ... of course, Herbert Pocket. Brilliant.'

Kafka inclined his head at the compliment from Brenda. 'Thank you ma'am. I am eternally obliged to you.'

Monk spoke next: 'I remember the book. But, where the hell was their flat? It must have been near the law courts somewhere.'

Gerry turned again to Kafka. 'Well? Where was the place?'

'Sorry, dear boy. I mean, Gerry. I'm fucked if I can remember.'

'We're all fucked if we can't.'

'Ah. It comes back to me a little. It *was* near the law courts. It was one of those

Inns of Court. Christ! Not one of the big ones. Get that fucking map Molineux left for us. It must be on that. I'm sure it was near Holborn somewhere.'

The map was hurriedly unfolded and Gerry took charge. 'This is the way. I'll find every place in that area that has the word "Inn" in its name and I'll shout it out. If it rings the right bell, then we're in business. Here we go. Clements?'

'No.'

'Let's see. Lincoln's Inn.'

'No.'

'Here's another one. Staples' Inn. How about that?'

'No. I don't think it was that. No.'

'Here's a small one. I can hardly read it. Barnard's Inn.'

'Say it again.'

'Barnard's Inn.'

'Yeah. That was it. I'm sure of it, Barnard's Inn. Where is it?'

'Bloody Hell! It's only about half a mile. This is going to be bloody tricky. If the Ghouls get it as well, then it's going to be a shambles. I don't think we can risk anyone riding decoy on this. No. I reckon there's only one way to play this one. Like this.'

Two office workers from Barnard's Inn were walking towards the main doors of their firm when they noticed a man standing on the steps, waving two papers excitedly at them.

'By 'eck. What's oop with him?'

'Happen it's the sun.'

'Aye. Happen it is. No, wait on. Those papers he's waving. They're copies of the *Leader*. You reckon... ?'

They were now close enough to the man to hear two things. One was the growing roar of powerful motor-bike engines. The other was the man's voice: 'Get out of the way. The Hell's Angels are coming!!' Having said that, the man suddenly threw both copies of the paper down into the car-park and ran indoors.

As the engine noise neared a crescendo, the two workers leaped for the doors. The car park was suddenly a melee of whirling bikes and fighting, kicking men, struggling over the papers, trying to find the one that would give their side a victory.

One of the riders in blue denim gave a scream of triumph as he leaned down out of the saddle of his bike and plucked out the copy marked *Last Heroes* right from under the wheels of one of the satin-clad riders. Bunching it in his fist, the bearded rider, chucked it out to another long-haired rider, circling a little away from the main band.

'I say, William. That's a girl.'

'True, William. True.'

In the half hour left to them before the third race started, Gerry and Brenda had slipped away down a back stairway and carried out a quick reconnaissance of the area. Realising that this one was likely to be a simple mad dash, there was nothing to do but make the most of what advantages one could. Running into a frightened junior executive of the *Daily Leader* getting ready to collect the two marked copies of the paper and deliver them to the two chapters – well, that was a bonus. It took less than a minute to convince him that he was asking for a dreadful beating if he waited around once the Angels arrived. How much better if he threw the papers on the floor and let the animals fight for them. The poor bastard was in such a nervous state that he never even realised that he was talking to two of those 'animals'.

The best thing was finding another way out of the Inn. Not marked on their map and, therefore, probably not known to the Ghouls either. The back entrance to the Inn was fairly wide, but not so wide that five determined men on choppers couldn't make it difficult to pass for a vital minute or so. And that was just what happened.

Kafka got to the paper first, expecting to find it on the floor, while the Ghouls wasted seconds looking for their contact. He was cowering behind the doors, safely behind the two office workers. Kafka threw a lovely pass to Brenda who flashed away, down a twisting and unsavoury narrow corridor that led out through white tiles right on to Holborn. A couple of heavy iron gates that were normally left open, swung shut as Cochise and Draig threw their weights against it. Eighteen inches of heavy-duty chain and one large padlock, and the bolt-hole was firmly blocked against all and any pursuers.

The five brothers held the other exit for long enough to give Brenda an unassailable lead. As Valentine Bergen took the paper from her, he smiled with his mouth and then turned to look at Molineux. The smile remained there, glazed in place, but the eyes were blazing with barely-contained anger. Despite the warmth of the day, Melvyn Molineux couldn't restrain a small shudder. One more win and it was all over for the Ghouls. And for him.

Back at Barnard's Inn, the car-park was pitted and torn up by the violence of the fight. Gouts of blood showed vivid red against the dull tarmac. The two workers stuck their respective heads round the doors.

'Never like this in Oldham, William.'

'True, very true.'

The day before last of the five day challenge. Friday 21st of June. Clue Number 4. 'First the Marsh in 1882. Then Northumberland Park in 1885. Now at the corner of Park and Worcester'

While it was being read out by the Editor of the *Daily Leader* and recorded by the swelling team of video and TV reporters and camera-men, Melvyn Molineux had wandered along to where the two teams stood by their hogs, waiting and listening. After Bergen had read it out once, and while the buzz from the crowd was abating. Before the second reading for the video boys who'd missed it first time around, he sidled alongside Evel Winter. 'Difficult, eh? Sorry I can't help you. Wouldn't be fair though, would it? Incidentally, are any of your boys football supporters?'

Evel Winter covered his surprise at the odd question. 'A couple, why?'

'Which teams?'

'I don't know, duckie. I think Howl and Alice used to go up to Arsenal. And Orc still creeps up to Tottenham. He thinks I don't know. Stupid chumsie.'

'Orc is that very tall, thin man, who wears orange? One of your reserves? If I were you, Evel, I'd pick him instead of one of the others. He's got a special knowledge that might ... might, be useful this one. Have a look at your map when you get into your room.'

'What the fucking hell are you pissing on ... Oh! Tottenham Hotspurs.'

'For Christ's sake.' An agonised whisper from Molineux. 'Don't tell them all.'

'Thanks sweetie. Come round tonight again, about ten, and ask for me.'

Molineux actually simpered. 'Evel, I don't think I can stand it again. My back is still raw from Wednesday night.'

Evel turned away from him, to lead his team into the huge office building. Over his shoulder, he said: 'Take your choice. But, I was going to wear my snakeskin boots, tonight. With the buckles.'

Waiting their turn to enter the office, Gerry and his brothers watched the exchange with interest. Monk commented to anyone interested: 'What did that little creep say to that big creep. Look at Molineux. He looks like a cat that's got the cream. He's licking his fucking lips. And grinning like a bloody cat. Bastard!'

Fourth time unlucky for the Last Heroes and Wolves. Not all of their combined brain-power, nor a chance stroke of luck, could solve that clue. Blank-faced they walked out to the start. Gerry's last-minute instructions – facing defeat – were the best he could do. 'Sit tight and watch them. We've got to let them make the play this time.'

Remembering what had happened when the Heroes had made a change in their team – the way it had given a clue to him – Evel decided against bringing in the towering Orc. He stuck with the same six, having first made sure that two of the roads that bordered the Tottenham ground were indeed Park Lane and Worcester Road. He didn't give a damn where their first two grounds had been.

As he, in turn, led out his five brothers, he looked at the Heroes and, with special care, at their reserves and their mamas and old ladies in the crowd. The previous three times, he'd noticed their enthusiasm – all times when events had proved that they had been confident and that they had the right answers to the clues. This time – dismal faces and silence. No cheering of their chapter. It could be put on, but it didn't seem it. No, you could never get those stupid cunts that followed them, their women, to act as convincingly as that. They really didn't know.

A lightning word along the line and then plump Valentine Bergen was again mounting up the rostrum, ready to wave them away. Engines revved up, blue smoke billowed protestingly from exhausts and eyes turned to the flag.

It dropped.

Bergen lifted it again. And dropped it again. The crowd gasped and began to shout.

None of the twelve Angels had moved. The Last Heroes and Wolves had been watching the Ghouls for the first move, looking for a clue from their plans that might help them. But Evel had second-guessed them. He chose to wait for them. Seeing that his guess had been right, Evel shouted across at the bitter-faced Gerry. 'Give up then. We all know where it is. I'll even tell you exactly what our plans are. We're going to leave at two-minute intervals. Alone. In ones. It doesn't matter if you send one of your smelly chummies after each of us. I know, and so do you, that you can't reckon on sticking with all of us. One of us will shake off our stinking tail, and then, when we're absolutely safe, not before, the one who's got clear will ride gently down to ... wherever it is, collect the paper and there we are. Toughers old cheese. Rotten tough cheddar.'

And, that's exactly what happened. One at a time, the Ghouls set off. Gerry tried to pair them with what he considered to be one of his team of roughly equal talent.

But, he knew he was on a loser. One by one they rode off, the roar of their engines fading away in the afternoon heat until they were no more than the drone of a wandering bee. Finally, it was Evel and Gerry.

It worked out like Gerry knew it had to. It took one of the Ghouls nearly twenty minutes to shake off his tail, but once one of them had, it was over. An easy ride up to Tottenham, the marked copy of the paper in an inside pocket of a bright silk jacket, and they were level at two each.

Which brother (or sister) was it that let the others down? Who lost the Ghoul they were supposed to be following? That doesn't seem a fair question. It could have been any one of them that was unlucky to be blocked off at a crucial junction. No, it isn't fair. To blame anyone. They all agreed afterwards, that it was just one of those things. But, tomorrow, that was a different thing.

Before they left the *Leaders'* offices that afternoon, both chapters were called to a surprise meeting in one of the top floor conference rooms, just along the corridor from the penthouse suite of Valentine Bergen. Melvyn Molineux presided and the large room was packed with other reporters. He clapped his hands to get everyone's attention. 'This extra meeting will come as something of a surprise to all of you. The owner of the *Daily Leader*, Mr Bergen, has agreed with me that we should have a slight change in the rules for the last leg of the challenge. He has had to leave immediately for Cowes where he is competing in a power-boat race later this afternoon, but he will be here for the final at mid-day tomorrow.

'Since the result depends totally on the last leg, and since we both feel that the last clue is somewhat more difficult than the others, we have agreed to give you the clue now, so that you can ponder on it overnight. There will be no eleven o'clock meeting tomorrow. Everyone will assemble at Marble Arch at twelve precisely for the off. Right. Any questions? All right, then. Here's the last clue. It's very short. "Rossetti on one wall, Turner on another, and Constable on a third". Gerry and Evel, here are your copies of the clues. Good luck, and may the worst chapter lose.'

In the privacy of their room, the Last Heroes were far from happy. The Ghouls had, for once, not bothered to have a meeting on the premises and had ridden straight off to their club-house by the canal in Camden Town. Quite rightly, that had been interpreted by Gerry as a sign that they felt they didn't need a formal meeting. Which could mean that they had already given up. Or, it could mean that they thought they didn't need a meeting. Because it was all fixed up. Or, just fixed!

'Anybody got any ideas? I'll read it out once more, for all the good that'll do. "Rossetti on one wall, Turner on another and Constable on a third". Kafka?'

'Sorry, Gerry. We're agreed that they're painters. So, it must be an Art Gallery or collection. That's as far as I can go.'

'How about the rest of you? Gwyn, Bardd, Draig, Rat, Cochise?'

The shaken heads gave the answer. The two options that most of them were agreed on were either the National Gallery in Trafalgar Square, or the Tate Gallery, though they all realised that there were a hell of a lot of other places it could be.

'Brenda, how about you? And Monk? Hey, where the hell is Monk? I haven't seen him since the end of the last leg. He looked fantastically pissed off then. Anyone seen him?'

'I saw him going off with Modesty. They probably think they've got time for a quick screw up in Bergen's office now he's away for the afternoon. Monk said that soft carpet was the best floor he'd ever screwed on.'

'He shouldn't just have fucked off like that.'

'Yeah, but he probably sodded off before creepy Molineux made his announcement. He'll meet us back at headquarters.'

'Well, he needn't fucking bother! If he reckons that he prefers a bit of cunt to coming and helping out, then he can just fuck right off!'

Gerry tried to pour a little oil on the troubled waters. 'If he didn't know, then we can't honestly blame him. Let's think of something to do, instead of sitting round on our arses and moaning at each other. What can we do that's positive? I know; it's still early. We can split up and go in pairs to all the main picture galleries and museums. The rules don't say that we have to rely on just the six. Get everybody mobilised, Gwyn. Mamas, old ladies. Everyone. Kafka ring up the Tourist people and get a list of all the places that might have these pictures. Come on! Let's get weaving!'

It had been a hot afternoon, with an even hotter day forecast for the following day. As the Angels lay around on the old lawn at the back of the ruined mansion that they had adopted for their own, there was no conversation. Cochise nuzzled on the vast breasts of Forty, his old lady. Rat whittled away on a piece of ash wood he had ripped off a tree in the grounds, carving a reproduction of his own penis. The other brothers and sisters of the chapter lounged about, idly brushing away the flies that gathered as evening grew near.

The six (or, rather, five) competitors, plus a few of the more senior brothers were huddled together passing around a couple of joints. Despair sat wordless on each man's shoulder. Despite frantic efforts by everyone during the afternoon, when every gallery of every size and location – Brenda had even managed to get as far as Windsor – had been covered, the score-sheet was blank. Dozens of Rossettis, cartloads of Constables and tons of Turners. But, nowhere were they all in the same room. Not even at the biggest galleries. Holly had found a Turner and a Rossetti in the same place. But, not all three.

'So, we're buggered. I'd bet any money you like that Molineux has leaked the answer to Evel Winter. I'd also bet that we'd never get the answer whatever we did. They'll have been laughing as we tore our arses all round London. I reckon it's a trick. What's that?'

The low hum of talk stopped. In the distance, far and low, they could just hear the sound of a hog, coming closer. Near the overgrown road to the big house. Getting nearer. Then braking to a halt, spattering gravel over the group on the grass. It was Monk, with Modesty hugging his back.

'Greetings oh my droogs. Welcome am I my brothers. What's wrong? Thou all look as though thou hast received a mighty kick in the yarbles?'

Gerry walked across to the grinning Monk. 'Where the fuck have you been all this afternoon? Screwing?'

'Yes my beloved pee. Giving young Modesty the old in-out with gusto. Not all afternoon. We went to a Classic this p.m. to viddy a screening of the mighty *Clocky O*. Wondrous still, my brothers.' Seeing that Gerry was not amused by his chat, Monk became more serious. 'Christ, Gerry, that bastard Bergen doesn't half do himself proud. We had it three times in about an hour on that smashing office carpet of his.

Oh, I forgot. None of you lot have been in there, have you. Fucking enormous place. Very Design Centre, with lovely furniture and nice picky-wicks on the wall. So, what's wrong?'

Gerry told him what had happened that afternoon. About the clue and the way they had combed London and the whole South-East of England trying to find the answer. Without success.

'And now we're trying to think of some way of stopping the Ghouls. Cochise has suggested an all-out attack on them tonight. Frankly, I think that's a shitty idea. Equally, I can't come up with anything any better. So, that's going to be what we've got to discuss. The only alternative is to try and pair with the Ghouls and just hope that we manage to get a break this time. Perhaps, we could all fake losing touch, and hope to trick them.'

'That's a long shot, Gerry.'

'Right. But, what about you. You've had a whole afternoon of fucking and relaxation. Haven't you got any ideas?'

'You haven't even told me what the clue is.'

'Rossetti on one wall, Turner on another and Constable on a third. Don't say it's a picture gallery, because if you do I'll personally kick you in the crotch.'

'Rossetti, Turner, Constable. All in the same place. My God, Gerry. That's absolutely impossible. What a cunt that Molineux is! What a cunt!!'

17. SOME IS WINNERS AND SOME IS LOSERS
A video news item dated Saturday 22nd June, 1998.
Interviewer – Tom Melling.

'Do you work at the *Leader*?'

A frightened girl, her face a lace-work of blood and cuts, cries hysterically, her shoulders shaking helplessly. She is unable to answer.

Melling moves through the crowd of weeping girls. 'Is there anyone here who saw any of the people who started all this?'

A tall girl, her left eye a pool of oozing blood, her hair covered in dirt and ash, nods at the question. 'I was on the third floor when it started. I was with my friend...' She breaks down, sobbing, unable to go on.

'Was your friend killed? How did she die?'

The office girl chokes back her tears and tries to go on. 'I think she must have been ... been killed. When the ceiling fell, she was underneath. I saw her trapped on the floor, by her desk, with her ... her hair on fire.'

'I'm sorry to press you at a time like this, with so many of your young friends slaughtered around you, and so many more scarred for life, but people will want to know what happened. Can you tell me any more?'

'No. No. No. Just leave me alone.'

Melling turns from the crying girl, with his most concerned look. 'That poor girl, who may well have lost the sight of that eye, sums up this staggering tragedy. What went wrong? Perhaps you, sir, [bending down to a man lying on a stretcher, with a bloody blanket across the lower part of his body] could tell us what happened?'

The man's face is contorted with spasms of agony, but he manages to gasp out a reply. 'I saw the leader of them come in. The winner. Then a lot arrived. Then there was screaming and then the fire and we tried to get the young girls out. Oh! Oh, God help me!'

'Can you go on?'

'No. That's all. Just the fire. Ceilings falling, desks over-turned, killings. Burnings.'

'One last question, sir. How badly are you injured?'

'I suppose I was lucky. I was on the stairs, near the bottom, when the worst explosion came. Part of the iron bannister caught me across the legs, and they tell me they're broken, but I can't sit up to see. I know I can't feel them. At least I'm alive. But, heaven help some of those poor girls.'

Melling looks down with revulsion at the lower part of the man's body, where the blanket has fallen away. Without any attempt to lower his voice, he goes on. 'As I can see only too clearly, this man has actually lost both legs, just above the knee. The final casualty total here is not known yet. Some informed sources speak of hundreds. Who knows what started it? Who can tell what really happened? Once again, the outsiders of society have been allowed to reap a terrible toll of death and maiming. These girls here [puts arms round two white-faced girls, standing waiting quietly for an ambulance] will pay their price for years to come. They both face hours of pain on operating tables; skin grafts to try and heal these dreadful facial scars. Learning to live when children in the street point fingers and laugh at their disfigurements. Knowing that many of their closest friends are dead in that mound of smoking rubble behind me. [Both girls begin to cry, quite uncontrollably.] That, is the result of a victory. But, these, these are the losers. Tom Melling, Video News, London.'

18. THE SKY'S ERUPTED,
WE MUST GO WHERE IT'S QUIET

Some facts are true and some facts are only alleged to be true. Some of the following facts are true and some are not. Guess which facts are accurate and piece them together, and you will have all the information you need to work out what is going to happen. But, remember, some of these facts are not facts at all.

The last day of the challenge was Saturday 22nd June 1998.
Both teams started out from Marble Arch at mid-day.
The starter was the assistant features editor of the *Daily Leader*. Both Melvyn Molineux and Valentine Bergen were waiting at the finish to acclaim the winners.
There had been rumours of fighting and bad trouble amongst the Last Heroes over their course of action.
One of the lesser brothers of the Ghouls' chapter, named Barron, had vanished during the previous night and had not been found.
The clue was "Rossetti on one wall, Turner on another and Constable on a third".
When the Last Heroes arrived at the start, their numbers were sadly depleted and most of those there wore bandages and plasters. Of Gerry's team of six, plus reserves, only five appeared to be fit.
Evel Winter had been given the answer to the last clue and had rewarded the giver with a session of sado-masochistic, homosexual activity until late the previous night.
None of Gerry's team knew the answer to the last clue and were relying on a miracle to help them to victory.
The naked body of an unidentified male had been recovered from the River Lee near Ware by local police at eleven-thirty on that Saturday morning. Hands were missing and the face had been flayed of all skin with a sharp Finnish flensing knife.
The Ghouls had a full team of six – the same as their original team.
Hardly any of the Last Heroes had even bothered to turn out to watch.
Melvyn Molineux had reassured Valentine Bergen that nothing could now go wrong.
The team for the Last Heroes and Wolves consisted of only five members. Gerry, Brenda, Gwyn, Bardd and Kafka.
At the last minute Gerry made a special appeal direct to Molineux to be able to draft in another member of the chapter to make up his numbers.
Suspecting a trick, Molineux had refused point-blank.

The starting-flag dropped on what was obviously an uneven contest.

Those are your clues. Most of those facts are true. All of them seem to be true. The flag has just dropped. What happens next?

Marble Arch at mid-day on that Saturday was hotter than the hobs of Hell. There was a gigantic crowd of onlookers and the viewers at home outnumbered those for the Cup Final a few weeks earlier. The tarmac was bubbling and soft and sellers of soft drinks were making vast profits, charging more than a pound a bottle for watered-down cokes.

The faded denims of the five Last Heroes contrasted dully with the rainbow jackets of the Ghouls. All six of Evel's team had gone to town with heavily-permed hair and sequin-splashed faces. All but Shelob wore swept-wing shades against the dazzling sun.

As the flag dropped, the heavy chromed and enamelled hogs edged forwards through the dense mass of onlookers. The few Last Heroes there gave a weak cheer for their chapter, but the biggest roar from the crowd was for the Ghouls. Looking like a show-biz circus, they had many supporters in the crowd, some wearing the silks and satins and many of them riding similar bikes. Which didn't make it any easier for the Last Heroes.

They had to try and keep track of six Ghouls with just five of them. Try and follow and hope to cover any break that might come. Shadow against all the odds and hope for a chance that might tip them off where the last clue would lead, and then beat that Ghoul back to the offices of the *Leader* with the winning copy of the paper.

Bikes streamed past them down Oxford Street, towards Oxford Circus. To Gerry's surprise, the six Ghouls kept together at first, and rode slowly, waving to the street-lining throngs and laughing and singing. The one thing worse than a bad loser is a bad winner. And that's what Evel was. He even throttled right back to walking pace and eased alongside Gerry.

'Don't wait for us, dearie. You just go right ahead and roar off and win if you want to. We're only here for the glory of competition. You don't have to wait for us. Anyway, in another mile or so we're all going to split up and since there's six of us and five of you, one of us won't have anyone to dodge and that one will ride softly ahead, collect the paper and win. I'm looking forward to seeing you all burn those poopie jackets of yours. Byesie-bye.'

As he rode forward again, Gwyn collected a lot of jeers from the crowd by spitting accurately into Evel's face, leaving him with a trail of spittle over his sun-glasses onto his make-up.

The race that had turned into a triumphant procession moved across Oxford Circus and finally reached the Tottenham Court Road Junction. There the Ghouls suddenly accelerated away from the Last Heroes, breaking away like falling leaves, a star-burst of colour for the helicopter following the race for the B.B.C. sports team.

And, they were away. Sunk in defeat, the Last Heroes didn't even make any effort to try and catch them, they just rode on, a tight-knit formation of five, back towards the offices of the all-powerful *Daily Leader*.

In the luxurious penthouse office suite of the boss of the *Leader*, the champagne was already flowing. One or two carefully chosen young ladies were in attendance, and the photographers were testing light. This was to be an exclusive. The winner taking the paper from the hands of Melvyn Molineux and passing it ceremonially to Valentine Bergen. For, in case any of you missed the liberally-sprinkled clues, the three painters referred to in the fifth challenge question all had pictures, even though they were only reproductions, hanging in his office. One by each painter.

Watching the progress on his video-viewer, Valentine called Molineux over to him. 'You don't think any of them will give it away do you?'

'No chance V.B., no chance. I did it all verbally. Evel got it all from my own lips.' Melvyn smiled to himself at his own private joke. Very private.

One of the girls squeaked as she looked out of the double-glazed window. 'One of those lovely bike-boys has just stopped down there. In a lime-green jacket.'

Bergen clicked on his speak-phone and rattled into it: 'When that Ghoul fellow arrives show him straight in. No hanging around.'

Conversation in the suite languished, as they waited for the winner. Cameras were raised and Molineux held out the marked paper, stretching his smile as far it would reach over his cosmetically-straightened teeth.

The muted hiss of the private lift up to that exalted floor and then the office door slid open. In walked the representative of the top chapter. Bulbs flashed and he paused for a moment, putting his hand up to his eyes, even though he was wearing a large pair of butterfly-wing, diamante shades.

Down below, the throb of more powerful hogs arriving. Both winners and losers.

Up above, Molineux, Bergen and the Ghoul. The only three that matter. The first two in their tropical light-weight suits and thin suede ties. Almost identical. Cast from the same company mould. One older and one thinner. The Ghoul in a bouffant upswept hair-do, bright-green jacket, silver platform-soled boots and darker green denim jeans. Sequins decorating both cheek-bones and crazy patterns of eye make-up starring and circling what could be seen of the eyes. A mouth that was a swollen cupid's bow of Scarlet Flame. Hands in tight black leather gloves.

Molineux placing the two copies of the marked papers, one bearing the letters for the Heroes and the other for the Ghouls.

'Very well done, er, I don't think I know which one you are. Frankly, you all look very much the same. Anyway. Well done. There's the paper you've been racing for. All you have to do is hand it to Mr Bergen there.'

Valentine Bergen beamed hugely and bellowed out: 'Jolly well done, young man,' while secretly thinking: *What a nauseating little poof!* He took the paper and the cameras clicked. A TV camera also recorded the historic moment for millions of eager viewers.

There was a moment when Molineux spotted a slight mistake and turned it into a joke. 'Look out there. You've picked out the wrong copy of the paper. That's the one for the Heroes. The losers. This is the one you should have given to Mr Bergen.'

'No, it's not,' said Mick Moore, also known as Monk.

What happened during the next half hour or so is still so confused and contradictory that it's impossible to get a truly clear picture. All that can be done is to try and piece together the fragmentary memories and observations of a number of people who were involved.

After Monk had clinched that shatteringly unexpected win for the Last Heroes, there were a few moments when Molineux tried to salvage something from the wreckage of his plans. He accused Monk of cheating.

'You can fucking talk. We know you leaked at least two of the answers to the Ghouls, because you were sucking off Evel Winter. We didn't cheat. Nothing in the rules to say that anyone had to wear any special colours, is there? I didn't start before the flag dropped and I was at Marble Arch on time. Our chapter only seemed to have five members in the challenge at the end, but I was there. Nobody cheated but you bastards. Now you pay the price.'

It was at this moment that the video producer finally decided that things had gone far enough and pulled the plugs. For the millions watching and listening, the rest was silence. Until their news programmes later.

What happened, looked at over-all, was relatively simple. The Ghouls arrived at the offices of the *Leader* expecting victory and finding only a bitter defeat. At the same moment, the five Last Heroes also arrived in the forecourt. Large screens round the building had been showing live pix of what had happened inside, so everyone knew. All the Ghouls and all of the Last Heroes fought as they tried to get inside the building and reach the penthouse floor. Battles spread throughout the whole office block and small fires were started on several floors. The staff tried to flee and only got mixed up in the carnage. There were the fights between Ghouls and Heroes – and the security trying to beat the hell out of both. Cochise, Holly, Lady, Brenda, Modesty, Forty and Geneth trapped three of the Ghouls in a corner near a lift shaft. A flash of knives and the three Ghouls were down and bleeding. Boots went in and the screaming stopped. The Last Heroes moved on, though Lady and Holly stayed behind for a minute collecting three unusual souvenirs with their sharp little knives. Finnish knives.

On another floor, Draig fought a brutal battle with two of the Ghouls, Rohan and Vanya. They beat him unconscious and ripped off his colours. They ran for the nearest lift and slammed the double doors shut. Doors made up of diagonal bars on both outside and inside, with gaps between. Draig pulled himself to his feet and staggered after them, blood pouring from his mouth. Seeing him coming, Vanya held the denim jacket temptingly in the air, dangling it at him. Dazed by blows to his head, Draig pushed his hands through the double doors to try and grab his beloved colours back. At that moment, Rohan pushed the button that took the lift plunging downwards.

The gates acted like a guillotine and, after a judder of protest from the mechanism, both hands were nearly severed at the wrist, soaking the Ghouls in the spray of blood. As the lift dropped from sight, Gwyn came charging along the corridor, brought by the yells from Draig. He found the big man sitting against the wall, stupidly watching his life's blood stream from his arms.

The albino dropped to his knees and held the dying man's head to his chest. Draig whispered: 'Vanya and Rohan. Got my colours.'

'Don't worry, boyo. They won't keep them.'

Life faded from the brother's eyes, and he even smiled at the end. 'On the wing of the gull and in the eye of the west wind, I ride always towards the sun.' And, so he died.

The penthouse room had cleared quickly of press and television as soon as

Molineux had tried to grab the copy of the paper from Monk, and Bergen had come to his assistance. As they chased him round the large office, Monk was seen to be pulling out a knife from the back of his jeans.

That was the last anyone saw of either Bergen or Molineux alive. Many of the bodies were so badly burned that identification was impossible, so no-one can know what happened during their last moments on earth. Monk knew, but he wouldn't talk. Once, when he was spaced far out of his skull, Modesty took a chance and asked him. All he did was smile a beatific smile and murmured: 'Sliced them lean and streaky. Like the pigs they were. Sliced them.'

Gwyn picked up Kafka and the two of them went hunting for Vanya and Rohan. Despite a minor diversion when two security guards tried to hold them up with sawn-off shotguns, they pressed on. The guards made the elementary mistake of expecting Hell's Angels to behave like ordinary folk. Most people would, at least, have paused when challenged. Not Gwyn and Kafka. They launched themselves at the men and took them both crashing into a side office. There was a scuffle and the sound of blows in the office, then Gwyn and Kafka walked out, each carrying a sawn-off shotgun.

Rohan and Vanya were with Shelob, trying to find a way up the back stairs to where all the action was going on. Between the tenth and eleventh floor, they found the way blocked by piles of burning furniture. As they turned round to run back down, they froze. Like two dread avenging angels, there were Kafka and the blazing eyes of the white-haired Gwyn.

Gwyn spoke: 'Three rats in a trap. Draig said two Ghouls had cut off his hands. Vanya and Rohan. He didn't mention Shelob. So, you keep very still, close your eyes and don't even breath. You might live. You two, come here.'

Hands held hopelessly, palm outwards, in front of their bodies, the two Ghouls climbed down to the landing below. As they stood there, side by side, both Last Heroes fired simultaneously. The pellets sprayed out in a double star pattern, ripping first through the thin silk jackets, tearing through the belts of the trousers, slashing through skin, then muscle, then intestines, then bone, then more muscle and skin and finally exiting through the flapping backs of the jackets, splattering blood and guts in a dreadful action painting all over the white stucco wall. The two bodies were lifted off their feet by the force of the double hammer blows and flung back against the wall together to lie in a tangled, undignified heap of mewing flesh.

On the roof was a huge tank, holding five thousand gallons of fuel oil, for the central heating. Telephoto lenses on cameras had picked out some activity on the roof, spilling out of the offices on to the patio. A figure in a lime-green jacket dashed out, doubled up, and vanished. Security men were seen chasing an elusive figure, small and difficult to spot, that wheeled and dodged, until it vanished as well. The security men went back to he centre stairwell and walked away, leaving the heavy door open. On to that deserted roof, insulated from the noise of battle below, came the figure of Evel Winter. He looked round desperately for support and found none. He ran out into the middle of the concrete desert and turned to face the door. Out of it came Gerry. For the final confrontation.

It was blazingly hot up there, under a blue, cloudless sky. Far, far away below them, in the dusty streets of Holborn, an occasional woman screamed, and police and fire sirens howled. But, on the open expanse it was quiet.

'This is it, Evel.'

'Yes. Yes. I reckon that I have to agree with you there little Gerry. Look over there, at those little pin-points of light. Cameras. We're on viddy. Now, let's not disappoint all those watchers. Load of ghouls, if you'll excuse the expression.'

All the time he'd been talking, Evel had been backing away, towards the edge of the roof. A low concrete wall over a death-drop. Gerry felt a fluttering in his mind, a memory unexpectedly unlocked. For the second time in his life he was on top of a cliff with the President of a rival chapter. A man who aimed to kill him.

The white satin suit looked tired and smudged. Round the eyes the make-up had run, leaving stains over the high cheek-bones.

As Gerry walked closer to him, the Ghoul climbed on the parapet wall. He turned one last time and half-smiled at the leader of the Last Heroes and Wolves. 'You'd like to smash me to a bleeding pulp wouldn't you? Sorry, but I'll let you into a secret. I don't like pain. There comes a point when you've done everything you can. Life seems empty and dull. There's nothing left. You'll come to it, as I have. I hoped this challenge might lead to something a bit new. But, we lost. We cheated, you know?'

Gerry nodded and stopped where he was, feeling almost pity.

'Yeah. That little pervert Molineux used to come round and I'd kick him about a bit, then let him blow me. We knew most of the clues. But, we still lost.' He looked outwards, across the canyons of the City, to where the sun blazed off the gold of St Pauls. 'One kick left, Gerry. Flying. Byesie-bye.'

Gerry didn't move. Didn't go to the edge to see the spinning figure plummet to the pavement. Didn't need to. Didn't want to. All he wanted to do was get back to the sea and the mountains, where the air was cleaner. Feet dragging in the molten dust, he walked to the door. From behind two of the air vents on the roof came two figures. A long-haired Ghoul in a lime-green jacket, and a tiny, rat-like Angel. They met together and talked briefly. Then, the Ghoul went off down the stairs after Gerry. Rat, for it was he, connected the thick hose-pipe to the fuel supply tank and dragged it to the top of the central stairs.

Walking down the stairs, towards the street, Gerry heard clicking heels behind him. He turned and saw a Ghoul running down towards him. He flexed his fingers and waited.

'Gerry, it's me. It all worked. Great. Fucking great. Oh, it was so good. Just like you said. And then old Evel doing his "look no hands" stunt. Listen, Rat's on the roof, and he and I have a great plan to finish off the Ghouls. All...'

Gerry interrupted him. 'I don't want to know, Monk. Suddenly I feel bloody tired of death. I'm going to collect all the brothers and sisters and get out of here. Back to Wales. Before the police pull us all in. If we go now, we can get away. I'm fucking tired.'

Monk looked at him in surprise. 'All right, then; get them all away and Rat and I'll try to catch you up. See you.'

With a wave of the hand, he was gone.

By moving quickly and silently, Gerry spread the word for his chapter to withdraw. Filtering away from different exits, those who were still able managed to get out. They were helped by an announcement from the tannoy system that originated in

Bergen's office. 'Ghouls!! On the roof! They've caught Evel. Quick!'

Any who doubted were convinced by the lime-green figure of one of their brothers shouting and beckoning from near the top of the main stairway.

Virtually all of the surviving Ghouls made for that stairway, to aid their President. The lime-green figure vanished.

A hand turned a valve. Oil gushed down the stairs, soaking the centre of the building. Drenching the Ghouls. Flooding off at every floor to pour through every office. A touch from a cigarette lighter to the end of a narrow trail of fuel. Two pairs of feet sprinting for the narrow, service stairs at the rear of the building.

The whole block rocking to the explosion. Anyone on the stairs was killed instantly as the pillar of flame dashed their charred bodies to oblivion. The flames spread uncontrollably through each floor, burning all they touched. Desks, floors, drapes, corpses, computers, carpets, the living.

Death came that day, as it so often does, to the innocent and to the guilty. It came to the *Daily Leader* as it had to its owner.

There is one last question for you to consider. In a tale of much guilt and little innocence; where lies the main guilt? Where?

19. ALL ALONE, ALL ALONE, ALL ALONE.

All alone, all alone, all alone.
Blood on the road,
And a white heron flying.
Blood on the road,
And a grey mist rising.
All alone,
All alone,
All alone.

Angels running, riding free.
Blood in the eyes.
And a grey goose winging.
Blood in the eyes,
And a red sun rising.
All alone,
All alone,
All alone.

I'm going to run and ride and die.
Blood in my brain.
And a black eagle stooping,
Blood in my brain,
And a dark river rising.
All alone,
All alone,
All alone.

Not alone, not alone, not alone.
Blood in my mind.
And a white hawk rising.
Blood in my mind,
And a free road waiting.
Not alone,
Not alone,
Not alone.

Book Three:

GUARDIAN ANGELS

1. TO SMILE AND DO MY SHOW

'End of May 1940 it was. I'd been lying there on the bleeding beaches for three days with bugger-all food and only half a canteen of water. Finally, we get our number called and this major comes poncing down to us. "You there," he says. Very high class. "You there. You men can go and form up as a rearguard over beyond the canal." Well, we all knew that Jerry was waiting there, itching for the go-ahead from Berlin to run all over us. But, orders was orders, so we gets up and he leads us over the dunes.'

'Was there much shooting?'

'Not much. A lot of them Stukas – Christ only knows where the Brylcreem boys were – but not much else. Anyway, we gets over the back of the sand-hills, all among the trucks and equipment that had been busted up, and he calls us round him and goes into this speech. About how proud he was to be able to lead us on this mission and how proud he was sure we were about having the chance to make the ultimate sacrifice.'

'Bloody hell, Tom. That was a short intermission. Looks like we're going to be back in business soon.'

'Yeah. Anyway. Just time to finish me story. This Major went on about home and country and King and mothers and babies. How we'd lay down our lives and that it showed no greater love. Something like that. He did it really well. I was nearly crying with the emotion. In fact, I found me eyes were all blurred. I had to wipe them before I could see. Then I shot the silly little fucker in the back and we all sodded off and got on a boat back to Blighty.'

'Good days, eh Tom? Good days. Here we go.'

The theatre lights dimmed once, then came up again as though it had all been a mistake. Then, they made their mind up and slipped off into darkness. The screaming that had been going on through the interval, barely above conversational tone – as though the teenies and middies were keeping their hands in – now boomed up to a level that neared the pain barrier.

A solid row of navy-blue power stretching along the front of the stalls, the aging commissionaires winced and some put gloved hands to ears. Most of them braced themselves for the second half of the show, knowing that this would be the big test. That the few girls and women who'd made runs at the stage in the first half were just feeling the way for the others. Waxed moustaches bristled, trouser seams were straightened, fingers flexed, watering eyes were wiped, and thudding hearts crept faster. On the dark chest of every man there was the bright splash of colour of rainbow medals – gallantry awards, stars from Burma, the desert, NAAFI medals, and, in one case, the subdued purple of the bronze cross – "awarded for the most conspicuous bravery or pre-eminent act of self-sacrifice or extreme devotion to duty in the face of the enemy".

One searing light, bursting through the dust and dope-smoke, stabbing at the centre of the stage. The screaming doubled, trebled.

Several years earlier, just before the inevitable decision was made to scrap it, an enterprising T.V. journalist had made a decibel test which compared the engine noise of the Concorde at take-off against one thousand fans of the then-popular group, Mealy Plum. Few people were surprised when the plane lost. Apart from having a certain surreal beauty, the plane never won anything.

A slim figure minced on the stage, wearing a tight-fitting black suit with a tightly-knotted silver tie. The hair was cropped short – not as severe as the skulls, but shorter than usual – and the eyes twinkled under a dusting of silver powder. Facing the black pit of screeching females, he waved a negligent hand, the silver finger-guard catching the spotlight and bouncing it back into the audience.

The voice was harsh, surprisingly loud for such a small man. Amplified and double-echoed, it thundered out. 'Lovely! Lovely! Glad to see you're all still here. Quiet, hush a minute. Shut your gobs! That's better. Now, Roland Porringer Supershows have got a second part here for you that's just packed with jean-creamers. Two acts. Only two. Shame!! Here's the first. Specially for the middies. Let's hear it for Mucking Punt. Lovely! Lovely!!'

This was for the middies. The teenies would get their kicks later when the top of the bill came on. The line of commissionaires braced themselves as waves of middle-aged – and older – women hurtled forward in an attempt to get at the stage. Tom found himself facing an Amazonian figure, nearly as tall as himself and probably twice the weight. Her face painted in the garish fifties fashion of the middies, her mouth a crimson cavern, she struck blindly at him. The lilac silk blouse she was wearing tore across the front with the effort of her blows and her enormous breasts spilled out, distracting Tom for a moment. In that instant, she brought up a nylon-clad knee smartly into his groin.

Things went black and he clutched at his savaged genitals, sinking to his knees. In a second, the woman was trying to climb up to the stage over him. When the blackness cleared, he felt her weight on him, kneeling on his shoulders. Pressing down with all his aging strength, Tom managed to rise to his feet, throwing her back towards the auditorium. She fell on other women, crashing into a chaos of flailing limbs. Tom caught a brief glimpse of her breasts, jiggling apart, then she vanished as another woman planted her foot in the centre of her stomach to help her own progress.

Chivalry be damned thought Tom, crossing a swift right to the middie's face. Cutting his knuckles on her teeth. Watching a flower of blood blossom in the middle of her face. Getting ready for the next one.

It took a full, savage five minutes of fighting to get the women cleared from the front of the theatre. Legislation aimed at checking the hysteria and casualties at pop concerts had made it illegal for police to enter theatres unless a serious breach of the peace seemed imminent. This measure had been intended to minimise provocation, but seemed to have had little effect. It had placed the onus for security on promoters, who had tried dogs and hoses, but adverse publicity had caused the cancellation of several tours.

No private firm would handle a pop concert, so the publicity agent for this package, Rupert Colt, had been forced to enlist the help of the Corps of Commissionaires. They were willing to help – the payment was more than generous – but some of their members had reservations about possible danger. 'Gang of kids and a few frustrated housewives.' That was what they had been told. 'Probably get a chance to cop a feel with some of the ladies.'

But, it wasn't working out that way. Tom groaned as he surreptitiously rubbed the damaged part of his anatomy. 'Bloody cows.' Still, they'd been hurled back and there was only one act to go.

Behind him, Mucking Punt were coming to the end of their first song, oblivious of the frenzy in the audience. There were four in the group – all under fifteen. They were all dressed in a similar fashion. Bare to the waist, with tight jeans, supported by garish braces, and heavy working-men's boots. Their hair was shoulder-length and back-combed to give a bizarre bouffant appearance. They wore no make-up at all – unusual among pop groups – but their teeth had been filed down to needle points and tipped with vermilion paint.

The stage was littered with gifts, tied with ribbon or brightly-coloured paper. The thing that had shocked Tom most was when some of the middies – old enough to be his daughter – had ostentatiously taken off their knickers, bits of lace to his thinking, and thrown them at the young boys.

At the end of the first song the leader had picked up one of the pairs of pants and wiped the sweat from his face with them. Then, he had wiped suggestively at his crotch, getting more cries and screams. Finally, he had spat into them and thrown them back to the howling mob.

Then, boots stamping heavily, guitars swung low on their hips, Mucking Punt moved on into their second song. Called "I live in an old body and I'm young", it was aimed deliberately at the middie-boppers in the audience. Tom couldn't hear most of the words, as the volume was set way up high, but he could have sworn he heard a line about how this woman thought her breasts were like 'wrinkled prunes'.

In front of the thin blue line, the mob of middle-aged women screamed and howled at their idols. On the stage, the group played on regardless. A third and fourth song followed, heightening the mood. A thin woman of forty, just to the left of Tom, dressed in a light blue denim jacket and absurdly short skirt stood, tears rolling down her powdered cheeks, hardly aware that she was touching herself and that her arousal was self-induced.

'Disgusting!' screamed Tom to his neighbour.

'What?', he yelled back, unable to hear, though they stood together with arms linked against the pressure of the middies.

Tom shook his head hopelessly. The noise was really getting to him, numbing his mind and making it hard to think with any kind of coherence. It penetrated though that Mucking Punt seemed to have finished playing, though the screams from the older women carried on. He had noticed vaguely that the young half of the audience – the teenies – had been comparatively quiet during the set, just keeping the moans going to stay at a high ready for their own special idols.

The lead vocalist sidled up to the mike, sweat streaking his naked chest. 'All right. All right. Me and Chris and Dick and Jeremy are splitting now. Nice doing it for you. Sorry these senile old bastards kept you away from us. See you all again and think of us when you're in your beds.'

Another onslaught on the commissionaires from the middies and Mucking Punt were gone.

Tom's mate banged him on the arm to attract his attention. 'Rude devils! If it hadn't been for us those women might have torn him and his poof friends to shreds!'

He nodded his agreement. The noise was building again, and talking seemed more effort than it was worth. But, he tried. 'Nearly over. Last damned time I get involved in this. I say, it's the last time for me. Never again. Still, it should be only the little girls this time. Easier than some of those heavies. Eh?'

The screaming had built to a crescendo of agony, and the compere was finding it impossible to get into his build-up. For his own special climax, Tiny Tony Nelson had changed into a silver suit with a tightly-knotted black tie. The shining finger-guard was gold, and a ruby ear-ring dangled fetchingly.

His voice cracked with the effort of trying to climb above the bedlam, and he finally gave it best. He pointed up into the shadowed flies, high above the proscenium arch of the old theatre. His mouth opened, revealing a twinkling of diamond fillings to his teeth. 'Erection Set!!!'

Total blackness.

The keening sound of a bass guitar on full feedback, throbbing round the echoing cavern. Above it all, the distorted voice of a man, whispering obscenities. Or, were they obscenities? The distortion was so arranged that nobody could ever be quite sure. The words could mean whatever you wanted them to mean.

When the blue lights flicked back on, the steel cables had lowered the gondola-shaped stage to the centre of the stage proper. It had unwound from the roof of the theatre where a helicopter waited to whisk them away at the end of their set. Erection Set would hardly leave that stage-within-a-stage for their entire act, and a roadie was always on the watch for any threatened invasion by fans. The steel cable could be operated within seconds to lift them up, up and away.

Tom glanced over his shoulder for a second, just so that he could tell his envious grandchildren that he had seen the magical duo. The taller one – nobody knew the real names of either man, and they refused to adopt any stage names as individuals – wore his hair very long, secured to silver nipple rings. Apart from a minimum of leather, his only other adornment was a cluster of little bells hung over his groin.

His partner, who was shorter and much fatter, wore only a see-through lace dress. Nothing else. He played electric lute – painted pink and shaped like no lute you've ever seen. The taller one played a bass guitar, with a beautifully-engraved reproduction of a naked girl exactly where his pale fingers plucked the steel strings.

Their opening number was mainly an instrumental, with repetitions of the phrase 'Rub yourself on me' at decreasing intervals and at increasing volume. It ended with the shorter one on his knees, rubbing the end of his flute faster and faster and faster against the strings of the taller one's guitar.

Several attacks by the teenies had been repulsed without too much trouble by the blue line. Tom was nursing a ragged scratch on his left cheek, and his epaulettes had been torn off, but the men still held.

'Now, one for all the Angels and all the friends of the Angels. Here's "All Alone".'

The song from a year or so back had almost become the anthem of the reformed and revived Hell's Angels movement. Since the catastrophic explosion at the London offices of the *Daily Leader* a few months ago, little had been seen or heard of Gerry "Wolf" Vinson and the chapter known as the "Last Heroes". It was assumed that they had once again retreated to their mountain fastness in the wilderness of North Wales. In the meantime, the country was plagued by a resurgence of the "skull" movement – an ultra-violent culture based on the mindless rampaging of the skinheads of the sixties and seventies.

Flute and bass were discarded and the couple sang together to a background of a wailing Moog.

'Blood on the road,
And a white heron flying.
Blood on the road,
And a grey mist rising.
All alone,
All alone,
All alone.'

The song hammered through two more verses, the background noise rising until it reached an almost inaudible pitch that vibrated the small bones in the face and caused teeth to quiver.

Erection Set began to stamp louder and louder. Faster and faster. They reached the final verse.

'Not alone, not alone, not alone.
Blood in my mind,
And a white hawk rising.
Blood in my mind,
And a free road waiting.
Not alone,
Not alone,
Not alone.'

The last phrase was repeated hypnotically, on and on and on and on. The strobe lights played faster, shining epileptically over the gyrating audience. With a sudden movement, the taller one ripped off the cluster of silver bells and threw them into the audience.

Underneath, he was naked.

Tom knew nothing of that. All he knew was that the noise and the lights had made him feel sick. That his false teeth seemed somehow too large for his mouth. That the scratch on his face was beginning to sting. His groin ached. If only it would stop!

The baring of the singer's sexual organ was the catalyst that transformed the audience. Pushed them finally over the brink.

Eyes wide open, staring blankly, mouths gaping, the young girls came at the stage. Tom and his colleagues linked arms and tried to repel them by becoming immoveable objects. But, they failed. And, the girls *were* an irresistible force.

Even so, in normal rock concert riot conditions, that were becoming almost acceptable, they might still have held.

Tom smashed his fist into the face of a girl – hardly fifteen – hurling her backwards, blood spurting from her nose. The noise from the stage hammered on, and the lights still flickered, lighting the mindless faces of the teenies. The screaming had died down and had been replaced by an eerie, obscene moaning.

For a second of frozen time they withdrew, leaving a narrow space in front of the stage. Several girls lay there, groaning, some with bleeding faces. The commissionaires also drew breath. Some of them – most of them – had scratches on hands and faces, while few had a uniform that wasn't torn.

Then, as Tom watched in confusion, the girls came again. And the lights in the theatre sparkled and spun about, whirling off the brass buttons on the commissionaires' jackets.

And off the sequins that were scattered in the hair of many of the girls. As well as on something else. Glittered on things held in the hands of the teenies.

Short, shiny knives.

Four of them converged on Tom at once. He was too shocked even to fight back. To explain why he was there.

As the thin blades pecked out his life, he began to cry.

2. WE'RE GONNA RAP IT UP
An interview with Rupert Colt, from the British rock magazine, 'Telescopic Knife'. February, 1999.

Telescopic Knife: Rupert Colt, you are handling the publicity and promotion for the tour that is now ending of Mucking Punt and Erection Set. I believe you are also the man in charge of security arrangements.

Rupert Colt: Yes, dear. That's right. But, after last night's awful happening at the Sundance Theatre, I'm not sure whether "security" is the right word.

T.K: Yes. This morning's papers call it a "bloody battle" and "a pop charnel-house".

R.C: You missed the one about the abattoir of rock.

T.K: We've seen figures quoted of up to forty dead and as many as one hundred and fifty injured.

R.C: I think that you can quote me as saying that those figures are considerably exaggerated. I rang the Royal Northern Hospital just before I came along here. The number of actual dead – actual dead – is no more than forty-four and the injured who have been kept in hospital number less than eighty. Seventy-nine if you want the exact figures.

T.K: How many of the dead were your security guards?

R.C: I'd rather not answer that one, if you don't mind.

T.K: Fair enough. It has to be said, though, that we've also been seeing people this morning, and we were told, officially, that over half of the fatally injured were these old men. Would you care to comment on that?

R.C: All right sweetheart. If you insist. Yes, that is correct. But, I honestly don't feel any blame over it. We had no way of knowing that the bitches would all be carrying knives.

T.K: There were warnings. Mick Houghton – and no better music critic there is – said weeks ago that the teenies were building up, wanting some rather special souvenirs, and that he'd heard some of them were going tooled up to concerts.

R.C: No comment.

T.K: After this, will the final concert of the Mucking Punt and Erection Set tour take place?

R.C: Unfortunately not. I got out when they started to come over and only went back after they'd shifted the bodies. The whole Sundance smelled of dope smoke, of piss, of blood and of death. No, after that, the rest of the tour is O.F.F. – off. In any case, they got Erection Set up the cable and into the helicopter in time, but they've split and

I don't know where the fuck they are. Of course, ticket money will be refunded.

T.K: We've heard about another big tour you've got lined up, including some of the biggest names from both sides of the Atlantic. Can you tell us something about that?

R.C: No.

T.K: Just 'No'?

R.C: Just 'No'. But, it will be big – probably the biggest package this country has ever seen. But, for contractual reasons, I can't give you any details. There'll be at least one big name from the old days. An American super-group. A great English group with a lead singer who used to be a great science-fiction writer. It's not certain about their booking yet; so, don't jump to any conclusions. And some names that'll make this package that's just ending look like an evening with Cliff.

T.K: One last question, please. If this show is as big as you say...

R.C: No 'ifs', about it, love.

T.K: Well, what will you do about security?

R.C: [after a long pause] I want to go for a drive out into the clean green God's country and try and track down an old friend of mine.

T.K: What makes you think he'll come?

R.C: I'll just look up at him with my baby blue eyes and tell him I'm in trouble. I know he won't let me down. He's a real angel like that.

3. TO GATHER FLOWERS CONSTANTLY

Spring had come late to the secluded valley on the Lleyn Peninsula in North Wales, named after the rebel chieftain, Vortigern. The first green shoots of the ferns were bursting through the dank, brown deadness of the previous year. The winter had been hard down there, close to the sea-wrack and the barking of the seals.

The two rows of cottages, set at a sharp right-angle to each other, had been almost destroyed by hooligans in the sixties and seventies. Roofs had been partly stripped and all the wooden floors and ceilings had been burned out. Only the shells remained. Plus the shells of one smaller house, and of the bigger building – that must have belonged to the manager of the lonely quarry, high on the grey hillside above.

But, the walls remained. Granite. Heavy block cemented to heavy block. It would have taken a bulldozer to flatten them. And there was no way that you could get a bulldozer down there. Or a car. Even a jeep would have found the twisting path impossible. Since the Welsh Freedom Society had destroyed what path remained several years ago, to check an attempt by the council to sell the village off, there had been no way down.

The handful of walkers who used to brave the stiff climb dwindled away. The Lancashire middle-class who had hoped for a country cottage were disappointed. In those days, it had seemed a cause worth fighting for. Now, the desolation of the whole area had gone too far. In summer it was crowded. But, out of season, the villages of weekend-dwellers stood empty and alone. From ghost villages, there had come a web of ghost communities. The Welsh-speaking population of Caernarvonshire had shrunk by half in the last six years.

Nant Gwrtheyrn remained. Gulls and cormorants soared above it, and the sea mumbled sullenly across the shingle beach below it. And, it had found a new life. With new residents.

The offices of the *Daily Leader* had erupted in a plume of death, and many had breathed their last. Again, the premier chapter of Hell's Angels in Britain – the Last Heroes, linked with the Wolves, affiliated by charter to the great chapter of Oakland in California – went underground. But, times changed. Many of the dead had been members of a rival chapter – the Ghouls – and the public were not that concerned. Of far more interest was the news, only three days after the Holborn cataclysm, that a Minister of the Crown had paid a high-class prostitute to beat him with bunches of thistles, while he stroked her Alsatian. Not only had he admitted this absurd perversion, but a leading paper actually had photographs of him taking his pleasure.

And the lady was reputedly of foreign extraction.

The Hell's Angels were off the front pages, and that meant they were out of people's minds. Which, decided Gerry, their President, wasn't a bad thing.

So, quietly living, and partly living, they had survived the cruel grip of winter. They had enough money – the benefits of a raid in Llandudno saw to that – but their village had been cut off by land. Fortunately, the rotting jetty along the beach held together to enable them to bring in supplies by motor-boat.

Now, spring, and it was all worthwhile. But the coffers were perilously low, and change was in the air.

Gwyn, the white-haired, white-faced, red-eyed leader of the Wolves, was becoming restless. Cochise and Kafka, with Rat, Riddler, Dick the Hat and Gerry the sole survivors of the Last Heroes of two years ago, wanted to move south again. They had seen enough of hills and rivers.

But the most interesting development concerned the ladies of the chapter. Brenda, Gerry's old lady, had always been militant, and two other women – they were no man's old lady, yet they weren't mamas either, who called themselves Holly and Lady – joined with her in a sort of splinter movement.

They didn't burn their bras – they didn't wear any – nor did they withdraw from the men members of the chapter. But, when they engaged in sex with any of the brothers, it was always on their terms. This had caused tremendous opposition at first, because it ran against all the laws and beliefs of the Angels. But, all three were clever, and very tough. In some ways more ruthless than most of the brothers. Between them, they had killed more than a dozen men. They walked together, and they walked alone.

The rest of the brothers still hung around the village. The new boy was Monk, a.k.a. Mick Moore, who had played such a large part in putting down the Ghouls. He spent a lot of time roaming round the Ballard landscape of the ruined quarry and rock-processing plant at the far end of the beach.

One freezing bright day, Gerry had walked along the pebbles, dusted with ice, the sea crackling in through a heavy mist, towards the quarry. Monk's old lady, Modesty, hadn't seen him for several hours, and had begun to worry.

The sandy path up to the wrecked offices was normally slippery, but the small stream that flowed over it was frozen higher up. The mud had rutted hard and gave an easy climb. The metal supports of the main shed were exposed and thrust sharply at the air. A light wind whistled through them, bringing a variety of pitch and resonance. Far below him, Gerry could just see the beach, speckled with vast logs from the summer storms. In the corner of the cove, the skeleton of a basking shark lay stark and white, sea-weed draping itself lovingly around the bones.

Far away, at the edge of seeing, a small group of brothers were riding their hogs round the pillars of the jetty, the wind bringing the thin note of the engines to his ears. Shrugging his denim jacket up round his neck, Gerry climbed inside the frame of the building.

Inside, all the noises were cut off. Red rust dripped silently from the rotting roof, splashing on the blown sand. The only movement in the emptiness came from the flapping, loose corner of a faded picture, stuck to a sheltered wall. Stained by time, it was still recognisable as a portrait of the anguished figure of Jacqueline Bouvier Kennedy, her pale dress stippled with the blood of her assassinated husband.

In front of the picture, like a daemonic altar, lay the red-frosted hulk of an old engine, the product of a crash years before between the manager's car and a loaded ore lorry. When the quarry closed down, the smashed engine had been left behind, coated with the crystals of time, a useless ornament in a dead landscape.

Gerry peered about this drowned world, looking for Mick Moore. Finally, he spotted a hint of movement, high among the thick girders, near the only window in the shed. 'Monk! Monk!'

The eyried figure made no movement. Sighing with irritation, Gerry swung agilely up into the maze of beams. He climbed towards the solitary man, noting in passing how fit he felt, despite their winter exile. Finally, he reached the side of Monk, and stood with him, gazing into the depths of the cliffs, down into the white water and sharp rocks.

Neither spoke. Finally, it was the younger man who turned, the wind plucking at his long hair, blowing it across his face. He raised a hand to push it out of his eyes and grinned at Gerry.

'Hello Wolf. Nice up here, isn't it?'

Before he answered, Gerry reached in his pocket and pulled out a battered joint. Hand-rolled. A few months earlier, the Government had yielded to liberal pressure and taken a faltering step towards the legalisation of marijuana. Under strict licence, one manufacturer had been given permission to market a branded line of cigarettes. There were rigid controls over any advertising, and the new line – named Rainy Day Women by some sharp young merchandising executive – was launched. But, there was one thing wrong with them. The amount of dope in them was minimal, and it wasn't even good quality grass at that.

It came from Government farms in Southern England and gave about as strong a buzz as dried banana skins. It became known as Berkshire White, and the cigarettes were called Enids, to indicate the contempt of the users.

So, the scheme failed, and everyone went on using the old illegal stuff.

'Modesty said she thought you'd be up here.' There was a question implied in the statement.

'Silly cow. She's worse than my old lady used to be. My mother that is.' There was a brief silence. Then, he went on to answer that implied question. 'You want to know why I come, don't you. Well, Gerry, I'm pissed off. We seem to have been stuck here, freezing our balls off for bloody years. I tell you, I'm about ready to pack it in and get away.'

'What would you do?'

Mick took a long slow drag at the joint, holding the smoke deep in his lungs. Then he expelled it, watching it circle away into the cold air. 'You'd laugh. I haven't told anyone about it; not even Modesty. I thought I'd pull a job and get some bread. Then, I'd straighten up and buy a shop somewhere. Maybe in Birmingham. A head shop, with a bit of magic and some science fiction. I've even got a name for it. I thought I'd call it "Agaric", after the mushroom.'

Gerry thought before he replied. 'I think it's a nice idea, Mick. Very nice. Going straight. I've thought about it during this winter, as well. But, I keep thinking about spring, and going on runs again. All together. No shit from anyone. Nobody hassling us. Spring's nearly here. Something's bound to come up. If it doesn't in the next week or so, then we'll go looking for it.'

Monk grinned. 'You're a clever bastard, Gerry. You're a fucking manipulator. You know that people fall for your freedom and the open road crap. Even me. But, there's a lot of aggro building up.'

Gerry started to swing down towards the sandy floor, and stopped half-way. 'Who from? I know the women are getting their knickers in a twist, but I reckon that'll pass. Who else?'

'Some of the Welsh. They used to like being the Wolves. They didn't mind too much being The Last Heroes and Wolves. But, they aren't the happiest brothers about being back to the Last Heroes again.'

Gerry spat. 'Shit! I thought it was that. Gwyn's been quiet for a couple of weeks now. Relapsed into bloody Celtic mysticism. Christ! The Last Heroes are years older than the Wolves, and I even put it to the vote. I'm the President, and I could have pushed it through. The majority voted for the name change back to the Last Heroes.'

'Yeah. But it wasn't much of a majority. And now they think they might split.'

Gerry dropped the rest of the way to the floor, cursing as he banged his ankle on a hidden splinter of metal. 'All right, Monk. Thanks for letting me know. I reckon we're going to have to get some action going, to take their minds off all this. Maybe a run in a week's time. We could go to a rock concert – something like that. Come on, let's get back for some dinner. Maybe God will send us a good fairy to give us some action.'

'Get your hands off my mohair suiting, sweetheart! I tell you I knew Gerry a year or so back. I was even in the quarry with him. And I knew Vincent and Kafka and ... and Rat. My name's Rupert Colt, love. If I might coin a phrase quite stunning in its originality, would you please take me to your leader?'

The small publicity man was finally hauled down to the village, where the Angels were just finishing their mid-day meal. Two of the Welsh brothers brought him in – Cyllell and Bardd – the latter holding a large porcelain pill-box.

'This poof reckons he knows you, Wolf. I think he's a pusher. Look at this bloody big box. There's speed for you. He's a dealer.'

Rupert wriggled in the grasp of the big Angel. His silvered shades had been knocked crooked in the struggle and his voice was shriller than usual. 'Gerry baby, good to see you. Get this gorilla to put me down and give me back my uppers and downers.'

Gerry grinned at the familiar face. And voice. He waved his hand at Bardd, and Rupert was unceremoniously dropped by the fire.

'Nice to see you, Rupert. To see you, nice. Give him back his little helpers. Sit down, mate. If you'd been here a few minutes earlier you could have shared our sumptuous repast of sausages, beans and baked potatoes. As it is, I can still offer you a few cast-off skins. No? How about a mug of coffee and a shot of Comfort?'

The small man grasped eagerly at the chipped blue and white mug of coffee, nursing it to warm his fingers. When one of the mamas brought in a cup of the thick, amber, peach-scented liquor, he drained it in one, feeling its warmth seep into his stomach.

'Jesus H. Christ, Gerry. This is one hell of a place to find; you know that? I left my Impala about a mile away at the top of those fucking hills. I've nearly ruined my best boots climbing down here.'

Brenda had joined them. Although she had disliked him at their first meeting, he had tried to make the film venture work, and had gone out on a limb after the slaughter in the quarry to try and convince the media that the massacre had not been the fault of the Angels. Now, Brenda was more prepared to be tolerant to the little man.

She sat down, stretching her long legs out towards the crackling fire. She wore a thick sweater under her blue denim jacket, and jeans tucked into the top of thick-heeled boots. The leather was whitened by the salt air, and steamed in the warmth of the blaze. She refilled Rupert's cup of Southern Comfort.

'Nice to see you again, Rupert. What can we do for you?'

He brushed dust off his coat and grinned at her. 'Straight to the point, eh, Brenda? Right. You get papers down here? Then you've seen about the rock tour that ran into a spot of trouble?'

A group of the other Angels had come into the room and stood leaning against the walls. At the words 'spot of trouble', one of them laughed raucously. It was a tall, slender figure, with white hair pouring icily over broad shoulders. A stark, pale face, with mad, red eyes gleaming like twin rubies set in polished bone.

Gwyn.

'Wolf's told us about you, Rupert. You've got a hell of a bloody nerve coming here and talking to us about having your "bit of trouble". Over a hundred dead and injured. Jesus!!' He whistled his admiration. 'You think big, boyo, if that's only a bit of trouble. What the hell would you call having a *lot* of trouble?'

Rupert looked serious. 'How about a rock tour without any kind of security? Is that big enough for you?'

This time it was the voice of Kafka. One of the oldest of the brothers, who'd lived through all the good old days; then the bad days of darkness and the underground life; now the days of the sun again.

'That isn't trouble. That's fucking suicide. For the groups and for the money men.' A thought suddenly struck him. 'Hey! Wait a minute, Rupert. You haven't come all the way up here just to show us your new coat and talk about the good old days. You cunning bastard! You and Rat could be brothers for sheer devious nastiness. Jesus! What a bastard!'

His eyes wide in bewilderment, Rupert turned to Gerry. 'Honest to God, Gerry, I don't know what...'

'Stop wasting your breath, my little mate. He knows why you're here. I know why you're here. You know why you're here. Some of these other brothers will have guessed as well. So, stop pissing us about and straight with us about this tour you've got coming up.'

Before he answered, Rupert opened his pill-box and tipped a handful of mixed colours into his palm. Following them down with a last gulp of Comfort, he knocked them all back. He looked round the low room, lit only by the flickering light of the fire. The plaster was chipped and missing in many places, exposing the broken slats. Graffiti smeared over the dirty walls, perpetuating the old jokes and the old myths. Many of them – the later ones – advocated activist politics for Wales, and they stressed the superiority of the natives against the English middle-classes that ravaged the land with their money and their second cottages.

At least one visitor from outside Wales had chosen to reply in verse. Not the usual ill-spelled poems that you find on walls, but a bitter summation of the troubles of the land, by a local priest and poet from Aberdaron – R. S. Thomas. Somehow, the bitter lines seemed the stronger, set among all the other trite scrawls.

There is no present in Wales,
And no future;
There is only the past,
Brittle with relics.

Then, someone had managed to rip through the next couple of lines, obscuring the words with a stump of burned wood. But, the last four lines could still be read:

Mouldering quarries and mines;
And an impotent people,
Sick with inbreeding,
Worrying the carcase of an old song.

Rupert looked back from the wall to the Angels ranged round the walls, many of them Welsh, and he wondered whether what he was going to ask was, after all, a good idea. These were not men of the nineteen-eighties, used to slick suits and the soft answer. There was a primitive violence and strength in the Angels. A strength that he needed to tap and try and channel for his own ends.

For a moment, he shuddered as he remembered going to a cold, white-tiled morgue in Birmingham to identify what was left of his old boss, movie maker Donn Simon. He'd tried to use the Angels. Things had gone wrong, and he'd misjudged the situation; expected them to act in a civilised way. And, they'd killed him for it. Brutally and savagely.

He drew breath. 'Well, Gerry. Right as ever, my love. I need your help, and I'm prepared to lay out a lot of bread to get it. We'll iron out all the little wrinkles later, but this is basically the idea. I've got this big tour coming up in a week or so, and I need some heavies. Some very heavy heavies.'

Across the crowded room, Gerry saw Mick Moore looking at him. They exchanged grins. This was going to be it.

4. I LAY TRAPS FOR TROUBADOURS
**An Extract from *There's No Failure Like Failure*
by Mark Olsen, published by Ortyx Press, 1998.**

Grab hold of the inside of your fluttering and heaving brains and latch onto one solitary Alcatraz idea. Security ain't just a lock on the door or a bolt on the shuttered window in the west wing room that's never opened. It's not fuzz on every street corner, making sure your too numerous progeny make it back from schoolies without being flashed at by some lonely old pervert with a fat gut and a bald head.

Security starts inside. It's what happens when the egg springs in the shell and the blue yonder comes rushing in with the Seventh cavalry. 'Never apologise, Mister; it's a sign of weakness.' And, God only knows, Big John Wayne knew about security if anyone did. But, the country was on the young side and God only came along for the ride.

Remember Woodstock? Holy Jehosophat; you're older than you look! Peace, love, beauty and a lot of lovely bread for those sweet innocent organisers. And for the record companies. And for the film-makers. And for you? Forget it, man.

Remember Altamont? Just another of those bitter days that the music died. I saw Satan dancing with delight. The Hell's Angels were dancing as well. On people's faces. Beating their skulls in with lead-loaded billiard cues. That wasn't the festival of peace that everyone hoped it would be. Maybe some of the people enjoyed it for some of the time.

You want to know one guy who didn't enjoy it? His name was Meredith Hunter and he was black. The Angels didn't like the way he looked so they outed him. Wiped him. Snuffed him. Made him defunct. Bye, bye, now baby, bye, bye.

Back in the white-cliffed palaces of England, it had seemed a good idea to use the Angels for security. Greasy kids' stuff. Their mothers used to wash their colours for them! That was the crack. But, they were kids. Fresh out of school with no future and precious little past. So, that meant that life was for now and for living. But, they were still a little on the light side, compared with the San Berdoo heavies. Too many of them rode forty-nine c.c. Hondas, instead of the big Harleys. Electra Glide in pale pink.

It worked well to use them to keep back the mob in Hyde Park. So, why not still use their American brothers at the Altamont Festival? Now, you know why not.

Because the American Angels were the greasiest, dirtiest, meanest, heaviest mother-fuckers since the Mongol hordes took apart half a world.

Now, a new tour – in England this time – and again the Angels were called. But, this time it was different. The boys had grown up into men. And what happened? Everybody knows.

5. THE HIGHWAY IS FOR GAMBLERS

So, it came to pass that the Angels agreed to help out with Rupert Colt's rock tour, acting as the security cover to a million pounds worth of stars. The package was arriving secretly – for secrecy was the key to all the publicity. The only man in England who knew what groups were coming over was Rupert Colt. And the promoter. The man who put up all the money. Not even Rupert knew who that man was. He got all his instructions either by letter or by phone call. To get in touch with the man, Rupert had to go through a tortuous web of intermediaries – the front-man was Albert Donegan.

The press were going crazy trying to find out who it was that would be headlining. One paper's aging pop correspondent had suggested that it just had to be Elvis, at last making the return from the grave his fans had always promised. But, as usual, it was Mick Houghton who got nearest the truth. In his regular column in *Rolling Stone*, he said : 'The mix of middies and teenies has proved so successful in the last few months that it's bound to be repeated in this "Magical Mystery Tour". So, that means someone for the old and someone for the young. Despite all this facile concealment, there can only be two possibilities.' And he named them.

Rupert, of course, denied the names. Then again, he was bound to really, wasn't he? Otherwise, all that carefully arranged secrecy was going for nothing.

The tour was due to open in Birmingham on March the first, then run to Glasgow on the second, Liverpool on the third, Cardiff on the fourth, Leicester on the fifth and two shows in London on the sixth and seventh. Single shows each night. Otherwise security was impossible. It wasn't getting the audience in for the first show. It was getting them out so that the second house could get in. There had been a fearful scene in Coventry when the first audience totally refused to move. Finally, the second house would wait no longer and stormed the theatre. Several people were killed in the ensuing crush, and nobody got to see the show. After that, it was once a night, one-nighters only.

The Last Heroes were due to appear at the press launch a couple of days before the tour. Rupert had discussed his plans in outline with Gerry and his inner council, but they had a final briefing in London, when they would actually meet the stars.

So, they had to get to London.

So, the best way was on a run.

When the Angels went on a run, they travelled in a surging convoy, weaving in and out through the traffic, sending the fear of God into the scurrying straights. The wind blew the wild hair of both brothers and old ladies, tugging at the frayed edges of their worn colours.

From the valley hideout, they had begun the run in high excitement. There had been a fantastic party on the night before, with music bursting out of their sound system. Oldies, from the great days at the end of the fifties and the beginning of the sixties. Holly and Eddy. Del and Gene and Chuck. Raves from even beyond the grave. Some precious forty-fives and some of the great revival albums from the nostalgia group of the seventies – the immortal ShaNaNa.

A mass of food sizzling over open fires - sausages, franks, beans, baked potatoes. Plenty of insulation against the freezing Welsh wind that would rip at them on the run. Booze and dope. Vodka and Southern Comfort, with speed, acid, coke, hash and, of course, Angel Dust. Monk had introduced them to the pleasures of mescalin, and Rupert had come prepared with some fabulous synthesised psilocybin. The chapter were heavily spaced-out and the party began to degenerate.

When they had wiped out the Ghouls in London in the previous year, there had been few survivors from the decadent outlaws. But one brother had not only survived; he had even managed to get adopted by the Last Heroes. That was the fat, smiling Shelob. A righteous from well-back – whose memory of runs and action went as far as Kafka. The two older brothers had become close, and spent a lot of time in each other's company.

That night they had danced together in the light of the fire, stamping at the springy turf. Moved doubled over, hands covering their crotches, shaggy and thick-set, like some dreadful Stone Age hunters, celebrating a ritual kill. They bellowed out the words of the songs, 'He rides through the jungle tearing limbs off the trees!!'

Despite his age and experience, Shelob had not yet been made a full-patch member of the Last Heroes. There had been a lot of opposition, particularly from a group led vociferously by Rat, but Gerry had decided that this would be the best time to initiate him. He still wore the faded silk and satin finery that had been the colours of the Ghouls, but these were now ritually stripped from him. It was Kafka, in his role as Sergeant-at-arms, who brought in the denim jacket and jeans, hard and stiff with newness, and laid them gently on the ground.

Slowly, to the applause of the rest of the chapter – those who hadn't crashed out – Shelob drew on the crackling clothes. On the back of the jacket was painted *The Last Heroes*, under a feral skull. Holly suddenly shouted: 'The fat bastard's got no marks.'

Shelob looked round and grinned at her. Without any humour in his smile. 'Right, bitch. I'm just about to get to tattooing. You can watch and fork yourself off on the blood.'

The reply brought a yell of approval from most of the brothers, who resented the female chauvinist attitude of Holly and Lady.

'Anyone got a little knife?'

Almost without anyone noticing, a slight figure was standing alongside Shelob, a glittering blade in its hand. A tiny, needle-pointed stiletto. An ideal weapon for a murder in the dark. A stabbing in the back.

'Thanks, Rat.'

The big man took the knife and moved nearer to the fire, so that he could see better for the delicate work he was about to do. Although it was a cold night, and he wore nothing but the new jeans and armless denim jacket, he was still sweating.

'Get back and give us a bit of elbow room. That's a bit better.'

Using the point of the knife, Shelob tattooed himself on the left forearm, pricking out the words *Last Heroes*, and the date. Pearls of blood oozed thickly down the arm, spitting into the smouldering edge of the fire. Some of the wood had turned to charcoal, and Shelob put the knife down and crumbled the ashes into powder. Then, grinning steadily into Holly's eager eyes, he rubbed the black ash into the bleeding wounds. Rat picked up the knife and passed him a dirty rag, thinly disguised as a handkerchief, to wipe off the surplus blood and ash.

Shelob proudly turned his arm about, so that all the brothers could see the clearly-marked letters and numbers.

'Bloody nice! What d'you want. A fucking medal and a testimonial? Let's get on with the initiation.'

The words had only just left her lips, when Gerry stepped forward and smashed Holly across the mouth, throwing her on her back into the fire. Cursing through the blood bubbling on her lips, she rolled away and stood up, brushing the sparks from her denims.

She wiped the blood from her mouth. 'What the fuck was that for?'

Gerry smiled thinly. 'You want to split and form your own chapter, then you go right ahead. If you don't then you ride with us and you obey the chapter rules like everyone else. Those rules say that only a President runs an initiation. Not any jumped-up little scrubber who wishes she'd been born with a prick. Right?'

Holly stood silently. Gerry was aware of a slight movement behind him. Without turning round he said: 'If your dyke lover moves another breath, I'll personally take you both apart. You stupid cows!' His voice was thick with his anger and contempt. 'You play around with kids and old men and that makes you tough. You plate each other and that makes you able to live without men. All right. But, don't try to play with men. Because you'll get hurt.'

Another woman's voice. Hard, with a silken touch of menace that probably only Gerry recognised. Brenda's voice. 'Cool it! Holly, Lady! Don't try anything with Wolf.'

The moment passed and the tension went. Gerry breathed a sigh of relief to himself. For a moment there he had thought that Holly and Lady might both move against him, and he wasn't that sure he could take them together. He'd seen them in action and they were lethal. Totally ruthless against men. Cripplingly effective.

After the interruption, the ceremony went ahead as planned. The details aren't for the squeamish. The idea, you see, is for the full-patch prospect to show that he is so in tune with his brothers (and sisters) that he is prepared to undergo any humiliation at their hands. Endure any discomfort. Be ready to subdue himself to any ruling of the President and a majority of his brothers.

So, Shelob, late of the Ghouls, skull fighter, survivor of an unprecedented seven ton-plus wipe-outs on his hog, came to the Last Heroes. He lay on the ground on his face, hands and feet stretched out like a Saint Andrew's Cross.

Gerry, who had been drinking heavily ready to play his part, stepped up first and took the honours as President. He unzipped his trousers and urinated over the prospect's back, shoulders and legs, reserving a little for the last to spray into

Shelob's hair. Kafka came next and showed great class by putting his fingers down his throat and flashing a nauseous mixture of partly-digested food all over his friend's colours, christening them in righteous Angels' fashion.

The rest of the brothers followed, Gwyn emptying a large slop bucket of excrement over the prostrate figure. Shelob won a lot of praise for not moving a muscle, or saying anything as he was drenched in the filthy, stinking mixture. Once all the brothers had finished, it was the turn of the old ladies and the mamas. But first it was Brenda, Holly and Lady.

Gerry had seen them whispering on one side, as they waited for their turn, and he guessed that Shelob was likely to pay a price for the insults that he had thrown at them. Sure enough, Brenda went first. She stepped up to Shelob, as he lay in the pool of excrement and vomit. And dug the toe of her boot into his ribs.

'Not like that, brother,' she said, unzipping her worn jeans. 'We ladies may be the weaker sex, like our President says, but we do like to see what we're doing. So, over on your back. Now.'

Shelob, his hair still rank with the proceeds of the initiation, his colours still showing damp patches – he would, of course, never wash them – led the front-guard of the run. By unanimous consent, he had been allowed to put up his wings from the Ghouls, and not show the class necessary to win them over again. He had all three – red, black and brown.

His bike was one of the big old Nortons, throttling up with a heavy roar that battered at the ears. The two other brothers who rode with him were Kafka on a 650 Yamaha and Ogof on a Bultaco-Metralla. Leading the way through the roads of the borders, heading east and southwards, towards London.

The rest of the pack were strung out about five miles behind, led by Gerry and Brenda, with Gwyn, his hair streaming like a mane of snow, screaming a Welsh folk-song at the cold Spring air. After them came the rest of the chapter, on an assortment of hogs. Gerry's chopper was the big Electra Glide, with Brenda on the Super Glide. Both Harleys were chopped of their extras, and both could get easily up to the hundred mark.

Back along the Lleyn, up into Snowdonia, then slowly through the Marches, towards Shrewsbury. Over the death-trap of Watling Street, through Weston-under-Lizard and Ivetsey Bank, until they reached the busy M6. Even the drivers of the heavy articulated wagons moved over when the Angels ran past. Most brothers carried lengths of polished chain, either round their waists or in special holsters snug against the tanks. Ready to snap off mirrors, shatter screens, or whip the flesh from the body of any driver stupid enough to anger them.

There were no outdated ideas of chivalry or fair-play among the Angels. Pick a fight with one of them and you pick a fight with all of them. As many poor bastards had found to their cost.

Picking up speed, and moving along with their heads free, the front-guard neared the service station where they had agreed to make a stop for fuel and food. The Watford Gap, just south of where the quiet M45 snaked in.

The three bikes peeled off onto the service area car-park, and rolled gently to a stop near the toilets, in a place marked *No Parking*. An elderly attendant came hobbling across, his voice raised in a querulous whine, which died away to a resentful mutter when he saw who the riders were.

'Anything wrong, uncle?' asked Kafka politely, but the old man turned away without any further fuss.

Shelob and Kafka paused a minute by their machines, making slight adjustments to the highly-tuned hogs. Ogof was in a hurry to get at the food and went leaping away towards the high, open bridge.

'That Welsh git'll have raving gut-rot if he stuffs any of this stuff down him too fast. Still, serve him right, eh. Finished Shelob? Come on and ... what the fuck? Come on!!!'

Above the rumble of the motorway traffic, Kafka's battle-trained ears had caught the faint sound of a cry. That meant aggro. That meant trouble.

Ogof had found the trouble, without even noticing it. He had run up the steep stairs of the bridge, and turned the angle at the top, to find himself barging into the middle of a crowd of more than a dozen skulls.

After the skinheads had their day in the early seventies, police and magistrates combined to stamp out hooliganism on the terraces at football and in the streets. But now, the steadily falling gates – the slump after England's pitiful failure to qualify for the ninety-four World Cup was never checked – dipped still more. George Hayes' rule as Home Secretary ended and the way was clear for more liberal men and women to ease many of his restrictions. These made life easier for all youth movements – including, of course, the Angels and it sparked off attempts to get the young back to football.

A hectic publicity campaign followed with discos, girls, films, better spectating arrangements and the cult of the individual player being built up. Also, many of the old best-sellers about skinheads were re-issued. And, the skulls were born.

Ogof barely had time to recognise what he was into. Young lads, mostly pale-faced with hair cropped so short that it gave their heads a curiously elongated look. They all wore faded and bleached jeans tight across the hips with white or pastel shirts. The most elegant had ruffled fronts to their shirts and sported embroidered waistcoats. Black high boots with metal-studded platform soles completed their get-ups. As it was still cold most of them wore either long jackets or the navy-blue 'Crombie overcoats of their skinhead forebears.

They too were on their way south to the lights of London. First Division leaders West Bromwich Albion, the team they supported, were playing in a fifth-round replay against the third division leaders Crystal Palace, managed for the third time by Mal Allison.

They had parked their Transit vans in the park and eaten their fill of burgers and chips washed down with the cheap wine that had become their cult drink. Now on their way back to their wheels there was a bonus. Something to whet their appetites on before they got to the real battleground at the Whitehorse Lane end of Selhurst Park.

A real live Hell's Angel.

Better than that. A real live alone Hell's Angel.

Ogof was still running forwards when the first fist hit him. It was a straight right to the face cracking solidly on his cheek just under the eye. He was brought up short in his tracks by the force of the punch. He had just the time to get out one yell for help when they were all on to him.

No weapons were out – with a dozen to one there really wasn't any need. A boot caught him in the groin, crushing and pitching him forward in retching agony. An elbow hit just behind the ear knocking him to the ground. Ogof managed with a superhuman effort to get to his knees but another battery of kicks smashed home in his kidneys and back, throwing him face-down on the dirty concrete.

Kafka and Shelob arrived at the top of the bridge steps at the moment that the final furry of boots were thudding in. So many of the skulls were eager to take advantage of the opportunity to get at their bitterest enemies that they were even kicking each other in the confined space.

Ogof had rolled into the street-fighter's defence position, legs together and knees pulled up, with the elbows in tight over the ribs. Head tucked in and hands over the ears. The trouble with that is that it only provides minimal cover for a short time. In only a couple of seconds most of his fingers had been smashed with kicks and the stabbing metal-tipped heels were getting through to his neck, head and body. His life was saved by the appearance of Kafka and fat Shelob, bursting on to the scene like a couple of primitive demons of anarchic violence.

There had only been time for a flung sentence of tactics from Kafka. 'Get 'em off and hold 'em till the others get here!'

That's right, old brother. The rest of the pack are speeding nearer, second by second at seventy miles an hour. They can only be a scant minute away by now. Then, like the avenging angels of doom, they would sweep in to the rescue, knocking the crap out of these vicious bastards.

Right!

No.

Wrong!

Pull up; up and away to the north. Look back over the miles of roadway, and you won't see the run. Not for nearly ten miles.

An efficient highway patrolman had heard the harsh note from one of the bikes – Dick the Hat's Yamaha. He flagged them down and pointed out the offending silencer. All very friendly. Not like it had been once. The Angels played it straight – being good citizens. The cop kept his finger down on his radio, just in case.

They rigged up a silencer from a perforated can of peanuts, and then revved it up to show the boy in blue that all was well. A wave of the hand and they were off again.

But, minutes had been lost. And they were due to meet at the service station.

Gwyn yelling to Gerry, 'That sod Ogof will have eaten the place as empty as a Tory Treasury.'

'Right. And Shelob will have licked up all the bloody crumbs.'

Brenda overhearing: 'One day those fat bastards will bite off a bit too much for them to chew.'

Still seven miles away. Not even at the A5 junction yet. Six minutes away.

After the Carradine cult of the mid-seventies, Kafka had got very into Kung Fu, enjoying the mixture of lethal brawling and Oriental mysticism. Now, he launched himself at the gang of skulls like a two-fifty pound bird of prey. Sad to say, at that moment, he forgot all the basic ideals of humility of Kung Fu, and merely wanted to knock the shit out of the scum.

He leaped head-high, feet-first, cracking into the mob. His right foot struck one of the kickers cleanly on the base of the head, snapping the neck like a dry branch. The skulls scattered like chaff before a winnower, and the violent whirlpool about Ogof was stilled. The Angel lay still on the floor, only his head moving slightly, a thin mewing coming through the dark blood that ran from his pulped lips.

Kafka landed awkwardly, but still cleared the whole bunch and so had no problem about protecting his rear. Behind him, the bridge was clear of people, except for a middle-aged school-mistress who had slumped in a faint.

A fine rain began to fall, misting the fighters on the open bridge. The skulls were just getting to their feet and readying their charge on Kafka, when Shelob – silent-footed for such a big man – took them from the rear. There was none of the subtlety of Kung Fu for Shelob. None of the 'brushing of the grasshopper's wing can be more deadly than the thunder of the tiger's claws'. With Shelob, philosophy was always a simple matter. Get there first and kick the crap out of them before they do the same to you.

He dived with his meaty shoulders at the nearest of the skulls, who was still off-balance from the savagery of Kafka's attack. The thin boy was bashed sideways, tripping over his own boots, until his head hit the bridge wall with a sickening crack. Blood and brains stained the ridged concrete.

Two down and ten more to go. Kafka and Shelob faced the group of skulls, ready for the next attack. A handful ran together at the Angels, two swinging rubber coshes. The melee was short and savage. Three of the skulls withdrew, leaving two of their number stretched out on the bridge. One had a broken arm, and lay whimpering until a kick in the face from Kafka shut him up. Permanently. The second had received a stiff-fingered jab to the head that had crushed his nose and impacted splinters of bone all through his face.

Shelob held a third in a bear-like grip, heaving him up off his feet. The skull screamed in panic, flailing helplessly at the big man. Blood ran from a deep cut in the Angel's scalp, but he ignored it, shaking his head to keep his eyes clear.

Slowly. Very slowly. Shelob hefted the skull above his head.

'No! Mother of God!!'

'Is this the end of Rico?' muttered Kafka irrelevantly.

The rest of the skulls stood paralysed by this scene of potential and actual death. Except their leader – a short skinny man whose cropped hair showed signs of curliness – who fumbled under his crombie.

The rain had stopped as soon as it had begun and a watery sun glinted down on the motorway and on the bridge and on the bodies and the trickling blood. And on the gold ear-ring worn by the leader of the skulls. And on the double-barrelled sawn-off shotgun in his hands.

His voice was surprisingly quiet. 'Put him down you gross fat bastard.'

But it carried along the few yards of bridge above the motorway rumble. Above the faint far-off whine of a large number of highly-powered hogs.

Shelob looked at the smaller man and grinned contemptuously. 'You want your mate put down? Right!'

With a heave of his powerful shoulders he swung the limp figure up and over the parapet of the bridge where it crashed down on to the road thirty feet below.

You know those plastic blocks – clear plastic – where you can freeze things forever? Bits of watches or flowers. Trapped for eternity. That was what the scene was like on that bridge for a split second. Nobody moved.

On the road many things were happening. Roland Hall, his wife Ruth and their children Scott, Tracy and Tarquin were roaring up the middle lane at sixty-nine miles per hour. Maximum speed for their old Austin 1100. They had Trini Lopez blaring away on the stereo cassette. Ruth was just handing round a bag of jelly babies.

That was when the skull dropped in on them.

He hit the bonnet of the car with his right arm which broke instantly with the impact. Next, as the arm crumpled, his head was smashed into and through the windscreen. The speed of the car coupled with its mass and momentum meant that the skull's neck was severed on the edge of the splintered screen.

Ruth Hall had time to scream as the severed head dropped in her lap, straight on the Iris Murdoch novel she'd been reading splashing blood all over the bag of jelly babies.

Unfortunately there wasn't time for anything except that one scream. Roland lost control of the car as the body hit it and it swerved inexorably sideways towards the apparent safety of the hard shoulder. In the way was a Continental juggernaut loaded with thirty tons of imitation dog turds.

So the Hall family went sailing into eternity buried beneath a mountain of "Naughty Fidos". The lorry went into the crash barrier (which was only designed to take the impact of a heavy vehicle at a maximum of ten miles per hour) and bounced back into the three streams of traffic flooding northwards. It would be tedious to list the multiple pile-ups that followed with cars and lorries spread over all six lanes and both hard shoulders.

Everyone knows that drivers go too fast too close. So, when something cataclysmic happens, then everyone buys it at the same time.

The Last Heroes were now only a couple of miles from the service station. Still hitting better than eighty.

Up on the bridge, things were happening. The slim leader of the skulls, the one with the golden ear-ring, watched his mate go over the bridge. Perhaps he never really believed that Shelob was going to do it.

Once it was done, the skull smiled, his lips whitening over his stained, rotting teeth. The shotgun was steady on the unmissable target of Shelob's guts. His finger tightened on the trigger. Squeezed slowly.

The spring was released and the hammer sprang forward that crucial fraction of an inch, making contact with the percussion centre of the cartridge. The shot exploded out in a star pattern. Shelob was a dozen feet away, and he was a hell of a big man, but the impact lifted him clean off his feet, and threw him on his back. The slugs would have cut through a thinner man. As it was, they demolished his stomach and spread his intestines in shredded pulp throughout his lower body.

If you're gut-shot by a powerful shotgun at short range, you don't live long. The hole in the front was comparatively small, yet the blood gushed from it as though tired of occupying the same body for so long. Shelob scrabbled at the concrete with his fingers, trying to get up and rend the man who had killed him. But, it was too late.

He sighed and turned his face towards Kafka. His mouth opened and he tried to speak. But, his brain failed him and he died. Mute.

The skulls' leader maintained his thin smile. 'I always said these Angels had no guts.'

His friends laughed dutifully. The nervous laugh that so often follows a sudden shattering shock. Like seeing one of your mates thrown to his death off a motorway bridge. Or seeing a human being murdered with lead pellets in front of you.

Three quarters of a mile back to the north, the Last Heroes had just run into the tailback from the massacre at Watford Gap. Gerry scented trouble and revved past the lines of stationary vehicles. Those brothers who could, followed him.

Ahead, at least one of the crashed lorries had caught fire, and the screams of the trapped driver could be just heard above the other noise.

A large tanker carrying concentrated sulphuric acid had been dented and was spilling its load in a flood of fuming death towards the rest of the shambles. A vicar was making his way through the tangle of metal, getting in everyone's path, when he walked straight into the stream of acid.

The soles of his shoes immediately began to dissolve but he felt no pain and walked deeper into the liquid. Only when his shoes had gone and his feet were beginning to burn did he suspect what was happening. He yelled out for help and tried to hop back. but his soles were burned through and he finally fell full-length. Nobody could get near enough to drag him out and he rolled and splashed for over a minute before dying.

Kafka saw his brother die and saw the skull laughing. There was another barrel left and, presumably another round to be fired. At times like that, you don't weigh the odds and decide what seems the best course of action. Kafka was hardly aware of the shouts and crashing going on below him on the motorway. Not even of the cloud of choking smoke that was billowing about from burning cars and lorries. All he was aware of was Shelob's death. A yell began, deep in his chest, and he moved at the surviving skulls, hands groping for necks to break and flesh to tear. Particularly, he wanted the leader.

In fiction, he would have made it, perhaps getting injured on the way. But, he would definitely have taken some of them with him.

So much for fiction. The skull with the ear-ring merely moved his aim and pulled the other trigger. The shot caught Kafka in the centre of the chest and smashed him against the wall like the hand of a berserk giant. Blood spouted from his mouth and his eyes closed with the shock and the pain.

The skull calmly put the gun back in the holster under the smart crombie and beckoned to his mates. They were off the bridge and back in their transits in seconds, and away down the clear southwards lane off the motorway.

Ogof? He's dead as well. How? Bookie Wyatt – the man with the ear-ring, called Bookie because he once worked for three days in a bookshop – had bent down as he walked past the injured Angel and carefully slit his throat with a short knife – a throwing knife – he always carried.

The tangle of vehicles grew thicker as Gerry neared the service area, and he was forced to slow to a weaving crawl. The thick, oily smoke obscured the bridge, and the clear road beyond, and he was too late to even see the bright yellow vans rocket away.

Up on the bridge, Kafka lay still, trying to hold what was left of his chest together with crossed arms. Waiting for Gerry to arrive, so that he could tell him who it was that had done this to him. He was conscious of the smoke, and of the sparse rays of the sun piercing the gloom, lighting up the furrows in the concrete.

He rested his cheek against the rough stone, feeling it cool and slightly damp. Getting tired, he closed his eyes, and thought back into the past. Of the friends he'd seen wiped out. One of them – the tall, satanic Priest – murdered by a brother on this stretch of motorway. He remembered back to his older brother, killed on the Brighton road, way back when they were rockers and not Angels.

Kafka was not in much pain. There seemed a large hole of numbness at the centre of his chest, and breathing wasn't easy. A little blood still frothed to his mouth as he breathed in shallow bursts. It made it taste like the dentist's.

He knew he was dying, and he wasn't sure that he minded. Kafka was old, an ancient by Angel standards, actually the wrong side of forty. Now, so many of his friends were dead, and the times had been a-changing for too long. If he'd have gone on, he'd have been a boring figure, constantly looking back to what he felt had been the good old days. But probably weren't. A long time seemed to have passed, and someone was shaking him gently by the shoulder. He tried to open his eyes, but it took almost too much effort. Finally, he opened them and made out a small group of figures, standing and kneeling round him. The smoke must be getting thicker, or it was already dark.

Gerry had his arm round his shoulders, and Brenda was wiping the trail of spittle and blood from his face. Their faces were blank with shock and anger.

Kafka smiled softly at them. 'Hello, Gerry. Brenda. Forgive me for not getting up to...' His voice faded away.

Gerry tugged at his arm. 'Kafka. Who?'

The big man looked vaguely at him. 'Who?'

'Kafka. Come on brother. Stay with us just a bit longer. Who did this to you and Shelob and Ogof?'

A coughing fit racked the dying man. 'Skulls. About a dozen of them. All tooled-up. One of them had an ear-ring. And a shotgun.'

There was no point in rushing off. If they'd gone, then they'd gone. But, there couldn't be that many gangs of skulls who got tooled-up with shooters. Nor many that had a leader who wore an ear-ring.

'There'll be time, mate. We'll find them. Don't worry about that.'

Again that gentle smile, sitting oddly on that ferociously-bearded face. 'Gerry, burn me hog. Please.'

His eyes dry, Gerry nodded his assent. Angels shed no tears for one another.

Brenda whispered to him, 'He's going love.'

Kafka peered painfully round at the growing circle. 'Tell you one thing I always dreaded. Snuffing some time when I didn't have me colours on. Still, this is all right. Isn't it?'

His body suddenly jerked. 'Christ! I wish it'd stop hurting.'

Even as he said it, it stopped and Kafka was dead.

6. THEY'LL PINCH THEMSELVES AND SQUEAL
An extract from the proceedings of the special Coroner's Court convened to examine the deaths at the Watford Gap Service Station, on February 26th, 1999.

Coroner: But, Chief Inspector, I am not entirely concerned with those unfortunates who died as a direct result of the road accidents. It seems to me, from the medical evidence we have had presented here, and from the mass of evidence we have heard from your own officers, that these deaths are not particularly mysterious. Would I not be right in saying that these people – with certain exceptions that I will come to in a moment – that these people died because they were driving too fast and were, therefore, unable to cope with the unexpected events?

Chief Inspector Simmons: You would be correct in saying that, sir. But, there were others who do not fall strictly in that category.

Coroner: I am aware of that. Indeed, I thought I had made that clear in my question. Having disposed of that, I would like to come to specifics. For instance, have your inquiries yet ascertained how the head – and only the head – of the young man named, let me see, Stokes; Desmond Stokes, came to be in the crashed car F, driven by the man ... Hall?

Chief Inspector Simmons: Yes, sir. We have a witness, a schoolteacher named Angela Shire, who was present for much of the fighting on the bridge, though she was only semi-conscious for some of the time. She says that one of the motor-cycle gang, we are not clear which, picked up one of the skulls, pardon me, sir, one of the other group of young men, and threw him over the bridge onto the motorway. His falling body struck the Hall's car, F, and we believe his severed head, amputated by the fall, came as a consequence to be in the Hall's car. We found what was left of the rest of his body nearer to the bridge.

Coroner: Apart from the youth's hand. I cannot be sure without referring back to my notes, but I recollect that one of the hands was not found.

Chief Inspector Simmons: That is correct, sir.

Coroner: How about the corpses that were found on the bridge? What evidence do you have on how they received the injuries we have heard about?

Chief Inspector Simmons: The left, sir.

Coroner: What?

Chief Inspector Simmons: I said, the left, sir.

Coroner: The left what?

Chief Inspector Simmons: The left hand, sir. That the youth Stokes lost. Or, that we didn't find.

Coroner: Chief Inspector; we have finished dealing with the affair of the missing hand some minutes ago. I would be more than grateful if you would lend a little more of your attention to the matters we are now examining.

Chief Inspector Simmons: Very sorry, sir.

Coroner: Very well. Now, I asked you how the young men who died on the bridge itself came to their ends?

Chief Inspector Simmons: Three of the young men with cropped hair, known as skulls, with an unknown number of their friends, were engaged in conflict with three members of the motor-cycle gang known as the Last Heroes. The three skulls – Griffiths, Morgan and Howell – suffered injuries during this brawl from which they all subsequently died.

Coroner: Can you form any opinion, bearing in mind the weight of the medical evidence, as to whether these wounds were inflicted by weapons, or by fists?

Chief Inspector Simmons: Although some of the wounds were extremely savage, I nevertheless came to the conclusion that they had been made without any extraneous implement being used.

Coroner: The most disturbing feature of this disaster seems to me to be the use of firearms by at least one of the main protagonists. What can you tell us about that?

Chief Inspector Simmons: We know that one of the skulls was carrying a sawn-off shotgun of the calibre mentioned in the pathologist's report. It seems that the Hell's Angels attacked the other gang, causing the injuries we have seen. In self-defence, one of them, quite wrongly, but, perhaps understandably, chose to use a gun to protect his life and the lives of his friends.

Coroner: Quite. Very wrongly. Do we yet know the names of the three motor-cycle hoodlums who were slain?

Chief Inspector Simmons: No, sir. The one with the throat injury was Welsh, and the other two were English members of their gang. Beyond the names Ogof, Sheila and Kaftan, we have no more information.

Coroner: Thank you, Chief Inspector. I am sure I speak for all decent members of society, when I say how unfortunate it is that so many upright citizens died as a result of this gang fight. We can only hope that there will be no repercussions of this. Oh, one last question. Did you manage to find how that one motor-cycle caught fire, so far from the scene of the other accidents?

Chief Inspector Simmons: Well, sir; all I would like to say at this stage is that our enquiries are proceeding, and that we expect arrests very shortly. My belief is that it was some kind of ritual. Sort of purging by fire. Obscene ceremony I reckon it.

Coroner: Thank you.

Chief Inspector Simmons: Course, it might have been a stray spark.

7. SO YOU WANT TO BE A ROCK AND ROLL STAR?

'Listen, man. I don't give a fairies' fuck what you think's a good idea. I'm telling you that we don't want any English kids playing round at being Hell's Angels as the security for this tour. I want professionals!'

Rupert let the fat man's tirade blow itself out, then tried yet again to explain the facts of stage security to him. 'Albert. I understand your concern, sweetheart. Truly, I do. But will you just take a tiny peek at that list I had one of my girls drawn up for you to peruse. It's every security organisation in the British Isles. It shows when I spoke to them and it gives the tone of their replies. None of them would even consider doing this tour. Not after what happened at the Sundance.'

Albert Donegan was not only the heaviest promoter of pop superstars, he was also the best. There was hardly a major name in the galaxy of magna-novas that wasn't under his protection and paid dues accordingly. Now, Albert was cross with Rupert Colt, his hired publicist.

'O.K. Rupert. How much did you offer them? Double it.'

A look of weariness and pain crossed Rupert's face. 'In the name of God, Albert, will you listen! How can you double nothing? I offered them twenty thou...'

'Dollars?'

'Dollars, schmollars. Pounds, Albert, pounds! They laughed. Times have moved on, sweetheart. The little girls who used to stir up the crap when the Osmonds or Cassidy came to this country were sweet babes of light, compared with some of these bitches. I tried to get Roscoe to take it on. He reminded me about the way he lost four dogs – Doberman Pinschers – when the bitches fed them acid. They all tripped out and he had to shoot them.'

'Yeah, but we paid him. What about Lunt? He ran cover for us on a tour a year or so back.'

There was a hollow sound from Rupert, that might almost have been a laugh. Yeah, Lunt. *He* reminded me about the last show – in Southampton. He hired eight of the toughest bastards he could find and gave them some special anti-riot truncheons. Fresh from Alabama. There was a lot of fuss in the Press when it leaked out about those truncheons. Remember how they were all found round the back of the theatre. The big tough guards. No clothes on. Tied up like turkeys. And, remember where those monsters had put those truncheons. No, forget about Lunt. Forget about Roscoe. And Blount And Copland. And Biggs. All of them.'

'Can't we offer something to those old guys again?'

'Jesus!! Our last insurance company'll be paying off for centuries after the Sundance. No, Albert. I promise you on my knees that the Angels are our best bet. Our only bet. And, we'll get some mileage out of them.'

Donegan tugged himself breathily to his elegantly shod feet and walked to the window of his suite. From behind the white lace curtains, he gazed unspeakingly across the snaking traffic, into the green depths of the park. Visibility was cut by the fine, cold rain that sheeted down from the west.

'My God, Rupert. You know this fucking country better than I do. You've lived here. Does the sun ever shine?'

'Sometimes. Round about the tenth of August to the twelfth. Miss it and that's it for the year.'

The temperature in the room was over twenty-five, but Donegan still shivered. 'I've seen some of the girls. Pale little thin things. The record company laid them on for me, and you know me, Rupert, I never like to offend anyone, so I let them stay. It was like screwing with a xylophone. All bones.' He drained his brandy glass and walked to the decanter for a chunky refill.

'Your trouble, Albert, is that you wish they all could be California girls.'

Donegan missed the allusion and nodded seriously. 'Damn right, Rupert. Did I tell you I'm not staying for this tour. Me for the Big Sur and a bit of sun.''

Rupert's jaw dropped at the bombshell. 'If you just fuck off, then who runs the show?''

Donegan grinned round his cigar. 'You do, Rupert.'

'And who carries the can back when the shit overflows on the table?'

'You.'

'Forget it.'

'Now, now, Rupert. Don't get your frilly nylon panties in a twist. I'm doubling your money.'

'Double?'

'Right.'

A long silence, while the computer that had replaced a brain in the head of Rupert Colt whirred and clicked. Finally, it came up with an answer.

'Treble.'

'Done. But, there may be one small problem. Freddie Dolan has his own contacts with the American Angels. We may have a little trouble there. But, I figure I can handle it. Tell you what, Rupert, baby, you get your man along here for breakfast at nine tomorrow, and I'll get Freddie here as well. I promise you, there'll be no hassle.'

'No way! No way!'

The table in the hotel was laid with a full breakfast. A crystal jug of fresh orange juice, jostling a tureen of steaming porridge. Silver chafing dishes stood in military rows, with devilled kidneys, thick-cut ham, golden fried eggs, sliced tomatoes, kedgeree, smoked haddock, pork and beef sausages, crisp fried bread – even baked beans for those with more ordinary palates. Toast racks spiky with thick and thin slices of bread, and small dishes of farm butter and jars of assorted marmalades. Silver pots of boiling coffee stood untouched on warming plates.

Rupert had nibbled at a slice of slimming biscuit and poured himself a cup of black coffee, which he hadn't even raised to his lips.

Albert Donegan had breakfasted on three Dexamyl capsules, three Ritalin, five Preludin and a handful of Dexedrines. Washed down with orange juice. 'You get the Vitamin C this way,' he explained.

Freddie Dolan had arrived late and refused to eat anything, worried about maintaining his lean and hungry look. All he had taken was a mixed assortment of Albert's uppers.

Gerry had been there on time. The rest of the inner council of the Last Heroes were breakfasting downstairs – some sixty floors below. The remainder of the chapter had gone back to their old headquarters in Hertfordshire – once a missionary training centre, and the war-time H.Q. of the Special Operations Executive. There they had found a colony of squatters moved in and well-established. There had been a few moments of tension, but an acceptable compromise had been reached.

The squatters had been pressured by a band of heavies controlled by Harry Hudson, and they were expecting another attack. In return for food and shared shelter, the Angels would give the unspeakable Mr. Hudson and his mob a nasty shock.

The prospect of some action cheered up the chapter, depressed by the sudden loss of three of their most popular members. Cochise had been promoted in Kafka's place, and Deintydd had moved up through the Welsh echelons. Life went on.

There were two pressing problems on Gerry's mind as he rocketed up in the lift that morning. One was the coming tour and what was going to be expected of him and his brothers. The other was how he could find a band of skulls led by a small man with a gold ear-ring. But, that would have to wait for a time.

Not too long, though.

Of the four of them in the hotel room, only Gerry had eaten anything resembling a normal meal. Fruit juice, porridge, at least one of everything from the chafing dishes, plus several slices of toast, thickly smeared with butter and lashings of marmalade. He was well into his third cup of coffee when Dolan burst in.

'No way! No way!'

Donegan waved his hands placatingly. 'Listen Freddie. Listen. I give you my solemn oath on my mother's grave that I've been all through this with Rupert last night and there's not a single alternative possibility that has any viability. No security firm will consider taking the job, so we have to fall back on amateurs. That means we have to make sure we have someone who's prepared to stand in line against the animals who call themselves fans. Gerry, here, leads just about the toughest bunch of men available. Now, what do you say. Huh. Freddie, baby?'

The skinny singer sat still in a deep chintz armchair, picking his nose and listening intently to the tranny ear-phone he had plugged in. Donegan might just as well not have spoken. His head stopped nodding and he opened his eyes and looked up at his manager.

'This bunch of pantie-waists couldn't fart their way out of a wet paper bag. Let me bring Rick and the Laurel Canyon brothers over. Ten of them could handle it better than fifty of these fags.'

Anxiously, Rupert watched Gerry for some sign of movement. He just carried on drinking his coffee. Not until the quiet had stretched uncomfortably, did he bother to reply.

'Dolan? How long has this chapter of yours been going?'

'Nearly two years. Why?'

'Because I know as well as you do that there wasn't a Hell's Angel left in the whole United States once Reagan got cracking on them. They didn't just go underground. They fucking vanished. Now, the Last Heroes have been up and running for round about fifteen years, with a charter that was signed personally by Sonny Barger. Despite all the shit we had thrown at us by the last Government, we kept together and we kept on riding.'

Throwing his radio on the floor, Dolan walked across and stood by Gerry. The Angel's President wasn't much above average height, yet the singer was several inches shorter.

'I don't give a flying monkey about that. All I tell you is that Rick and his boys would eat you alive.'

Rupert saw a chance to pour some of his unguent on the warming waters, and slipped in between the two men. He put an arm round a shoulder of each, and grinned confidently.

Well, treble money!

'Now, fellows. Come on. Freddie, I just ask you to believe that these boys are the very best I can get. It's them or the whole tour's off. Right? So, we can't get your friends over here in time for a tour that starts in just two days. Now, can we?'

Dolan shook his head angrily, and pulled away from Rupert's hold. 'For Christ's sake! This isn't the fucking Stone Age. Maybe they can't be here for the start, but the London gigs are going to be the tough ones. Right? So, I cable Rick now to come over here and get the lead out of his ass. He can be here with, say, fifteen brothers and their hogs by about the third.'

Behind Freddie's back, Gerry saw Donegan make a hand signal to Rupert, and the two men edged over to the far side of the room. Gerry was left grinning into space, three inches from the top of the head of one of the greatest rock stars in the world. The conversation, whatever it was about, took only a minute. Then, Albert came back, all beaming bonhomie and pep pills.

'Freddie, my little jean-creamer, Rupert and I have discussed your suggestion, and we think it may be workable. Gerry will run the security on the first shows on his own – well, with his boys. Then, when your amigos show up, they can split the job with Gerry. Say, fifteen of each chapter. Chapter? Is that the right word? How does that sound?'

Gerry grinned at the promoter. 'Fine. But it's going to cost you double.'

There was a muted grunting, as though a pig had choked on a turnip top. Donegan turned red in the face, and Rupert had to bang him on the back to try and clear his breath.

'Double! Double!! Double!!! You little schmuck! You cock-sucking limey bastard! Nobody screws me around like that. We're talking about taking work away from you and splitting the risk.'

Helping himself to another cup of coffee, Gerry waved a finger at the raging man. 'Temper, temper. That won't help anything. You're talking about halving the job. Fine. But, we've also been talking about how you have no chance on this earth of finding anyone else to smile and run your show. Not till these American Angels arrive. So, what do you do? You pay the price. All of us have paid our dues, love. Now it's your turn. Supply and demand. How far do you think this pimply streak of shit would get with nobody to save him from the little girls' knives? Eh? And, Rupert;

I'm ashamed of you. You've forgotten what it's like dealing with me. Tell you what. You agree – in writing – there'll be no mention of two gangs of rival Angels trying to prove who's top, and we'll do it for the flat fee. Otherwise, double. What's it to be?'

Donegan laughed flatly. 'I tell you right out, sir, I'm a man who likes talking to a man who likes to talk.'

Gerry looked puzzled. 'I'm sure I've heard those lines before. Funny. Never mind. Go on.'

'Very well. Double. We'll see you in Birmingham at nine-thirty sharp on the morning of the first March. Rupert will give you all the details of who's appearing. Oh, it includes Warsun, but they can't make it.'

Gerry nodded. 'Two groups is plenty to look after. Specially with superstar here,' pointing to Freddie Dolan who was back with his radio pressed to his ear, 'camping all over the place like a tart in a tantrum.'

Rupert took his arm and showed him to the door of the suite. 'Cool it, will you, sweetheart? Just for me. I'll see you're all right for the money. You do trust me, don't you? I mean there's no money problems. The tickets go on sale in about half an hour and they'll sell in minutes.'

Gerry turned in the corridor. 'Yeah, of course I trust you, Rupert. If you rat on us, I'll personally nail both your knees to the floor. See you in Brum.'

The tickets for all the concerts went as Rupert had predicted. The Sundance, despite the last disaster, had been chosen as the venue for the last show of the new tour – on the seventh.

In a pub nearby, a group of skulls were drinking happily, flashing the tickets they'd just obtained by waving knives at some young girls who'd been queuing for three days and nights. The leader of them strolled to the bar and ordered another round of vodkas. While he waited he unconsciously fingered his ear.

And his ear-ring.

8. ABOUT SOME USELESS INFORMATION

Publicity Notes for the Projected Rock Tour. Dates and further information available from Rupert Colt at the address and number below.
NOTE: We regret that Warsun will not now be available for this package. No replacement will be used. The two other groups will play longer gigs. We acknowledge the source material used here from *Rockary* by Harvey Barton, published by Ortyx Press, 1999.

WARSUN Ben Sidla (lead vocal and tambourine); Kes Murel (clarinet); Crisp Reece (organ); Jon Rennur (drums); Henrietta Slib (moog). Previous members: Nical Peters (bass); Jim Colvin (vocal and guitar); Ed Bradbury (drums).

WARSUN were one of the English groups who succeeded in cashing in on the mystic-rock revival in the mid-nineties. Their musical style was not unlike the earlier combo, Hawkwind. They had a big Transatlantic smash with the title track of their first album – *Flowers of Madnof* – which reached second place in British charts and third in the *Billboard* hundred. The science fiction writer, Mike Dempsey, produced some of their best material in the earlier months, but his involvement in the film world and tragically premature death from cancer has affected their songs. They have also been plagued by personnel changes. Once they can settle down, they should produce some better tracks and make a more consistent impact.

NOTE: Page three gave details of WARSUN's albums and single releases. This has been removed.

FOOLSGOLD Jak Whiteson (vocal and guitar); Pete Greane (vocal and guitar); Thom Wilder (vocal and guitar); Chris Kenyon (organ); Little Tommy Bowdesire (vocal and drums); Al Durer (vocal).

FOOLSGOLD are one of the newest and very, very biggest sensations around the pop/rock scene. Almost singlehanded they have built up the phenomenon known as the 'middies'. Middle-aged women go into orgasmic ecstasies at the sight of this extremely young group of boys performing. Underwear is often thrown on the stage by these women; psychiatrists suspect that there is often a strong mother-fixation involved. Mob scenes at the concerts of Foolsgold are believed to be worse than any with other contemporary group.

The boys, none of them older than fifteen, met at the Chester Goldsmith Seminary in Des Moines, Iowa, where their music teacher introduced them to the music of the legendary Blind Boy Grunt. Black blues inspired them to learn their instruments and start playing at junior proms. Record producer, Albert Donegan, happened to be visiting the College and signed them on the spot.

Each of their singles has scaled the topmost peaks of the charts, and they currently have all three of their albums in the top ten on both sides of the Atlantic. As long as the cult of the middies lasts, Foolsgold will also last.

ALBUMS

Foolsgold Now – Love Is Strange; Fools In Love; Goodbye To Love; True Love Is Forever; Poor Little Love; You're So Loving; Love Is Sweeter Than Candy; Mother Love; No Baby Love For Me; Teach Me About Love.

Foolsgold Country – I Walk The Line; Don't Take Your Love To Town; Long Black Veil; Nothing Was Delivered; The Night They Drove My Lover Down; Jackson; Dutchman's Gold; Two Little Boys; Lightning Express; Put My Little Shoes Away; Barbara Allen; It Doesn't Matter Anymore.

Foolsgold Glitters – Walk On The Wild Side; Big Man; Diana; Born Too Late; Bridge Over Troubled Water; Leave, Love, Live; Rave On; Every Day; In Praise Of Older Lovers; Go Now; So Long, Mama; We've Gotta Get Out Of This Place.

SINGLES

Fools In Love; Poor Little Love; Mother Love; Put My Little Shoes Away; Diana; Every Day; In Praise Of Older Lovers.

CENTRAL HEATING Freddie Dolan (guitar and vocal); Hal Marx (guitar and vocal); Jim Lawrence (guitar and vocal); Matt David (drums, moog and vocal).

This foursome from wind-washed Wisconsin erupted, or maybe vomited would be a better word, on to the stage about the same time the lovable Foolsgold came into prominence. It just wouldn't be possible to imagine two more disparate groups. Where the young boys wear clean white – admittedly rather tight-trousered – suits and sing light little ditties about love lost and love found, this foursome of old men (their average age is over thirty) sing songs about how screwing can give you the clap.

Mick Houghton described them as 'musical excrement' and he's not wrong. They have a devastating stage act that sends the young girls who make up most of their fans screaming into hysteric frenzies. They are as big and dirty as anything around, and their lyrics go with the looks. The name 'Central Heating' has a certain erotic ambiguity that is no accident.

Noel Coward had a nice song filled with advice for Mrs. Worthington. I would say: 'Don't even let your daughter anywhere near the stage, Mrs. Worthington.' Not when Central Heating is anywhere around.

They have roots back to Frank Zappa, and the Fugs, but the sound is way ahead of anything else. So are the lyrics, which are all written by the same man. Tall, thin, young, Adrian Moore. I wake up screaming in the night when I think about what he must have inside his head.

With long songs, full of sexual depravity, half-whispered and half-sung, Central

Heating may go on for a long time. I hope not.

ALBUMS

Central Heating – Little Liz Is The Biggest Turn-on I Know; Take It Out And Use It; My Tongue Can Creep In Anywhere; I'll Untie You If You Let Me.

Central Heating – Meat Injection – Sixty-nine Ways; Did You Ever Meet A More Cunning Linguist Than Me; Meat Injection; Wild Thing; Fumble And Squeeze; Let Me Press Your Button, Baby.

Central Heating – Rape Is Inevitable – Down On Me; Let Me; He'll Be Along Later; Your Mother's Not Going To Get It; I'm Not Superstitious.

SINGLES

Little Liz Is The Biggest Turn-on; Meat Injection; Wild Thing; Down On Me.

A separate hand-out is available on the security angles for this most dangerous of rock tours.

9. ON A TOUR OF ONE-NIGHT STANDS

Birmingham. The second city. In the fifties it was a true stronghold of all that was best about Victorian commercialism. Then the developers came along and ripped out the heart and the guts of the city. All the old sturdy red mansions of insurance and banking were torn down. Old roads vanished and familiar shopping areas disappeared from the face of the planet.

What came in their place? Roads. Just roads? Well, there were some shopping centres designed for the cave-dweller or the intrepid hermit. And some concrete blocks that were dirty before they were even a year old.

But, mainly there were roads. Cars ran everywhere, like mindless lemmings, speeding across and through and over and under. Gradually, people stopped coming into the very centre even for shopping. Shame, really.

Nice Pre-Raphaelite Art Gallery and one or two interesting shops. But, not at the centre. Mainly little places, for the specialist. The best record shop in Britain – the Diskery. And a combined head books and health food shop right at the top end of Corporation Street. The end that had still resisted planners' blight.

And a big new concert hall. Out to the north, near Perry Barr. A place that visiting orchestras came to; where poets read their works, and important political speeches were given. And rock groups came and did their own particular thing.

The Angels rode north from London in the early morning, when the sun crept unwillingly over the tops of the eastern trees, and morning seemed a long time a-coming. The hogs thundered through the misty stillness, mamas and old ladies clinging sleepily to denimed backs.

As they went past the Watford Gap, over the smoke stains and rubber burns, and patches of sand still on the hard shoulder where blood had been soaked up, Forty – Cochise's generously endowed old lady – let drop three single, long-stemmed, crimson roses.

Round the M6 into Birmingham as the rush-hour traffic was building to its shrill crescendo, and up on to the Walsall Road into the city. They reached the concert hall, angular and brooding, just before nine o'clock. Two police cars had picked them up – one at Intestine Corner and one at the Scott Arms junction – and followed them at a cautious distance to the hall.

Gradually, one by one, the brothers switched off the powerful engines, letting the distant sound of arterial traffic slowly filter through. Ignoring the fuzz, several of the

Angels strolled across to a wall, right by the cars, and unzipped themselves. The urine steamed in the cool air as it splashed on the bricks, and ran in an amber stream across the car park.

Riddler, one of the old Last Heroes, seized the chance to show a bit of class by walking to the side of the nearer car. Grinning amiably in at the two policemen, and urinating all over their front wheel.

The driver of the car was out in a flash (to coin a phrase) and started round with his hand hanging over the holster of the revolver that all motorway police now carried. Riddler stepped back a pace and one hand groped at the back of his belt, where he carried a short-handled axe tucked down his jeans.

At his side, Hanger John let his favourite weapon slide down into his hand, from up the sleeve of his jacket. A coat hanger, made of wire, twisted and sharpened until it formed a lethal weapon.

The potentially explosive tableau froze when another police car – a big White Jaguar – sprayed gravel as it dug on to the car park. Riddler, Hanger John, and the rest of the Angels froze. The policeman stopped half-way round his squad car and suddenly leaped to attention.

A tall man in a smart burgundy velvet suit got out of the Jaguar and strode up to where Gerry stood. He put out his hand and shook vigorously with the inner circle of Angels, acknowledging them all by name.

It was the same officer who had nearly succeeded in taming two chapters of Angels in the affair of the *Daily Leader*. The failure had not been his, but had resulted from crass stupidity on the part of the paper's owners. They had paid with their lives, and he had been cleared at the official inquiry. Then he had been Chief Superintendent Israel Pitman Penn.

Now he was Assistant Chief Constable Israel Pitman Penn.

'Hello, lads. Nice to see you all again. I bet you're a bit surprised to see me here again. Eh?'

Gerry replied: 'Glad to hear you're moving up in the world. Like the suit, too. Very sharp. Don't let it all go to your head, though, will you?'

The policeman smiled. With his mouth. 'I'll try not to, son. With you lot around, it won't be easy.'

Sidling round the fringes of the group, as usual, Rat added his contribution to the conversation. 'Shouldn't talk to us like that, now. Like, now we're members of a legally-appointed security organisation.'

The smile wavered, but Penn managed to keep it pegged in place. 'Not for the want of my trying to get it stopped, lad. This is my patch, and because the first of these happenings takes place here, I get lumbered with security liaison for the whole damned tour! So, we're going to be seeing a lot of each other for the next seven days. Gerry, I think you and I might get together for a cup of coffee after we've both had a chance to look out all the angles for this particular show. Right?'

'Right, Chief Superintendent.'

'Wrong, lad. Assistant Chief Constable now.'

Penn marched towards the theatre with a squad of his men. Dick the Hat began to whistle the theme music from *Bridge On The River Kwai*. Sometimes known more familiarly as *Hitler Had Only Got One Ball*. The rest of the chapter took it up, fitting the metre to the marching of the police. One of the sergeants tried to break out of step, but tripped inelegantly over his own feet. There was laughter.

Inside, the theatre had all the warmth and charm of a deserted public lavatory. Together, the police and Angels toured the entire building, sussing out likely trouble spots, and planning where danger was most likely to come. Under the Public Order Acts, Penn was unable to have men stationed within the theatre, but it was something of a relief to Gerry to know that there would be an unprecedented number of police outside, ringing the place.

'Nobody gets in without a ticket, and nobody gets in without, at least, a flash search by police men and women. And, we'll keep things cool outside. All you've got to do, my old son, is look after the valuable superstars inside. Got any ideas about that?'

Gerry grinned at the Assistant Chief Constable. 'Now, now, Israel. If I had and I told you, then you might not like them, and you might feel that you should do something to try and stop it. So, let's say I've got an idea or two, but I want to talk them over with the brothers first. Right?'

While the talks and the planning went on, one or two of the Angels had slipped away to get on with their own thing. Or things.

One of the results the city had achieved with its superb concert hall, was to cater for the class system. It was possible for the rich to rent boxes for a whole year, for an exorbitant price. The nearer to the Royal Box, and the centre of the action, the dearer it was. But, the Royal Box suite was sacred. It wasn't for Lord Mayors, or Dukes, or even for visiting Heads of State. By an overwhelming vote, the Council had agreed that it should be retained solely for the use of members of the Royal Family. That meant if you weren't a Prince or a Princess, then forget it!

Mick Moore had eased away from the main tour of inspection, taking with him his old lady, Modesty. Together, they had followed the discreet arrows that pointed the way to the Royal Box, until they came to a narrow corridor, guarded by a vast constable.

As soon as he heard them coming, he swivelled round on his size twelve heels, mouth open like a striker appealing for a penalty. 'All right; that's as far as you two go. This is private. So, bugger off.'

Monk said nothing at first, merely standing still where he was and looking up at the policeman. Then, when the man's neck had reached an agreeable shade of puce under his stiff blue collar, he finally spoke. 'My name is Monk and I'm the chief security officer in this theatre for tonight's show. And, what I say here goes. And I say that you go.'

'Why you cheeky young bastard. If you don't sod off in just three seconds, I'll really...'

'You'll really what? Listen you fat bastard; if I go down to Israel Penn, your fine Assistant Chief Constable, and tell him that constable 2875 is proving obstructive, what do you think he'd say? Eh? Or, if I told him that this same man, 2875, had threatened both me and this young lady. I reckon you'd be on permanent patrol in the enticement squad, hanging round public shithouses for the rest of your life.'

The red faded to a lighter shade of pale. 'Well now, look here! I mean. Blimey! I didn't know that ... that you were one of them. Is Mr. Penn here?'

'Very much so. Now why don't you sod off and let us get on with our job.'

Perspiration now damping his shirt, the constable eased down the narrow passage past them. 'Is there anything I can do for you, sir? Or for you, madam?'

Modesty smiled gently at his discomfiture, and reached up to straighten his tie for him. Her breasts, unrestricted by a bra, swung against his chest, hardly restrained by the thin denim jacket.

'Yes, there is one thing.'

'What's that, Miss?' His voice had gone up a couple of octaves with the strain.

Modesty softly pinched his ear-lobe between her finger and thumb, and tugged his head down, so that his ear was level with her lips. 'You could kiss my arse, if you really wanted.'

The colour returned to his face in a rush, and she thought for a moment that he would strike her. 'You filthy-mouthed little slut! If I had the...'

'Constable!' Monk's voice cracked out. 'Go and have a drink and snatch a bit of a rest. Off you go. We'll be all right up here. And we'll keep an eye on your Royal Box for you.'

Muttering under his breath, the fuzz stamped off, out of sight.

Giggling, Modesty grabbed Monk's hand and pulled him to the door. A blue velvet rope hung across the sacred portal, which she kicked casually out of the way. The door itself was unlocked. 'Aren't you going to carry me across the threshold? Come on.'

Bowing so low that his curly hair pitched about his face, Mick picked up his old lady and pushed sideways through an ante-room, with a door to their right, marked *Retiring Room* in elegant Gothic script. Ahead of them was the shadowy, plush interior of the Royal Box itself.

Still holding her round the waist, Monk let Modesty slide down until her feet sank into the deep pile of the maroon carpet.

'Neat, lover. Very neat. Almost peachy-keen. This is one hell of a carpet. It's like walking on a load of dead, skinned cats. Soft and clingy. Hey, what does "Retiring Room" mean?'

'A right regal shit-house. Here, have a look inside and see how the other half craps.'

A light came on automatically as the door opened, bathing the toilet in a soft, pink glow. Apart from the wash-basin and polished mirror, there were the closed doors of two stalls.

'All mod cons, baby.'

'I wouldn't like to use those crappers very much, Monk, you know.'

'Why not?'

'No sign on the door, to let you know whether they're vacant or not. Imagine bursting in on Her Royal Majesty, while she was ... well, you know. Very embarrassing.'

Monk laughed at the thought. 'Suppose you were in there and you were just on the verge of going. And you heard the Queen go into the one next door. I mean, it must be frightfully bad form to crap noisily when she's around. You'd just have to sit there and hold it, until she'd finished and gone. Hey, look at all this soap and everything. Fantastic.'

Modesty ran her fingers critically through her tangled and not-all-that-clean hair. At the side of the wash-basin were three virginal tablets of toilet soap, each with a different colour and each with a different scent. Modesty picked up each in turn, and sniffed at them. 'I don't think I like any of them. Give me a good old Pear's any time.

I like it when it's gone all transparent near the end.'

Monk was leaning against the door, laughing silently to himself.

'Hey what the bloody hell's the matter with you? What did I say?'

'Nothing, love. Nothing. It's just that it always makes me laugh when I see soap on a wash-basin, all laid out like that. Reminds me of Gerry's story.'

'Which one?'

'About the fat old bloke he used to have who taught him all that unarmed combat stuff when Gerry was in the army. You know, the one who had the awful wig they used to call his "dead rat".'

Idly turning the gold-plated taps on and off, Modesty smiled. 'Yeah, I remember about him. Gerry's got a bags full of stories about that bloke. I reckon he makes them up.'

'No, it's true. Anyway, this Sergeant Newman used to have his bathroom absolutely full of all sorts of medicines and special tooth-pastes for soft gums. All that crap. And, he used to have a big piece of soap. That strong, yellow soap. This Newman was very bald on top, and they used to reckon that his pubes must have been moulting as well. This soap was always covered in masses of pubic hair. One time, his C.O. came round on an inspection and he gave Newman a right rollicking over it. So, next time, the morning of the inspection, he gets the soap, and he *shaves* it! Honestly.'

Modesty began to giggle. 'So, what happened?'

'Well, Gerry had this mate called Gordon Krays, and he managed to get in to the quarters, before the C.O. came round. He had time to get a pair of scissors and cut off handfuls of his own pubic hair and stick it to the soap.'

Modesty had moved closer to Monk and was slowly running her fingers up and down the front of his jeans, feeling the swelling grow. 'That's class to do that. What happened?'

Finishing off the story, Monk responded to her touch, by slipping his left hand inside the denim top she wore, and gently caressing her breast, feeling the nipple harden under his fingers.

'In the end, it was this Newman bloke who had the last laugh. You see, the C.O. was very short-sighted and he'd broken his glasses. So, when he came in the bathroom, he saw this great hairy lump of soap. Of course, Newman couldn't believe his eyes, 'cos he knew he'd shaved the bloody stuff all clean. The C.O. peers at it, and asks him if he can explain it. Quick as a flash, he looks all upset and says: "That's Dinsdale." The C.O. looks at him. "Dinsdale," he says. "Who's Dinsdale?" "My pet hedgehog," says Newman. "He died this morning, and I put him there until I can bury him." Of course, the officer is a bit dubious about this load of crap, but he can't see properly, so he has to believe him and Newman gets away with it.'

By now they were in the dim depths of the Royal Box proper. The seats were stacked at the back, and the luxuriously carpeted area stood dark and empty. The two Angels had peered quickly over the padded balcony, making sure that neither the other chapter members nor the prowling police could see them. Then, they had slipped quietly to the floor.

Monk had his hand down the front of Modesty's unzipped jeans, his finger moving softly in the depths of her body. As he reached the end of his story, he had felt her muscles contract about him as she laughed.

Her jacket was open, and she moaned as he nuzzled on her firm breasts. Her hands sought him, stroking him to a hard readiness. She pulled his face to her, licking his face. Her teeth met on his lips, nipping hard, making him jerk back. But, she still held him, biting harder, until he could taste the salty hotness of his own blood.

Modesty wriggled her hips upwards, so that Monk could slide her jeans and pants down and out of the way. In his turn, he tugged down his jeans and rolled out of his colours, pitching them to one side. His hand reached up to the top of her thighs, feeling her ready warmth. She lay on her back, feeling the plush of the thick carpet tickling her skin. As he raised himself above her, she opened her legs, and used her hand to guide him into her.

Below them, as they thrust and panted to a mutual climax, Gerry and Penn walked the theatre together. Its modern design made it easier to protect than some older halls. Blocks of seats were cut off from each other by heavy partitions, and the nearest rows were still a good twenty feet from the high stage.

'I'm putting some of the meanest mothers in a row at the front here. There'll be four more on the stage itself, and half a dozen in reserve in the wings. Also, there'll be a few brothers, with most of the old ladies and the mamas mingled in among them.'

Penn nodded at the plan. 'Sounds fine. What about giving them a warning?'

'Rupert Colt's arranged that. There'll be a message printed on the front of the programme, plus special sheets handed out at the door, plus a fucking great poster that's going to be hung up there over the stage, before the show starts. And the compere's going to lay it on the line for them all.'

The policeman sat down with a sigh in one of the stalls seats. 'Who's the compere?'

Gerry grinned. 'Well, they are having what you might call a bit of trouble over their compere. After the Sundance killings, nobody seems that keen to get on stage in front of these little creeps and risk having his cock ripped off in the rush. So, I reckon it's not absolutely out of the question that it might be yours truly. Unless, of course, you fancy the job yourself?'

A slow shaking of the head was all the answer that question got.

Meanwhile, back in the Royal Box, events had just reached a satisfactory conclusion, though Monk had found it necessary to jam his fist into his old lady's mouth as her back arched with the strength of her orgasm, otherwise her screams would have brought every copper and Angel in the place running to the Box.

Modesty wiped between her thighs with Monk's colours, the stains making no noticeable difference to their filthy state. After they were both dressed, she led the way back out towards the main body of the theatre. But, before she closed the door, Monk took her arm.

'Wait a minute. Bit of unfinished business in there.'

And he walked back into the Royal retiring room, automatically lit by the dim lamp. Both the closet doors were still shut.

He raised his voice. 'I count three, then I kick these doors in and knock the crap out of anyone I find inside there. One ... Two...'

Before he reached three, first the right-hand door and then the left eased open. Round each door, two faces peered. 'Out! Come on, out here!'

Four young girls, the oldest who couldn't have been more than fifteen, walked nervously into the centre of the floor. They wore the traditional teenies' gear. Skinny, tight jackets of brightly-coloured cotton or silk, across their budding breasts, with either jeans or very short skirts. Spike-heeled shoes in shiny leather completed the outfits.

Their faces were thin and pale, almost entirely without make-up. The tallest spoke in a whining, nasal, Black Country accent. 'We didn't mean no harm, no road. We just wanted to get a chance to see Central Heating. The tickets went before we had a chance. Here, you're a Hell's Angel, aren't you? You won't turn us over to the fuzz, will you?'

Monk scratched his nose. 'I don't know. We're supposed to be in charge of security, you know. That means not letting kids like you four into this place.'

'They wouldn't know. Come on, be a sport. We all like the Angels, don't we?' Three heads nodded in unison.

Monk pretended to be considering their request. 'Just how much do you like Angels?'

Blank incomprehension. 'What do you mean, "How much"?'

'I mean what would you be prepared to do for me, in return for me not ratting on you?'

'Like sex? Anything you like.'

Monk winked at Modesty. 'All right, then girls. I want each of you, in turn, to blow me. Come on, plate me; you know what that means? Right then. And, one more thing. After that, you each do the same for my old lady here. Right?'

The teenies looked horrified. Not at the thought of having it with him, but at the thought of giving head to another woman. But, the threat of police action was pressing, and they did want to see Central Heating. So they performed.

And, Monk kept his word.

He didn't turn them over to the fuzz.

That wouldn't have been sporting; especially after the fine job they did.

But, he did tell his President, as all loyal brothers should. And, Gerry was delighted to hear about it.

'Where have you hidden these little darlings? I reckon we can find a use for them. Where are they?'

It was Modesty who answered, unable to hide her laughter. 'They can't come down at the moment. They ... well, they're a bit tied up at the moment.'

10. GET BACK, GET BACK, GET BACK TO WHERE YOU ONCE BELONGED

WARNING!!!
WARNING!!!

This is a WARNING to all fans of Central Heating and Foolsgold who are attending any of the eight concerts held during March.

Events at recent tours of pop singers have produced more than their fair share of tragedy. Rupert Colt, on behalf of the promoters, announces here and now that every effort will be made to ensure no repercussions of this kind of behaviour.

Therefore, we urge all fans, of whatever age, to read this WARNING, and pay strict attention to it. There are only two words that you need to remember.

COOL IT.

Try and think of that when the time comes for your favourites to appear on the stage in front of you.

COOL IT.

On behalf of the promoters, we wish to make it clear that security is being handled by people who will not react gently to any attempt by ANYBODY to rush the stage or interfere in any way with the performances.

This WARNING also applies before and after shows.

The Hell's Angels who you will see at the front of each theatre have been given a completely free hand to run the security any way they think fit.

The Hell's Angels are not gentle people. BUT, they will not initiate any violence. Their job is to protect the show and to keep things moving. NOTHING will stand in their way to achieve this aim.

COOL IT.

Rupert Colt and Albert Donegan Enterprises take no responsibility for any person harmed, wounded, maimed, killed, or for any property damaged as a result of any illegal activity by any member of the audience.

No claim as a result of any such action, especially by the Last Heroes' chapter of the Hell's Angels, can be entered into by the promoters.

The show is for you to enjoy. Do that, and nobody will get harmed. Step out of line, and you'll imagine the WORLD HAS ENDED.

So, just COOL IT.

And, don't say that you haven't been WARNED.

This WARNING appears on all authorised publications connected with this tour. Ignorance of this WARNING will not save you from any action.

Rupert Colt and Albert Donegan Enterprises end this message, by hoping that you all ENJOY yourselves, and have a FUN TIME.

PEACE AND LOVE.

KEEP ON TRUCKING.

11. THE TIMELESS EXPLOSION OF FANTASY'S DREAM

'My name's Gerry Vinson. I'm the leader of the Last Heroes. You've heard of me and my brothers. This is the first show of the tour. Two acts. Great acts. Two halves. Foolsgold open in a couple of minutes, and Central Heating come on for the second half. Nobody else. No crap fillers. Just the top. Before we start. One thing. Look at this, and learn from it. Any of you try and cross us up and this is the sort of thing you'll get. Bring them on, Gwyn. These stupid tarts tried to get in free and fuck up our plans. Look at them.'

The capacity audience, who'd paid minimum prices of a hundred pounds to get in, had been screaming and shouting as they waited for the show to start. When the denimed figure of the almost mythical Wolf Vinson came on instead of the expected glam compere, they shut up for a bit. By the end of his brief intro the noise was again building up. When the crowd, mixed between middies and teenies, saw what came on from the side of the stage, the silence became total.

First, stripped to the waist, was the nightmare figure of Gwyn. His body was as white as light, and so thin that the ribs stood out as dark, smudged shadows. A wraith of hair toppled onto his shoulders, framing that face of evil purity. From the centre of the ivory face, twin red lights glowed at the audience. The ruby eyes of Gwyn, the albino. In his black-gloved hand, he held the end of a silver cord. It reached back into the wings of the stage.

Against the heavy blue plush of the front curtain, Gwyn was a creation to stop the heart of the nervous. Grinning wolfishly at the paralysed throng, he tugged at the silver cord. Once, twice, three, four times.

A collective gasp.

WARNING.

KEEP COOL.

Four young girls, though it was difficult to see at first that they were girls, and not some product of a Salvador Dali dream world. The four young girls that Monk had discovered hiding in the Queen's lavatory. He had promised not to turn them over to the fuzz, and he'd kept his word.

The rope ran to the neck of the first girl, then onto the necks of the others. The spotlights gleamed off their heads. Off their bald heads. Their hair had been brutally shorn by Holly and Lady, and the scalps coated with thick gold paint. Sequins had been scattered on the top to give the glittery effect.

They were totally naked, and even their body hair had been shaved. Hands were bound behind them, and ankles were hobbled so that they could only mince along in steps of not more than eight inches.

Strips of sticking plaster sealed their mouths. Some of the brothers had spent an enjoyable time finger-painting all manner of bright, jolly designs on their bodies, during the afternoon.

Bringing up the end of the line was Brenda, in her colours, with a short riding-crop in her hand, which she swished with alarming vigour and carelessness in the region of the girls' naked backs.

When all four were roughly in the centre of the stage, Brenda made them turn to face the audience, then kneel awkwardly down, and bow till their heads nearly reached the floor.

Gerry had retained the hand-mike, and his voice swelled to fill the silent theatre. 'I have told you why these girls have been treated this way. I would ask you to note that they have not been physically hurt, and they have not been sexually assaulted. When they go off the stage, they will be taken, as they are, to the centre of Birmingham and there released. The hair will grow back.'

Voices began to shout out, protestingly, from the crowd. Particularly from the older women. Gerry ignored them, and went on. 'But, if any person attempts to wreck this concert, or tries to get on to the stage, they will be treated without any mercy. The brothers are under my instructions to hold back nothing.' Finally, he acknowledged the growing protests with a wave of the hand. 'It's easy to scream now. But, the last concert resulted in deaths. Lots of them. I don't want that. But, if there are to be people dying, they will not be the stars on this stage, and they will not be any of my brothers. No more of this unpleasantness. Gwyn, get these bitches off. Ladies and girls. Scream all you wish now. But, nothing else.'

From the centre of the stalls, a large lady, the wrong side of forty, in a pink, fun-fur skirt and jacket clambered from her seat, and began to squeeze through the seats towards the front. Above the noise of the rest of the audience, she managed to make her voice heard. 'Sisters! Don't let these male animals dictate to us. Look at the way they have treated those children. Let us rise against them. Now!!'

Nobody knows whether the lady would have roused her comrades to storm the barricades. Although both Holly and Lady were sitting in that part of the auditorium – disguised as teenies – Gerry was concerned to see that neither of them made any move to expend the troublemaker. It was Rat, sneaking among feet and knees, who suddenly popped up directly in front of her.

She towered over him, fully nine inches taller, armed with the righteousness of her own anger. But, she omitted to do anything to protect herself. There was a swirl of movement and Rat was suddenly standing alone. The lady vanished. As completely as though she had never been.

Distraction came with the perfection of timing, from Gerry up on the stage. At a wave of his hand the house lights flicked out. He shouted one word: 'Foolsgold!!!' Blackout.

In that darkness, the unconscious figure of the woman was dragged hastily out and given over to the tender hands of the Assistant Chief Constable's men, who ringed the concert hall three deep.

Six angel-brats, each bathed in a cone of white light. Snowy-suited and halo-headed, Foolsgold swung into their first forgettable number. Middies bounced in their seats, and a cascade of knickers fluttered to the floor of the theatre. But, the line of brooding, righteous brothers wasn't even approached.

Gerry watched from the side of the stage, his fingers crossed. And he wondered why Holly and Lady had withheld any movement.

Foolsgold ran through their samish repertoire with the professional gloss and expertise that their fans expected. 'Poor Little Love', 'Mother Love', 'Diana', 'Put My Little Shoes Away', 'In Praise Of Older Lovers', followed each other with the same gentle and – some said – boring rhythms. It was what Mick the rock critic had christened 'simp-rock', and found his abusive mail multiplied a hundred-fold overnight.

The group did a country medley, with some of the immortal Johnny Cash's best songs put through the pulper. The teenies got in on the screaming act when the youngest of the six-boy ensemble – Little Tommy Bowdesire – hopped nimbly down from behind his drum kit and capered across the stage with his own version of the old Lou Reed biggie – 'Walk On The Wild Side'. With slightly amended lyrics.

In the wings, Gerry was conscious of Gwyn standing at his elbow. As they watched the child star, noticeably overweight in his doeskin suit, hop through his act like an invigorated doughnut, the Welshman brought a grin to Gerry's lips by giving a convincing impression of someone in the throes of agonising stomach pain, culminating in a superbly mimed technicolour yawn.

'At least they're staying more or less in their seats,' shouted Gerry to be heard by Gwyn, less than a foot away.

'Don't speak too soon, boyo. The night is still young, and the action hasn't started. By the time the next lot get on, half the audience'll have forgotten our lesson.'

'Maybe we'll get a chance to give them another.'

The chance came as Foolsgold moved into their last number. They had a new album out, called *Night And Foolsgold*, which was the usual easy-listening mixture. The ace track off it was called 'I'll Let You Do Anything For Me', and the words catered to all the imagination and fantasies of the middies.

The thought of being able to do anything for any of the fine young dudes was just too much for one of the middies. She forgot the WARNING and lost her COOL. Tears of passion streaking through her heavy make-up, her breasts swinging heavily inside her puce blouse, a middle-aged lover from Handsworth Wood made her run at the stage.

Maybe some of the brothers had just lost that edge of sharpness from the winter's lay-off. Maybe the first part of the concert had gone so easily that they thought there wasn't going to be any hassle at all.

Anyway, the middie made her run and actually got past the row of Angels, and scrambled inelegantly on to the stage, her short skirt riding up over her better-than-ample thighs, showing her laddered tights and crimson knickers to the world.

Deintydd and Hanger John were both on the stage patrol, and they went for the middie at the same time.

Hanger John's sharpened coat-hanger hissed at the woman's out-stretched arms, making long, but shallow cuts. Deintydd got there slightly second, but his method was far more direct. Without checking his run at all, he launched his leather-booted right foot in a savage kick, which cracked home in the woman's ribs.

The air whooshed out of the stricken middie's lungs, and her scream was strangled at birth by a chronic lack of breath. The kick sent her rolling to the very edge of the stage, clutching at her body, and fighting for air. One of Foolsgold – Pete Greane – moved forward, as though to interfere, but he was checked by an urgent yell from Gerry in the wings.

The row of brothers at the front of the stage grabbed the woman, and hauled her off on to the floor of the stalls. There they worked her over, not causing any permanent damage, but giving the audience a salutary lesson in mob control.

There was no more trouble during the first half of the concert.

'Two things, brothers and sisters. One, when the middie made her run near the end of the set, you were all too slow to get to her. Except you two on the stage. She should never have got that far. It'll be worse if the teenies get up on stage, tooled-up. Stop them at the first moment. Once they're ready moving, they're going to be that much harder.'

'No way, man. No way!' It was, of course, Freddie Dolan. Lead singer with Central Heating. 'We're used to having the chicks balling their way right up on the stage. Then, we have one or two men to pick them up and drop them back in to the front seats. That's what I want to happen here.'

Without even looking at the skinny figure, Gerry went on. 'Forget about what the old men up there on the stage want. Maybe they get their kicks being cut to bits by a mob of girls. But, we aren't going to let that happen. Now, the second...'

'Listen, man. I said I want the girls allowed to get near us.'

Finally, Gerry acknowledged Freddie by facing him. 'I don't know why I bother with cunts like you, I don't. Tell me just one thing.'

'What?'

'Do you want your cock cut off and pinned to some teenie's wall?'

'No. But it's absurd to think that...'

'It's not anything, baby. Gerry's right. Your girls are in a different league to some of the harpies they have here.'

Gerry took Rupert by the arm. 'Listen, sweetheart. I run this or you find another man. If I run it, then it's my way. I say this only one time. This bastard stays away from me, and stops moaning on about how I run things. That way, I've got a chance of saving his rotten body from being chivved. And you stay well back as well. Now, both of you. Out!'

Rupert patted Gerry's arm reassuringly as he walked out of the room. Freddie turned in the doorway, and spat out: 'Just you wait till Rick and his boys get over here from...'

'We know. From Laurel Canyon. When they get here we might play a few games. Just to see who's got class and who hasn't. Now, fuck off!'

Once the door was shut, with what was intended to be a slam, but was defeated by the pneumatic device that closed it with a gentle hiss, Gerry continued his intermission tactics talk.

'Time's getting short, and we've got to be back in a couple of minutes. One other thing I noticed that worries me. Something that we're going to have to talk about a lot more. Brenda, Holly, Lady; we'd be sorry to lose you all, but if you want to pack your things and split to form your own ladies' auxiliary, then you'd better go. No,

Brenda! There isn't time here. There isn't going to be enough time over the next few days either. So, what happens? When that old bag out of the audience started shouting, you two ignored her. It was Rat who outed her. I'm not having that pulling-out shit at this time.'

Brenda moved forwards to speak, but stopped when she saw the look in Gerry's eyes. She had seen that look before, and knew that there was a time to talk and a time to shut up. This was one of the times to shut up.

'You're all members of the Last Heroes, and that means you play your part for the chapter. When this tour's over, we'll get everything out in the open. That includes some of your old brothers from the hillside, Gwyn. Don't look so fucking surprised, mate. I'm not blind. So, we all pull together, as they say. Until after the concert on the seventh. Anyone not want to go along with that?'

He looked particularly at Gwyn, then at the militant old ladies and mamas. All of them met his eyes, and all of them finally looked away. None of them argued.

The second half of the concert passed off quietly enough. Both Freddie Dolan and Jim Lawrence were more provocative and outrageous than usual. Lawrence wore crocodile-skin pants, and had a lot of trouble with the zip.

At the best of times that would have caused a near-riot. The teenies made their run. But, only some of them, and a lot of those went straight back when they saw what happened. Some were chopped down in their seats, while most got knocked back by the brothers along the front of the stage.

Only a couple reached the actual performing area, and they were heaved off with a surprising lack of violence. After the excesses of the Sundance, Gerry – and Assistant Chief Constable Penn – had anticipated the use of knives. It may have been the WARNINGs, or the lessons so brutally demonstrated by the Angels, but the girls obviously decided that – at least in Birmingham – that kind of game wasn't worth the risk.

There was only one fatality that evening. A teenie – near the end of the act – charged towards Freddie Dolan, with a long carving-knife gleaming in her dimpled fist. Gwyn stopped her with a chop to the neck, and the girl fell on her own blade, dying in hospital later that night.

After that incident, Freddie cooled his moaning for a bit. And Jim Lawrence's trousers stayed together for the rest of the tour.

While the stars relaxed in their dressing-rooms – they either made a very fast getaway or they sent out stand-ins on dummy runs and remained behind themselves – sometimes for hours – Penn joined Gerry and the senior brothers for a glass or two, or three, or four, of good old Southern Comfort.

The theatre was quiet, though they could hear chanting and screaming from the thousands who still waited impatiently outside. Some of the chapter had already begun the long haul north towards the next gig in Glasgow. Gerry was due to lead the others on a run some time after midnight.

Penn raised his glass. 'To you and yours, Gerry. You did a good night's work.'

Cochise lurched over from a corner. 'What about the press, eh? There were dozens of reporters and cameramen there. What do you think they're going to say about tonight in the papers?'

Rupert Colt was also there. Grinning all over his new lilac evening suit. 'I can answer that, Israel. I've talked to a lot of the boys about that, and Mr. Penn here has also had a quiet chat. Some of them'll have a go at strong-arm tactics, but most of them have been yelling for stronger security at concerts for years. Now, they've got what they wanted. Cochise, my big lover, you needn't lose any sleep over that.'

Gerry spoke quietly. 'What was the score?'

The policeman pulled a small notebook from his pocket and opened it, peering at his own tidy writing as intently as if it contained the wisdom of the ages.

'Not counting the four we had to start with. The girl that our pale friend over there knifed has been...'

Gwyn stopped him. 'The one who fell on her own bloody knife. You remember that, copper.'

Penn carried on, unflappable. 'The girl that fell on her own knife has been taken to the General Hospital. My latest information is that she has severe internal bleeding and that it is more than possible that she will not live through the night. Outside, my men had a bit of trouble with pushing and crowding, and about thirty girls were taken away either to the hospital or the nick. From the ones you sent out to us, twelve have gone to hospital with injuries ranging from broken ribs to facial cuts and bruises. Not really a bad night at all.'

Brenda drained her mug. 'Gerry. Time we were off.'

Penn watched them preparing to leave. It would be easy for him; sleeping the night away in the back of his white Jaguar as he was carried towards Glasgow in style and comfort.

He waved his finger, beckoning Gerry over. 'One last thing. My informants in Glasgow tell me that the local chapter up there feel that they might be rather better at providing security cover in their own city. They might try and prove something with you. Thought you'd be interested. Drive carefully, won't you.'

Astride his Harley, Gerry warned his brothers-in-war that there might be a rumble up north. 'The fuzz says that the Blues reckon they might be better than us.'

Riddler said what they all thought. 'I hope the bastards really try something, Gerry. I'd like a go at something different from women. It was like I was either putting the boot to me kid sister or me mother. Bloody shame!'

It was raining for most of the long run up the teeming grey ribbon of the M6 to the border. Some of the hogs had ignition trouble, and the journey was less than fun and slower than fast. The worst moment was when the huge Mercedes armoured coach, carrying Foolsgold, Central Heating, and a crew of roadies and groupies, crashed past them when they were stopped on the hard shoulder.

Spray soaked over them, and they had one taunting glimpse of the warmth and light of the interior. Then the blackness and cold ripped back around them.

Gerry had hoped to get some sleep in Glasgow, but the trip took longer than anyone had reckoned, so it was straight round to the theatre – a gloomy Edwardian mausoleum disguised as a palace of entertainment. Penn arrived half an hour later, looking cool and immaculate, followed by the roadies and followed around midday by Foolsgold and by Central Heating.

Last of all, tripping away on – something – came Freddie Dolan, his high cheekbones stark against his pale face. The liveliest thing about him were his eyes, flickering like those of a malign elf.

He went straight to Gerry and flung his arms round his neck, kissing him on the cheek. Effortlessly, Wolf back-handed him across the face with an open palm. To everyone's surprise, Freddie just sat there, spread-eagled on his ass, and roared with laughter.

'I told them you weren't fairies.'

'Told who, Freddie? Told who?'

Dolan pulled himself to his high-heeled feet, still grinning. 'A bunch of brothers from round here. They said to tell you that they'd heard that all English Angels were fairies – poofs, they said – and that they were waiting outside to show you that the Blues could,' he hesitated, pretending to have forgotten the exact words; just to heighten the effect, 'could beat the shit out of the Last Heroes.'

Gwyn dropped a crow-bar he'd been fooling around with, the noise sounding thunderous in the suddenly quiet theatre.

'Have we got time, Wolf? Have we?'

Gerry stole a quick glance at his watch. It was just after twelve. The show opened at seven. He and Penn had already sussed out the main features of the place – noted the particular dangers.

'There's time.'

The area outside the theatre was a mass of over-walks and under-passes, with steps spiralling up and down, and ramps and blocks everywhere. The Angels' hogs were stored safely away in a back-stage area – away from the main car-park. It was on this car-park that the Glasgow Angels – the notorious Blues – had gathered to taunt their rivals.

'Where're yer hogs, Vinson? Have yer ta'en to walkin' now?'

The leader of the Blues was a gross man – over twenty stone – named Wee Georgie Bond. His hair dangled greasily over his shoulders, and his eyes were like two small marbles almost buried beneath layers of fat. Like most Presidents of long-established chapters, he wasn't young.

There were about fifteen of his brothers ranged in a half-circle around him, mostly on the old Triumphs and Nortons. Gerry had roughly an equal number of Last Heroes. Behind the Glasgow contingent waited a couple of local police cars, with fuzz sitting tensely, fingers poised over their calling radios.

'Wait here Fatso, till we get our hogs.'

'We'll be waitin'.'

By the time the Last Heroes had revved their choppers from inside the theatre and down into the car-park, word had got around the city, and a hundred people lined the walls. Hundreds more were flocking in from surrounding streets. A lot of local teenies, all ready for the action of the night were there, urging on the local boys. The papers had carried stories of the Angels' security operation, and the girls knew what to expect.

Gerry throttled back, sitting easily back on the seat, hands drooping on the ape-hanger bars. The sun was just breaking through, and the chrome on the hogs glittered with a watery light.

A police siren came vibrating unevenly from a street nearby, and a white Jaguar came scattering through the crowd, braking in a shower of gravel between the two chapters. Out leaped the dynamic figure of Assistant Chief Constable Penn.

'Blimey, Israel! Do you always have to roar up like the bloody masked avenger?'

Unsmiling at Hanger John's greeting, Penn went straight up to Gerry, and the two muttered together for a few seconds. At first, the fuzz shook his head, but Gerry's earnestness convinced him of whatever it was they were discussing.

'Have yer sold us all up the Clyde, then? Yer fuckin' grass, Vinson!'

Bond's words were stilled as Penn strode back to his waiting car and, with the same scattering of gravel, roared away. After a minute's delay, the rest of the police cars also withdrew, leaving the park to the Angels. And their spectators.

'Right, Fatso. The blue meanies have all packed their tents and faded away from the scene. Like the old morning dew. Just you nutters and us. Come on, Fatso, the ball's bouncing in your half. How d'you want to play it?'

Wee Georgie heeled his heavy machine – a Harley like Gerry's, but with a lot of the original trim on – forward. The Electra Glide was painted in a flake enamel – orange. The rear wheel boxes had been stripped, but all the array of lights and horns on the weighty front remained.

'An all-out fight?'

'What a crude fellow you are, Bond. You do lack any kind of imagination.'

'All right, smartie. Just what the fuck do yer suggest? A university debate?'

'No, Fatso. Your top three against my top three. That's me, Monk here, and Gwyn. Each pairing to agree their own terms. How about that?'

Oily wheels clicked inside the fat man's skull. He'd hoped for a simple battle, so that he could call on his reserves as soon as fighting started and wipe the Last Heroes clean off the park. Now, Gerry had got in first.

'Of course, you chubby old fart, if you're afraid of losing?' Having planted his barb, Monk turned to Gwyn to give it a tug. 'I heard these Scotch bastards didn't have any class.'

The sergeant-at-arms of the Blues – Bond's right-hand man – was another fat man, Robbie White. Known as "Red-eye", because he permanently suffered from conjunctivitis, he came from one of the toughest estates in that tough city. And, he thought he could beat any skinny English sod. 'Oh, really! Come on Georgie. You can take that little one. I'll knock the crap out of big-mouth there. And, Wormie'll beat that white-faced streak o' rubbish. Come on! Nobody talks about us not having class!'

Faced with that kind of talk, a President has little choice on a course of action. A small thought crept out of the slush in Bond's mind and he wondered just how it was that he wasn't doing what he'd intended. But, he shook his head and washed it back below the surface.

So, it was agreed. While the other brothers formed an arena, mainly to hold the crowd – getting up towards a thousand now – back, rather than to keep the combatants in.

First off were Wormie, a silent Scot, and Gwyn, the white. They were to race across the park, up a ramp, then get up a steep spiral concrete staircase, once round the top and back. It was a course that the Blues knew well, and were confident of winning. Gerry, Monk and Gwyn got together for a quick word, but Gwyn shrugged off any advice. 'Leave him to me, boyo. The poor sod won't know what hit him.'

On the shout, Wormie thrust his heavier machine into the lead and was fifty yards ahead as he started the wheelie that would help to get him up the stairs. The Blues were already crying: 'Easy,' as he appeared on the block on top, before Gwyn reached the bottom of the flight.

Then, both riders vanished into the concrete stairwell.

Wormie on the way down. Gwyn on the way up. Time seemed to hang around. Then, there was a splitting explosion and a blossom of black smoke and livid flame from the stairs. For long seconds, nobody moved.

Then, at the top of the steps, a figure rode into view. With dead-white hair streaming behind him like a banner of light. Round the top and then throttled to a stop at the head of the stairs. Barely visible through the smoke. Still, nobody had moved.

A voice, lilting across the car-park to the ears of the listeners. 'You Scotch sods ought to be grateful to me. You won't have to worry about burying what's left of him. I just discovered instant cremation.'

Choosing his moment to perfection, Monk asked Red-eye where they were going to race.

'There's no fuckin' race. Get down off your chopper and fuckin' fight!'

Bond made no move to interfere. When Gerry started to speak, he said: 'Yer fuckin' chicken now. What's wrong wi' a fight?'

'Nothing, brother,' replied Gerry quietly. 'I just thought you might not want to have another full-patch member snuffed so soon after that one. A fight it is.'

Again that nagging thought that somehow he'd been manipulated crept back. But he looked at the huge figure of Robbie White, compared to the slight, curly-headed Last Hero, and he felt much happier.

'Rip his bollocks off, Robbie!'

Robbie had been reared in one of the toughest fighting schools anywhere in the world, and he could look after himself in any class of company. Fist or boot or bottle or razor. He was a fair hand with all of them.

And, as Mick Moore noted, the big man had all the scars to prove it. The one thing that Red-eye didn't have was much brain.

The two faced each other, Mick empty-handed. The Blue letting his hand creep round to the pouch at the back of his belt where he kept a honed-down chiv. Monk feinted an attack, making the bigger man move quickly back. But he still kept feeling for his blade. Which was stupid. It left him slightly off-balance, moving back, and it left his right side virtually unprotected. Kafka hadn't been the only Angel to get into Kung Fu. Well was it said: 'The speed of the gad-fly, will always defeat the power of the water-buffalo'.

Springing off his left foot, he thrust out his right foot towards the big man's knees. Monk hit him hard, the heel of his boot tearing into the delicate machinery of the knee joint. As he fell backwards, mouth open in agony, Red-eye still managed to get the razor out and wave it desperately at the sliding figure of the Angel. But Monk was quick, elusive as an eel in a weed-fringed pond, and the blow missed. He rolled back to his feet, watching the struggles of the fat man to get up. Balancing awkwardly on his one good leg, the Scottish Angel tried to pivot and face his moving opponent. Holding the razor low, he weaved it from side to side, trying to cover himself against the next attack.

Horse stance to scorpion blow to tearing-rock kick with right foot. Against the weak knee. This time breaking the bones of the joint. The pain from a broken or dislocated knee is one of the most extreme known. Robbie dropped his razor and fell to his back, hands trying to hold the wrecked bones and cartilage together. And crying for help.

Monk looked at Gerry. 'Do I out him?'

Gerry looked at Wee Georgie Bond, watching with horror and fear as his two top brothers were beaten.

'Well, Fatso. Does he out him?'

On the dirt of the car-park, the sergeant-at-arms of the Blues cried and rolled, clutching at himself. Mick Moore stood over him, waiting for the word. Thumbs up or down. It didn't make much difference to him. The fat man would have killed him if he'd had the chance.

While they waited for the answer, Gerry probed a little deeper. 'Fatso. If he dies, then I'd kill you. You've seen two of my best. I'm better than either. I'm even better than both.' The Blue opened his mouth in disbelief. 'You're just going to say that can't be true. You've got one way of finding out. I hope you feel lucky, Fatso.'

The crowd, mostly young girls, were impatient for more action and started to scream and yell at the delay. By his car, Penn watched patiently, a thin smile nearly making it on to his lips.

Bond's eyes dropped, and Gerry knew he'd won. 'Right, Fatso. Pick up that great piece of garbage off the mud there and move off. A lot of people here, and a few journalists around. So don't bother claiming any class in this city. Not while we're around.'

There was no more talk. A couple of the Angels picked up their fallen comrade. The burning bike had been put out, but the smell of oil and blazing flesh still lingered sickly on the air. Riding quietly with none of the bravado of their arrival, the Blues left the theatre car-park. The hordes of teenies, who had expected to see these English heavies stomped out of sight, booed and hissed their former heroes.

At the concert that night, there were no serious incidents.

In Glasgow, at least, the lesson had been learned. Mess around with the Hell's Angels, and you mess with the inside of your own nightmares.

12. THE MOTOR CYCLE BLACK MADONNA, TWO WHEELED GYPSY QUEEN

An extract from an interview with Brenda,
from the magazine 'Oral'. – March, 1999.

Clive Parkes, for 'Oral': Nice of you to come along and talk to us, Brenda. Could you tell us what you full name is?

Brenda: No. [Long pause.] You're wasting your time if you try that draggy old technique of sitting back silently hoping that I'll feel so embarrassed that I'll blurt out some appalling truths. That went out long ago.

Clive Parkes: Fair enough. Just Brenda, then. Tell us why you became a Hell's Angel.

Brenda: I used to be a member of the Young Anarchists, because I hated the restrictive negativism of the last Government. But, they didn't seem to have any activist concepts, so I decided to opt out completely. I met this ex-soldier at the meetings and we found we thought the same kind of thoughts. So, we went along to the local chapter of one of the very last left in the country – the rest had been driven underground – down in Hertfordshire – and after the usual initiation ceremony they accepted us.

Clive Parkes: The man would be Gerry Vinson, also known as Wolf, who became leader of the gang known as the Last Heroes.

Brenda: Chapter. Not gang. Yes.

Clive Parkes: Tell us about the initiation.

Brenda: It was much tougher in those days. Gerry had to fight a man – he killed him – and I had to pull a train.

Clive Parkes: Pull a train?

Brenda: You must have done your research, so you must know what that means.

Clive Parkes: I believe it means to have intercourse with all the men in the ... chapter? [Long pause] Tell us about your friendship with Gerry. How deep is it?

Brenda: I fuck with him and he fucks with me. That's all I'll tell you about that.

Clive Parkes: Fair enough. You're very outspoken for a lady. Are you very into the ideas of female liberation?

Brenda: I think that women should be allowed to be as liberated as they want to be. I don't believe any doors should be shut to them, but they have to face the fact that men are likely to do better in certain areas of work.

Clive Parkes: Could you specify those areas?

Brenda: No.

Clive Parkes: We'll come on to the way security is being handled on this current pop music tour in a moment, though it does seem as though the Hell's Angels' particular brand of barely controlled violence is working. First, I'd like to ask you a bit about the ethos of the Angels. The rules you live by. And, most importantly, whether you approve of some of the things that Hell's Angels actually do.

Brenda: There are plenty of fine books about what we do. They're all old – written in the early seventies, most of them, but you might still find a copy around of one of them. Some of the brothers have copies, but they look like the Dead Sea Scrolls. There are pages missing and what's left is held together by tape and glue. Try and read anything by either Stuart, Cave or Norman. They all knew what it was all about.

Clive Parkes: But, they were writing about what one might call the good old days.

Brenda: You might. You might also call them the lazy, hazy days of summer. Things haven't changed that much regarding what we do. You know. Runs, wings, colours, hogs, that sort of thing.

Clive Parkes: Would you like to say what you think about why Angels behave the way they do, and whether you approve of it?

Brenda: Second one first. I ride with the Angels. I wouldn't if I didn't want to. First one second. Why the fuck shouldn't they do what they want? Life is brutally short, and there's only one go at it. We don't go for the old myths about helping somebody as we travel along life's path or our living will have been in vain. It's for now. Not tomorrow. But now.

Clive Parkes: That seems a very selfish attitude.

Brenda: Screw you with your expense account and your three divorces and your little probing, prying mind. Ninety per cent of what the media puts out about us isn't true or is so slanted as to be unrecognizable from the truth. The other ten per cent is wildly exaggerated.

Clive Parkes: I think that perhaps we'd better agree to differ on that. I see the Angels as mindless parasites and...

Brenda: You know what that word means? Parasite? It's someone who makes his living fawning around the tables of the rich, flattering their egos. Picking up the scraps that they discard. A toady is another word. Whatever else you say about the Angels, I reckon that you're a lot more of a toady than any Angel that ever breathed.

Clive Parkes: Do you fear death?

Brenda: Subtle change of subject, laddie. Do I fear death ? No. I believe that death is simply Nature's way of telling you to slow down.

13. AND THE CORNER SIGN, SAYS IT'S CLOSING TIME

'Listen, son. I honestly don't care what you want. I know you skulls. You come in places like this and you take all sorts of things and when you're asked to pay for them, you just walk out. Safety in numbers.'

The thin boy, with his cropped, curly hair, stood unsmiling in the small café. His clothes were neat and expensive, with a pale green ruffled shirt under his coat. The boots gave him a specious height. The Greek proprietor of the greasy spoon sniffed disapprovingly at the strong scent of cologne that many of the top skulls used.

'Wait a minute, Mr. Cristinos. You saying that me and my mates are cowards? Is that it? Why don't you try putting me out of your stinking place then. Just you against me. Come on. Let's see you.'

The eatery owner weighed up his chances. He'd had trouble with the skulls in the past, and here was an opportunity to get his own back on one of them. His sleeves were already rolled up high over his strong, hairy arms, but he made the necessary gesture of rolling them up still further.

The skull backed away from him, waving his hands placatingly at the vision of this juggernaut of wrath. Fumbling behind him, he opened the door and jumped backwards into the ill-lit, empty street. Cristinos followed him on to the pavement, letting his anger build in a flood of insult. He blinked across at the slight figure, screwing up his eyes to try and adjust them to the dark after the bright neon within.

'You're a coward, like I said. You talk pretty big when you come in with all your friends. Friends! A load of work-shy loafers and no-goods. Why don't you wash out that stinking perfume, and take off that ear-ring and try behaving like a man instead of a poof.'

Finally, Bookie Wyatt had taken enough. The game was over and it was getting boring. 'All right, uncle. Get inside and start serving us.'

The big Greek shrugged his shoulders with a mixture of bravado and new-born uncertainty. 'Us? Where is this us?'

'Behind you, uncle. The rest of my mates.'

Cristinos looked nervously behind him. Fearing that he might see a cluster of skulls, waiting for him.

You know that there are times when you know you've made a fool of yourself and you wish that you could cut off your tongue. That was what the Greek felt. But he didn't have to cut out his own tongue.

They did it for him.

'So this is London, again. That's the trouble with being on the road; you lose all track of where time is and your head starts to slip. Still, two more gigs and away for the sun.'

Rupert Colt got up to pour Freddie Dolan another coke. 'You must admit, Freddie, that things haven't gone too badly on this tour from the security angle. Apart from that spot of bother at Birmingham, when Gerry was still sort of feeling his way. Glasgow, was fine. Liverpool, Cardiff and Leicester all went quietly. Assistant Chief Constable Penn told me that his men had made far more arrests outside the theatres than from inside.'

Dolan crunched his ice-cube in his teeth. 'Colt, I didn't want these English Angels here as heavies when we started this tour, and I still don't want them here now. Rick and his brothers arrived in town last night and they're just catching up on some lost sleep. They're going to be at the scene some time after lunch to take over.'

'Wait a minute, sweetheart. The term you want is not "take over". It's "share". That's what we agreed, and that's what's going to happen.'

'No way that Rick would agree to that.'

Amazing himself even more than he amazed Freddie Dolan, Rupert slapped him hard across the mouth, starting a thin trickle of blood.

'You jumped-up little prick! If it hadn't been for Gerry and his chapter, you and your lot of filth could have been chopped-up cats' meat. Raw head and bloody bones on anyone of half-a-dozen stages. If Gerry and Rick want to get into a hassle situation, then I'll back Gerry. I hired him and I'll back him. Even if it means losing your precious company for the last two shows.'

Dolan's thin face, and deep-set eyes were immovable. The red marks of the slap stood out lividly on his cheeks. For a moment, Rupert thought that he was going to attack him. But, the moment passed.

'Rupert.' The words seemed dragged out from a great distance. The voice was suddenly that of a tired man. 'I'll do a deal with you. I'll lay off Gerry if you'll do me a favour. I can't guarantee that the Laurel Canyon boys will agree to take any crap from the English Angels. But, I'll do what I can.'

Relief staining his face, Rupert sat down heavily in one of the deep, over-padded chairs. 'Shoot baby. You tell me what the favour is that you want, and I'll do what I can to help out. What is it? Bread, chicks? Boys?'

The unanswer stretched out. Far below them, Rupert was aware of the constant rumble of traffic, despite the lateness – or earliness – of the hour.

He coughed, wondering whether to speak or not. Finally, he had to. 'Smack?'

The deep eyes looked up at him. Surprised. 'How the fuck d'you know? Someone split on me?'

Rupert smiled at the concern of the question. Though it really wasn't a funny thing at all. Heroin addiction in anybody is one of the least funny things around.

'You know when we had to do that pix-session at Glasgow. That one when we couldn't find you.'

'Yeah. I was having a sleep in my room.'

'No. That's not true, baby. That's how I know. When you came out of your dressing-room, you had on that new pair of white jeans. Remember?'

'Yeah. How the hell did that tell you I was on smack? Don't tell me you could see tracks through them. Because I ... Hey! Wait a minute.'

'That's it, Freddie. I was looking at the pix that they took. Only yesterday. There's a small circle of blood on the front of the right thigh. About the size of a nickel. Like you'd just shot and not had time to clean up properly after. Is that it?'

'You're a cunning bastard, Colt. Yeah. You're right all the way on. The trouble is that my pusher, a guy named Gallacher, got himself busted three days ago. And, the fuzz over here are so fucking tight on hard dope. I sent one of the roadies down to a place called G_____ Street, where it's supposed to be easy to score. A Chinese guy offered him what he said was some good smack. Got back here and the schmuck had bought some talcum powder!'

Rupert looked at his watch. 'I reckon that H is out. But I know somewhere I can score some methadone for you. If I do that, will you play ball?'

The mask cracked, and anger flared briefly. 'What the fuck d'you want, you bastard fairy? You want me to put my hand on your cock and swear an oath to pay my dues and stand in line? That what you want?'

'No. That's not what I want. I want no hassle to wreck the end of a good tour. You've told me about your problem. I dig that makes you feel one down to me. O.K., then. I'll tell you my secret. Once the lights go down and Foolsgold bounce on stage for the last show, then I'm long gone. I've bought a small homestead up in a place called Shropshire. Quiet sort of country. Not under my own name, even. Rupert Colt's going to vanish. For ever.'

Even as he told Freddie Dolan about his plans, Rupert began to regret it. If Dolan was really hooked on junk, then he would do anything and use anybody to try and get his script. But, somehow, he liked the short, intense singer. For all his faults, the guy had a kind of unshakable integrity. Maybe it would be all right.

'I've got what they call the "Gauguin Complex", when middle-aged men jack it all in and head for the sunny side of the hills. Keep in touch, baby, and you can come and sit with me and watch the grass grow. When things all get too heavy.'

Dolan smiled – a rare sight. 'Maybe, baby. I'll do just that.' Then the smile vanished, and the tenseness that is inseparable from the superstar came sidling back. 'Now, get your friend with the dope. I've got to go and see Rick and try and sort things out for you.'

Rupert puckered his lips in what he fondly hoped was a relaxing grin, and went over to pick up the phone. Freddie watched him. 'You sure you don't mind, man.'

'No, Freddie. No. No. I'm the original Freak Brother.'

A floor down, and a few feet to the south, Gerry and Brenda were also relaxing and preparing for the rigours of the last couple of days.

'Gerry.' The voice was muffled, as though it came from a mouth that was also occupied with other matters.

'Yeah.' His hands were idly running through her hair, pulling strands together, and knotting and loosening the skeins.

'How you going to handle the Americans?'

'I've brought along ... Ouch! Don't bloody bite when you're doing that.'

'Sorry.'

'I've brought along our original charter. I'm going to show them Sonny Barger's signature. That's for starters. Then, if talking doesn't do any good, I might get one or two of the brothers to show a bit of class. I've got a couple of ideas that might do some good.'

The conversation was interrupted for a few minutes while Brenda gave him his pleasures on a plate, and, in return, he showed her what a cunning linguist he was. Then, they both washed and, being clean people, brushed their teeth. After that, they climbed back into bed and carried on the talk.

'What if that doesn't work?'

'What? Oh, the class. Well, I thought I'd go right up to Rick Padrino and shake him by the hand, as a kind of welcoming gesture, and give his hand a tug, then break his neck with my other hand. How does that sound?'

Brenda laughed. 'I like it G.V., I like it. No more hassles then.'

For a few minutes, they lay together, passing a joint between them, watching the smoke ring around the white ceiling. It was Brenda who broke the silence.

'Do you want to talk about it?'

They had known each other too long and too well for him to need to ask her what 'it' was.

'When are you splitting?'

'You asked us to wait till after the last concert, and that's what we'll do. Holly and Lady wanted to split right away, but I wouldn't let them.'

'You reckon it'll work?'

'I don't know, Gerry. We want to try and this is the only way I know of.'

'I'll have to get another old lady, you know. It wouldn't do for the President to be single. The brothers would talk.'

'I know that.'

Stubbing the joint out in the ashtray on the bedside table, Gerry raised himself on his elbow and looked down at Brenda. 'We never talked much, did we? Didn't seem that much time for it. Tomorrow's the party, and you'll leave straight after the concert on the last day. So, this is about the last time.' He fumbled for the words he wanted, finding they lay uneasily on his tongue. 'I just want to say, Brenda, that I'm going to miss you, more than you'll ever know. That's all.' She reached up to him and pulled him down on her, and kissed him slowly and deeply. 'Let's have one more for the road then. Remember one thing, Gerry. I always loved you.'

At eight-thirty that morning, Gerry was woken by someone hammering on his hotel door. Brenda had slipped away from him during the night. Rubbing his eyes, he shouted for them to come in.

In burst Gwyn, eyes blazing redly in his pallid face. His hair was so tangled that he'd obviously come down straight from his bedroom.

It had taken the Angels several hours' talking before they had agreed to accept Rupert's offer of accommodation. Many of them still mistrusted the soft life.

'I've just had a call from my old lady, Geneth. The local radio back home have just run an item about a fight at Nant Gwrtheyrn. Seems a gang of thugs have moved in and taken over our village. They say that the Wolves are finished and have sold out to the English and they are the only chapter who uphold the rights of the Welsh-speaking minority. Fucking bastards.'

'Where did she hear this?'

'Well, she hadn't been well, so she went to stay with her old mum at Pwllehli. There was about five left down at the village. She said the radio talked about casualties. And possible fatalities.'

Gerry reached out and touched Gwyn on the shoulder. 'One favour, Gwyn. Stay until after the meeting with the Americans. It's only another three hours or so. Please. Then you can take all the brothers – Cyllell, Deintydd, Bardd – all of them, and get the Wolves riding again.'

Gwyn turned and flashed a grin at him. 'But, how about you? If you want, we'll stay till the tour's over.'

'No, boyo. The girls are leaving after the tour. Things are changing. We're all going to have to look to new roads to run this summer.'

'Even Brenda?'

'Yes. Shove off now, while I put me best colours on. Then come back here with a bottle of Comfort, and we'll talk tactics. Bring the council with you.'

Like a blown wave, Gwyn was at the door. Gerry shouted to him: 'Listen. If you Welsh poofs have trouble up there. The Last Heroes'll come and sort you out. All of you.' Under his breath. Very quietly, he couldn't help muttering: 'What's left of us.'

'Wolf, is there anywhere round here we can get any fucking food that isn't recycled shit?'

The speaker was Rick Padrino – known as "Greek" to the brothers in his chapter, and as the "Godfather" to the rest of underground America. He was extremely tall – six eight – and thin as a drinking straw. He wore his hair long and tied back in a pony-tail with a red velvet ribbon.

The Laurel Canyon chapter had roared up to the meeting-place at the theatre car-park at exactly one o'clock. They all wore black leather, rather than denims, for their colours, and they all rode immaculate Harleys. The flashlights of the Press and the glowing floods of the video people shone and bounced off the mass of chrome.

Gerry had deliberately tried to keep the confrontation as low-key as possible, by leaving their hogs out of sight, and only meeting them with a dozen of the top brothers, on foot. The rest of the chapter were around, watching from hiding.

Padrino had been cool – super-cool – and had shaken hands gently with Gerry. If he was aware of being watched from windows and behind walls, of gun barrels pointing at him, he showed no sign of it.

There, in the spring sunshine, the two chapters met and mingled, drinking the Southern Comfort provided by Rupert Colt. And charged to Albert Donegan Enterprises. As soon as the initial meeting was over, Rupert appeared, shaking hands everywhere, and making himself suitably effusive. The dark figure of Assistant Chief Constable Penn also appeared, introducing himself to the Americans. Even Freddie Dolan showed up, once more fully in control of himself.

He'd done what he promised, and there was no major confrontation between the English and American Angels. The drink flowed, and all the Laurel Canyon brothers gathered round in a sort of worship at the sight of the signature on the charter of the late and great Sonny Barger.

After the booze, and the introductions, and the initial sizing-up, thoughts turned to food. That was when Padrino asked his question.

The concert was at the new Hall in south-east London – not far from New Cross. It wasn't an area that Gerry knew well, so he looked around at the brothers to see if any of them could help. The answer came from a small man who seemed to materialize from the floor. Although it had been many years since Rat first had his colours christened, the smell of urine and vomit seemed as fresh as the day he was initiated.

'There's a smashin' chippie round the back of Nunhead. The owner keeps a stuffed parrot on the counter.'

The Last Heroes got their hogs and the two chapters rode together for the first time. Children on the pavement shouted and waved, and old men looked the other way or spat in the gutter. The Americans rode in pairs, while the English tended to go single. If they had anyone up, it would normally be their old lady.

The Laurel Canyon chapter had brought no old ladies with them at all. Just eighteen brothers. Gwyn rode next to Gerry, occasionally resting his hand on his shoulder. They both knew this would be the last time.

Although there was to be no violence between the chapters, a little needling over class started as soon as they crowded into the steamy little chip shop. It was getting towards the end of the lunch hour, and there were no other customers. The owner was a large Italian, who ran the place with his even larger wife. The vats of boiling fat bubbled and hissed behind the counter. On top of the marble counter was a long row of dirty jars, each holding two or three quarts of vinegar and a wide assortment of pickles and huge, lumpy gherkins, bobbing and weaving in the liquid like extra-terrestrial foetuses. In pride of place, at the far end of the counter, by the cash register, stood a stuffed parrot. There were still old people around who swore they could remember the time when Zeppo had a live parrot there. He had been intensely patriotic and had called the bird "Neville" after the then-Prime Minister. Now it was dead, and viewed the strings of customers with a baleful and glassy eye. To Zeppo, it was the love of his life and woe betide any man or woman unlucky enough to knock against it.

Cassady, one of the youngest of the Laurel Canyon chapter, was fascinated by the large gherkins, and ordered four with his cod and chips. Monk pointed out he wouldn't normally want more than one. That started it.

'Wait a minute, there. If I wanted, I'd eat the whole damned jar. In fact, I will eat the whole jar.'

Watched by an amazed Zeppo – and a mute Neville – the big Angel took the long fork and proceeded to spear and devour every one of the twenty or so green gherkins from the jar. By the fourth, his eyes were beginning to water, but he ploughed remorselessly on, encouraged by the cheers and shouts of the other brothers. When he finished, even Monk congratulated him.

Rick grinned at Gerry. 'Not a bad bit of class, eh? Any of your boys want to show us what they can do?'

Rat pushed the tall thin brother aside, with a contemptuous flick of the hand. Putting on an American accent, he swaggered through to the counter.

Narrowing his eyes, so that he thought he looked like John Wayne, Rat ran his gaze along the row of jars. And stopped at the one that had held the gherkins. Now all it held was a couple of pints of very old and rather dirty vinegar.

He gestured to Zeppo. 'I kinda reckon I feel like a little drink, barman. Pass me that there glass of sarsaparilla.'

Speechless, the Italian handed it to him. The watching Angels began to clap in unison, faster and faster, as the littlest brother drained the jar to the very bottom. For a moment, Rat stood there grinning proudly, then his already pale face began to turn paler. 'Pardon me, brothers. I feel like a walk in the good old clean air.' Then holding his hand to his mouth, Rat fled the shop.

To the amusement of the Last Heroes, Cassady had also been going a greener shade of pale and he followed Rat out of the door, muttering something about seeing how the little fellow was.

'Honours even, Rick?'

'I guess so, Gerry.'

But, at least one of the Last Heroes wasn't prepared to leave it like that. Good, brotherly love is one thing, but class is class, and it has to be shown. The chance came as they neared the end of the queue. Zeppo had been getting increasingly choked-off with the kidding and jokes of the Angels. When one of the Americans came to pay him, and fumbled for the right money, Zeppo made a crack about them getting out of the country.

That was the excuse Mick Moore needed. With lightning speed, he picked up Neville, and threw him with unerring accuracy straight into the hissing chip-fat. There are still people who swear that the bird squawked as it plunged into the boiling liquid, but all that bubbled to the top was a load of feathers and a lot of sawdust.

Zeppo couldn't believe it. He clutched his head, finding it near to bursting. The Angels fell about, English and American holding each other with helpless laughter. Yet, Monk wasn't finished. He looked at the Italian with a consoling smile. 'You know mate; you really ought to do something about that parrot of yours. If it goes on moulting like that, it's going to come to a sticky end.'

'Things went well, didn't they, boyo?'

'Yes, Gwyn. I reckon that cunning little Rupert had a word with Freddie; maybe even got him some junk. And Freddie had a word with, all together now, Rick and the Laurel Canyon boys.'

The albino laughed. But it was not his usual full-throated laugh. The tension they both felt still lay between them, like a heavy curtain. The parting was upon them, and they both found it difficult to talk.

After the meeting with Rick and the brothers, Gerry had taken him round the theatre, and they had talked, with half a dozen from each chapter, about problems they'd had and what should happen that night. It was agreed that the Americans would take the front line in the theatre – fifteen of them – and that the brothers and sisters of the Last Heroes would run the auditorium and the stage itself.

The news had been broken to all about the departure of the Wolves to clean up their own patch back in North Wales. With them gone, Gerry had lost in one swoop most of the top fighters in the chapter. All he had left, apart from the usual small number of prospects, old ladies and madams, was Mick Moore, Rat, Cochise, Riddler, Dick the Hat and Hanger John.

That meant that out of the whole of the old Last Heroes chapter who'd ridden under their last President, Vincent, only five were left, plus Brenda and Forty – the gargantuan old lady of Cochise.

The death toll for both the Wolves and the Last Heroes had been heavy, even since they joined together. Kafka, Draig, Ogof, Shelob, Gafr – all righteous brothers who'd got wiped in the best of ways; wearing their colours. Three of them still to be avenged. That would come. After the end of the tour.

Now, Gwyn and Gerry lay together, relaxing after the food and drink, passing a joint backwards and forwards between them. The rest of the brothers were getting ready for the run back home.

The sun shone almost painfully off the long white hair of Gwyn. In the caverns of his face, the ruby eyes glittered as brightly as ever.

'The Wolves are going back to their lair. Eh?'

'That's right, Gerry. I'm sorry it all has to end like this. More of a whimper than a bang, as my old sports teacher used to say. Still, when we've driven off the filth up there, you must come and see us again.'

They both knew that the amalgamation was over. That it had worked for a time, but all things must pass. From the next moment, they would still be brothers, but they would be leading different chapters. And, Gwyn would have the stronger. Gerry would need to open the doors to new members. The reputation of the Last Heroes was so strong that there would be a flood of motor-bike tearaways from all over the place wanting to join.

'I've been thinking about after the concert tomorrow, Gwyn. You know, there's not going to be much left.'

'Well, it's picking up the pieces again, then. Isn't it? It won't take that long.'

Gerry stood up, looking at his watch. 'Time you were moving. There's not that much light-time left.'

So, the Wolves mounted their hogs, collected their old ladies, and said their good-byes. And, one after the other, fists clenched in salute, they rode out of the car-park, heading for the South London Motorway and then the north and west.

Last to leave was Gwyn. Like Roman senators, he and Gerry clasped wrists. 'Remember the song that Gafr was singing when he wiped-out? "Ffarwel fy annwyl gariad". Fare well my own true love. Duw, Gerry, I'll miss you.'

Then the black glove twisted on the throttle and the power surged. The back wheel whined and spun on the concrete, spitting shards of gravel. And he was gone. Back to his hills and falling water.

The rest of the Angels walked inside, out of the cooling afternoon. Gerry waited on, until the high note of the engines had faded completely away. Then he shuddered, as though someone had walked over his grave, and he too went in to the warm.

14. IT REALLY WAS SUCH A NIGHT

An Extract from the Confidential Report of Assistant Chief Constable Israel Penn to the Home Secretary. Subject: The Music Concert at the South-East London Concert Hall. Dated: March 6th, 1999.

It must be born in mind that the previous appearances on this tour – at Birmingham, Glasgow, Liverpool, Cardiff and Leicester – have been comparatively free of major disturbances. There have been only two fatalities. The first, at Birmingham, was caused by a teenie falling on to a knife that she should certainly not have been carrying. The second, at Cardiff, was caused by a middle-aged woman falling to her death when she attempted to scale the side of the theatre to get near the dressing-room of the group known as "Foolsgold". She had borrowed climbing gear from her husband – a scaffolder with previous convictions for breaking and entering, who is currently doing a four year stretch in Walton – and had rigged it inexpertly. When it slipped, she plunged seventy feet to her death.

There have been many cases that required brief hospitalisation of some sort – mainly for shock or bruising. In total, the number of casualties have been less than one quarter of my original prediction. Also, injuries to my men have been less than half my predicted figure.

Although I was opposed to the use of motor-cycle hoodlums as an ad hoc security force, it must be said that my fears had proved groundless. Until last night.

My understanding of the situation is that a number of the English/Welsh members of the gang had to leave on unspecified business. My belief is that it concerned trouble back in Wales, and I have already passed on a recommendation to the head of Mercia C.I.D. to that effect.

Whatever the reason, a number of American gang members were used last night, and they proved less than adequate. My belief is that they remained unconvinced, despite the strongest warnings from Vinson and myself, of the true dangers of letting any popular music crowd get at all out of hand.

Fortunately, the so-called "Last Heroes" gang members were there in adequate strength to aid the Americans. But, it proved a close-run thing.

In fighting on the stage near the end of the act of the group called "Central Heating", three of the Americans received serious knife wounds, from which two of them subsequently died. Four girls were also badly wounded in the fracas, but all are expected to recover.

I am forced to admit that the wounding resulted from the weapons that numbers of the girls and women had managed to smuggle in. At my express insistence, none of the Hell's Angels carried any weapons.

One of the newspapers today carried an extremely inflammatory article about the American Angels and about the violence that happened last night. They make little mention of the fact that it was the motor-cycle boys who died. I fear that this might inflame the "middies" and the "teenies" to worse excesses on the last night of the tour this evening.

I am reliably informed that a number of the London gangs of "skulls" have obtained tickets for this last show and may be there in some numbers. Since they are the traditional enemies of the motor-cycle gangs – a rivalry that goes back to the days of the "Mods" and "Rockers" in the nineteen-sixties – the dangers that may result from tonight's concert must be obvious.

Therefore I regret that I must request the Home Secretary to use his powers to order that this final concert shall be cancelled. I can arrange for a sufficient force to be made available to ensure no breach of public order if this is done.

At the very least, I would ask that the Public Order Act should be amended so that I can place enough uniformed men inside the hall to check any trouble. Unless this is done, I am not prepared to take the responsibility for any casualties that may result.

Israel Penn, Assistant Chief Constable,
Birmingham.

Home Secretary's Recommendation:
Is this man losing his grip? I will not interfere in the simple and healthy pleasures of the young, merely to please some alarmist old woman. No. Recommendations rejected. Please send me this officer's record.

15. AND BID FAREWELL AND NOT GIVE A DAMN

The big new concert hall in the centre of London, where the old Covent Garden fruit market used to stand, had been designed by a Czech architect – the winner of an international competition – and held four thousand people. Shaped like a huge shell it had proved a great success with pop concerts. This hadn't been its original function, but the acoustics meant that anything much under a full-blooded scream was inaudible near the back.

Tickets were fetching absurd money on the underground market, but there were still buyers. The police, under the control of the bitter and angry Penn, had sealed off many of the surrounding streets, and only those lucky few with tickets were allowed through. At least that would keep the area immediately around the hall clear, and give Penn a chance to have a reserve force of men close outside for the trouble that both he and Gerry expected. The hall held a helicopter launch pad, and a shuttle service had been arranged to get first the stars and then the Angels away.

That was the idea.

After a cursory frisking by police men and women, the middies and teenies, with a sprinkling of skulls, screamed their way into the hall. The doors were opened at seven on the dot – just thirty minutes before the show was due to start. Anyone who hadn't made it by then was simply too late, and the doors were locked. There were a few exceptions, but it was generally only the powerful who got in after the show had begun. There had been a famous fracas when a titled lady, supposedly still happily married to her Minister husband, had turned up drunk with a transvestite pop star and had threatened to get the show closed if they didn't let her in. She didn't get in and the show went on.

The WARNINGs had been printed and distributed as usual, but they were losing that edge of fear that they had once instilled. Last night had shown that the Angel heavies could be almost ignored. Certainly they could be hurt, and even killed.

The deaths had badly upset the Laurel Canyon brothers and Freddie Dolan, who was on a guilt kick, claiming – with some justification – that he had been responsible for the killings. Gerry had tried to talk to the American brothers, but they had withdrawn into themselves, arranging for the bodies of the wiped-out to lie in a morgue until they could find the time for a true Angel burial.

All Rick had said was: 'Stay cool, Gerry. It won't happen tomorrow.' When pressed to find out why he knew it wouldn't happen again, he clammed up. The meeting over planning had been so brief as to be almost useless, and it had been left again to Gerry and Penn to produce any plan that might work.

The problem here was simply one of numbers. In the favour of the Angels was the narrowness of the stage, which gave a smaller frontage for any direct attack. In fact, it's worth noting that the stage was so narrow that a full symphony orchestra couldn't even get on it. Another reason why the owners were so glad to have pop concerts there!

For this last gig, Gerry decided that there would be little point in scattering his tiny forces through the audience. The element of surprise would not be there, and they would swiftly be overwhelmed. So, it had to be one line across the front – which would be Rick and the Laurel Canyon brothers – and the rest of the Last Heroes at the sides of the stage and in the wings ready to come to their aid if a serious charge developed.

Gerry parted the heavy green drapes and peered out at the crowd. The house lights were already dimmed and the noise was climaxing. He turned to Mick Moore at his elbow. 'You know what that is out there? It's a riot just waiting to happen.'

When the lights spotted clean out, and a single beam isolated a cone of brightness at the centre of the stage, the cheering and shouts were deafening. Gerry walked quietly into the centre of that noise and light, and the cheers became boos. Although he didn't see it, Gerry heard the hiss of a missile pass close to his head, and he felt the dull thunk as it struck the stage.

He glanced behind him, and saw an ordinary dart quivering in the wood, driven in so deep that the shaft was sunk right in. From the angle of the dart, it looked as though it had been thrown from the balcony, or even from the upper balcony.

Something like that had been one of Gerry's major fears, and it was damnably hard to check. But, he had a contingency plan, and he shouted the code word 'Throwing' to Riddler waiting in the wings. Immediately, the house lights came on again, and the American brothers ran out to make a ring round the front of the stage, peering intently into the upper regions.

'Anybody, anybody who's standing up, gets jumped on hard! Any cunt who throws anything at this stage gets hit! Hard! Right, this is the last concert in this present tour, and I don't want it screwed up.'

'Fucking get on with it, you big poof!!' A man's voice, from somewhere near the front of the stalls. There were a crowd of skulls down there.

'First. Here's Foolsgold!!'

'Thank you all for being just sweet. I'm only sorry we can't get to meet every one of you. I can see a lot of ladies out there that I'd really like to meet on a lot more intimate terms.'

The slush from the leader of Foolsgold – the lovable Jak Whiteson – was soaked up eagerly by the frustrated middies, eager for the fantasy chance to lose their grey identities in the sparkling world of the young boys with their lean bodies and the tight trousers.

It was too much for one woman, who leaped wetly from her seat and pounded down the centre aisle. That sparked off several more middies to make their run. From the side of the stage, Gerry got ready to go to the assistance of the Americans. But this time, there was no need. There was a confused melee in front of the stage, as bodies whirled and fell. There were a few screams and at least one pair of frilly knickers sailed through the air to land at the feet of the saturnine Al Durer.

It was difficult for Gerry to see exactly what happened from where he was, but the lights flickered off some metal, and when the flurry had cleared, none of the brothers seemed hurt. But, five women lay moaning on the carpet, staining it red. Two more didn't moan. Or move.

Or breathe.

At Gerry's instant order, the house lights were dimmed down, and Foolsgold did their last number – a waltz-tempo version of the Janis Joplin hit, 'Down On Me' – to a darkened and angry audience. The Last Heroes slipped to the front of the stalls and helped drag away the wounded women, as well as those who lay still.

With the fickleness of the big crowd, the middies and teenies forgot the dead and the dying in the excitement of that last song. When it ended, the Angels combined to hold back the rush that followed and there were no further problems. The women who mobbed the stage hardly noticed that their feet sank into the pile of a carpet made soggy with blood.

Somehow, in the caves and recesses of the huge theatre, Rick Padrino and his band of brothers managed to perform an impressive disappearing act during the intermission. Failing to find them, Gerry went looking for Rupert Colt.

Rupert found him first.

'Rupert! What the fuck is going on tonight? The Americans are all tooled up with knives. And guns for all I know. What are you...?' The words faded away as it suddenly penetrated that Rupert wasn't taking a lot of notice of what he was saying. And, that he was wearing a heavy overcoat and carrying a black leather case. And, that he'd recently shaved off the bushy moustache he'd been sporting since they met at Nant Gwrtheyrn.

Rupert saw the question leaving Gerry's eyes and moving to his lips and got in first. 'I know what you're going to ask my love, and I fear the answer is "yes". I'm buggering off. "Rupert Colt takes a powder" is the name of this particular game.'

'Why? And where?'

'Because I've had enough. It's the male menopause, baby. I've seen too much misery – does that sound corny? It shouldn't. It's one of the truest things I've ever said. If I don't get out now, I'll finish up as an old agent. Button-holing big men at boring parties, with sticky fingers and promises of the sensation that's going to make all our fortunes. I'm fed up of drinking too much and sleeping too little and popping too many pills. I know that I could be on smack within three months. And, I don't want it. In fact, I'm thinking of making a real effort to stop the pills. When I get to ... to where I'm going, the air and work should help a lot.'

'What are you going to do? Be a bloody farmer up in the Black Hills of Dakota?'

Rupert looked hurt. 'I'm not joking, Gerry. I'm sorry, but I thought you might understand.'

Gerry regretted his joke immediately. 'I'm sorry, mate. I was only taking the piss a bit. Honest. If you can get out, and you can make it work, then it'll be the best thing you ever did. Really.'

'Really? You think that? That I might be able to make it work?'

Despite all, Gerry truly liked the little man, and he put his arms on his shoulders and smiled at him. 'Listen, man. If you want it to work, then it's going to work. You really are going to drop right out of it?'

'Yeah. Change my name. Keep off the telephone. Only let a very, very few of my friends – whoever they are – know where I'm going. And, never come back. I've got a bit of money put away. I've bought a homestead on the borders of Wales. I've done all I can for this tour, and I just don't want to be around afterwards. So, I'm off. I was looking for you to say good-bye.'

Solemnly, almost formally, they pulled apart, and shook hands. The thought came to Gerry that yet another strand of his life had pulled loose. 'Where exactly are you going?'

Rupert shook his head. 'No. I want to make a few weeks there just on my own. See if I can. Then, if it works out, you're going to be the first one I ask up to see me. Don't worry about getting in touch. That's the thing I've always been very good at.'

Somewhere below them, a bell was ringing insistently, signalling the end of the intermission. Gerry patted the little man on the shoulder. 'Good luck, Rupert. I'll be waiting to hear from you.'

He walked away down the corridor, and turned at the end to see Rupert wiping his nose. Or, maybe his eyes? The small figure waved to him, and the familiar husky voice came floating down to him. 'Take care, now. Keep on trucking, baby.'

On the way to the stage, Gerry was stopped by Brenda. 'Jesus, man, where've you been? You know those Americans are all tooled up. Three of those old women are dead. Penn is rushing around like a fart in a colander, threatening to come in with the Seventh Cavalry. And, I reckon that one or two of Padrino's brothers have guns.'

'Guns! Christ, that's all we need.'

Brenda took him by the arm. 'I saw Rupert. You know he's splitting.'

'Yes. That's where I've been. There's not going to be much left is there, after this? Anyway, I've got to go on stage and introduce Central Heating. Tell everyone to take extra care. This could really be the big one.'

Just as he was leaving, Brenda grabbed him and kissed him hard on the mouth. 'Gerry.'

'There isn't time. Not any more.'

'I just wanted to tell you that I wasn't going. With Lady and Holly. I'm staying with you.'

Gerry looked at her, hardly able to take the news in. Then, ignoring shouts from the stage for him to get on, he took her in his arms and returned her kiss. 'See you after,' was all he said.

Then he left to go and announce the last act of the last show. Central Heating.

It was a fantastic act. Freddie Dolan had never been better, and the three others – Jim, Hal and Matt – drove him up and on to new heights and new depths. They opened with a chanted song, about the power of the occult, then slipped easily into a thirty minute string of their hits and big album tracks.

The excitement communicated itself to the audience, and it seethed and bubbled, screamed and moaned. Another dart was thrown, and it hit one of the Laurel Canyon Angels in the shoulder. Padrino desperately held back two of the brothers who wanted to go into the audience, and Gerry could see for the first time that they were actually wearing hidden automatics.

As usual, Mick Moore was with him, just behind the side curtain. Putting his mouth to his ear, Gerry shouted: 'Go and find Penn! Quick as you can! Tell him to stand by with everything he's got! Tell him some people are carrying guns! Tell him I said that I thought this one is really going to blow! Quick! Then get back here; I'm going to need you!'

The set went on, and Gerry waited anxiously for Monk's return. As soon as he got back he made straight for Gerry and told him the news. 'Penn's tied up with rioting outside. He says to try and stop it. He can't get to you for at least ten minutes. And, he said "Good luck".'

'Fucking funny, Israel.'

Two more songs went by, and the tension still boiled up, until it seemed impossible that it could go higher. The hall reverberated to the battering of the guitars, with the amps full-up. Screams and moans tore at the ears, destroying all thought. It truly was like a scene from a medieval hell.

Central Heating reached the end of the song, and Freddie came forward to the mike. Sweat streamed down his naked chest, and his trousers gaped open at the front. His hair was tangled into greasy string over his eyes, hiding the light in them.

Before going on, he'd taken a shot of synthesised psilocybin – which is harder to say than shoot – and the effects were just getting to him. Historians believe that it was eating hallucinogenic mushrooms, such as psilocybin and fly agaric, that gave the Vikings their strange berserk savagery.

Now, things were moving inside his head – things that he hardly knew about. His eyes dilated, and specks of froth hung at the corners of his mouth. There was only one song to go. And, Freddie Dolan swung on up to the mike to announce it.

'Thanks. Thanks. All of you. One number then we have to split from you. It's a newie, and it's dedicated to the brothers who've looked after us on this tour. They're my friends, whatever some of you may think of them. This one is for the Hell's Angels. "Grey Turns Green".'

Immediately, from the bunch of skulls near the front, the chant started to go up: 'Murderers! Cowards! Queers! Killers! Killers!! Killers!!!' It built up to a crescendo of noise, inflaming the teenies to explosive pitch.

Freddie and the rest of Central Heating ploughed into the new song, but they'd only got one verse through, when the drug freaked the top of Freddie's mind and he tripped out completely. The Vikings used to strip off their clothes when the fighting madness hit them, and Freddie did the same. He clawed at his trousers, leaving bloody furrows on his white skin from his own nails. The clothes scattered to the stage floor, and he stood there totally naked. His eyes rolled back into his skull and he wailed in a thin, high, penetrating voice: 'I want you all. Now. Come and take me. Please!'

The last word was drawn out to a grinding falsetto scream, rasping like a saw on the edge of a sheet of plate glass. It was all the catalyst and invitation that the little girls needed.

In an unstoppable many-headed throng, they poured out of their seats towards the stage. The American Angels saw the futility of trying to check it and all climbed on the front of the stage. Central Heating's driving sound wavered and stopped, the amplifiers hissing into silence. Matt and Jim fled to the back, but Hal dropped his axe and went to try and help Freddie who stood stock-still, arms at his sides, vulnerable in his nakedness, waiting for the mob to devour him.

From the moment the first wave broke against the high front of the stage, things became impossibly confused. All that can be done is to select odd incidents and try to report them.

Many of the girls had managed to smuggle in knives, and these were licking out of their hands as they ran. Two of the Americans were too slow in making the stage and they were dropped and trampled in seconds. The others tried to hold the front of the stage, kicking at the crowd. Several of the brothers also had knives and they slashed fruitlessly at the fists and hands that threatened them. Blood sprayed everywhere from cuts, but there were too many.

Cassady was one of the brothers who had a gun, and he emptied it into the air, hoping it would cool things. But, the moment the last shot was fired, fingers clawed him to the edge of the stage, and he was pulled to the floor. The last thing he saw were the forest of legs and feet, in chunky fashion shoes, milling about him before he was kicked to death.

Hal Marx failed to reach Freddie, being checked by one girl who'd come round the side. He saw her coming, and saw the slim-bladed kitchen knife she held in her hand. Yet, he did nothing to stop her or to protect himself.

What he saw was an angel-faced child of sixteen, with long blonde hair waving softly about her untouched face. By some freak of fashion taste, she was dressed exactly like a schoolgirl of the fifties. She wore neat little patent leather shoes, with white ankle socks. Her blue pleated skirt floated about her firm thighs, revealing a glimpse of her cotton pants. Her silk blouse was drawn tight about her budding breasts.

She was a vision from the dreams of lust, and Hal found himself paralysed by her. He even put his hands out in a vague gesture of welcome. The blade of the knife slipped between his hands and sank into his stomach. The force of the blow through his flesh flung him on his back, and the girl fell on top of him.

He tried to rise, tried to push her weight off him, but the effort was too much. But, the girl failed to get the souvenir she wanted. Other teenies came yelling over and the knives clashed and sparked off each other in Hal Marx's body. In all the action, the souvenir got so cut about that nobody finished up with more than one little piece.

In an attempt to save some of his brothers, Rick Padrino finally drew his own gun and fired into the press of struggling bodies. Five bullets ripped into the crowd, but it was like trying to slay the Hydra. Kill one and twenty more grabbed at you. Rick was about to fire again, when the heavy charge from a sawn-off shotgun nearly tore him in half. He was so thin that many of the pellets gouged their way clean through him, and hit the expensive amplification equipment behind him. Sparks flew from shorted wires.

The noise of the shotgun hardly penetrated the keening of the girls, and only those nearest to the man who fired were aware of it. Leading his band of skulls, the gunman jumped up through the gap left by Padrino's torn corpse and headed for the side of the stage. His gold ear-ring swung madly from his tightly-cropped skull.

Gerry, with his eye for tactical strategy that had saved him several times in the past, realised that there was no point in waiting around to die. The Americans were overwhelmed and only two seemed to be still on their feet. Mouthing his orders, he managed to get Monk to shepherd all the Last Heroes towards the emergency exit door, designed to be locked from the other side, and made of heavy steel. The first girls were only just getting a hold on the stage and were making for the dazed figure of Freddie Dolan.

'Hold the door for me!' Gerry shouted as he sprinted round the back of the amps and got to Dolan. As he was trying to drag him to safety, the eight skulls made their appearance. A feral grin split the face of Bookie Wyatt, as he recognised the leader of the Last Heroes. His lips tugged back over his rotting teeth as he aimed the twelve-bore, its barrels gaping hugely at Gerry.

Dolan had watched the happening with a vague, distant interest, until he saw the gun. His jaw dropped open, and a mangled shriek burst out, as he launched himself at the slight figure of the skull. Contemptuously, Bookie Wyatt smashed the sawn-off shotgun to the side of Dolan's head, cracking his face open, and sending him staggering towards the amplifiers. Before anyone could move, the superstar made contact with the bared wires hanging loose at the front. His body arced forward, his arms flapping uncontrollably against other live connections. His eyes opened wide, staring unseeing into the slaughterhouse on the stage. Smoke gushed from his skin, where the electric current scorched and seared it.

Finally, his own weight dragged him down the amplifiers, breaking the contacts. Freddie Dolan slumped face-down on the stage, his limbs spastically twitching. A dark thread of blood tricked from his mouth.

His death took only a second.

Gerry stood there and watched his own killer stepping lightly towards him, the gun unwavering. He poised himself on the balls of his feet, ready for a desperate leap if any half-chance came.

Wyatt stopped, maybe twenty feet away, and smiled. A very unpleasant smile. It vanished as he was hit from behind by Brenda.

She had waited to see if Gerry managed to rescue Freddie Dolan. They all knew about the skull leader with the gold ear-ring, and she ran through the narrow corridor behind the stage, until she emerged behind the drums to the left of the stage. There wasn't much space, but she took a few steps and jumped.

As she took-off, a trailing wire caught at her ankle and she half-leaped, half-fell against the skull leader. It was enough to throw him off-balance, but not enough to make him fall or drop the gun. Gerry had been ready, and he didn't miss the chance.

Fists and feet working, he attacked the skulls, joined by Brenda. And by a small, scurrying Hell's Angel whose knife flicked and darted like the eyes of a Rat.

Several of the skulls were down; some still and some moaning and thrashing about like dying fish. One sat upright, muttering to himself, trying to stuff his intestines back into the slit made by Rat's blade.

A cry, staccato and urgent, from the skulls' leader froze everyone. 'Get away from the girl!'

The tableau was still, the screams and yells from the fighting mob behind them almost forgotten. Bookie Wyatt was happy, as his lean finger squeezed the light trigger.

Even as he fired, and the pellets starred out, Rat jumped at him to try and save Brenda. He was too late by a fraction of time, but he was in time to sink his knife straight into the skull's right eye-socket, killing him instantly.

Riddler and Cochise led a charge from the safety door that scattered the remaining skulls and sent them scampering for the protection of the crowd. Rat paused only to pull out his knife, wiping it on Bookie's silk shirt front.

Gerry scooped Brenda up in his arms and walked slowly back, guarded by his brothers. The screeching mob of teenage harpies made no attempt to follow them, for there was death in the faces of the Angels. Even as they pulled and bolted the heavy steel door, the Last Heroes heard the crackling of small-arms' fire, and a voice bursting out over the bedlam demanding quiet. It was the voice of Assistant Chief Constable Israel Penn.

He had arrived too late to save the lives of twelve of the American Angels. Of two of the members of Central Heating. Of six skulls. Of eleven middle-aged women. And of over a hundred girls, mostly trampled to death in the hysterical charge.

He was also too late to save the life of Brenda.

Gerry had sent the rest of the brothers who remained, plus the mamas and old ladies, to get the hogs ready for a run out, as soon as things had quietened down a bit. Holly and Lady had disappeared as soon as the fracas started.

In the dark passageway, they could hear order being restored. Only Monk was left with Gerry. The single sound in that cramped space, was the painful bubbling as Brenda tried to breathe. To stay alive.

'Push off, will you mate, and make sure everything's ready. Tell them to head for the house in Hertfordshire as soon as they can. You go and lead them. I'll come when I can.' His voice was muffled, as he bent over his old lady, cradling her, holding her to him, feeling the life slipping away.

'Will you be along?'

There was a flash of anger. 'Mick. Do as you're told and fuck off!'

There was a knocking at the door, and the sound of someone heaving against the bolts. 'They'll soon be round the other way, Gerry.'

'Yeah.' The voice was tired. 'Yeah, you'd better go now. Thanks, Mick, for staying. I'll see you.'

Mick Moore dropped his hand to his President's shoulder, then walked away, to lead the tatters of the chapter to a place of safety. The Last Heroes would, yet again, have to go underground.

Behind him, Gerry felt the first pangs of cramp biting into the muscles of his legs. He stretched a little, trying to ease his position. The body of Brenda seemed to be getting heavier.

The shot had hit her in the chest, crushing her ribs in and demolishing most of her lungs. The blood loss was colossal, and he was amazed that she should still be breathing. Her eyes were open, and she twice tried to speak. He leaned over her, wiping the blood away that filled her mouth.

Brenda's lips trembled and she made a last attempt to lift herself. Gerry put his head down, until his ear was right by her mouth. The banging had stopped, but he could now hear footsteps away to his right, behind the stage.

In his ear, he could just catch the faintest whispering. Words, torn painfully from her ruined chest.

'Sorry ... love ... should ... got... gun ... Looks ... like ... no... more ... run ... I ...'
A coughing fit hit her, and Gerry thought she'd gone. But, she tried one last time.

'Hold ... me ... love ... I ... always ... loved ... you.'

Gerry still held her, even after the life had irrevocably left her. He was still there, kneeling awkwardly on the floor, when Assistant Chief Constable Penn strode in, a streak of blood across his cheek. He stopped at the sight, pausing uneasily in the doorway. Gerry looked up at him.

'Hello, Israel. I'm all alone, now.'

16. GREY TURNS GREEN
By the late Freddie Dolan, of Central Heating.

I opened up the window
And the sky climbed high inside me,
While the city blocks grew higher
And my lover slept unknowing.
The grey lay heavy on me.

The hands of friends are waiting
For my tears to fall upon them.
And I wake up from my darkness
With a flower at my table.
And the grey lay lighter on me.

My clothes brush me like strangers
On my brittle waking body,
And I must walk from my lover
And slide out to the highway,
Where the green is just appearing.

The dead in shrouds behind me
Touch their minds with splintered fingers
As I climb the purple mountains
While the air sings in my brain.
And the grey has turned to green.

Yes, the grey has turned to green.

Book Four:

ANGELS ON MY MIND

1. A TIME TO BE REAPING

The sun blinked a watery eye through the early summer haze. It was a quiet time among the green-muffled hills of Shropshire. Up on the slopes of the Long Mynd, sprawled like some gigantic sleeping monster above Church Stretton, a highly-powered motor-cycle roared along the narrow road.

The rider was alone, in that grey-green world. Alone among the bracken, with only the sheep trotting away from the noise of his passing, shying at the intrusion into their silence. Although Easter lay only a week or so back, the weather was warm, and the rider straddled his machine in short-sleeved denim jacket and faded jeans. His hair was long, blowing in the wind, streaming out behind him like a banner of protest.

If you could get close enough behind him, you would see that his jacket sported a colourful motif – a feral death's head in white and crimson – with lettering beneath it. Worn by wind and sun and time, they still stood out starkly against the pale blue denim. "Last Heroes" it said. The Last Heroes motor-cycle gang of Hell's Angels, affiliated by charter to the great chapter of Oakland, California. Their charter signed by the late and wonderful Sonny Barger himself.

Stretching back his shoulders, as though he was trying to shrug off some load, the rider throttled back the huge machine, and pulled slowly into the side of the road. All around him, the ground dropped sheerly away to shaded valleys, with dark pools at their centres. His hand pulled up on the brake, and the bike finally stopped. He kicked the rest down and got off, letting the powerful engine cough itself into silence.

Almost as a matter of habit he patted the tangerine-flake enamel petrol tank, with the silver words *Harley-Davidson – Electra Glide* glinting in the sunlight. Though, it's doubtful if the makers would have been very pleased to see what had been done to their Rolls-Royce of motor-bikes. All the heavy chrome trim had been stripped off, and the front forks raked back. Shorn of its surplus weight, it could easily reach over a hundred miles an hour, and was sufficiently manoeuvrable to shake off any official pursuer.

Humming to himself – the song written for the Angels by Freddie Dolan before he was electrocuted at a rock concert the previous year, "Grey Turns Green" – he walked over to a clear patch of turf and sat down. He was conscious of the growing heat of the sun, and he slipped out of his colours and let them lie by his feet.

The man was Gerry "Wolf" Vinson, President of the Last Heroes chapter. What was left of it. A presidency that he'd taken over from the previous leader – Vincent – about ... how long ago was it now? It seemed many years, but it couldn't have been more than a couple of years ago.

He reached the line about "The dead in shrouds behind me touch their minds with splintered fingers", and he stopped singing. There had been so many dead. Friends, enemies, brothers and sisters. It had been a long and bloody road since he first joined the Angels. His face set in hard lines, and he lay back on the springy turf, watching the clouds chase each other across the sky. A falcon stooped over his head, a tiny dot against the blue. He let his mind wander back.

So many dead.

He remembered bodies splashed along a motorway, leaving a trail of blood and loops of intestine. Bodies torn apart by bullets and by the blast of shotguns. Men crying with pain and the fear of death. Men who faced death with a grin, or with resignation.

And, not only men. Gerry wandered deeper into rooms at the back of his memory that he normally kept closed – even to himself. At the end of the rock concert, there had been the one death that had touched him more closely than any other.

The shot had hit her in the chest, crushing her ribs in and demolishing most of her lungs. The blood loss was colossal, and he had been amazed that she should still be breathing. Her eyes had been open, and she had twice tried to speak. He remembered how he had leaned over her, wiping the blood away that had filled her mouth.

By putting his head down, close to her mouth, he was able to catch the whisper of sound, painfully torn from her ruined chest.

He could even remember her last words. Always would.

'Hold ... me ... love ... I ... always ... loved ... you.'

He felt his face wet, and lifted a hand to wipe away the tear. There had always been Brenda – right from the start. Now, even she was gone.

With all the rest.

Vincent, blasted down in an abandoned quarry, the victim of his own anger and hatred. Priest, snuffed on his last run, the most righteous brother of them all. Legs, Moron, Crasher, Dylan, Tiny Terry. Wiped out.

Gafr, the mad, stoned Welsh brother, from the Wolves' chapter, beheaded on a weaving run.

With a song on his lips: "Ffarwel fy annwyl gariad"; Fare thee well, my own true love.

Draig killed in the fight against the Ghouls. The silk and satin Angels, most of whom perished in the cataclysm in the London offices of the *Daily Leader*; Evel, Vanya, Rohan – all dead.

Shelob, Kafka – oldest of the brothers – and Ogof, blasted off the world by skulls. The Laurel Canyon chapter, all murdered in the savage aftermath of the rock concert. Rick Padrino and Cassady.

Gerry sat up and looked over the hillside. Far below him, a tiny speck in the solitude, he could see the sun bouncing off the bald head of a stout man, pushing a loaded bicycle up the steep path.

Idly, he watched him, not really seeing him, letting his thoughts wander away. Away from the dead to the living.

In the last few months, the chapter had gone underground again. All that was left of the Last Heroes was a handful of hard-core, full-patch brothers.

One of them, the indestructible Rat, had been along there before Gerry even appeared on the scene, and would maybe be around after he'd gone. Cochise and his massively built old lady, Forty. Gerry grinned slightly as he remembered the suggestion from Rat that if she got any bigger, they'd have to rechristen her Fifty. Dick the Hat, Riddler and Hanger John. Fine brothers, that you could depend on in a fight. All capable of showing the sort of class that would blow the minds of any straight citizens unfortunate to be around.

And, there was Monk, and his lovely old lady, Modesty. Monk – or Mick Moore as he used to be called. Gerry knew that the day was coming when Monk would split from them. He kept talking about settling down, and one day the talk would stop, and there'd be another gap in the run.

The man with the bike was closer. As Gerry watched him, he stopped to wipe sweat from his head. Then, leaning forward against the handlebars, he pressed on towards where Gerry sat.

The Wolves still held the fastnesses of the Lleyn Peninsula. That desolate wilderness that became a crowded holiday area as summer wore on, then became a depopulated ghost land, where only the old now lived.

Gerry had been up to see them once, but there had been a subtle tension between Gwyn and himself. Once, the red-eyed albino had ridden with Gerry, but he was the President of his own chapter now. They had sniffed suspiciously at each other, like two stiff-legged old wolves.

The tension had eased, once Gerry had made it clear the old days were over for him. The firelight had glinted on the red eyes of Gwyn, ruby pools in that shocking face of wind-washed bone, and they had got drunk together. When they parted, Gwyn had told him to see them again. But, maybe there are things you can never go back to.

Now, it was time to stop looking back and keep on looking forward. To decide what road he would take. Above him, the hawk dived at a pigeon, but the slower bird side-slipped at the last minute, and the claws hissed harmlessly by.

Time to move on. Shropshire fell within the control of Assistant Chief Constable Israel Pitman Penn, a long-time enemy of the Angels. It wouldn't be a good idea to get caught on his patch. Not without a bit of support. The rest of the chapter were safe down in their headquarters in Hertfordshire, while their President went on this solo run, to get his head together.

The man with the bike was right up close to him now. To his amusement, Gerry noticed that the bike was one of the old sit-up-and-beg type of ladies' machine, with no crossbar. The saddle and handlebars were draped with all manner of bags and containers. The top of a head of celery peeked out of one, and a chicken's feet out of another.

The stout man, heavily built around the shoulders and with a deep chest that told of an athletic past, grinned at him as he came level, and shouted out a greeting.

'Good day to you! Lovely day to be alive, isn't it?'

Then he stopped, staring hard at Gerry. The Angel gazed back at him, wondering whether there was going to be any aggro. The way the tramp was screwing him could mean trouble. Although he was obviously getting on, he still looked as though he knew how to handle himself.

In fact, there was something familiar about him. Where the hell had he seen that squat physique before?

Wait a minute!

At the same time, recognition dawned on the man's face.

'I thought I knew you. Yes, of course. Two nine eight, three seven four two five. Vinson. Gerald.'

'Jesus Christ! It's Sergeant Newman!'

To Gerry and to the Last Heroes, Sergeant Newman had become an almost mythical figure. During Gerry's brief and lethal army career, Newman had been an enormous influence on him. Apart from anything else, he had been his combat instructor, and it had been Newman who had taught him all the tricks that had made him the efficient killing machine he had finally become.

All of that had been years ago. Now, here was old Newman, face as brown as a berry, his hairpiece – or 'dead rat' as they'd called it – discarded, pushing an old bike across a hill in the middle of Shropshire.

It was bloody unnerving. It was like meeting Count Dracula and finding he'd turned into a benevolent old Sunday School Teacher.

'Sergeant, what the hell are you doing up here? Don't tell me you quit the Army?'

Newman let his loaded bike drop to the spring bracken and let himself down easily beside Gerry. Before he spoke, he let his eyes roam unhurriedly over the Angel's body, taking in the biceps, the flat ridges of stomach muscle, and the general muscle tone.

Grudgingly, he spoke. 'You've looked after yourself, Vinson. You looked like a killer then and you still look like a killer. I've read about you, in the papers. Massacring coppers in Birmingham a couple of years ago. Blowing up a paper's offices and then running guard duty on a load of poof pop singers. You get around, son.'

It was impossible to tell from the neutral tone of Newman's voice if he was being disapproving or not. He picked up a blade of grass and stuck it between his teeth. For a few moments there was silence. Then, he went on.

'I always knew you'd do something like that. I've never seen you as the office type. I reckoned you'd either end up with a bit of power, or you'd end up dead. Well, you've got your bit of power, and you must have come bloody close to buying it a few times.'

Gerry nodded. 'Yeah. I reckon. But, come on, what about you?'

'Me? Well, a year or so back, I was just getting ready to sign on for another seven in the mob. It would have been my last round. Retirement after that. I had a spot of leave owing to me, so I took a small tent and went camping. Just on my own. All over the place. Saw lots of things. I ... what's the expression you lot use? Got my mind all in.'

Gerry laughed. 'Got your head together.'

'Right, son. Dead right. Basically, it seemed to me that I was working my arse into an early grave shouting my lungs out at a bunch of no-hopers. So, I just never went back, simple as that. I get by doing a few odd jobs. No problem. Find a nice quiet derry in winter and that's that. I'm my own man, son.'

They chatted for a couple of hours about the bad old days, and Gerry filled Newman in on some of the things that had happened since he left the forces. Time wore on. The Angel found it easy to persuade Newman to share a joint with him. And then another.

'I want to be in Woolaston by dark, so I'd better be moving.'

'All right. I want to get on the way back to our base. It's been, you know, really good to see you again. I'm glad things are going the way you want.'

Both men stood up. Faced each other. Gerry was the taller by three or four inches. Awkwardly, he held out his hand, and Newman took it, grasping it firmly. Gerry noticed that his ex-sergeant still kept up his karate training. There were no nails on the hand, and the edges of the palm were as hard and unbending as a chunk of oak. Gerry would have backed himself in a fight against most men. But, against Newman? Maybe. Maybe not.

He mounted the Electra Glide, feeling the leather of the seat warm through his jeans. The engine barked into life on the second attempt, and he throttled back, until it just ticked over. Now that he was leaving, it seemed hard to find any words.

'Look after yourself, sergeant. I'll maybe see you again. Bye.'

He began to move slowly away. Leaning on his overloaded pushbike, Newman watched him go. Suddenly, he shouted to him. 'Gerry! Always look out for your back!'

The Angel waved a hand to show he had heard, then revved the powerful machine up. The front wheel lifted for a few yards, then he pressed it down and sped away South and westwards, towards the sun. Over the top of the Mynd.

He didn't look back.

Funny, he thought, after all that remembering the old days, to run across old Newman. A gentleman of the road. Old Newman of all people. Doing his own thing. Man's got to do what a man's got to do. But, he never expected to find the immaculate instructor ending up a tramp.

It surely was a day for coincidences.

More than he knew.

Gerry rolled slowly and carefully down the very steep southerly end of the Port Way by the hamlet of Asterton. Then he rode to Plowden, turning sharp left on to the A489 towards Ludlow. Although the afternoon was wearing on, the sun was still warm.

Just through Cheney Longville, up on the right, there's the remains of an old Tumulus. A minor road comes on to the main road from the right. The remains of an old Roman thoroughfare.

Gerry was roaring along, the wind stinging his eyes, when a car pulled out of the side road, straight in front of him. He braked sharply, feeling his hog swerve, the back wheel snaking viciously. He yelled out a single word of insult, and thrust two fingers at the departing driver's rear mirror. In return, he got only his gesture repeated.

That was enough. He slewed the chopped bike round and shrieked off in pursuit. Neatly stashed away alongside the tank was a length of highly-polished drive-chain, and he snapped it off and let it dangle low in his left hand. Gradually, he closed the gap, oblivious to all other traffic.

The driver saw him coming and tried to accelerate away. But, nippy though his sports car was, it couldn't take the tight country corners the way the chopper could. Gerry stoked it right up, riding to the limit, and even a little beyond it. On one sharp left hand twisting corner, he sent up a shower of sparks from his foot rest. But, the gap was closing. He was within thirty yards, and he could see the driver – a young man in a bright check jacket – casting frightened glances in his mirror.

Twenty yards. The driver tried to snake to throw him off, but Gerry was in the catbird seat, and he could control the action. Already, he felt the warm glow of action spreading through his guts. This bastard had cut him up badly, and he was going to have to pay the price. It had been a long time since Gerry had been able to have some solo action. Too long, maybe.

He was delighted that the sports car was nearly new, with gleaming yellow paint. Ten yards.

Five. Then, he was within reach. Somewhere behind him, Gerry was vaguely aware of another car, tyres screeching in protest, as it rode with them. But, that was for later. If anyone else wanted to get in the action, then that was going to be all right with Gerry. Tangle with the Angels, and you mess with the inside of your own nightmares.

He dropped the one end of the chain, letting it swing free alongside his left leg. The rear bumper of the car was only a foot or so from his front wheel. Now!

With a crack, the chain swung over and down, ripping a dent of bare metal through the new bodywork. And again. And a third time. The boot was beginning to look as though someone had been jumping on it in studded boots.

Now it was time to move up for the wing mirror and the windscreen.

But, the driver had taken enough. Cutting up punk kids on low-powered bikes was one thing. A lot of fun after a night out with the boys, or after a boozy business lunch. But, this was way out of his league.

There was the warning dash of the red brake light, then he flung his car sideways in a spectacular skid. But, as police forces all over the country had discovered, you can't beat a chopped hog for manoeuvrability. Gerry broadsided his bike, churning up a shower of loose gravel, cutting past the rearing car. By the time the driver had his pride and joy under control again, Gerry was sitting astride the hog, grinning wolfishly at him, the length of chain dangling menacingly.

With a hiccup of panic, he tried to crash into gear and get away from the demon of evil that had ridden his tail for so many miles. But, in his nervousness, he stalled it. Twice he tried to start it while it was still in gear, and it bucked and coughed like a spavined stallion. Still grinning, Gerry got off the big Harley, and walked slowly towards the car. Out of the corner of his eye he noticed that a white Jaguar had pulled up on the left, and the driver was watching him through the windscreen. That must be the car that had followed him. But, he hadn't broken the law, so he hadn't got anything to worry about. Anyway, it wasn't a marked car, so it couldn't be the police.

While the driver, his mind blanked by panic, struggled to move, Gerry reached him, and leaned on the bonnet, smiling pleasantly. Without altering that expression, he whipped the chain over and round, slicing the offside mirror off as neatly as a pair of bolt-cutters.

That was enough. His mouth hanging open, his eyes wide in terror, the car driver wrenched his door open and ran across the road.

Across the busy road.

Halfway across the busy road.

In his fear, he made no attempt to look both ways before crossing. Or, even look one way. When the hounds of hell bay at your heels, the Green Cross code all seems rather remote.

A yellow Transit van, its multiple-track stereo blaring out an old New Riders Of

The Purple Sage song, its tousle-headed driver zonked from here to eternity, was bettering sixty along the road. The car driver – his name, by the way, was Derek Stokesley-Wyatt – never saw it. There was the flash of bright yellow at the edges of his seeing, then he felt the immense and agonising blow that tore his body apart and spread it over the tarmac.

The injuries were so massive that he died instantly, his ribs crushed into splinters of bone that ripped his heart to bloody rags. The violence of the impact threw the corpse clean over the top of the van, smearing its bright paint with red streaks. Like a discarded and ragged doll, the earthly remains of Derek Stokesley-Wyatt splashed into the dusty hedgerow, landing in a cluster of golden toadflax that splattered up around him, covering his staring eyes. The rest of his body was soaked in dark blood.

As the van skidded to a halt, its sound system continued to tear at the afternoon air. Gerry walked over to the corpse, the chain dangling forgotten in his hand. He'd wanted to beat the crap out of the bastard, to teach him some manners. But, he hadn't meant death.

He looked down at the sprawled body. An image from a forgotten Bradbury story came to him. 'Dark it is and golden-eyed,' he muttered.

'What's that, son?'

The voice made him start. The van driver was vomiting quietly in the ditch a few yards away, and he had thought himself alone. He swung round to face the speaker.

It was the driver of the white Jaguar, and he held a small hand-gun, with a barrel that looked as big as all outdoors. The new police issue .357 Minim. After the assassination attempt on Princess Anne, some years back, when the bodyguard's Walther had jammed, there had been a shake-up in police weaponry. The Minim was one of the results of that shake-up.

The driver was tall, and smartly dressed in a cream shirt and burgundy trousers. He held the gun with the ease of the professional, the barrel pointed casually at Gerry's navel.

'Hello, Israel,' said Gerry wearily.

Of all the men he wanted to see at a moment like that, it was Assistant Chief Constable Israel Pitman Penn. He and Penn had crossed swords before, though the security of the rock concert had caused an uneasy truce between them. One of the results of that tour had been a severe reprimand for Penn, and the hint that promotion might have been jeopardised.

Israel Penn did not love the Hell's Angels. Most of all, he didn't love Gerry Vinson.

'You saw what happened?'

The policeman nodded. His face was grim, the lips thin and tight. 'Yes, Vinson. I saw you murder that man by pushing him under the van.'

'What?' Gerry's face reflected the horror he felt.

'Yes. Murder, Vinson. Don't try anything. I'd be happy to shoot you for resisting arrest. Now, I must ask you to accompany me to the nearest police station where I believe you can help me with inquiries into a charge of wilful murder.'

The formal phrases dripped from his lips like leaden honey. For a moment, the mask of officialdom dropped. With all the hatred naked on his face, he spat: 'Got you! You cunt!!'

2. BALLAD OF A THIN MAN

Surname: Penn.
Christian name(s): Israel Pitman.
Age as at 1.1.99: Thirty-seven.
Height: Seventy-four inches.
Weight: One fifty-seven pounds.
Eyes: Brown.
Hair: Dark.
Distinguishing marks and scars: No lobe to right ear – birth-mark. Jagged scar on back of left hand. Scar on right side of abdomen, below ribs. Vaccination scars on left shoulder. Deformation of sterno-clavicular joint on right side, owing to poor healing of injury. Thumb joints both weakened by cricket accidents.
Joined force: September 24th, 1977.
Rank on joining: Constable.
Rank as at 1.1.99: Assistant Chief Constable, attached to Mercia Constabulary with peripatetic brief.
Marital status: Married once (Janet Compton), divorced by mutual consent on March 19th, 1997. No issue.

Comments: For all case histories, including the controversial incidents with the Hell's Angels, see attached sheets 2-18. His record is, basically, that of an efficient and hard-working officer. But, his attitude has occasionally upset high-ranking officers and, on one noteworthy occasion, the Home Secretary. Penn is too often prepared to bend the rules in what he believes to be a good cause.
But, this is a minor problem, compared with the trends outlined in the psychiatrist's report attached below. It is felt that this is of some significance, and could easily lead to a major incident unless it is checked. Attention is drawn to the C_____ case of the seventies when an officer who became unwell in this manner became the focus of a deal of adverse publicity. It was felt by many that the force dropped a brick over that. Without the utmost attention, the Penn case could be a repeat of that.
(*Signed:* Chief Constable Augustus Owsley, seconded to the Home Office on special matters of public concern.)

Psychiatrist's Report: I have been asked to keep this as simple as possible and avoid any technical terms. I assume this is to cater for the limited intelligences of Home

Office officials.

I met the subject, called 'P.' for the sake of anonymity, on several occasions during the winter and early spring of 1997 and 1998.

Although I place little reliability on first impressions, I must note that I was surprised. The man wore clothes that are called, I believe, 'trendy'. Far more so than one would expect for an officer of such a high rank. He carried himself confidently, and did not seem at all surprised to be interviewed by a psychiatrist.

His whole appearance is one of confidence, and I do not think that he is the sort of man who would suffer any kind of fool gladly. If at all.

I talked freely with him, and gradually I began to get glimpses of the state of mind that has worried other officers both above and below him. The phrase 'find out what makes them tick' began to reappear as he grew more at ease in my presence. By pretending to go along with his theories, I was able to draw him out more and more.

The key to his obsessional preoccupation with the minds of criminals lies with his private life. Since the failure of his previous marriage (incidentally, P. blames the failure on his wife's lesbian behaviour. Is this true?), P. has only had one sexual relationship of any depth. Interestingly enough, this has been, and continues to be, with a fringe practitioner of mental medicine. I hesitate to use a more specific phrase.

Her name is Doctor (although I doubt her qualifications) Angela Wells. She seems from his comments to be a very dominant lady, who has imposed her extreme theories on him. Her ideas, as far as I can understand them, involve digging back into the past adventures of young criminals to try and determine a pattern. Or, to find a reason for their anti-social behaviour. Once the clues to their past have been located, they can be used to change their present and make them useful members of the world.

That is her theory. Personally, I do not subscribe to it. I feel that a senior police officer such as P., when exposed to this pernicious twaddle, is in danger of losing his objectivity and trying to get criminals to pour out their tedious pasts while he plies them with tea and digestive biscuits. Instead of getting out and catching them.

On his last visit to see me, he was even more convinced of the rightness of his ideas. Over the period of several months that I have had consultations with him, I have been alarmed by his progressive deterioration. His idea is truly becoming fixed. The problem is that another analyst might well be deceived by his cleverness and his reasonableness for most of the time. But, when I risked contradicting him, the change in his manner was quite frightening.

I would advise that P. is relieved of his duties and is persuaded to enter a nursing home for a spell as a private patient. Having said this, I quite realise the difficulties of doing this.

If he is left alone, I cannot see any improvement in him. Indeed, if he once has a chance to put his plans into practice, I must stress that the consequences could be utterly disastrous.

Home Secretary's comments: On the advice of my experts, I am inclined to give this officer enough rope and then smartly hang him. I have been aware of problems connected with him in the past. Let things go, but watch him carefully. Was he not the officer who had the unhealthy preoccupation with the motor-cycle gangs known as "Hell's Angels"?

3. TALK THAT TALK

It hadn't been a fair cop – not in any sense of the word. But, Penn had the gun, and that was the kind of argument that Gerry understood better than most. But, there were other things that he didn't understand.

Like, why Penn paid no attention to the shocked driver of the Transit, who still sat at the roadside, his head sunk between his knees. Like, why there was such a tearing hurry to get away from the scene. Threatened by the Minim in the policeman's hand, Gerry managed to hoist his hog into the open boot of the white Jaguar and tie it in place. The Harley was too heavy for him to lift on his own, and Penn panted alongside him, the gun waving dangerously around.

Then, they were away, just as the first other vehicles started stopping. Most had passed unseeing, as there was little to see. The body was partly covered in the ditch, and there were none of the obvious signs of a pile-up that drew the ghouls like rotting meat attracts vultures.

Israel handcuffed him, clapping the steel manacles behind his back, and then fastened them to the reinforced door handle. It wasn't the most comfortable way to travel, but he was able to brace himself against the corners with his knees. Penn made no attempt to talk to him, concentrating on driving very fast, cutting off the main road as soon as he could and belting along twisting side lanes.

After about ten minutes of this zig-zagging, Gerry found that his doubts were being confirmed. When he first got cut up by the sports car, he had been fairly close to Ludlow. The chase hadn't gone on that long. Yet, they seemed to be heading away from the town.

'Israel. Can I ask you a question?'

The grunt from the hunched figure in the front of the car sounded affirmative.

'Where the fuck are we going?'

'Station.'

'Liar.'

They were in the depths of the country and the sun was sinking behind the high hedgerows. They hadn't seen another person for some miles.

At Gerry's words, Penn brought the big car to a skidding halt, sending splinters of gravel bursting into the long grass at the side of the road. He swung round, and he held the gun in his hand. The barrel gaped unwinkingly at Gerry.

'Listen, Vinson. Talk like that will get you fucking dead, fucking fast.'

Gerry sensed the tension in the voice, and felt the finger of cold fear inch down his spine. This wasn't the same man that he'd known in two previous encounters. There was something different about Penn. Something he couldn't quite put his finger on. Whatever it was, all his senses told him to step very lightly.

'What's the idea, Israel? You know bloody well that I didn't kill that man. It'd never stand up in court. So, what's the idea? Take me out in the country then shoot me in the back while I'm running away. Is that it? I'm disappointed in you, Israel.'

The sharp front sight dug a furrow in his cheek as Penn lashed out at him with the gun. His voice still calm, the policeman went on as though nothing had happened.

'It's "Mr Penn", to you, Gerry my boy. If you want to have a chance of staying alive and out of the nick. I'll explain it all when we get where we're going. But, you needn't worry about getting shot. You play ball with me, Vinson, and I'll play ball with you.'

Gerry kept his face calm, feeling hot blood trickle down his face and dribble on to the front of his colours. His face was calm, but his thoughts raced. What the hell was Penn up to? He runs an instant frame on a murder charge, and that could easily mean a thirty-forty year sentence. Ignores the driver that really did it, and drives off, chopper in the boot, with Gerry handcuffed in the back. Taking him where?

The last question was soon answered. In a way. After a few miles more of twisting and turning, Penn again stopped the Jaguar. He reached over into the back and pulled a black linen bag over Gerry's head, tying the drawstrings around his neck. The cloth was thick enough for Gerry not to be able to see out, but not *quite* too thick for him not to be able to breathe.

'True what my old schoolmaster said, you know Vinson. Always be prepared. Heard a little whisper from a little bird who owed me a favour that you might be up this way. Knew you liked hills, so I had the roads off the Mynd watched. Soon as I got the word, it wasn't hard to pick you up and follow along. That's the thing with you, Vinson, and the rest of your mob, you know. Trouble doesn't exactly stay away from you. If it hadn't been a murder charge, I could always have come up with something equally good. Now, you sit quiet, while I take us the last few miles.'

Gerry had a very well developed sense of direction, but he didn't know the area at all well. Even with the masking cloth over his eyes, the dying rays of the sun still penetrated, and he guessed that they were somewhere south of the Long Mynd. About twelve miles he reckoned. But, for all the good that knowledge might do him, he could as well be on Mercury.

Finally, after crunching over some loose gravel – probably a driveway – Penn stopped. There was the creaking noise that all cars make when they stop after being driven hard. Oil, petrol and water all find their own levels, and hot metal begins to contract.

Gerry heard Penn get out, slamming the door. There was a painful wrench on his wrists, as the back door was unlocked and swung open. The policeman was no fool. He unlocked the Angel from the door, but kept his hands securely cuffed behind him. By now the chromed steel was biting agonisingly into Gerry's wrists, but he wasn't about to complain.

Israel grabbed the cuffs and twisted the arms high up behind Gerry's back, forcing his head down. He didn't resist. There wasn't any point at that stage. Old Newman used to say: 'Don't waste your time when there's no point in trying. But, as soon as you see a half-chance, then you move, and you move fast.'

There was the sound of a door opening, and a muffled exclamation from someone. Then, he was pushed into a house. He guessed it was a house from the depth of the carpet, and the smell of polish. It was a clean house. Next thing he knew, Penn had pushed him flat on the floor, giving him no warning and no chance to save himself.

His kung fu training gave him the split second to pivot, even as he fell, so that it was his shoulder and not his face that took the shock of landing. Despite that, the blow was heavy, sending currents of agony lancing through his shoulders and arms.

For a moment, he passed out. When the blackness cleared from his mind, he realised that someone was fumbling to untie the hood.

There was a sudden flood of orange light that seared his eyes and made him blink. When his sight cleared, he found that he was gazing, at very close quarters, up a woman's skirt. He could only see her thighs, firm and well-rounded, without stockings or tights, vanishing up into the darkness beneath a green skirt, with the entrancing sight of the vee of a pair of light pants.

That was all he could see. Then she stood up, seeming to tower above him like the incredible fifty-foot woman. Flat on the floor it was difficult to see, but she seemed youngish, maybe in her mid-thirties. Nice hair, cropped short on to her shoulders. Then a boot slammed into his back, over the kidneys, sending him skidding across the floor.

'Keep your eyes to yourself, Vinson.' Then, in a different tone: 'Well, Angela, what do you think of him?'

There was a pause. They might have been examining a new specimen in a laboratory. When she answered, the woman's voice was cold and impersonal. 'He seems all right, Izzie. Is this the animal you told me about?'

Penn bent down and hauled him to his feet, pulling his head back by his long hair. Gerry was beginning to not like the tall, skinny policeman.

'Sorry, dear. I should have introduced you. Gerald Vinson, also known as Wolf, self-styled leader of the Hell's Angels gang who call themselves the Last Heroes. Doesn't look much of a hero now, does he? Vinson, this is my fiancée. Doctor Angela Wells. She's a psychiatrist. She and I are going to help you. Isn't that nice of us?'

Gerry tugged his head free of the gripping fingers. 'Oh yes, Izzie. Very nice. I can hardly wait.'

He had banked on the presence of the woman checking any violence from Penn. That was a miscalculation.

'Israel!' The voice was like the crack of a whip. 'Teach that animal a lesson in manners.'

Assistant Chief Constable Penn didn't need telling twice. With a restrained savagery, he beat Gerry brutally about the face and body. Restrained by the handcuffs, there was nothing that Gerry could do to protect himself. It was a great relief when a pool of darkness opened at the back of his mind, and he was able to sink into it.

'So, Vinson, that's what we want you for. This is why Israel brought you here. Now, if you will agree to be reasonably co-operative, then you will find that the murder charge will disappear as though it had never been.'

As the woman had talked to him, bathing the cuts and weals on his face, gently brushing ointments on the deeper scratches, Gerry had seriously wondered if he'd finally lost his mind. Or, maybe he'd got concussion. What she had said to him, in a reasonable, educated voice, was so bizarre that even now he couldn't really believe it.

'All right.'

'Miss Wells,' she prompted gently. 'We might move on to first name terms a bit later on.'

'All right, Miss Wells, let me run through it again to make sure I dig what you're saying.'

She smiled at him. For the first time. It was quite a nice smile. 'Of course. That's what I want you to do most of all. Talk to me.'

He shook his head to clear it again. With a struggle, he managed to find a more comfortable sitting position. Both Miss Wells and Penn had promised him that the cuffs would come off in a couple of days. After Penn had made some arrangements. Which sounded ominous. But, at least the atmosphere seemed more friendly.

He had sat at the table and shared their meal, with Miss Wells feeding him. They had frozen steaks with duchess potatoes and green beans. Strawberries and fresh cream had completed the meal. One wine was much like another to Gerry. As far as he was concerned, there were only three kinds. There was red, white and pink. With the steak, they had red.

The conversation hadn't exactly flowed, as the woman had to keep getting up to get a clean cloth to mop the worst of the blood off the Angel's face.

Penn had even made a sort of apology for that. 'Thing is, Vinson. You have to realise how precarious your position is here. One word from me, and you will serve a life sentence that will make the Great Train Robbers look like a load of lads on an extended vacation. So, don't mess us about. Angela here will explain it all to you.'

And she had. Now, it was his turn to make sure that this Alice in Wonderland world was for real, and that he hadn't been mysteriously transported to the magic land of nutters.

'Right, Miss Wells. You reckon that I'm about the hardest case in Britain, as far as the unconvicted criminal elements go?'

'Yes. Please don't feel ashamed about that. I asked Israel whom he recommended for our little scheme, and he gave me your name without a moment's second thought.'

'You've got me here, at what we might call a bit of a disadvantage. If I don't go along with what you want, then Israel gets me framed on a killing and I vanish into the stinking bowels of Durham nick for forty years.'

'Not framed, Gerry.'

This was something he hadn't sussed out at all. Israel had actually told her that he'd really killed that stupid bastard driver. For a second, he was on the verge of blurting out what a lying cunt Penn was. Then, caution took over. If she was in love with the policeman, then whose word would she take? His face would be bruised for days from the last beating. If he told the truth, she might well get all uptight again and dish out another knocking. No, that would be something for later.

'No, No, Miss Wells. Course not. Sort of a habit to say that when Old Bill pulls you in.'

The smile told him he'd said the right thing. He felt a bead of sweat edging its way down his forehead. This wasn't going to be that easy.

Over their meal, Penn had seemed under strain, as though the effort of being civilised with Gerry was almost more than he could stand. The Hell's Angels sometimes attract some right maniacs, and Gerry had seen this kind of tension before.

Way back, in the early days of the Last Heroes, there'd been a brother called Mad Mark. And, he had been. He'd had an old lady with breasts like wrinkled prunes, called, what was her name, Drooper? That was it.

Mad Mark had showed the same kind of odd behaviour as Penn. There had always been a suppressed lunacy about him. He was one brother that nobody crossed. Even big men like Kafka and Cochise would shuffle uneasily when they found themselves fixed by his glittering eye.

One day, he'd cracked. They found Drooper with her throat slit so savagely that the bones showed through the red lips of torn flesh. Nobody ever found out what it was that made him crack. In fact, nobody ever found Mad Mark either. Well, they found bits of him. As he'd crashed away from the camp, he'd cut at himself with the bowie knife he always carried. They found four fingers and an ear at intervals along the path that led to the pool of quicksand. That was all.

And, Israel Pitman Penn was showing the same sort of underlying tension.

He realised that Miss Wells was looking at him, a patient smile on her well-bred face. Waiting for him to go on.

'Sorry, Miss Wells. I was thinking about something. Where was I?'

'You were going to tell me what you thought of our little plan to help you. And hundreds like you.'

'Yes. I stay here for a few days...'

'Or as long as is necessary,' she interrupted him.

'Right. And, I answer all your questions as honestly as possible and I tell you everything you want to know about me and about the Angels. But, I'm allowed to change names in case I incriminate anyone else.'

She looked pleased, as though a lapdog had just managed to roll over and play dead for the first time.

'And,' he went on, 'Mister Penn will promise to forget all about the ... the killing. And, he promises not to take any action against me for anything else in the past that I might reveal while we're talking. Is that about it?'

Again she nodded and smiled at him. He wouldn't have been surprised if she actually applauded him for being a good boy.

'That's it exactly, Gerry. I can see we're going to get on ready splendidly.'

'But, one thing I still don't honestly understand.'

'What's that?'

'How are you going to keep me here? Remember, Miss Wells, that Mister Penn promised the cuffs could come off soon.'

The voice behind them made both of them jump. Neither of them had heard Penn come in.

'Easy as winking, Vinson. I've been on the blower to my County H.Q. while you and Angie were having your little tête-a-tête. Everything's organised. In fact, you can have the cuffs off in about an hour.'

Angela got up to make a pot of coffee, and Gerry was left alone with the policeman. Penn walked round the room, then sat down opposite him.

'Want to know what's going to happen here? I've locked your machine up in the garage. Double Chubb locks on all the doors. No windows. Safe in there. This house is isolated. Nothing else for a couple of miles in any direction. Told my boys Missl

Wells had been getting threatening letters and phone calls. Funnily enough, I said they were from you lot. Bit of a joke, eh Gerry? So, there'll be special patrols all round this place. Night and day. Armed too. Shoot on sight merchants. Anyone round here who looks vaguely like a motor-cycle man'll find his brains splattered all over the landscape.'

Gerry looked up, wondering how to pick his words to avoid angering the man. But desperately wanting any information he could get.

'But, what if I hurt Miss Wells? While you're away. What's to protect her?'

'Nobody, Gerry, my boy.' He was becoming distinctly amiable. Since before the meal he'd been knocking back cut-glass tumblers full of brandy. Inevitably, they were having their effect. 'But, I've thought about that. In the garage there's a steel belt that I'll lock round your waist. There's a pair of cuffs attached by bits of chain. Give you a reasonable amount of freedom. Feed yourself, wipe your arse, that sort of thing. But, very limiting in a barney. Angie's a black belt judo and karate. Very good she is. And, there's a set of steel leg-irons as well. You can hobble around like a tart in a tantrum, but that's about all. No running or riding a bike.'

The Angel said what he thought. 'Clever.'

Penn suddenly leaned across the table at him. 'Sir. Clever sir'

The venom was awesome.

'Sir. Clever, sir.'

A room had been prepared for Gerry on the ground floor. As an extra precaution, bars had been set in the concrete and a special lock fixed on the door.

But, Gerry had been taken upstairs by the smirking Penn, and he'd seen the armed patrols. It wasn't bull. He wasn't about to go anywhere.

Angela had fixed the belt and chains on him, while Israel stood by toying with the Minim, twirling it round his index finger. There was a certain amount of play in the leg chains, enabling him to take small, mincing steps, but, as Penn had said, there wouldn't be any running with them on.

Since he didn't seem to be in any direct danger, Gerry decided he had nothing to lose by playing along with them. He knew damned well that Penn wasn't bluffing about fitting him for the road accident. So, he'd keep the ball in play.

Penn and Angela went upstairs to their bedroom. Although he was exultant over his capture, Israel still couldn't perform. It had been several weeks since he'd been able to get an erection. As was becoming usual, he had to satisfy Angie by other methods. She was as understanding with him as she ever was.

'It's probably excitement over that animal downstairs, Izzie. Once you realise we've got him, it'll be all right again.'

She dropped off to sleep. Penn couldn't sleep and walked down, pausing outside Gerry's cell. Or, room. He had poured himself a last brandy, and clutched it in his left hand. His eyes flickered through the Judas window set in the door, watching the sleeping figure of the Hell's Angel.

In the half-light of the hallway, the policeman's lips drew back from his teeth in a strange, humourless smile. Still grinning, he began to squeeze the glass tighter.

Tighter.

And tighter.

When it splintered in his palm, he still smiled, looking vacantly at the leaping threads of red that broke from his flesh.

And he laughed, deep in his throat.

Gerry murmured in his sleep, disturbed by the sound.

4. DRUNK MAN – STREET CAR – FOOT SLIP – THERE YOU ARE

Youth Jailed On Driving Death Charge

Twenty-three-year-old Marvin Simmons was sentenced today at Ludlow Magistrate's Court to eight years in jail for causing the death of Derek Stokesley-Wyatt.

The defendant, a Birmingham record seller, who had four previous convictions for offences under the abuse of restricted drugs rulings, had pleaded "Not Guilty". His story had been one of the most amazing ever tried in such a case, and it was its very absurdity that contributed to the correctly severe sentence passed by magistrate Sir Thomas David.

Intolerable Fantasy!

Simmons claimed that he had been returning to Birmingham after a festival at Glastonbury to celebrate the so-called 'Ley-Day' and was driving carefully along at thirty miles per hour. He saw the deceased pursued by a Hell's Angel motor-cyclist roaring towards him. The car skidded to a halt and the driver of it ran straight in front of his van. He said he had no chance to avoid him.

Phantoms Of A Drug-Crazed Mind!

Not only did the guilty man claim to have seen a ghostly motor-cyclist, but he also claimed that he also saw a man in a white Jaguar, a tall thin man, he said, pull up at the scene of the death and help the motor-cyclist away.

Sir Thomas David remarked at this point whether or not the defendant was also going to claim to have seen a coach and four, a headless hound and Anne Boleyn.

The sally was greeted with laughter in court.

Children In Custody

The magistrates did not even need to retire to consider their verdict, so obvious was the man's guilt and so absurd his attempted defence.

'I will not bother to discuss the attempted defence. That the dead man was pursued to his death by twin spirits of doom. A black man on a motor-cycle and a white man in a car. They were obviously the phantoms of a drug-crazed mind!' said Sir Thomas David, just before passing sentence.

'I dismiss this intolerable fantasy and will only comment that we would have been better minded towards some leniency if the defendant had pleaded guilty like a man.

'As it is, we are agreed that a salutary sentence is called for. In view of the man's appalling record, we have decided to make something of an example of him, in the hope that other like-minded hooligans and anti-social elements will take note and avoid this area.'

As stated above, Marvin Simmons was sentenced to eight years preventive detention on the driving charge. A suspended sentence of two years for drug offences was also implemented.

Simmons' wife was in court to hear the sentence, and fainted when it was announced.

An appeal has been denied.

© *Shropshire and West Midlands Gazette and Weekly Bulletin.*
May 2nd, 1999.

5. LISTEN CLOSELY TO ME

He heard them moving about upstairs for some time before he saw either of them. The first sight was of Penn as he unlocked the greased tumblers of the security lock on the bedroom. His left hand was bandaged.

But his face looked more normal, more at peace. Gerry wondered about the risk of asking about the bandage, or making a joke about Angela closing her legs on him. But, he thought better of it. And, he was probably right.

'Morning Vinson. Sleep well?'

He stood up and stretched, feeling the sinews crack in his shoulders, still stiff from the hours in handcuffs. Penn still had the Minim .357, only it was now tucked back in the waistband of his neatly-tailored slacks.

It wouldn't have been that hard, even allowing for the new steel restrictions on him, to take Penn and reach the gun. He had second thoughts. It would have been hard, but not impossible. Then, what? He's in a house with a gun and two possible hostages, with the gardens and land around positively crawling with fuzz.

Gerry had woken early, and given a lot of thought to his predicament. Planning when you were in a tight corner meant you were on the way to getting out. Panic, or risk committing yourself to hasty action, and you were on the way to getting dead.

He mentally ticked off the points. Firstly, and maybe the most important, he reckoned that Israel Penn, Assistant Chief Constable, was well on the way round the bend. Maybe it was this bird, the lady shrink. She seemed an odd mixture. Nice some of the time and a bitch at others.

Gerry had served in Ireland at the time of the Paisley Riots and knew all about interrogation techniques. For a spell he'd been involved in it himself. He'd been a hard, ruthless soldier and his dedication to the problems of staying alive in ravaged Ulster hadn't escaped the attention of his superiors.

They tried to get him to use this vicious streak to break other men. Suspected assassins, killers, bomb-makers and carriers. Men and women. Even children.

He'd given it a try. He'd always been prepared to give most things a try. But, after a few days he'd jacked it in and gone back to facing the Armalite snipers and the bullet from the passing car.

It wasn't so much the physical side of it. That was as old as time, and twice as nasty. But, at least you knew where you were. If you got caught, you could always expect a boot in the bollocks or a cigarette stubbed out on your back. That was the way of the world.

But, since the Korean War, every armed country in the world had been working on more sophisticated methods of torture. No; that wasn't the word to use. Not torture. It was called intensive interrogation. Made it sound better. Cleaner. And, in some ways it was cleaner. There was very little blood nowadays.

But, the end results were just as devastating. Even more permanent. The sensory deprivation. Being slung upside-down in a webbing cradle, with your eyes and ears blocked. A rubber tube probing at your intestines that fed you a trickle of sweet pap at irregular intervals. Sometimes being lowered into tanks of liquid at body heat, wearing a mask that enabled you to breathe. Never knowing which way was up.

Music in your ears that played endlessly, sometimes increasing in volume beyond the pain level. Hallucinogenic drugs that sent you screaming into your own guts. No sleep. Too much sleep.

Of prisoners released after that sort of treatment, a terrifying twenty-three per cent attempted suicide more than once. And well over half ended up in permanent psychiatric care.

Gerry shuddered as he remembered some of it. The blank faces, and the dribbling, slack mouths.

That had been the top stuff. But, at the beginning, there'd simply been the old stick and carrot routine. Sometimes with two men and sometimes with only one. Start off by being a real hard bastard. Then, suddenly become Mr Nice Guy. Or, call in your nice partner. The contrast is so great the prisoner becomes disorientated.

And, that's what Gerry was. A prisoner. So, he'd play it very cool. Go all the way along with them and then see what happened. Trouble was, he didn't have many cards in his hand at all. Not even the physical freedom to play it.

'Morning Mister Penn, sir. Lovely morning.'

Penn nodded, pleased to see his prisoner so obedient. Yet, also disappointed at it. The thrill as he pounded the Angel's face and body with his fists had been indescribable. Sending a warm glow powering through his body. He almost giggled at the memory, then held himself in check.

They breakfasted together, as a bizarre little family. Conversation was limited, with long silences between the crunching of the Sweetie-Bobbles and the sipping of coffee.

Penn finished his meal with an appreciative belch and went into the living-room to read the morning papers. Angela and Gerry remained behind. Nodding his head in the direction of the open door, Gerry whispered: 'Excuse me, miss, but is he going to stay here all the time? While I'm talking, that is?'

She was reading the *Times*, and only gave him half her attention. 'What? Oh, Israel. No, he won't. He has to be back at work this morning by ten, and we'll get down to things after he's gone.'

At nine-thirty, Penn came in and checked the locks on Gerry's manacles. Satisfied they were still secure, he pushed him back in the chair.

'Listen, Vinson, and listen good. You play ball here, and things'll be easy. Maybe you'll even find some good out of it all. You step out of line and I'll ... I'll kill you. All right?'

Gerry watched his mouth working. 'Yes, sir. I believe you. Have a good day.'

They sat together in the long work-room. Lined with book-shelves in natural wood, the lines of leather-bound volumes, interspersed with paperbacks. On one shelf, he noticed a well-worn set of the books of Cave and Stuart – the early chroniclers of the Angels.

Her desk was functional, with chromed steel legs and a black leather top. It held only a notebook and a tape recorder. The angular microphone pointed accusingly at Gerry as he sat opposite her, trying to get comfortable in an upright chair.

Angela had poured out a glass of vodka for herself. He had asked for a drink, but there was no Southern Comfort in the house. He'd settled for coffee, although she'd offered to get some in.

She switched on the tape recorder, and began muttering into it, trying to find the right sound balance, getting him to talk as well.

'What should I say, miss?'

'Anything you like, and you can drop the "miss" bit now that Israel isn't here. You can call me Angela and I'll call you Gerry. Is that O.K. with you? Good. Now, just say something so that I can get this set up.'

Gerry grinned at her. 'All right. There was a young girl from the Azores, whose...'

Her face had gone cold again. 'Gerry. Don't push it. And, for God's sake try and sit still. What's the matter, have you got threadworm or something?'

'No! No. It's just that it's bloody impossible to sit still on this chair, wearing half the chains of the Tower of London.'

She looked at him more sympathetically. 'They really are a bit much, aren't they?'

Shuffling and wriggling, he made it look much more uncomfortable than it really was.

'All right. If you promise to co-operate fully with me, then I'll unlock the handcuffs. But you must keep the leg-irons on. Is that a deal?'

Anything to make the chance of escape seem better was a deal. He wasn't that big at keeping his word. Specially not when he was being forced into it.

What surprised him, as she unlocked the steel belt and the wrist bands, was that she hadn't asked for a promise not to escape.

She must have read his mind.

'You're surprised I didn't ask for your parole and your word of honour not to escape. Obviously you are. I'm slightly insulted by that. It means that you think I'm a fool. I'm not, Gerry, and you'd better believe that. I know that you could probably overpower me, and get out of the house. Probably, but not certainly. Israel told you I can look after myself. Then you've got to get past all the police out there, and you can't get at your bike. Israel has the only key to the garage. There you are, is that better?'

'Nice to be able to pick my nose again,' he grinned.

After that, she became totally business-like. They spent the first hour or so on simple facts. Name, age, birth-date and place, parent's occupations and ages. The usual things that you get filling in forms everywhere.

Gerry told mostly truths, altering a few of the numbers and dates slightly. He was interested to see how thorough their checking system was. At the end of the hour, he pleaded a headache, and they broke for a couple of hours.

She locked him in his room, and he heard her on the phone for most of the time. When she released him again, her face didn't betray any emotion. But, she was holding a gun. A twin to Penn's automatic. He made to leave the room, but she waved him back with the gun. 'Those things you told me this morning. Were they the truth,

Gerry, or were you just stringing me along with a load of lies?'

So. She'd been busy. She couldn't have checked one tenth of everything he'd told her. But, he guessed that she'd managed to check enough to know that it wasn't all true.

Angela had been watching his face closely. 'That's right, Gerry. I know, and you know that I know. Now, I have ways, with Israel's help, of checking more or less everything you tell me. This whole exercise is going to be wasted if you lie to me. So, I have to go out shopping for an hour or so. I'll leave you locked in here. Think about it. When I get back, then we'll go over this morning's tape again, and you can correct your ... mistakes. Right?'

'Right, Angela.'

The door closed in his face, and he heard the key make its double turn. He sat down on the camp bed and thought things over.

'Even at school I suppose I was what you might call a bit of a rebel. I didn't like any kind of authority, and they weren't fond of me. We're going back to the seventies now.'

Angela sat forward interestedly, occasionally making a short note. The rest of the time she sat and listened, prompting him when he seemed stuck.

'Was it at school that you first encountered or heard of the Hell's Angels?'

Gerry thought. It all seemed so long ago now. Back to the days in Birmingham, when he'd read about Altamont – just one of the days the music died. Meredith Hunter, lying dead under the knives and lead-loaded billiard cues of the Angels. Days of easy riding and watching Corman's biker movie so many times he could deliver any line of dialogue from it.

Trying to buy his own bike. Not being able to afford it while he was still at school. But, still getting one.

'How on earth did you do that? Steal it?'

'Sort of. It happened like this ... Hey, it's a shame your tape machine can't do flashbacks like on the films, when a man says it happened like this, and the whole screen goes fuzzy and wobbly. Anyway, it happened like this.'

The Beatles' *White Album* rocking and rolling away on the turntable. The sun shining in an early summer frenzy. Term over and the endless holidays stretching before them.

A group of schoolboys strolling together along a quiet side road, not far from school. A rattling and creaking behind them along the way.

'Christ, it's old Slimy Cook!'

Desperate straightening of ties and digging out of caps. All too late.

The noise screaming down from its crescendo as the motor-bike wobbled to a halt. Sadly neglected, it was still a basically serviceable machine. With a bit of care, it was good for a few more years. Nortons really lasted.

A thin, high voice, bitter and frustrated, arid with chalk and generations of pedantry.

'You boys! I have never seen such a disreputable bunch of scruffs in my life. The Chief Master will hear of this. Don't you worry. Let me see now. Williams, Butler, Packham, Tracy, and, of course, Vinson. Wherever there is rudeness and dirt and a lack of any decent quality, then there is Vinson. Stand up straight, boy.'

The five of them stood, sullen-browed as the master carried on buzzing his own ego at their expense. Cook was the least loved of the masters, and well-merited his nickname of Slimy. Gerry Vinson had been unlucky enough to be in his form in the fifth, and suffered under him with English Literature.

Ever since Gerry had placed a number of alarm clocks, set to go off at ten minute intervals, around Slimy's classroom, there had been little affection between them. But, Cook carried his dislike above and beyond the call of duty. He really enjoyed disliking some boys.

Under the heavy crash helmet, sweat trickled down the master's pale face. He looked intently at Vinson, watching for some sign of insubordination that he could pick on and exploit by keeping him in on that last day. But, Gerry had been taught the hard way and he remained impassive.

'Very well. I am returning to write out the last of the reports, and I will not expect to find you loitering here when I come back.'

He turned away, then paused as an afterthought struck him. 'Vinson.'

'Yes, sir.'

'Don't look so mulish, boy. Your parents depend on your grant, do they not?'

'Sir.'

'And that grant depends on your obtaining average reports throughout the year? I fear that your marks are scarcely at the average level, dear boy, and my marks are yet to come. I hold out little hope for your parents receiving the money for next year. Goodbye.'

With that parting shot he revved up the bike and chugged away. Gerry spat in the gutter.

'That sod! If I had the chance I'd bloody kill him. He's been down on me ever since I refused to play his little games in the bogs after scouts. Come on.'

Later that afternoon, Gerry was on his own, walking to the bus on his way home, to try and break the news about the impending report. His father had been off work for nearly a year with lung trouble, and his mother was crippled with arthritis. It would bite hard. Somewhere behind him he heard the familiar chugging of Cook's Norton.

Much farther away, he could also hear the whining of a number of high-powered bikes, coming closer.

He turned round ready to face Slimy. Unconsciously, he clenched his fists.

Yet again, the master braked to an unsteady stop, wiping his brow.

'You are all I need to round off my afternoon. It was bad enough to come across that gang of Satan's Devils, or whatever ridiculous name they choose to call themselves. Riding all over the road, and frightening innocent people.'

Despite his desire not to involve himself in any way with the master, Gerry had to ask: 'What did you do about it, sir?'

'Do! Do? Why, I did what any right-thinking citizen would do. I telephoned for the constabulary and they arrived in quick time and gave the rascals a good telling-off.'

In the background, Gerry could hear the petulant note of powerful bikes, coming gradually nearer. Sounding as though they were quartering the streets. Looking for something. Or, maybe, for somebody.

'I was lucky enough to be there when the police caught up with them, and I told them it was I who had acted so public-spiritedly. I must say that the police did not seem as grateful as I think they should. Anyway...' he suddenly realised that it was

Gerry that he was talking to. 'I told you what would happen if I caught you up here when I came back. No doubt you've been drinking pot or injecting opium again. I warned you what would happen.'

A detention now would throw out all of Gerry's plans. And, it meant that his parents would have to wait at least another hour for their tea.

Cook laughed. With his mouth, but his eyes remained little flecks of black plasticine in his oily face. 'That upsets you, doesn't it, Vinson? I fear your poor old mother will have to wait for her tea. Anyway, once the governors see my report – here it is in my case – your wretched parents will have no further worries about your future here. They will no longer be able to sponge off the state, and we will not have to put up with you any longer. Now, where are my detention notes? And, what is that noise?'

The noise was the sound of the bikes. Now, very close. Several bikes. The crack about his parents had been the end of the road for Gerry. He didn't even hear the motor-cycle engines. His only desire was to wipe the smile off the master's face.

With an animal cry, deep in his throat, he launched himself at the older and bigger man. The force of the attack threw Cook half off the bike, and they grappled clumsily for a moment.

Just then, across the road that ran at right angles to where they were, Slimy saw three Hell's Angels ride past. It penetrated even through his blanketed mind that they must be following him, and that he must hide.

'Vinson! Are you mad? Let me go, or I'll have you expelled. Let me go!'

Gerry managed to lock his fingers in the master's collar and haul him off, sending him sprawling on the pavement. Then, he saw the Angels. Coming down the road from both directions.

Slimy Cook saw them coming for him, and he panicked, lashing out wildly at Gerry. One punch struck home in his mouth, and blood jetted from smashed lips. The master bolted for the dubious safety of his own bike, but Gerry caught him by the ankles, sending him flat on his face on the dusty pavement. The boy was up first and he got off one punch to Cook's head, knocking him back again to his knees.

But, Slimy wasn't quite finished. With strength that owed its existence to despair, he flung his case at the boy. It hit him in the chest and burst open, scattering papers all over the road. In retaliation, Gerry took one shuffling step nearer to his tormentor. Shifted his weight to his left foot, and whipped the right up and in. It hit home with the sickening crunch of splintered bone. On the side of Cook's cheek.

His head snapped back as though he'd been shot, and he fell full-length in the dirt. His hand went to his face, gently probing the swelling. He was crying.

Gerry was suddenly conscious that he was at the centre of a group of Hell's Angels. The stench of their unwashed levi jackets and jeans was rank in the warm sun. The stench of urine, sweat, oil and excrement. For a moment, he knew a depth of fear that he had never experienced before. It was as though the shadow of some dark being had passed before the face of the sun, veiling its warmth.

A hand dropped to his shoulder. 'All right, son. You piss off now, and leave him to us. He tried to play a game with us, so we're going to play a little game with him.'

Two of the brothers picked up the almost fainting body of the schoolmaster, and led him off the road, towards a large industrial tip, among high hedges.

Papers blew about the gutter, and the abandoned bike was left, like some unwanted toy, leaning desolately up the kerb. The President of the Angels saw Gerry looking at it.

'You want the old hog son? It's yours.'

'What about him?'

There was a burst of noisy laughter. Laughter that was almost as frightening as their appearance.

A grossly fat brother pushed forward. 'Fuckin' twat. He won't fuckin' want the fuckin' hog any more. Not where he's fuckin' goin'. You have it mate.'

The President again patted him on the shoulder. 'Right. You take it. You did us a big favour there. Getting that snot. Any time you want to come along to see us. Just ask for the Silver Surfers. See you mate.'

Then, they were all gone. Like smoky demons in some satanic pantomime, they just seemed to melt into the fields. If it hadn't been for the scattered papers and the abandoned Norton, Gerry might almost have dreamed it.

He noticed that the papers were the reports. It took him only a couple of minutes to gather them together and light a small bonfire. As the thin column of smoke climbed into the silent summer heaven, he mounted the old bike and rode off.

Just before he went, he thought he heard a single high scream, from over near the old tip. But, he couldn't be sure about it.

For a moment, there was silence in the long room, broken only by the hiss of the tape-recorder. It was Angela Wells who broke it.

'That's really a dreadful tale. I'm not surprised you have this preoccupation with violence. And that was when you joined the Hell's Angels?'

'Christ, no! I was still at school. I wasn't at all keen on all that anti-social, dirty business. Remember when this was. Before that bastard George Hayes came in with all his bloody restrictions. Put the Angels out of business in weeks. That was when they all really went underground.'

She got up and walked round the table, rubbing the tips of her fingers together. Gerry watched her closely. He noticed that her one hand was rubbing, unconsciously he thought, at her breast, and her thoughts seemed miles away. She wasn't wearing a bra, and the thin cotton of her blouse was stretched tight over her nipples.

'What about the bike, Gerry? Did you keep it, or did you return it?'

He looked at her with the pitying sort of look that you normally reserve for the mentally deficient. 'What do you think I did with it?' He answered his own question. 'I kept it of course. Lasted me for three years. It was better when I sold it than when I got it.'

Angela walked out into the kitchen. 'Do you want a cup of tea or coffee? You must be thirsty after all that talking.'

'I'll have coffee please, Angie.' He risked the pet name. But, there was no response. 'Yes, I don't reckon I've talked as much as that for years. Hey,' he followed her into the small, fitted kitchen, 'how much longer do I have to keep this up? Will we finish it this afternoon?'

She turned from the stove, jumping slightly at finding how close Gerry had moved to her. Her hands leaped up to cover the front of her blouse, but he was quick enough to see, before her fingers covered them, that the nipples had become erect.

He laughed at the expression of shock on her face. 'Don't worry, Angie. There's not enough of me for a gang-bang.'

She laughed back, but there was a tension there. For the first time he'd managed to penetrate past her guard, and it had made her uneasy. She could be caught. The knowledge gave him a strange feeling of relief.

'Gerry, it's not that. Just that you made me jump. I'm not frightened at the prospect of being raped by you.'

That was what she said. But, it was obvious to both of them that she could have said more. In fact, she'd said too much.

'Boiling over,' said Gerry, conversationally.

'What?'

'The kettle. It's boiling over.'

To cover her embarrassment, Angela started making the coffee, turning away from him as she did so.

'Didn't the master ... Slimy Cook, take it out on you when he got back to school?'

'Christ, Angie!' he was genuinely amazed at her naivety. 'He tried to get the fuzz to bust an entire chapter. They snuffed him.'

'Snuffed. Do you mean killed?'

'Snuffed. Outed. Zapped. Wiped. Zonked. Wrecked. Killed. Stomped. Look, Angie. There's no chivalry with the brothers. Tackle one and you tackle all. When they found what was left of him, he was in a municipal sewage disposal tank.'

'What on earth was he doing there?' Her face reflected her horror.

'Nothing much. Just going through the motions really.'

6. AND DON'T SPEAK TOO SOON
An extract from: *Think It's Good And It Ain't – A Study In Popular Sociology* by Mark Olsen. Published by Ortyx Press, 1999.

What mind bubble, psyche-blasting pie of chaos do they think we want? A collective cornucopia of cataclysmic categorisation to catalogue our cancers? A phantasmagoria of fantastic flickering figures to dim and dazzle the eyes of Mr and Mrs Middle-Class in their semi-detached suburban little boxes?

Just who do they think we are? Children to frighten with the bogeyman. A fearful fiend that doth behind all of us tread. The voice in the night that rattles at our roofs. Remember what Eliot said about a man sitting at meat and feeling the knife in his groin.

What we want to know, you people of power and money and influence with your high-rise wives and your expense account children, is just who is the smiler with the knife under his cloak? And, we have the right to know the answer to that. And the wrongs to flee along with it.

It won't wash and wipe any more folks. We know better. They may have seen the torn girl trembling by the millstream. We've seen the good days come again. Like we were promised. And we want our rights and we don't care how. We already have our revolution now! So, stuff your nightmares. We don't need them any more. Not with the night-light of affluence to keep us from harm.

They say, beware of the skulls and the Hell's Angels. Angels know the angles. Skulls bone up on sociology.

Where are they? Gone to nice kids every one. In the dim, dark days of yesteryear, then there were some of them. I know it. I even wrote about it. But, I was a voice crying in the wilderness. Wasting my time, babies. Wasting my time.

Not any more. I cry 'Hosannah' for the peace has come at last. Verily I say unto you, be of good cheer and play the man. The candles are lit and we're all off and flying. The blind shall see and the deaf shall hear and even the mute shall speak with an infinity of tongues.

What about the cripples? I heard that question. I say with you, what about the cripples? Let them run. Run through the streets that are as clean of violence in this day as they ever were.

In the bad old days, every street corner had its own mugger and popper. No, God be thanked who has given us of this hour. They are gone. Swept away in the purging wind that has cleansed and burned away the chaff. All that is left is the wheat. Some of it shredded, but most of it whole.

Eat of it, for it is good. Good. Good.

So, forget the gangs. Not with a gang-bang but with a Wimpy. Every mothers' son is all right. There is no more danger on the streets. No more mayhem in the country lanes. Turn the corner and there's light where there was once only dark.

So, remember my sermon. Mount it in your books. Carve it on your tables.

There is no more danger.

There are no more youth gangs to terrorise you and rip the tender loins of your virgin daughters. Let them forget their loins.

There are no more skulls.

There are no more Hell's Angels.

There are no more Hell's Angels!

7. THE SMOKE RINGS OF YOUR MIND

The woods around the headquarters of the Hell's Angels' chapter of the Last Heroes were green and blooming. Despite what Mark Olsen said – or, rather screeched – there still were Hell's Angels. And there were skulls. Youth cults came and went, but there were always new ones. Teddy Boys to rockers and mods and greasers and skinheads and Angels and skulls.

The remnants of the Last Heroes had waited for the return of their President, but he hadn't showed. Gerry wasn't the sort of brother who'd have crashed out somewhere stoned out of his mind. Nor was he likely to be shacked up with a tart somewhere. Since Brenda's death, as far as the chapter knew, he hadn't laid so much as a finger on any of the mamas or made a play for any of the old ladies.

'So, where is he?' The speaker was Cochise, one of the oldest brothers. The sergeant-at-arms now that Kafka was gone.

'I don't know. I know he was going to get his head together up in the hills somewhere. Maybe he looked up the Wolves and got stuck overnight.'

The words didn't convince anyone, least of all the speaker. Mick 'Monk' Moore, one of the youngest of the chapter, and one of the hardest. In the shifting hierarchy of the Angels, where death helped in the promotion battle, Monk had risen fast. Now he was the accepted number two to Gerry. If he didn't know where the President was, then nobody did.

The discussion was interrupted by the arrival of one of their sentries. Skulking among the bushes, sidling between the patches of shadow, came Rat. Nobody knew how old he was. Nor his real name. Nor where he came from. Nor why he never bothered with the scrubbers who hung around the Angels like groupies round a big plaster-cast. All anyone knew was that you didn't turn your back on Rat.

His hiss of warning broke the talk up. Monk got up and ran to where Rat beckoned.

'What is it? Trouble?'

'Don't reckon so. One man. A brother. He's waiting by the gate. He knows I sussed him out, and he's not trying to get in. Dick the Hat's watching him. I reckon it's the Welsh git. The one with the long hair called Bardd.'

If Rat, or any Angel, describes someone as having long hair, then you can bet they've got long long hair.

'Could be a decoy.' The thought was from the cautious Riddler.

Monk smacked his fist into his open palm. 'No. Not from the Wolves. Maybe he's got news about Gerry. Come on Rat. Go and invite him up. He's a righteous brother.

Remember that time we went out to the Tower of London? Just for laughs. He nicked that fat American cow's vacuum flask, tipped out her decaffeinated coffee and pissed in it. Then put it back in her bag. Class, man. Class.'

It only took a few minutes for Rat to reappear, shepherding Bardd before him. The Welsh Angel was tall and agonisingly thin. His hair was knotted at the back with a strip of leather and hung to his belt. When he saw Monk, he gave a whoop of joy and clasped him to his chest, kissing him in the passionate way of a good brother. This french-kissing was what blew straights' minds more than anything else.

'Good to see you, Bardd.'

'Good to be here, Monk, boy.' He looked quickly round the fire-lit group. 'Hey, where's Gerry?'

There was a silence. Finally, Monk answered. 'We don't know. He went off a couple of days ago and we haven't seen him since. He said he'd be back by now.'

Bardd sat down, looking disappointed. 'That's bad news. Gwyn specially told me to talk to him.'

Cochise asked the inevitable question. 'Come on, Bardd. We're all brothers together. What's happened?'

'Yobbos. Heavies from Manchester, calling themselves the Star Trekkers. They've tried twice to take us over, and we've managed to hold them off twice. But, things are getting tough up there, and we wondered if...'

He let the sentence drift away into the evening air.

Monk wasn't one to sit around while his arse sprouted weeds. If a brother asked for help, then you gave it. It was as simple as that.

'We'll leave first thing in the morning. I'll have to leave a few here, because we've been having a bit of aggro from some local skulls. Not serious, but we don't want this place wrecked.'

Hanger John stopped picking shreds of corned beef from between his teeth with the point of his sharpened steel coat hanger and belched. 'Hey, what about Gerry?'

'He's going to have to take his chances. This shouldn't take more than three days to clear up, then we'll run back. If he's still not turned up here, then we'll go out and look for him. There'll be brothers here to tell him where we've gone.'

'Suppose we don't find him?'

That was a question that Monk hadn't really thought about. He knew that Gerry wasn't happy with the fragmented remains of the Last Heroes, and shared his own desire to break and get out. Some time. Monk's other pressure came from his old lady, Modesty, who was constantly pushing for a real Angel wedding. That left him a simple choice. Throw her back in the pool as a mama who was anyone's property. Or, marry her.

He'd decide soon.

'I said, what if we never find Gerry?'

'Then, John, we'll have to wait and see. All right?'

Hanger John looked up at him out of the depths of a coke world and grinned. 'Right.'

Dawn crept up over the Lee Valley, flicking at the tops of the pine trees that surrounded the old missionary college where the Angels now ran and lived. It gleamed off the chrome and bright paint of the hogs that were getting their last polish and service. Gerry had installed a giant petrol tank for them to use – hassles with filling stations were the most persistent aggravations in an Angel's life – and it held five thousand gallons of the high octane fuel they used.

Finally, at seven, they were ready. No old ladies, except for Forty and Modesty, were coming along. The rest of the women stayed with Riddler and a few of the younger brothers to guard their turf. Monk held up his hand, and boots stabbed at starters. Birds flew shrieking out of their nests at the thunderous bedlam. Rabbits dived back in their burrows.

Clutches were slipped, wheels dug gouges in the soft leaf-mould under the trees, and they were off.

The Angels were running again!

There had been too much trouble on motorways, and the white patrol cars would always pick up any band of motor-cycle outlaws they saw riding in a pack. So, although it was a lot slower, Monk led the raggle-taggle file up along the quieter A5.

They cut through St Albans, scaring the crap out of the early rush-hour traffic, twisting and cutting among the cars and lorries. Up Watling Street and under the M1 at Harpenden.

The sun shone, and they were able to enjoy the run. Rat got his huge chopped B.S.A. moving well, and took his feet off the rests and put them up on the ape-hanger bars. Riddler and Cochise terrified a motorist in an old Humber Hawk by roaring past him, one on either side, and then linking hands in front of him.

A police car rolled in with the convoy at Fenny Stratford, manned by a young copper in his first week with the force. It did little for his hopes of a man's life in the police force when he discovered Bardd riding alongside him, then leaning his arm in through the open driving window to pat him affectionately on the cheek.

At seventy-five miles an hour!

He had just enough sense left not to try anything. He realised that they were friendly and played his luck. He even managed to pull out a stick of chewing-gum from his top pocket and hand it to the grinning brother. That gesture brought a round of applause from the rest of the chapter, and they all gave him a wave as they accelerated past him.

After they'd vanished over the crest of the hill in front of him, the young policeman pulled over and sat for quite a while before he could stop his hands from shaking.

By then, the Angels were barrelling through Wilnecote, on the fringes of the industrial Midlands. It was getting on for nine o'clock.

Cochise leaned across and shouted to Monk: 'Glad we came this way. Nice and quiet. Brings back some good memories!'

Four miles ahead of them, pushing their old Dormobile van to its limit, were a crowd of skulls. These cropped youths, with their embroidered waistcoats and their anarchic violence, were the true successors of their skinheads of the sixties.

There were ten of them cramped into the van, huddled on benches jammed down both sides. Led by a Birmingham tearaway – Duggie Whitehouse – they were off to cause the maximum damage they could over a weekend on the North Wales coast. They were all tooled up for action, with knives and small axes in fitted holsters inside their long, draped jackets.

Duggie had their pride and joy broken open in his lap. Every time they passed what they thought might be a suitable target, he would slip in a couple of cartridges and pretend to squeeze the twin triggers. They all thought that was a load of laughs.

It took a long time for the Angels to close that gap, and the van was nearly at Nesscliffe – close to the Welsh border – before one of them spotted the leading Angels through the dirty rear window.

'Angels! A run coming up fast behind us!'

Duggie took over immediately, pushing the others out of the way, so that he could kneel behind the back window with the sawn-off shotgun ready. Cocked and ready.

Hanger John was out in the lead, showing some fine class in a fit of exuberant high spirits, weaving in and out, standing up on the saddle, passing vehicles on the wrong side of the road. They were reaching a long straight patch of road, and he opened up his hog, and managed to get upright, pulling down his zip as he did so. To the cheers and encouragement of the rest of the brothers, he succeeded in having a piss while belting along.

He was so involved in avoiding splashing himself with the golden shower that he scarcely noticed that the old van in front of him – the one with the dusty rear windows – had slowed right down.

Hanger John got closer, still peeing over the road. Slowly, almost imperceptibly the window inched down, and the snub nose of the shotgun peeked through.

The only one of the Angels to see it was Rat. His mouth opened and he screamed a warning to the clowning John, but the noise of the bikes was too loud, and he never heard it. Rat frantically throttled the chopper onwards, but he was way late.

The boom of the gun shook the air. The double charge of shot starred out and struck the Angel in the abdomen and chest. The impact lifted him clear off his machine, hurling him up in the air. It seemed like a slow-motion replay of a doll being thrown in the sky by a wilful child. Blood gushed from the torn flesh, sprayed high, and dappling the following brothers, making the road greasy.

Duggie immediately shouted at the driver to move it, and the van accelerated away from the shambles behind it. The skulls had expected to get away in the chaos caused by the murder, but they showed little awareness of the manners and way of life of the Angels.

It was obvious that Hanger John was snuffed. Although his bike still rolled on for another hundred yards, causing a woman driver coming the other way to faint and steer her car through a hedge into a herd of Jerseys.

The following convoy skidded round and through the spilled blood, machines weaving and sliding as they struggled to keep upright. Rat was well in the lead of the pursuers. Where the skulls went wrong was assuming they would at least stop to see how Hanger John was.

He was dead. Nobody stops both barrels of a shotgun and falls off a speeding motor-bike without being dead. One of them would pull in and collect the bike, if it wasn't scrapped. Probably either Modesty or Forty would be dropped off to make her own way along.

A dead brother wasn't an important thing. Just a load of meat. What was important – more important than even drawing breath – was getting the bastards who'd wiped him.

Duggie looked back out of the window, ready to grin at the carnage of his victory. His face changed when he saw Rat creeping up at over eighty, only a hundred yards behind. Closing fast.

'Step on it, Harry. For Christ's sake. They're right up our arse!'

There were few Hell's Angels who didn't carry special weapons on their hogs. Rat was no exception. Indeed, he was a one-man arsenal. There were Molotov cocktails, three knives, the obligatory length of chain, and even one hand-grenade. There used to be two, but one had gone a year or so back removing an awkward police car from their path.

The gun barrels again poked out at him, but the road was winding, and the shots went wide, cutting a swathe through a fence on the far side of the road. It takes a little time to reload a shotgun in a crowded, swaying van, and Rat took the chance to draw right up alongside the rear off-side.

The driver steered wildly back and forth, narrowly missing oncoming traffic, but he couldn't shift him. Again, the window wound slowly down.

Rat grinned.

He'd bought the two grenades from an ex-I.R.A. man years back. Now, at last, the second one was coming in useful. He slipped it from its pouch, tugged the pin out with his teeth, and wheeled in close behind the van. He dropped it, rather than threw it, through the gap near the top of the window.

Inside the van, things began to happen. If it hadn't been anything as lethal as a grenade – say a stink-bomb – then it could have been hilariously funny.

It rolled forwards, under legs, banging on the steel sides of the van. The driver could only hear confused screams and shouts, so he pushed his foot even harder on the accelerator. Duggie dived down, trying to find it in the tangle of legs and bodies. Some of the skulls hadn't seen what had happened, and had no way of knowing they were less than four seconds from death.

Duggie, being the quickest-thinking of the band, abandoned his search, and concentrated in trying to get out. Concrete at eighty miles an hour was preferable to a hand-grenade in a small van.

But, the doors were jammed.

Rat had been joined by Cochise and by Monk, and he screeched to them what he'd done. They throttled back, watching the van.

Rat had been counting, and he dropped the last three fingers. Two fingers. One finger.

None.

It wasn't quite as spectacular as he'd hoped. There was a rather muffled explosion, followed immediately by the tinkling of glass on the road. The Dormobile swerved to the right, bouncing off the wing of a laden lorry. The glancing impact sent them off to the left, and they hit the kerb and overturned into a field.

This time, the explosion was more satisfying. A crescent of orange flame, white at its centre, throwing up a column of oily smoke. The screaming had nearly stopped. The run braked to a halt and watched in silence. Revenge had been swift and lethal. The rear doors swung up and open, freed by the flames. Out of it clambered one of the skulls. It would be nice to claim poetic justice and say that it was Duggie Whitehouse. In fact, whoever it was, was so badly burned that it hardly resembled a human being at all. More a staggering charred piece of wood, flames pale in the light of the sun.

It ran around, mewing quietly to itself for what seemed a long time, but was probably only half a minute. Then it fell to its knees, then on what remained of its face in the cool grass.

The van burned on, the sickly smell of roasting flesh picking at the nostrils of the silent watchers.

'Let's go,' said Monk,

And they went.

Things hadn't been good when they reached the coastal village where the Wolves lived. The ruined houses of Nant Gwrtheyrn showed signs of recent battles, and there were two new mounds where the Angels buried their dead.

Gwyn had been delighted to see the Last Heroes, though he was concerned to hear about Gerry's strange disappearance. The red eyes had burned in that ivory face, and he had promised the co-operation of his brothers, should it be needed after they'd sorted out the Star Trekkers.

There'd been plenty to drink and plenty to eat, and the fire had blazed long into the night. There'd been music – the old rock songs so loved by the Angels. The Everlys, Buddy Holly, Duane Eddy, the King, Gene, Eddie and all the rest.

It had been a good night. Forty had duly arrived, straddling Hanger John's hog, the vibration of the rough path shaking her vast breasts, to the ribald amusement of the brothers. Cochise had used his boots on one of the Wolves who'd got a bit carried away by the sight, pointing out in the friendliest way that she was his old lady. Nobody else's. But, it was all in good spirits.

Later, Gwyn and Monk walked together along the pebbled beach, beside the murmuring sea, and talked about the coming fight with the Star Trekkers.

'Thing is, Monk, we've not had the numbers to defend this place from all sides. The bastards have got boats, and they're camping round the bay, somewhere near Nefyn. I'd love to have a go at them in their own camp, but that would leave us too stretched here. Now, with you here, we could have a go.'

Monk bent down and picked up a stone, skimming it across the low waves. Far behind them, the noise of the party was fading into the distance.

'No. I reckon it's better to fight on your own turf, if you can. Let them come. They won't know we're here, so we can hit the bastards from behind. Probably get their boats. When do you reckon?'

Gwyn pondered. Although it was almost full dark, it was eerie to see the pale figure of the albino so clearly.

'Maybe tomorrow. Maybe the next day. No later, I reckon.'

They walked on, in silence, to where the ghost of a great rock-crushing plant loomed over the cliffs. Part of it had slipped down into the sea, and vast timbers lay, covered in weed and shell-fish, half in and half out of the water.

Suddenly, Monk started and put his hand on Gwyn's arm. 'Don't look round, but I can hear someone coming up behind us. They're walking on the earth at the very base of the cliffs, but I still heard them.'

They sat down, talking quietly of this and that, both straining their ears for another sound. Finally, it came. Monk was on his feet in a flash, diving into the pools of darkness where the rocks met the beach.

A figure moved, and he was on it, sending it crashing down painfully on the shingle. From the yelp, and from the soft feel, he guessed instantly that it was one of the women. It was only when she spoke, that he recognised who it was.

'Modesty!'

'Get your knee off my tits, you big, heavy sod. I wanted to talk to you.'

Gwyn left them together, and they talked about it. Finally, Monk knew that there was no way round it. The only thing that would satisfy Modesty would be an Angel wedding.

When they got back to the camp, their announcement was greeted with whoops of delight. A bike was got ready, and the sacred maintenance manual was dug out.

Modesty washed – an unusual experience for her – and Monk got as pissed as he could without actually crashing.

Then, under the guidance of Gwyn, as the President of the host chapter, they stood together in front of Monk's own hog. The purple paint gleamed in the flickering light of the fire and the chrome shone with an evil splendour.

While Gwyn read out the words, Modesty and Monk held hands. They both promised to honour the chapter and the bike, nourishing and caring it above all their own interests. Not letting anything come between them and the chapter. Honouring the President. And the chapter. And aiding all other brothers when càlled upon to do so.

When they had each promised to do all these things, Monk was handed a highly-polished steel washer, which he slipped over Modesty's ring finger. Then, amid obscene yells and cheers, he kissed her hard on the mouth.

Modesty got her own share of the cheers by drawing down his zip and fondling him in front of all of them. That was class.

Later, after all the fuss had died down, they walked together on the beach. The tide was in, and the strip of pebbles was narrower than ever. The night was warm, and Monk made no protest as Modesty pulled him gently down on to a small patch of sand, under the lee of the cliff. Close to the ruined remains of a rotting jetty.

Her hands were careful, helping him out of his jeans, caressing him, until he reached the edge of readiness. Fingers and mouth took him, lovingly carrying him on to a bursting warmth. Only when he had finished did she allow him to take her and make love to her. Not brutally, as it so often had to be, but with caring.

He licked her breasts, rolling the nipples between finger and thumb. She moaned and arched her back as his tongue moved lower down her body, leaving a wet trail, that dried in the warm air. Modesty took his hand and brought it to the core of her body, pressing his fingers against her.

Only then did he roll on top of her, and she guided his swollen firmness into her. Together they thrust and rose and fell, until they climaxed together.

Afterwards, they lay together, holding each other close, covered only with a blanket that Modesty had brought draped over her shoulders. The sea whispered at the pebbles by their feet, and the rest was silence. Above them, the camp was, at last, settling down into sleep.

She touched his lips with her finger. 'Mick?'

'Yeah.'

'What about getting out? Like you said you wanted. Have you thought about it at all?'

'I tell you, love, I'm always thinking about it. When I saw poor John buy it today.

One day that'll be me. I want to help out here. Then, get back to our place, and talk it over with Gerry.'

The mention of the name brought an uneasy moment of quiet. Modesty broke it. 'Do you think he's all right?'

'Gerry? Yeah. He's probably living it up somewhere right now. Probably screwing some young bird. Lucky bastard.'

She nipped him with her nails, and he rolled back on top of her. Later, they got back to the camp, and slept.

8. THAT'S WHAT HAUNTS ME
An extract from an interview given by Professor Angela Wells in the magazine 'New Social Conscience' – January, 1998.

New Social Conscience: Professor, you have been called the stormy petrel of modern psychiatric research. Would you like to comment on that?

Angela Wells: Everybody wants to put labels on everyone else. I'm sorry, but I'm not prepared to play that game.

N.S.C: But, it is fair to say that you have built up an enormous international reputation for some of your outspoken and controversial views.

A.W: Yes.

N.S.C: You're very young...

A.W: You make that sound like a crime.

N.S.C: No. Not at all. But, do you not think that a lot of the antipathy among the traditionalists is due as much to the fact that you are an attractive young woman as to the validity or otherwise of your views?

A.W: Christ! Every time I hear that tired old phrase 'attractive young woman' it makes me want to throw up. It's like that great old actor – Jack Palance. Every interviewer used to ask him about having the face of a prize-fighter and the voice of an angel. I know how he felt. Can we just get this one straight? I am a psychiatrist, with a particular interest in penal sociology. That's what I want to talk about, not whether I've got big boobs or not.

N.S.C: All right.

A.W: And, as for the traditionalists did you call them? As for them, I have not a shred of respect for their hidebound and outdated ideas. They are living in the seventeenth century. It would be better for the whole area of penal psychology if those dotards retired to sit in the sun and weave baskets.

N.S.C: As you rightly say, let's try not to get involved in any kind of argument about personalities. Let's keep it to your views.

A.W: Very well.

N.S.C: What, as simply as possible, is so different about your concepts?

A.W: Basically, I'm not saying anything that is radically new or different. All I want is for penal psychology to take a tip from psychiatry, to get right back to a criminal's roots. Spend a lot of time with him – or her – and dig deeply into seminal events. Those happenings that really seem to matter in the development of that person's psyche. What makes his character into a criminal one. I suspect that this kind of really deep digging will turn up some interesting facts. The trouble is that it is virtually impossible to get the prison and after-care authorities to co-operate with one on such a lengthy scheme.

N.S.C: Of course, as you say, there isn't anything very new in that.

A.W: If you weren't so eager to leap in, I could go on and expand on the new areas I want to touch. I also feel that there is a tendency among criminals, when they are confronted with the full panoply of the psychiatrist, to lie. They will tell you what they think you want to hear, rather than what is true.

N.S.C: There may well be something in that.

A.W: It's not a question of 'may be'. There definitely is.

N.S.C: How can you check it?

A.W: What I want to do is to find some top criminal and spend several days with him.

N.S.C: I notice you didn't qualify that by say 'or her' as you did earlier.

A.W: Quite right. Before I was talking about the ordinary criminal. Now I'm talking about major crooks. Sad to say, there are very few major criminals among the female sex. That is also something I propose to look at later.

N.S.C: Please go on.

A.W: By doing this, I can win some sort of confidence. Also, I really want to have some kind of hold over him so that he will be under pressure to tell me the truth. I wanted to offer remissions in return for the truth, but the authorities wouldn't think of it.

N.S.C: What is the alternative then? Or, is there any alternative for you?

A.W: There's always other possibilities.

N.S.C: Such as?

A.W: I might kidnap someone and threaten to have him killed if he doesn't co-operate.

N.S.C: I hope you're joking.

A.W: Well, what do you think?

N.S.C: When do you hope to get your plans moving forward? We've heard that your rivals have suggested that you will never be able to operate under the conditions you want. What do you say to that?

A.W: I suppose that they might be right. All I can really do is keep waiting. And trying.

N.S.C: As long as you don't have to kidnap anyone to do it, we wish you luck.

A.W. Thank you. We'll see the way the prune wrinkles.

N.S.C: Professor Wells. Thank you.

A.W: Thank you.

9. AND YOU HIDE FROM MY EYES

Angie cooked supper for them both. She seemed happy with the sort of stuff he'd handed out to her during the afternoon session. Not that it wasn't true. It was. Every word of it.

More or less every word. The only change came at the end. He had actually followed them and watched the end of his tormentor. And, he'd enjoyed it in a weird way.

Supper was good. Israel had rung late in the afternoon to say that he was hung up on a case in Birmingham and wouldn't be back that night at all.

So, it had been a meal for two. Gerry wasn't a great expert on food, but he enjoyed it all. There were avocadoes with prawns for starters. Veal cutlets with a superb sauce to follow and a mixed salad. The afters was ice-cream and fresh strawberries. Just about his favourite.

They had a chilled white wine with it, and she had managed to get some Southern Comfort for afterwards.

Over coffee, she asked him if he'd mind doing one more session that night.

'I work best at night, Angie.'

She grinned at him. 'I'm sure you do, Gerry, Now, come on. Hobble into my work room, and we can get started.'

She followed him in, carrying the coffees on a tin tray, heavily ornamented with flowers. He sat down in his usual chair, and she set up the tape machine.

'You've told me about the first time you ran in with the Angels. Now, I'd like to know about the time in your life when you first came into contact with violence. It seems to me, from what Israel has told me, that you have a strange preoccupation with death and violence.'

'Maybe.'

'Well, I mean, don't you think that you have less of a regard than most people for human life?'

Gerry thought about it for a time. 'Yes. I suppose there's something in that. But, I don't put that much value on my own life either.'

The sun was just sinking over the hills to the west. He knew they were somewhere in Shropshire, but he couldn't guess where. Over on the horizon, he could see a small white house, with a white fence around it.

Angie had stood up and had now walked near him. He was conscious of the scent of her body, close against his shoulder. Almost without thinking, Gerry put his arm around her shoulders. She moved a little away from him.

'No Gerry. That's a dangerous path to start down. If Israel ever found out that I'd been unfaithful to him, I think he would kill the man. I think he might even kill me.'

He swung round to face her. 'Then why do you go with him? Leave him.'

Her face changed, frighteningly. Her eyes widened, the nostrils flared, and the mouth tightened. Her voice was cold and hard. 'Leave him? You must be mad, Vinson. It's only through him that I have this chance to carry out my ... my tests. How could I possibly leave him?'

It was time to change the subject. He pointed over the fields, to where the distant house was just visible among the trees.

'Who lives over there?'

She stood by him again, but not close enough for him to touch. 'In the white house?'

'Yes.'

'An American. We know nothing about him. Small man. Moved there a few months ago. Does a bit of smallholding. Name's ... let me see. Remington. Richard Remington. I've seen him a couple of times. He's put on weight since he's been here. Must be the country air. Personally, I think that he's a homosexual.' Hastily, she went on: 'Of course, that doesn't make him a bad person.'

They both sat down again.

'Back to life and death, Gerry. Tell me about when you first started to hate the system. And, when you first came to realise that life wasn't all that valuable after all.'

'I don't know.'

'I think you do. Was it soon after school?'

'What good will it do you to know all this? I still don't understand.'

Patiently, as though teaching a half-witted pony to jump over a rope, she explained it. He noticed that her words were just that little bit slurred. The Southern Comfort was getting to her. He remembered how Brenda had started to go, and the signs that showed him how pissed she had been. There was a momentary pang of loss.

Now, this woman was showing the same signs. The eyes opened that bit wider, and the lower lip seemed to get bigger. Sort of flubbery.

'Gerry, my dear man, I will try again to make all clear for you. By spotting these key times in your wretched life, we might get clues as to what has made you the way you are. Then, we might be able to help you. And those who come after you. Now, come on, there's a good boy. Otherwise I'll have to smack your bottom and send you to bed. When did you find out about the value of life? And, when did you start to hate authority?'

'In the army.'

'Yes. Come on. I want a bit more than just "in the army". Come on.'

'Well, it was after I'd left school...'

Gerry Vinson had got his degree, from a good provincial redbrick university. As a result of the saturation induction into the profession in the seventies, there was a glut of teachers. There was little that an arts degree qualified him for.

He didn't fancy selling himself up the river every day in an advertising agency. Publishing was a profession for a gentleman. At least, that was what he'd always heard. Journalism often had a bad effect on people, and he didn't want to shuffle off with blood pressure, or ulcers or cirrhosis before he was forty.

So, that left the army. He'd signed on for a five year spell, although he only just scraped through on the tough physical qualifications. He'd done well in training, thanks largely to the untender care of Sergeant Newman. He'd learned things there that he'd never forget. Things of greater value than the quadratics, or Boyle's Law, or the limewater equation, or declensions or conjugations.

Newman had taught him how to kill a man. Quickly and efficiently. How to defend himself. How to turn himself from mild-mannered Gerry Vinson into a lethal fighting machine. That was something he'd never forget.

After basic training, with its incessant drills and practicing, Gerry found himself in the real thing. He was drafted to Northern Ireland, then at the worst period of its bitterly troubled history.

He found himself less than two hundred miles from his home, yet in a country that might have been centuries away. He saw things in Belfast that would stay with him for the rest of his life. Things that the newspapers either glossed over, or just ignored.

He saw a child's head burst apart by the powerful bullet meant for the soldier who was taking it across the road. What was left of the man who one of the illegal movements suspected of being a traitor. A mentally deficient youth gunned down in his own bedroom.

Gerry had been on duty the day that a bomb tore the heart out of a crowded bus station. He picked up the arms and legs, swept up shattered fragments of bodies with a stiff-bristled broom, shovelling up dripping loads of intestines. Dropping a woman's handbag on the stretcher, because the hand still held it.

But, the wrongs and the brutality and the senseless slaughter weren't all one-sided. A young corporal in his platoon panicked when a crowd of women started to heckle him. He forgot all about the warning card. His finger squeezed the trigger, and carried on squeezing. Set on automatic, the rifle cut a bloody swathe through the women.

It went on all the time. You got used to the muffled blasts of the car-bombs, or the milk-churns packed with weedkiller and the other simple ingredients necessary to make a lethal bomb. There were things that took longer to settle to, like the toddlers of four and five who marched after you down the street shouting obscenities at you, and heaving stones at your back.

Eventually, even that became commonplace, and you forgot about it.

Gerry Vinson did well, showing himself sufficiently tough to survive and sufficiently tactful and self-controlled not to make waves for his superiors. After six months he was seconded to one of the special undercover units that patrolled the Bogside and Creggan in unmarked cars and vans. Working in twos and threes, their job was to watch for the top men in the I.R.A. and the U.D.I. and snatch them if there was evidence of illegality.

'Of course, Vinson, if you get caught, you must expect to get killed,' said his captain. 'In fact, if that happens, we shall officially deny all knowledge of you. Good luck.'

The army had supplied them with a van, painted up to look like a laundry van. They had a tough, bitch woman officer with them who actually ran a laundry round, collecting information with the dirty washing. Gerry and a lance-corporal were there to provide any muscle that was needed.

One morning, the woman came back in a high state of excitement. 'O'C_____'s staying the night at twenty-seven. If we move now we can have him.'

That was Seamus O'C_____, high on the army's wanted list. In this sort of situation, to try for his capture would mean that their cover would be blown. It was up to the officer to take that decision.

They got in contact with their base by the short-wave radio they carried. There was a deal of excited squawking above the static, and they finally got confirmation to go in.

This was at a time of the 'No-go' areas and there was no chance of an orthodox unit getting and snatching O'C_____. So, it was up to them.

Their plan was simple. The woman would stay with the van. That wasn't chivalry – she just happened to be the best driver of the three of them. Gerry and the lance-corporal – a dour Glaswegian called Andy Brown – would rush the house and hope to catch him. It was risky. but there was no other way.

Twenty-seven was just the same as any of the other neat little terraced houses in the long road. The curtains were drawn when they pulled up outside. Gerry and Brown cocked their automatics and sprinted up the front path. The officer – Gloria Shuckburgh – stayed in the driving seat with the engine running.

Gerry shouldered his way through the front door, finding himself in a narrow hallway. Leaving Brown at the bottom of the stairs, he ran to the top, pistol in his hand. All the bedroom doors were shut, and he paused.

'In here, soldier-boy.' The voice was quiet and controlled. Gerry stopped dead. That meant bad news. It was a set-up. He turned to look down the stairs and saw his lance-corporal, hands raised, ringed by masked men with levelled pistols.

Again, the voice came from in one of the bedrooms: 'Come on in. You'll catch cold standing out there.'

There wasn't much choice. Keeping his gun ready he pushed open the door.

As he'd expected, the room had several men in it. All but one wore the balaclavas and sunglasses of the Irish guerrilla fighter. All but one held a gun. Two had sub-machine guns, the rest pistols.

The unarmed man was Seamus O'C_____. He lay on the bed, his hands and ankles tied. He had been subjected to a heavy beating. His nose was broken, and his lips swollen and covered in dried blood. One eye was buried beneath a purple bruise, and there was a ring of small burns on one cheek.

The bad news looked worse. Not only was it a set-up to get them. It was also a death plot to get rid of O'C_____. There had been guarded whispers that he had fallen from favour. Now, it was obvious that those rumours were true.

'Put your gun down on the floor, soldier. You'll not be needing it for a bit now.' He saw Gerry's hesitation and laughed. 'Come on son. You don't have the look of a man who wishes to die here and now. Your friend downstairs will be of no help.'

There was just a chance that Gloria might have got away. But, that hope was dashed by a whistle from the street outside.

'That's your lady friend as well. Come on!' This time there was the unmistakable crack of command. Gerry threw the automatic to the lino.

The man – Gerry guessed it was Sean M_____, regional head of operations – had them all brought in the same room as the bound O'C_____, and explained to them what was to happen. It was a clever and simple plot, that would bring home to any potential traitors the risk they ran, as well as showing the army that their special operations were a dangerous hazard and could be broken.

Three out of the four of them in that room were to die. O'C_____, obviously. And, two of the soldiers. The only questions was, which of them was going to live.

'What about you? Which of you would like to live?'

None of them answered.

'Normally, I'd spare the lady, but we think she's an officer, so maybe she'd better go. What about you two?'

It was too much for the young Scot. He hadn't signed on to get shot down by a laughing assassin in a Belfast back-street. At seventeen, there seemed a lot of living to do. He pushed forward, face working with his nerves.

'Not me! She's an officer all right. And the other one,' pointing at Gerry, 'is a killer. He's a specialist in murder. He's killed lots of your men. And women. And children. Kill him. Not me.'

All eyes turned curiously to Gerry. His mind raced furiously, trying to see a way out of this one. Trying to think how Newman would have acted. He'd probably have suspected a trap and not got caught in the first place. Or, just lobbed a bomb through the front door and waited safely outside to pick up the bits.

'Well?' There was no laughter in the voice now. 'Is it true what the boy says?'

'Answer the officer!'

It was a toss-up. Lie and they might shoot him. Tell the truth and they might shoot him.

'I've killed some of your men.' There was a hiss of indrawn breath in the quiet room. 'But, I see this as a war, not like most of my officers and the politicians at Stormont and Westminster. It's war. Your men have tried to kill me, so I've tried to kill them back. So far, I've been luckier, or better, than them!'

'Kill him!' the words came from several of the men. But, their leader was looking at him steadily.

'That's a good answer. At least it's an honest answer. You came here as a spy, pretending to be what you're not. Why shouldn't I shoot you?'

'Because I'll do you more good alive.'

'How come?'

'I'll do the killing for you. After that, I'll get out, and you'll not see me again.'

The woman screamed at him: 'You can't do this to us! We're your friends. You're a soldier. It's mutiny. You're a traitor, Vinson.'

He turned to look at her. 'I'm sorry about that, Gloria. But I'd really rather be a live traitor than a dead hero.'

Back in Angela's living-room, the tape hissed on, and the coffee had grown cold. Outside, it was pitch-dark. Far away, through the window, Gerry could just see a light at the farm-house of Remington, Angela's neighbour. There was something about it that rang a bell. When he had time, he'd give that some thought.

'Well?'

'Well what?'

Angela tutted irritably. 'Come on Gerry. What happened? Obviously you're here and alive. What about the others? What happened to them?'

'Sorry. Both Gloria and Brown got killed.'

'Who killed them?'

'Me.'

Despite her desire to avoid any kind of moral judgement or comment, she couldn't hide her shock. 'My God! You really are a hard bastard, aren't you?'

'Why?'

She got up and walked over to the window, trying to keep her voice level. 'You know damn well why. To murder two of your friends. And then be so damned indifferent.'

He got up and walked awkwardly over to stand near her. The chains between his ankles clinked and rattled. He was pleased. He'd managed to get to her. Make her get involved and show weakness. That was another step in the battle.

'First, they weren't my friends. Brown was a cowardly little snot who shot two schoolkids and then claimed they'd shot at him. Paraffin tests showed otherwise. And as for Gloria. She was just a career-minded dyke who'd rat on anyone to get herself promotion. That's one.'

Surprised by the cold note of angry triumph, Angela had spun round on her heel to face him. The only light in the long room came from a spotlight near the tape-recorder. Apart from that pool of light, the room was nearly dark.

'Two. I didn't shoot them.'

'You said you did!'

'No I fucking didn't. You're a psychiatrist. You're not much bloody use when you don't listen to what I say. I just said they got killed.'

Angela began to suspect he'd tricked her. In turn, she began to get angry. 'If you didn't kill them, then who did. You told me you did. Listen.'

She turned to the recorder and played it back, until she found the spot she wanted. Her voice came in, sounding flatter than it really was. She was asking what happened to the others. Gerry replied: 'Sorry. Both Gloria and Brown got killed.' Her own voice came back, the note of anger clearly detectable, asking who had killed them. Finally, Gerry saying simply: 'Me.'

'There. Now do you deny that you shot them?'

He sighed. 'There you go again. I've never known anyone get her knickers in such a twist. I said that they died and that I killed them. That doesn't mean I shot them.'

Forcing herself to keep calm under his sneering, she sat down and sipped her coffee, forgetting that it was stone-cold. 'Come on then. How did you kill them and not kill them? Both at the same time.'

Walking like a child that has wet itself, legs forced apart by the chains, he joined her at the table. A silent witness to everything that went on, the tape spools revolved inexorably.

'They both died when I pulled out another gun. My own. Not army issue. Things got a bit warm in the room. But, some of them had left, including their leader. They believed me when I said I'd do their executions for them, and they'd dropped their guard. But, there were still a lot of them. Gloria and Brown both got hit several times. She died at once, and he died in the ambulance.'

'How did you get away?'

'Through the bedroom window. I shot three of them in the room, and got two more when they made a run for it out the front. The rest all got away.'

Angela sat back. She'd learned about violence from Israel, and she'd read the books and seen films. But, sitting there in her own room, listening to this slight young man talk casually of death and torture, she began to feel a little sick. To wish she could get out of the room. Away from the foetid smell of the Hell's Angel, with his rank odour of sweat and grease and other unmentionable smells.

'O'C_____?'

'What about him?'

'What happened to him?'

'Well, after I got out, and shot a few of them, the rest made off like shit off a shovel, and they forgot to do anything about him. I went back upstairs, dragged him down, put him in the van and we were away. None of the locals tried to interfere. I'd have shot them down where they stood if they'd tried anything on.'

That was that then. Another episode from his past safely on tape and in her notebook. She reached out to switch off the tape-recorder.

'Wait a minute.'

Her hand hesitated over the off-switch, not sure whether he was teasing her or not.

'What's the matter?'

'Nothing.' He looked away.

'Yes there is. What made you say that?'

Gerry grinned inwardly. She's nibbled at the bait, as he'd known she would. 'Well, I thought you wanted to know all about things that sort of shaped me. Seminal events you called them.'

'But, we've finished that one. You were a hero, got your man, like the Mounties, and two other members of your unit got killed. What else is there to say.'

'Oh, nothing. I thought you'd be interested in what happened to O'C_____ after I got him back.'

She could feel one of her migraine headaches creeping up, and it was getting late.

'Is it important?'

'I thought so at the time. But, if you don't...'

She picked up her pencil again, ready. 'Well, go on.'

'After I got him back to our H.Q., they gave him a bloody long interrogation. I was in on it, and it was soon obvious that he had been a spy. And a traitor. His mates had him dead to rights. The officer in charge of the questioning was right pissed-off that they'd rumbled him, and he could hardly care about the beating the poor sod had been through.'

The pencil flew over the pages of Angela's notebook. This could turn out to be more interesting than the actual fight at the beginning of the story.

'After ... I reckon it must have been getting on for six hours, the officer suddenly turned all smarmy and nice to poor old O'C_____. Told him what a splendid chap he'd been and how grateful the British Government was for all the information he'd found out. I was surprised.'

'Why? Surely the man had risked a lot to get information to you?'

'Maybe. He got well paid for it. I always reckon that anyone who does that sort of informing for money is a bit of a shit.'

'Go on.' Gerry had stopped talking.

'There's not very much more to say. I went off duty, and got pissed. I never saw O'C_____ again.'

'Well. What on earth happened to him?'

'He had an accident. Fell out of a helicopter on the way from the camp. From about fifteen hundred feet. They had to dig him out.'

There wasn't anything that Angela Wells felt she could say. You read about betrayal in papers, and called it propaganda. This was different.

'Of course, it was called an accident. But, I knew better. I'd heard the officer talking to the sergeant detailed with getting O'C_____ out of the camps.'

'Why? What did he say?'

'Didn't hear it all. Just the phrase "from a great height", and a lot of laughing.'

That night, she locked him away with scarcely a word. He could tell that his stories were beginning to get to her. Gerry guessed that she didn't believe some of them, but she could check all she liked. She'd find that the basic, background facts were correct, and she'd never manage to get anything on the rest.

With Israel not due back that night, he'd had the faintest of hopes that he might manage to lay the snotty Miss Wells. But, she seemed to be making every effort to avoid any sexual contact at all, and even got uptight if he made any kind of doubtful remark.

Despite that, Gerry hadn't entirely given up hope.

His only worry was where to move next in his stories. In one day he'd got through both school and army days, and they seemed to expect him to stay for several days. That meant that there would have to be a lot on the Angels. Which was obviously what she was most interested in anyway.

Before he dropped off to sleep he heard her making two or three phone calls. Who to, and why? Gerry reckoned that she must be trying to check up, and probably reporting to Israel the progress she'd made in her first day with the patient. Was that the word? Patient? Guest? Subject? Straining not to make any noise, he crawled across the carpet of his room, holding the tinkling chain in his hand, and pressed his ear to the panels of the door, to try and overhear what she was saying. But, it was impossible. There was only the low drone of her voice. All he heard was when she raised her voice and repeated a phrase. Twice.

'No. No, he hasn't. No, he hasn't.'

For his second night in the lonely Shropshire house, Gerry slept well. The sleep of the just.

10. PEEKING THROUGH HER KEYHOLE

Dearest Izzie,

I was terribly sorry to hear from you that this wretched business in Yorkshire is going on and on. Can't you take leave of absence? I'm only joking, really. I know that you can't.

Seriously though, love, I'm getting worried at the amount of work you seem to be doing. Are you the only keen policeman in the whole force? I know we've talked about it before, but I do wish you could see your way clear to getting out. I mean, with your official retirement coming up next year. Why not take advantage of it and get out? We could get away then and do what we talked about.

Is this surveyor really as big a criminal as the papers seem to be implying? I don't see how he could have that sort of influence over so many people for so long. Still, I suppose it is possible to fool all of the people for most of the time. Do you know yet how much longer you're going to be on it? Not more than another couple of days, I hope.

Our phone calls always seem so difficult. I suppose that's one of the troubles about going out with an Assistant Chief Constable. If it hadn't been for you I'd never have suspected how many phones are tapped. With our 'guest' we can't be too careful.

I expect you're itching to know how things are going, and whether I've dug out anything really worthwhile. Since you insist on putting your job before me and my simple needs, I've got a good mind to keep you waiting and not tell you.

Don't worry, Izzie! I'm only joking. Please forgive me. I know you will.

Well, the first day was the best, with lots about his school days and his career in the army. My God, Izzie, I honestly had no idea what I am getting into. I imagined that someone like Vinson would have some redeeming features. Not necessarily cultural. But, his indifference to human suffering is quite incredible. The first tapes reflect over and over and over again how he feels society has given him what he calls a 'bum trip'. That since society doesn't care about people – he has a point here – then why should he?

His whole code or philosophy of life is that he's only here once and he's going to make the most of it. He really is fantastic. I wish I could take him back to Oxford and present him to old 'Collar and Cuffs'. It'd really shake the old duffer out of his dream-world of ids and alter egos.

He always used to say that there could not possibly be such a creature as a totally psychotic egocentric. Yet, that's exactly what Vinson is.

I've given a lot of thought to your involvement in all this and I'm sure there'll be no problems. It is becoming increasingly clear that Vinson is on the verge of leaving the life of a motor-cycle outlaw, and will not worry unduly about the way his statements are used.

The real information will start to appear in the next two days. Names and places and dates, so I suggest you ring me on Friday – after eleven, we're working late – and I'll give you all that I've found out so far. But, remember that you promised not to start anything moving your end until I've finished my study.

All for now, I think. Do try and relax Izzie. The last couple of times I've seen you, I've been a little worried. You're always so tense. Relax. Please.

Must go. It's very late, and we've another long hard day coming. Incidentally, I suspect that Vinson thinks his friends – his 'brothers', must use the right word – might come after him. You told me they wouldn't move from their base without your men knowing. I hope you're right.

I'm one gang who doesn't want banging. Except by you.

Fondest love,
Angie.

11. I FELT THE EARTH MOVE

Friday was another lovely day.

The temperature rose to twenty-four degrees centigrade. The humidity was low, and the wind only two on the Beaufort Scale. There were no earthquakes reported in Western Europe. No rain fell.

The days had passed slowly for Gerry Vinson. Each morning he rose at the same time and ate breakfast with Angela. As time went on, he was increasingly conscious of the growing sexual tension between them, and he had done nothing on his part to lessen it. Angela Wells was an attractive lady, and it was months since Brenda had bought it. He was getting tired on the loneliness of the hand-job. Also, if he could lay her, it might help to open a door or two to his future.

Right now, he was beginning to wonder just where that future lay. Each day the digging had been a little harder and a little deeper. She had returned again and again to the school days, and to the horrors of the army years, until he finally refused to go through it yet again.

Only on the previous day had they begun to touch on the central subject of the Angels themselves. He had described how he'd met Brenda at the Young Anarchists, and how it had been her who had persuaded him to take both their lives in his hands and join the Last Heroes. She had been an idealist in those days of political frustration, and she had called them the 'last hope for the free left' and 'the apostles of ultimate freedom'.

They had found a savage pack of animals, driven underground by the restrictions of a restrictive government. Gerry had fought for his life against one of them, killing him cruelly and efficiently. Brenda had qualified by pulling a train. That phrase had fascinated Angela.

'I've read it, but I can't remember what it means. Please tell me.'

He grinned. Whenever he could, he took the chance to shock her. 'It means that she had to get fucked by every one of the brothers who was capable of action. As many times as they wanted. In any way they wanted. You'd have been amazed to see how many orifices in the female form can be quite accommodating.'

He paused, waiting for the inevitable question. There had once been a popular lady journalist who had interviewed him for her magazine, and had been similarly intrigued. After he had told her, she had come back with him to the turf, and she had there been persuaded to take part. The article had been a mind-blaster.

'Er, Gerry. How many did she...?' She let the question tail off.

'How many fucked her? In one way and another, she managed about thirty in an hour.'

Angie's voice hardly stirred the shadows. 'My god! The poor girl.'

Gerry sighed, as soft as a razor-cut. 'No. You don't get it Angie. She enjoyed it. In the end. You know the record's nearly double that.'

The first days, when he was just a prospect, and the way he rose to full-patch status. Finally challenging the President, Vincent, for the leadership. And getting it.

It was here that Angela first encountered the trouble that she and Israel had expected. Although he'd given names quite happily in the first few days, detailing school and army – she'd checked he'd told the truth with the aid of a few calls – he now started using different names for characters, hardly bothering to conceal his ruse from her.

After half an hour of this, she reached forward and stopped the tape. Silence flooded in. He grinned at her.

'What's the matter, Ange? It can't be time for our coffee break already.'

'Why are you lying to me?' The chill in the voice took him aback, with its surprising depth of venom. 'Why are you changing names all the time, and dates?'

'I wouldn't rat on mates. That wasn't part of the deal. Just to tell you about me. What difference do names make?'

'Israel gave you his word that nothing would happen to you or to anyone you named. Now, come on.' Again, she pressed the switch to set the spools revolving.

But Gerry was adamant. Not under any circumstances would he give real names or times and places of events. There were far too many skeletons buried here and there that he didn't want to see unburied. Too many bodies that the police would love to hear about.

Angela threatened him, even saying she would put him back in the handcuffs, and ring Israel up to collect him and charge him with the wilful murder of the motorist. Nothing worked. He simply refused.

'Look, Angie. I'll tell you all about these "seminal" events that you think are so important, but I won't rat on a mate. I'm sorry, but that's that.'

And, that was that.

They did no more taping that morning. Over lunch, she tried to convince him to change his mind. But, he could tell that she had accepted his decision, and she was just going through the motions.

They had iced orange juice for starters – or, rather he did, she didn't join him. Roast lamb with fresh mint sauce and green beans. Summer pudding for afters. She even allowed him a glass of wine with her.

Then, saying she felt tired, she locked him up for an hour and a half. He used the time working at the chain with a small penknife he'd lifted from her desk. Although the blade was wearing thin, so was the chain. After a bit, he felt surprisingly tired, and he slept for an hour.

When he woke, his door was open, and he could hear Angie singing to herself as she worked in her room. Feeling decidedly wobbly – probably the wine after a lay-off for a few days – he joined her and they spent the afternoon taping.

The words flowed faster than he could remember before, and she was obviously happy. The trouble of the morning, that he could only vaguely remember, seemed to have passed away like the morning dew.

He talked about the mass slayings in the quarry north of Birmingham, when large numbers of police and Angels were killed. Although he tried hard to avoid names, it somehow seemed that some slipped out.

'What happened to the small American? The one you called Rupert Colt? Did you ever see him again?'

He was surprised at her interest in little Rupert, with his gay life and his taste for purple shirts, that they used to joke about.

'He ran the pop tour that we were security for. Israel could tell you all about that. Rupert skipped at the end. Said he was going to change his name and run a little farm somewhere. Hey! I think he said it was near Shropshire.'

'What was his new name going to be?'

'Don't know. Rupert Colt. Like the gun. Nice guy. A really nice guy.'

The afternoon sped by, and Gerry fell asleep at about six in the evening. Unusually, they had no night session, and he didn't wake till ten the next morning. Angie was sitting on his bed with a glass of orange juice and a plate that almost groaned under the weight of the mixed grill it carried.

'Gosh, you must have been knackered last night. I had to put you to bed.'

'Sorry about that. Christ, have I got a fucking headache! You got any aspirins?'

'Yes. Of course. Come on though, drink this orange. Then, eat your breakfast, and we'll make a start in an hour or so. Give you time to feel a bit better. Then, as a treat, I thought we might go for a ride in the car this afternoon, if you like.'

'What, just you and me?'

'Yes. Israel phoned while you were out last night, and the Yorkshire business I told you about looks as though it's going to drag on for another week. He sends his love, incidentally.'

Although he laughed, Gerry was just wide awake enough to spot that she wasn't easy about Israel. Why, he wondered.

But, she sidetracked him by continuing about their afternoon jaunt. 'You must give me your parole, Gerry.'

'Course.'

This time she laughed, and it had the ring of genuine amusement. 'You must really think I'm naive, Gerry. After all you've said and told me over the last few days, you must realise that you're one of the most amoral men in the world. You'd swear anything that was in your interest. Still, I partly believe you. You can't get at the bike in the garage, and I think I'll put on the belt and cuffs. Just in case. It's a deal. To get some fresh air?'

He nodded. It was peculiar, but he was feeling the effects of being stuffed up in the house. He needed to get away.

The morning fled by, and Gerry was amazed when the tape ended and she decided to break for lunch. There had been so much on the tape, that he couldn't remember what was new and what was recapping over old material. He was actually beginning to enjoy talking about the good old days and remembering the names of all the old brothers. She had been particularly amused by the tale of the bank robbery they'd pulled in Holloway, and she got him to repeat some of the funnier details. And some of the not so funny ones.

After a lunch of cold chicken and salad, he stood passively by while she fastened on the belt and cuffs. With them on, it would be impossible to drive a car or ride a bike, and walking was hard enough in the leg-chains. So, he still had to play along with her.

She brought her car – a nippy little two-door saloon in cerise – round to the side door, so that he could hobble in without attracting the attention of any of the watching police. She packed some tea, and a bottle of what she claimed was a very good wine.

He took it out in the back of the car as they hurtled dangerously round the lane, and read the label. It said *Gewürztraminer 1971*. Not that it meant much to him. It was white and chilled, beads of moisture clinging to the sides of the bottle. It seemed ideal on a hot, sweltering day. Maybe it would clear the fuzziness from his head.

This time, there was no blindfold, which was an oversight on her part. They passed a sign that said *To The Goggin*.

'What the fuck is a Goggin?' he asked, amazed at the name. 'It sounds like a bloody dinosaur.'

'It's a hill. You shouldn't really have seen that. I forgot the blindfold. Still, now things are going so well, I don't suppose it'll do that much harm. You can't really get away, and we'll be finished in another week at this rate. Then it'll be all over.'

There was a finality about that last phrase that he didn't like. 'What happens when it's all over, Angie?'

'We'll see.'

And that was all she could be persuaded to say. They drove for about another two and a half miles, he calculated, through some of the most beautiful lanes he'd ever seen.

Tall trees towered over them, the branches meeting high above, cutting out the light with a cool green filter. The lane narrowed, and there were no houses to be seen.

At one point, they saw a huge figure of a man, standing alone at the side of the roadway, watching them. He was so enormous, and the lane so narrow, that Angie had to slow right down to a crawl to edge past him. The man wore a long, grey raincoat, almost down to his ankles, and his hair was long and uncombed. Gerry stared at the giant's face – for he stood near to seven feet – as they passed, and was horrified by the blank gaze that met his eyes.

The face was heavy and brutish, with flickering animal cunning in the tiny eyes. Very pale blue eyes. A dribble of mucus ran from the flattened nose, and the mouth dropped swinishly open.

He felt a prickle of fear raise the short hairs at the nape of his neck. Angie accelerated fast as soon as they were past.

'Fucking Christ! Did you see that?'

Her voice, when she answered, wasn't as much under control as she wished. 'Gerry, this is a very, very old part of the country. You have to live here for at least three generations before they begin to accept you. Odd things go on. Even rumours of fertility rites, and intermarrying, and sun kings ruling for a year.'

A mile or so farther on, they reached their destination. She pulled off the lane, which was now almost non-existent with a belt of grass running down its centre. Then bumped down a grassy slope, hidden from the roadway, and finally stopped in front of a tumbledown, half-timbered cottage.

Gerry scrambled awkwardly out and stretched his legs and shoulders, glorying in the freshness of the air, and the chuckling of a nearby brook. Angela got out of the car, carefully locking the doors, and unpacked the hamper from the back, spreading a white cloth on the springy turf. She beckoned him to sit down beside her.

Clumsily, he did so.

Her eyes confused, she looked at him. 'For God's sake! This is silly. Please give me your word not to try and escape today, and I'll unlock you from the belt.'

'All right. Cross my heart and hope to die. I give you my word as the President of the Last Heroes chapter of the Hell's Angels motor-cycle outlaws, incorporated by charter to the great chapter of Oakland, California. Honest.'

'All right.'

The meal was good. Light and right for the occasion. The wine was excellent. Cool, with a tang of fruit to it that he'd never encountered before. Afterwards, while she lay back sleepily in the shade of the ruined house, he walked down and idly threw small sticks in the stream, watching the sticklebacks dart and flash in the shallows. Back through the trees, he could just see Angela, stretched out, apparently asleep. He looked around, weighing up his chances. He decided not to try it. Not because of his promise - that weighed less than dandelion down. Simply because he didn't fancy his chances. Not with the leg-irons on, and he hadn't scraped them thin enough yet to snap.

So, he walked back. Angela raised her head and smiled at him. She was a little drunk. He had noticed she didn't wear a bra during their first session, a habit she still had. Her cotton blouse was almost opaque in the strong sun, and her short skirt had ridden up high over her thighs. She looked very attractive, and he told her so.

'Why thank you, kind sir,' she laughed.

He sat down beside her, and lay back, watching the clouds chase each other whitely across the deep blue sky. He felt better, and the muzziness of the previous couple of days seemed to have worn off.

Without any warning, he felt a hand on his chest, undoing the front of his colours, baring his body to the sun. He froze, waiting to see what would happen. The fingers traced a path down his chest and stomach, only stopping when they reached the top of his levis. Then, while he kept his eyes closed, the hand worked his zip silently down.

Only when he felt the fingers grasping at the swelling maleness did he open his eyes, and roll over on his side. Angie was watching him, her face flushed, lips parted. She smiled at him.

'I think that this is the time and the place. Don't you, Gerry?'

He wasn't about to argue. The crushed grass beneath their bodies smelled heavy and sweet. As they thrashed their way to a climactic satisfaction, a flock of crows circled and cawed above them.

The fluttering of her stomach muscles told him that she was near the brink, and he quickened his thrusting. She moaned as he filled her with his strength.

After it was over, she walked alone to the stream and cleaned herself up. When she came back, she seemed different. Cooler, less friendly.

'Come on, Gerry. Time we were moving back home again.'

As he sat in the car, and they started to roll through the quiet lanes, he asked her there was anything wrong.

'Wrong? No, nothing. Why, what makes you think something's wrong?'

'It's just that you seem a bit distant. Wasn't it any good for you?'

She laughed, but there was little humour in it. 'Christ! What an ego-trip fucking is for you men.' He was surprised to hear her swear like that. It was the first time since he'd met her that she'd used any kind of really strong language. 'No, it was fine. I felt the earth move and all those other tired clichés they use. Is that what you wanted to know? So that you could get a big kick from having done a good job on me?'

He leaned forward in the back seat, so that his mouth was only inches from her ear. She was startled by this, and the car swerved, clipping the grassy bank.

'Don't do that! What's wrong with you?'

'Listen Miss Wells. Just because you get the hots to find out what it's like to be screwed by a Hell's Angel, then that's your hang-up, not mine. Lots of women feel like that, and they expect to be raped and dragged screaming to submission. Well, I'm sorry, but that's not my scene, baby. I like it, and I like my women to like it as well. No tart I've ever screwed at a bang really got much out of it.'

Angela drove in silence for the next mile or so. Finally, with a jerk, she pulled into the side of the road. She tugged savagely on the hand-brake, then sat back and looked at him in the mirror.

'Gerry. I'm sorry. I shouldn't have said that, and you were right about what wanted. I thought it might be a new thrill for you to take me, out there. I expected violence and rending lust. I didn't get it. Instead I had a gentle and considerate lover I was too stupid to realise that I ought to be grateful for that.'

There wasn't anything that he could think of to say in reply. Instead, he touched her gently on the back of the neck. After a minute, she took off the handbrake, put her car in gear, and moved off.

They were nearly back, he calculated, coming in by a different route, when he saw the house the American lived in.

'Isn't that the farmhouse you can see from your place?'

She glanced to the right. 'Yes. Yes it is. Mister Remington's place.'

'Remington. Like the gun.'

'What?'

'Nothing, Angie. Just thinking aloud.'

As they went past, they saw a little man riding a bike up the lane towards them.

Angela was preoccupied with squeezing by, and took hardly any notice of the cyclist. But Gerry watched him, staring closely at him as he went past the car.

He was short, and plumpish, on the way to middle-age. He wore a bright purple shirt. Not bothering to look at the occupants of the car, he rode steadily off.

'Was that Mister Remington?' he asked.

'What? I didn't really notice.' She peered in her mirror. 'Yes. That looks like him. Why, do you think you might know him?'

'No. No, I don't think I know Mister Remington at all.'

He turned round and watched the slight figure disappearing round a bend in the lane, near his house. The last thing he saw was the flash of the bright purple shirt.

After he'd been safely locked away for the night, Angela Wells made a long phone call to Yorkshire. Then she went to her room and spent a long time with her tape recorder and her notes.

Gerry would have been less than flattered to hear what she had to say about the afternoon's adventure.

'I gave him the chance of some freedom, and he sadly abused that by trying to rape me. I managed to fight him off and calmed him down. But, it was an undeniably unpleasant experience and not one that I would like to have repeated. It typifies the attitude of this young man to other people and to property. It was perfectly clear that he saw it as his God-given right to have intercourse with me, and he seemed surprised at the strength of my resistance.'

She paused to take a sip of a very dry Martini. Then, she continued with her version of the events, until just after midnight.

It wasn't until she was getting undressed for bed that she remembered a chore undone. Tutting irritably to herself, she went downstairs again to the kitchen. She opened the tall fridge that stood against the wall, and took out a large glass jug of orange juice from the middle shelf. She poured out a breakfast dose into a crystal beaker, and put the rest back in the fridge.

Holding it carefully, she carried the glass into her working-room, and through into a side-room. One that Gerry had never seen open.

Putting the glass of orange juice on the small table, she took a silver key from a ring in her pocket and unlocked a stripped pine cupboard. The cupboard was full of bottles and vials, all neatly labelled.

Angela took one of the vials out, and carefully tipped a measured amount into the orange juice. Using a glass rod, she stirred it round. After she'd put the vial back, she locked the cupboard, locked the room, put the drink back in the fridge and went happily to bed.

The label on the vial bore the neatly-type words: *Scopolamine-Hyoscine*. Underneath, in her own precise writing, she had added the words: *Truth Drug*.

12. IT'S BAD FOR YOUR HEALTH HE SAID
Extract from *Uses Of Psycho-Therapeutics In The Treatment Of The Recidivist*, by Beulah-May Howell.
Published by Ortyx Press, 1997.

It has often been suggested that there is no such thing as a "truth drug". Too many medical experts are prepared to discard the overwhelming body of evidence that shows that such drugs do indeed exist, and have been used under practical conditions for many years.

Their basic principle is the same as that used in certain forms of anaesthetic, where resistance is lowered in pre-operative conditions to ease the way for the final anaesthetic. This lowering of resistance is exactly what is needed to take a person to the position where he finds it difficult to resist any question. Where it is simply easier to tell the truth than to lie.

There was long held the opinion that it was only possible to make someone confess to things that he actually wished to confess to. And, that it was not possible to make anyone reveal anything that he or she did not wish to confess to. In other words, that a simple determination to resist was sufficient to keep the truth from an inquisitor. Subsequent events have repeatedly shown how outdated this idea is.

There are three main drugs used in this form of interrogation. All are forms of barbiturates. Perhaps the least used is Amobarbital, which has long-lasting effects and is generally felt to be one of the least effective of this group of so-called "truth-drugs".

An anaesthetic sometimes used by dentists is Sodium Thiopental. Administered intravenously, it has the effect of a general anaesthetic. Because of this, it is less than satisfactory when used as a drug to break down resistance in cases of psycho-therapeutics.

It must be administered in doses subject to the most careful control, otherwise the subject will simply either not go under at all, or will lapse into total unconsciousness.

At this stage, it must be stressed that I am not advocating any kind of illegal use of these drugs, nor should they be used for ascertaining military or criminal information. That would be a gross invasion of privacy. Nor should they ever be used without a patient's consent, as their identity may become confused.

It is only in cases of recidivists and quick-return criminals that I advocate the use of such drugs. This is to try and discover any deep-seated blocks that may give a psychiatrist a clue to any personality disorder. I cannot stress enough the dangers of illegal or uncontrolled use of these drugs.

The last of them, and the most commonly used, is Scopolamine-Hyoscine. There is an increasing use of this in cases of difficult childbirth, as it can – when combined with morphine – produce a state known as "twilight sleep".

An alkaloid of the belladonna family, it is found in nature in Deadly Nightshade. In small doses it depresses the para-sympathetic nerves. It is in this state that it can be used as a truth drug. It has a particularly wide use because of its easy solubility in any liquid.

But, caution! It is a highly toxic material, and extreme care must be exercised if it is to be used in any larger dose. Apart from its effects when used in moderation, in higher it affects the autonomic ganglia. That is to say the main motor functions of the body such as bowels and, more importantly, the heart. It can stop the heart.

Used in moderation, it can have the effect of putting the subject into a slightly confused and forgetful state, whereby his resistance can be broken and he will reveal facts that he would otherwise not do.

NOTE: All of these materials are dangerous if improperly used, or if a dosage is repeated with any frequency.

13. THE DEATH COUNT GETS HIGHER

The attack was two days in coming. The weather stayed warm, but Gwyn and Monk insisted on sentries being posted, while a couple of the old ladies, organised by Modesty, dressed up in pretty summer dresses and kept an eye on the camp of the Star Trekkers. It was on the evening of the second day that Modesty came running up to where Monk lay asleep on one of the broken pews in the quiet of the shattered school-house.

'Tonight, love. Geneth was up on the hill watching them and she saw them cleaning guns through her glasses. Guns love. That means big trouble.'

Monk rolled over on one elbow and looked up at her through his sunglasses. 'Thanks, love. And thank Geneth for us. You've done well. Yeah, guns are always fucking trouble. Looks like they really want to make this a big one. Wipe the Wolves right off the fucking map. I'll go and talk to Gwyn. Better get our plan ready.'

The plan was nearly ready. It was just a question of whether it was to be a day plan or a night plan. It now looked as though it was going to be a night plan.

During that early evening, the old ladies and the mamas gradually dropped out of sight, making their way by a devious and secret route out of the ruined village, to camp high on the eastern slopes of The Rivals. Yr Eifl, as the Wolves called them. Near the ancient camp of Tre'r Ceiri. There, they'd be safe, whatever happened.

Because it wasn't going to be any easy win for the Wolves and the Last Heroes. They were both out-numbered and certainly out-gunned. Between them, they could muster about twenty-five fighting brothers. Only half of the Manchester chapter. And, they had no guns. But, they had local knowledge on their side, and they were probably more ruthless and experienced in real eyeball confrontations.

As the sun went down, Gwyn and Monk made their rounds of the camp, checking that all the brothers were where they should be and that they were sober.

After the checking, it was just a matter of waiting.

The President of the Star Trekkers was called, predictably enough, Kirk. His second-in-command was called Spock. He'd even taken the extreme step of having his ears altered so that they resembled the pointed shape of the old Vulcan hero. The sergeant-at-arms was Scottie, and other brothers were called Bones, Sulu, Chekov, Kang, Koloth and Korax (these three all admired the warlike Klingons and had taken their names) while Kirk's old lady had changed her name from Tunnel, to the more beautiful Uhura.

As a chapter, the Star Trekkers had only been established for a couple of years, but they had already built up a reputation in the North of England for being the meanest bunch of hell-raising mothers ever to straddle a hog. In those two years they had challenged and beaten every other chapter of any note in the North and Midlands.

What galled them, was the romantic magic still attached to some of the old names. Chapters that had actually been chartered before the great clampdown and had, somehow, managed to survive through the seventies into the eighties. These were the ones they wanted. The Last Heroes were too far away, and there were many good reasons for leaving them till last. The most pressing of these reasons was that they were the best.

After them, the most magic of the chapter names was the Wolves. The white-maned albino and his band of Celtic brothers, riding the desolate cwms of the northern Welsh peaks. They were the ones to try for.

The first two skirmishes had been inconclusive, with losses on both sides, but no sign of a final result. Now, tonight was to be the big one.

Kirk had called his council-of-war and had decided on a simple sea-borne attack. Their previous sallies had involved subtle plans and split forces. Now, since they had an overwhelming numerical advantage, Kirk had decided to make one great rush and end the affair. But, he didn't realise that the odds weren't quite as much in his favour as he thought.

They stole their boats from Nefyn, after the last holiday-makers had left the sweep of fine sand, using engines stolen from a marine supplier in Caernarvon. Petrol from a garage near Abersoch. Guns, ammunition and knives from their own home city.

They chugged round the bay, heading out to sea in a tiny armada of overloaded boats. All of them wearing their colours, with heavy boots. They were lucky the tide was on the turn, and the waves quiet and flat. When they were a mile out to sea, Kirk gave the signal, and they all cut their engines. Moaning and cursing, they got out the paddles and oars and started the long trek in to the elevated beach at Nant Gwrtheyrn.

Using night glasses that he'd liberated from an army camp when he was showing a bit of anti-English class, Gwyn watched them plodding in.

'I make it seven, no eight boats. Jesu, that's not many for all that lot. Unless they're a diversion and there's another lot coming over the back.'

'Relax, Gwyn. We've got men out along the top, and they'd have let us know by now if there was anything.' In the blackness, he could easily make out the pale face of the Wolves' President, the lips pulled back from the teeth in a feral grin. He thought, as he had before, that this was not a man he'd like to have to face on a dark night.

A night like that.

It wasn't until they were within fifty yards of the beach that Gwyn's first-row defence came into action. Most of the Wolves could swim, and swim well. Few of the Star Trekkers could swim at all.

Quietly, secretly, they were creeping closer. Suddenly, a hand came over the side of one of the boats, and pulled down hard. With twelve men in, plus their weapons, the dinghy was already crowded to the gunwales. Immediately, icy water sloshed over the side. The Angels panicked. In the blackness it was hard to see where the beach was, and the boat wobbled and rocked. Spock was commanding it and he yelled at his men to sit still. All pretence at secrecy was forgotten in an instant.

Despite Spock's shout, the panic didn't cease. And, when a Welsh brother appeared over the other side of the boat and knifed a Star Trekker in the chest, screaming with wild laughter as he did so, there was a rush to get out of the boat. It tipped over and filled instantly, throwing them all into the cold sea.

Cyllell swirled among them, his flensing knife pointed upwards. Fifty yards is only one length of a big swimming pool. Not far at all. But, at night, wearing heavy clothes, with a man after you with a knife, then it's not so damned easy.

The Wolf did his work so well that only three of the twelve made it to the shore at all. The rest either drowned, or bled to death in the salt green depths.

Two other boats went the same way, until Kirk managed to get the others to start their engines and roar for the dubious safety of the beach. One Angel died, losing an arm to the tearing teeth of a propeller. That was tough on that brother, but it was a cheap price to pay for that stunning blow at the onset of the battle.

The Manchester Angels straggled on to the shingle, looking round for the attack they expected to come at any moment. Their guns raked the hill above them, looking for the silhouettes of their enemies.

This was a crucial psychological moment. Monk had urged that they hold off, in case they didn't manage to sink enough boats. If they had attacked, there were still enough guns to cut bloody gaps in their ranks.

Hidden on the bluff, Gwyn passed the heavy glasses to the acting President of the Last Heroes. 'See. You were right, boy, there's still a fucking crowd down there. I make it at least twelve with shotguns.'

Monk was also busy counting. 'Eleven shotguns. Their President, if that's the big guy, looks as though he's got a fucking Luger. Have to watch him. Bloody good, though, Gwyn. I reckon they lost nearly twenty men there. Stupid bastards. Wait till that hits them.'

It had already hit Kirk, and most of his senior brothers. It had seemed a game when someone suggested they set out to be top chapter. And, the first few fights hadn't been too tough. They'd only lost two men in the first year and a half. Three more had wiped out trying to show a bit too much class on a crowded motorway. Then, things had started getting much tougher. They'd got the guns, and that had tipped the balance. Until these Welsh bastards, nobody had wanted to tangle with them. Preferring to simply back down. But, they had grievously miscalculated over the Wolves. They were the gutsy, old-fashioned brothers. And, they fought for keeps.

Kirk was shattered by what had happened. Spock had crept among the survivors, reporting that their original party of forty-eight was now only twenty-nine.

'Dead. All of them! Fucking God! What went wrong? Listen, we've got to wipe them all out. Every single one. And their women. Otherwise, we'll have the police on our backs.'

Still the attack didn't come on them. Minutes passed, and tension stretched nerves to breaking point.

They spread out to form a loose ring, about fifty yards apart.

That was what Monk wanted. He waved his hand, and the second phase started.

Stones were lobbed accurately into that circle, and all around it. They bounced off the shingle and rattled around like a charge of cavalry. At the same time, Monk shouted out at the top of his voice. 'Come on Wolves! And Last Heroes! At them!'

It was enough to spook the Star Trekkers. First one, and then another of the brothers with guns started to use them. Spinning around in the blackness, blasting away at each other. Pellets bounced and ricocheted off the shingle, lodging in bone and muscle and flesh. It took over a minute before Kirk managed to regain enough control to stop the firing. By then, five more of his landing party had died, while several more were coughing and moaning on the rocks.

'Hold it! Hold it! You stupid bastards! There's still only us on the beach. Group together. We're going in.'

Privately, he was demoralised, and that's over half way towards being defeated. The thought of the police who must inevitably be brought in with that number of dead and seriously wounded tore at his mind, making it hard to concentrate on what he was doing.

That was something that the other Angels in the ruined village, higher up the mountain, didn't worry about. There'd been other killings and other times when they'd had to go underground. This time, though, the bodies were going to be many more and take a lot of explaining. So, they'd make sure that none of them were left alive to give any explanations.

Kirk split his men up into three separate groups, hoping to outflank and encircle the defenders. With their advantage of height and the night-glasses, and now even a numerical advantage, it would have been better if he'd cut his losses and gone home. But, he pressed on stupidly. Above him, with all those advantages, the Wolves and Last Heroes waited.

And watched.

The first group was led by a thin brother called Sulu, and consisted of eight of the toughest members of the chapter. The slippery cliff rose sheer above them, so Sulu tried to cut round by what was left of the old quarry. Creeping along in single file, they climbed through a narrow ravine, with a fast-flowing stream to their right.

They froze as the voice of Cochise echoed from in front of them. 'Let there be light! And there was light. Close!'

At the last word, the ambushing brothers all tightly closed their eyes, pressing their palms to shut out what they knew was happening. Deintydd was a bit of a chemist, and he'd made a string of magnesium bombs, that all ignited at the same moment.

The glaring white light blasted at the night, turning it to a ghostly pale day. The Star Trekkers, their pupils ready for blackness, were immediately blinded. Although they closed their eyes at the first dazzling flash, it was still too late. One of the Wolves who had wrecked his own night-vision to watch the flares gave the shout the second blackness had fallen again.

It was all too easy. Like taking shotguns from blind men. The three who fought were clubbed quickly into unconsciousness. The remainder never knew what was happening till they felt the prick of a sharp knife nudging at their jugulars, threatening them with an instant one-way trip to eternity.

It took less than five minutes to subdue the best third of Kirk's floundering command. Over to the right, the second third had got themselves lost and were sliding and cursing as they tried to climb an unclimbable rock face. Monk had taken command of that flank, and simply waited at the bottom, until they slid down to where he waited with his men. Since the Star Trekkers fell in ones and twos, he was able to take them easily. Only one of the Manchester brothers died there. He'd broken free and was running along the shingle, breath rasping in his throat, when a small, almost dwarf-like figure appeared out of the beach at his feet and opened him from groin to neck. The shock was so great that he tried to keep on running, despite his hideous wound, finally falling when he got tangled up with his own intestines.

'Never did have any guts, these bastards,' muttered Rat, looking down at his handiwork.

That left the middle eight, with Kirk and Spock. The brother with the mutilated ears had played a mute role in the battle. If such a one-sided slaughter could properly be called a battle.

While they looked up at the steep climb that faced them, they suddenly saw a vision from the depths of hell, grinning down at them. The face was as white as scrubbed ivory, and the red eyes seemed to gleam at them, in that deep darkness. The voice was as soft as a caress, and as vicious as a scorpion's sting.

'Brothers. Can you hear me? Brother Kirk and what is left of your Star Trekkers?'

In answer, Kirk wildly fired both barrels towards the face, which promptly disappeared. And reappeared some yards to the left of where it had been.

'Naughty, naughty. That will only get you all dead. You ought to know that all the rest of your party are dead or captured. Which may amount to the same thing, depending on whether you decide you're going to be sensible or just fucking stupid!'

On the last two words, an edge crept into the voice.

'You're bluffing. We'd have heard something.'

Gwyn smiled. He knew that Kirk really believed him. 'Do you think that? Call to them. See if they answer. Or, would you like me to have them brought here and cut their throats one by one while you watch.'

All but two of the Manchester Angels surrendered. One ran for the shrubs that clung to the soft sandy edges of the beach, and dived in with his shotgun in his hand. From there he held the Wolves and Last Heroes off for two hours until he had only two shells left.

By now, first light was nibbling at the blackness, and the watching Angels saw a remarkable sight. After the crack of the gun had kept them low, they heard muttering, as though Kirk was talking to himself. Then, there was the double bang of both barrels being fired. But, it sounded more muffled than it had. They saw the body of Kirk rise vertically in the air, as though a mighty hand had thrown him, then it flopped down again into the grass.

By putting the barrels in his mouth, he had muffled the bangs. But, the power of the charges had lifted him clear of the ground, ripping the back of his head off in whitened splinters of bone. So, he boldly went where no man had gone before.

That left one. The psychotic Spock. He got to one of the boats and managed to paddle it away.

By dawn he was back at their deserted camp, breaking the news to the mamas and old ladies that the Star Trekkers were finished. Before this could really penetrate, he was astride his Norton, eyes staring insanely at the pale eastern sky, roaring off southwards. On a lone run.

By nine he was already near Shrewsbury, his face a mask of dust and sweat. His lips moved incessantly, and tiny bubbles of spittle frothed at the corners of his mouth.

By midday he was getting near his destination.

Just after one thirty, he reached it.

Behind him, at the village of Porth-y-Nant, in the valley of Nant Gwrtheyrn, the carnage was cleaned up. As many of the bodies as possible were retrieved from the sea, but some had drifted away during the night, and some had sunk, to reappear days later, miles along the coast, with all the soft flesh gone from their faces and bodies.

Gwyn and Monk held a last hasty meeting. They had sent the remnants of the Star Trekkers off on foot. Barefoot. With their colours shredded from their backs. The village was cleared up, with the help of the returned mamas and old ladies, and they all prepared for a hasty farewell and exit.

Amid all the bustle, Gwyn and Monk snatched a few quick words.

'Come down and see us when things get quieter, Gwyn. In a few months.'

The albino grinned. 'I will, boy, don't you worry. Hey, but what about Gerry? Almost forgot him in all the excitement. What about him?'

'We'll find him. But, he's probably turned up by now, and he's roaring up here on his way. Keep in touch, mate.'

'Right. And you.' Monk walked to his hog, where Modesty sat waiting for him. Gwyn shouted above the revving of the engines: 'Hey, Monk. Thanks for coming.'

Monk grinned back. 'Thanks a lot for having us. Take care now.'

And they were gone.

At Shrewsbury, Monk shouted for the others to carry on back to their turf without him. Didn't give them time to ask where he was going or why. Didn't even say when he'd be along after them.

He rode on, with Modesty clinging to the back of his colours, through Shropshire lanes. After a couple of miles, she asked, her lips pressed close to his ear, shouting above the slipstream: 'Where are we going?'

He shouted back. One word. 'Away.'

14. AND HANDED OUT STRONGLY

"The Country's Conscience" – the weekly social leader in the Sunday paper, 'The Clarion'. Sunday, May, 1999.

Well, it's happened again. I wonder as I read the news tapes how much longer we are going to have to put up with these desperate animals. The self-styled "apostles of the open road" with their filthy habits and depraved rules and regulations.

I'm sure that many of you, like me, made extra checks on your locks and bolts when you read about the shocking outbursts of killing and woundings that took place in different parts of the country last week.

I know North Wales well, and I love its people. I love their quietness and their respect for the summer visitors. Most of the Welsh love the English, as a horse loves its hay, and I mean no disrespect by that. What, you may ask, have these soft-spoken folk done to deserve this mass slaughter on their doorsteps? It is not an easy question to answer.

According to most reports, as many as thirty young people perished in a fight between several gangs of thugs. These young men, mostly from Manchester – a city that I know well and love – chose to live their lives in this mindless way, ending them in as futile a manner as it is possible to imagine. They never walked hand in hand with their young women through fields of summer green. They never walked along sandy beaches, dreaming of the family they would raise. No, they walked in darkness, knives and guns their only loves. And, so they perished, by that same violence by which they lived.

I for one can shed no tears.

And what of the folk in the quiet hamlet in Hertfordshire, who had their afternoon peace ripped apart by the violent explosion? Are they not entitled to protection? I am a firm supporter of the police in their vigilant and ceaseless battle against the forces of evil and corruption. But, I wonder why they did nothing to stop this slaughter. Perhaps they were too busy harrying parking offenders, as I myself was harried only last Thursday. Priorities should be examined with greater care by the senior officers.

We learn that a camp of these Hell's Angels was devastated and most of the occupants killed when a tank of petrol – did they have a licence for storing that sort of quantity, I wonder? – exploded. One of the few survivors, a teenage girl, claimed that it had been a member of a rival gang who had caused the blaze. A man who thought it clever to mutilate his own ears and name himself after a television programme of years ago. It is some relief to know that this "Spock", as he called himself, was among the dead.

I have attacked these hooligans in the past, and I shall, doubtless, have to attack them again in the future. I cannot allow my function as the "Country's Conscience" to falter or waver.

Perhaps the days will come again when a man can take his family out into God's green country, at the end of a week's honest toil, without having to look over his shoulder for the looming spectre of Gerry Vinson and his self-styled "Last Heroes". Gradually, my friends in the police tell me, his gang has been eroded, and this last blow to his headquarters may prove the last nail in their coffin.

As all my regular readers tell me so often, they appreciate the cool impersonal way that I make my points and put my grievances. The reason for this is simple. I feel that I am putting your grievances, and that is why I remain cool.

But, I will relax that dispassionate calm when I think about the Hell's Angels. If they are finally buried, I will go and dance on the grave. And, I feel that I will be doing that for all of you.

Next week I'll be looking at the softies who bend over backwards to help unmarried mothers. I'll be asking why they can't help themselves.

Until then; so long my old chinas.

15. YOU ASK WHY I DON'T LIVE HERE

Assistant Chief Constable Israel Pitman Penn was due back from the north that evening. His case had been neatly wrapped up, and he couldn't wait to get back and see how things were going.

Angela was satisfied. The last three days had seen Gerry unwittingly pour out to her all the innermost secrets of the Angels. The killings, accidental and deliberate. Where they got dope and guns from. Friends in straight jobs who would help out now and again, when they were in trouble. The pile of tapes stood several inches high, each tape loaded with names. Enough to break the back of the Angels in Britain from here to eternity.

All supplied by Gerry Vinson.

She had kept him in a semi-twilight sleep state since their afternoon out, knowing that he would start to suspect what was happening if she once took him off the truth drug. Each morning she gave him the large glass of orange juice with a second helping at lunch, and a third to get him to sleep.

Exhausted by the shattering effect the drug was having on his mind and body, Gerry had collapsed and she had put him to bed, locking him securely in. Allowing herself the luxury of a drink with lunch. Lying on her bed, relaxing, idly letting her fingers feather down to touch herself. Literally hugging herself with pleasure at how well things were going.

There'd be another session later, maybe after Israel came back, so that he could see for himself what she'd done to the big, strong, villain, Gerry Vinson. He was almost literally eating out of her hand. Maybe one, or two at the outside, more days, then Israel could have Vinson and the tapes, and she would begin to work on her thesis. The book that would bring the name of Angela Wells out of the shadows into the glare of the spotlight. The book that would make her.

Grinning at the sheer beauty of that thought she reached over and poured another drink. Opened the small drawer at the side of the bed. Took something out, and turned it on. The soft hum filled the room, and she slipped away into another world. The sun crept round.

Downstairs, Gerry woke up about five. The clock on the wall of his bedroom wasn't all that reliable. He was surprised to see it was that late. Normally they had a long afternoon session. Maybe they'd had it, and he hadn't noticed. He stood up, shaking his head to try and clear it. He'd collapsed just before lunch, and he'd had nothing.

Not even the usual glass of orange juice.

Strangely, the muzziness seemed a little easier after his sleep. If only he could get his thoughts together, he reckoned he could work out what was wrong with him. But, concentration was out of the question.

Vaguely, he gazed down at the chain between his feet. Just visible, a nick on one of the links, was the silver cut he'd been making, trying to sever it. That had been ... how long ago? It seemed ages. Maybe it was only a few days. Maybe he ought to try.

But, it wasn't easy to get through one of those steel chains. They had enormous strength. He grinned as he remembered something one of the brothers had once done with a chain. It had been ... who had it been? Cochise. That was who. He'd crept up behind a parked police car, attached one end of a forty foot chain to the rear axle. The other end to a concrete post just behind the car.

Then, he'd gone out in front of the police car and shouted out they were a crowd of fucking queers. Then, waving two vertical fingers, he'd ridden slowly away.

The moment the police woke up to this insult, the driver slammed the car into gear, and stamped hard on the accelerator, intending to knock the crap out of the Angel. If necessary, ride him into the road in a smear of blood and guts.

When the chain snapped taut, it ripped the rear axle clear away from the chassis, and the car veered sideways in a shower of exploding sparks and ground splinters of torn metal.

In the silence of his lonely room, Gerry laughed out loud at the story. He remembered that Angela hadn't seemed to think it was that amusing.

It was a hell of a good job he hadn't mentioned the name of Cochise to Angela. Despite all her promises and those of Penn, it would be a temptation not to try and bust the big Angel.

'Fuck! Fuck!! Fuck!!! Oh, fucking bloody bleeding sodding bastard!' As suddenly as he exploded into blind rage, so he managed to bring himself under control. His anger was so intense that he actually rolled on the bed, biting on the pillow to stop himself screaming out again. The anger burst through his body, helping to push back the effects of the scopolamine.

Like someone switching on a powerful light inside his brain, he realised what Angela had been doing to him. He *had* given her the name of Cochise. And all the other brothers. Given her descriptions and places where they hung out. Who had done this and that and when. He'd given her enough on tape to bring in every Hell's Angel he'd ever known. Not just the Last Heroes, but some righteous brothers from other chapters. Notably the Wolves.

It took him a moment to fully regain his composure. Even then, he found his hands shaking at the extent of his treachery. Would Penn keep his word? Would he hell! That meant two things he needed to do. One was to get out, and the other was to destroy the tapes and all her notes.

First, there was an even greater urgency. To find out how she was drugging him, and stop her without her noticing. Unless he could do that, he'd be easy meat if he tried to escape.

What could it be? Not an injection. It was virtually impossible to give anyone the needle without them noticing, though he'd once O.D.'d a bent pusher without him knowing. That meant it had to be in food. Or drink. What the hell did he have that she didn't?

Mind racing, because he could hear someone moving around upstairs, Gerry tried to think what he had to eat and drink at each meal. Something that maybe Angela didn't touch.

The muzziness was easing with every minute that passed. What about breakfast? Orange juice! Of course. The one thing he had three times each day, and Angela never had at all. Said it brought her out in spots. Right. That was the game they were playing. Now that he knew what the rules were, he'd be able to take a much bigger part in it.

The sound of someone fumbling at the lock, rattling the key. Angie pushed her head round the door, a lop-sided grin barely pasted in place.

'Hello, little Gerry. Sorry to keep you waiting. I was just catching up on a bit of sleep. How do you feel?'

He forced a dreamy, vague note into his voice, telling her he was all right.

'Good. Izzie'll be here in about an hour. Is there anything I can get you before he comes? I'd like to have a session with him sitting in. I think he'd be interested. How about a drink?'

'Yes please. I'd like a glass of orange.'

He watched her face, seeing that she didn't bother to hide her amusement that this was what he wanted. Yes, that had to be it. The orange. Some kind of drug in it that had made him vomit up everything he knew.

After she brought it, she locked him in again and went upstairs to take a bath. Carefully, he poured the drink on to the carpet under the bed, where the shadow would hide the dampness until it was dry.

Then, he sat on the bed, thinking out what he would do. His plan had to be a good one. With Israel there, he wouldn't have much room for error.

'Ask him about the bank raid again. Where the money went. That's what'd interest a few coppers around the place.'

There was a nervous tic right between the eyes that hadn't been there when he went away to Yorkshire a week ago. His face looked thinner and more drawn, the eyes never still, flicking from face to face, stopping at the pile of tapes on the cabinet against the wall.

Angela looked at Gerry, pitching her voice low, so that he would feel secure, and wouldn't want to fight against the influence of the drug that she imagined now had him in its grip.

'Gerry, my love, can you tell me what happened to all the money you stole from that bank?'

He gazed at the table for a moment, gathering his thoughts. He knew he was going to have to act fast and soon. Everything he'd said in the past had been true, and Israel would have it all later that night, or by tomorrow at the latest.

'We spent quite a lot on dope and booze and tools for the hogs. The rest we buried in our camp down south.'

'Exactly where?' asked Israel, sharply.

'Underneath the petrol tank that held all our fuel. In a wooden box.'

There was a crash as the policeman banged his hand on the table. 'Bloody damnation! That explosion at their camp that killed a lot of them was centred on that fuel tank. Some bastard from one of the other gangs got to it and blew it up!'

It took an enormous effort of will for Gerry not to show his shock at the news. The money wasn't really buried there, but that didn't matter. There'd been an explosion, and some of the brothers were dead. And, there'd been a rumble. He prayed that Israel would say more.

Fortunately, Angela had been so busy taping and keeping her copious notes together that she'd not bothered to watch the news or look at the papers for several days. She asked what had been happening, and Israel put her in the picture. The story he told – broadly accurate as it was – shattered Gerry. Deaths on the scale he was talking about meant big trouble. It meant a police purge bigger even than the one under Hayes. And, it meant that the police would need and use every single scrap of information they could against the brothers.

To his relief, Angela had been so thorough that there were only the most minimal gaps in the picture that Penn wanted filled in. By eleven that night, they were done, and Angela led him to his room, giving him his glass of orange juice.

They had become so used to his dullness and lack of interest in what was going on around him that they were speaking freely without worrying if he could understand or not. While she was getting him ready for bed, Penn had been talking about tomorrow.

'I'll get him to London in the morning. We needn't get up too early. Plenty of time for a bit of relaxation first. But, with all these explosions, and the Home Secretary wetting himself, I don't think we can wait any longer. I'll take all the tapes and all the notes with me, and get them transcribed straight away. I'll charge him with a few things to start with, then I'll get as many men as possible out on the road, tracking down the rest of his bastard friends.'

And he laughed. Laughed until the tears ran down his thin cheeks. Laughed and kept on laughing, until Angela shook him by the arm and almost hit him. Then, spinning on his heel, he left the room.

Gerry sat apathetically, ignoring this bizarre cameo, the glass of drugged orange held tightly in his hands, hoping that she would leave so that he wouldn't have to drink it. To risk slipping back into that half-world of living and partly-living would mean his own end, and the end of many of his closest and oldest friends. That was, if any of them had survived the slaughter in Wales and in Hertfordshire.

But, he was out of luck. Angie stood by the door, looking worriedly up the stairs after Israel, her mouth set in a tight, worried line. She turned round to face Gerry.

'Drink up your orange. Otherwise you won't grow up to be a big strong boy.'

There was no way round it. Israel had been flashing his automatic around, like he could hardly wait for a chance to use it. If he didn't drink, then they'd know he'd been faking.

And the shit would hit the fan in the biggest way possible.

So, as fast as he could, he drank, draining the glass. As he handed her the empty glass, he looked up at her, wondering whether there might be any touch of kindness or compassion in her.

She was hardly paying attention, and the glass fell to the floor, where it rolled across the carpet. Her voice breaking with anger, she slapped him hard across the face, knocking him backwards over the bed.

'You stupid little bastard. Thank Christ I won't see you again after tomorrow until I see you in the dock, collecting forty years without remission.' She looked down at him, as he struggled to get up. 'Maybe I'll chain you up properly for the night. One round your neck, so you can't even sit down. Teach you one last lesson. Then you can think about me upstairs in bed with Israel. Not that you can think about anything with that inside you.'

He waited, ready to try and kill her if she tried to do what she threatened. But, from upstairs came the bull's bellow of Israel Penn, shouting for her to hurry up. Picking up the glass, she spun on her heel and walked out. He heard the key grate in the lock, then her footsteps going upstairs. The slamming of her bedroom door, then silence.

The marks of her fingers burned on his cheek.

Apart from the muffled noise of voices, the big house was quiet. Already the drug in the orange would be passing through into his stomach. He didn't have much time at all.

He dropped to his knees in the corner of the room farthest away from the door, and put his hands to his mouth. If she'd chained him at all, there would have been no way he could have saved himself. He jammed his fingers into his mouth, probing at the back of his throat. He gagged, but kept his fingers there. He gagged again, and his mouth filled with saliva. Breathing hard with the strain of what he was doing, he spat it out, trying again. He felt his stomach muscles heaving, telling him he was progressing. At last, with a great gush, his throat and mouth filled with vomit. Head down, he retched and gasped, bringing it all back home. His supper was fairly digested by now, but he brought it up. He was relieved, in the pale light of the moon, to see a flood of liquid. In the time he'd taken, the drug would have had no chance to get into his system.

Still he thrust his fingers down his throat, heaving and straining until he was only bringing up thin bile. It was done. He'd managed stage one.

The chain broke at eighteen minutes past one. By half-past, he had wrapped the tinkling ends up in rags torn off his sheets. The noises from upstairs had ceased nearly an hour ago. That left the bars to the window.

During supper, it hadn't been difficult to pocket a fork, keeping it down the front of his levis. Now, working steadily away, he managed to chip the concrete away from the bottoms of two of the bars. Exerting all his strength, he forced them apart, leaving a gap just wide enough for him to wriggle through.

The tearing noise as the bars gave under his pressure made him grit his teeth, and he waited in the darkness for a moment. But, all was as silent as a sealed tomb.

The garden was pitch-black. The moon had been obscured by heavy cloud. That was to his advantage. Gerry was a skilled and cautious tracker, and his time in the jungle warfare section of the army had left him with few equals at this sort of game.

He ran, lightly, over the lawn, keeping to the deeper shadows at the edges, slipping into the shrubbery like a ghost of vengeance. He'd noticed the guard patrols in his first couple of nights, before the scopolamine took its toll. He guessed there were four, patrolling in linked pairs.

Among the trees, he paused as he heard the church clock in the distant village strike the hour. Silently, he counted the strokes. One. Two. Three. Christ, time was passing much too fast! It would be dawn in less than three hours.

As it turned out, the patrols were easy. He could hear them coming a long way off, chatting amiably about the cricket season, and the controversial appointment of a

Pakistani-born West Indian as the new captain of the national side.

After they'd lumbered past, making more noise than mating elephants, he struck quickly across the country. In less than a quarter of an hour, he was there.

The white gate had a strict notice on it. It said, in bold black letters: *Keep Out. No Admittance. Keep Out.*

That figured, thought Gerry. Maybe he wouldn't want many people coming round looking him up. Not Mr Remington – like the gun – with his taste for purple shirts, and his desire for secrecy.

The gate was locked, and Gerry scrambled over, scratching his hand on a strip of barbed wire as he did so. There were no lights showing in the cottage. Gerry walked quietly round the path, breathing in the deep odour of honeysuckle that clustered round the side wall.

Near the back door was a tub of clean, fresh rain water, and he used the opportunity to wash some of the stale, brackish taste of vomit out of his mouth.

It wasn't hard to guess which was the main bedroom, and he stopped and picked up a handful of earth from the edge of the neatly-trimmed border. He flicked it up at the bedroom window, hearing it rattle on the glass. He had to do it three times more, using slightly larger lumps of earth, before he got the reaction he wanted.

A bedside lamp clicked on, and then the window inched open. A high-pitched American voice drifted across the garden, sounding like the sweetest music in the world to Gerry's ears.

'Who the fuck is that and what the fuck do you want?'

A blast from the past. Not Remington, like the gun, but Colt, like the gun. Purple nightshirt and all.

'Hello, Rupert. It's Gerry. I was just passing by, and I thought I'd drop in.'

16. THAT'S STRUNG A KNOT IN MY MIND

Extract from a confidential memo from assistant Chief Constable I. P. Penn, to the Home Secretary, 1999.

You will find attached to this introductory note a selection of data from a number of tapes made by Professor Angela Wells. They will incriminate many members of the outlawed motor-cycle gangs, in many cases linking them with crimes going back several years. I will not mention any of these here, but I would just ask you to note that the suspicions of many of my fellow officers about me – I heard about these suspicions, all the whispering behind my back – are completely without foundation. I have produced in this document the most comprehensive and damning indictment against a criminal culture since the days of the big London gangs.

Miss Wells, who I know personally, is a socio-criminal psychiatrist of proven ability. I only hope that her growing relationship with me will not jeopardise her professional position. I know too well what it is to be the subject of a malicious witch-hunt. People you once thought were your friends conspiring in corners, imagining that one is losing hold of one's sanity. Well, sir, with the greatest respect, I can only say that this will vindicate my single-minded devotion to duty that I hope has always characterised my attitude to the police force.

I found myself in the position of asking one of the leaders of these Hell's Angels – indeed, I would venture to say that he is the leader of them all – to help her out with a project into the criminal motivation of violence. I feel sure that there will be jealousy over my coup, but I would ask you to believe that there was little luck in my choice. I had planned and schemed for years, giving up everything, to help bring these animals to justice.

Investigation might suggest that I bent the rules to try and entrap this man and his nefarious associates. I deny that. I deny that absolutely. He came with me of his own free will and he stayed of his own free will. Anyone who says otherwise is simply out to bring me down and help these creatures of night and death to escape. Well, you have my word that I will not let a single one rest until they are all safely behind bars for the longest sentence the law can possibly pass. I only hope some bleeding-heart liberal judge doesn't set them free with a smack on the bottom and a lecture on civics.

That is all I want to say. In a day I will have all the information I need to present you, and that will make certain folk – I name no names – laugh on the other side of their faces.

I remain, respectfully,
Israel Pitman Penn.

Comments of Detective Inspector Peter Gudgeon, Shropshire Constabulary.
This piece of paper was found in a charred brief case that we believe was the possession of the Assistant Chief Constable. There was nothing else attached to it. Nor was there any sign of anything in the house that might have supported his strange fancies.

Unless there is any evidence still to come to light, I fear that I can only imagine that the Assistant Chief Constable might, as has been suggested, have been suffering from overwork.

I present a fuller report in the dossier on the incident.

17. TIME WILL TELL JUST WHO FELL AND WHO'S BEEN LEFT BEHIND

Over a hastily-prepared mug of coffee, Rupert Colt and Gerry caught up with the main essentials of what had happened to both of them since their last meeting, backstage at the apocalyptic concert in London.

Then, the little American had told Gerry he was getting out. That the rat-race had finished for him and that he was going to get right away from it all. Change his name and live on a small farm in the country.

And he'd done all that. It had been even better than he'd hoped. He felt twenty years younger and he'd already stopped gorging himself on handfuls of uppers and downers.

At first, he obviously didn't believe Gerry's amazing story. Until he was told about the involvement of Israel Pitman Penn.

'Right baby. Now I know it's for real. That man was a psycho in the making if ever I saw one. The guy was bound to crack up sooner or later. Happens it's sooner. And that's the chick who lives over there? Well. I've seen her a few times around, but we just exchanged the usual pleasantries. You know. See how English I've become, Gerry. It's great. But, what the hell are you going to do?'

Gerry shook his head wearily. 'I just don't know, Rupert. All I know is that I've got to get back to that house tonight, and stop them spilling it all.'

Rupert nodded. 'I need someone to come and live in here and help out. It's all a bit much for me. After you've finished over there, why not come and stay a bit. I'm a respectable fellow. There are places in this old place they'd never find you. I can even hide your hog.'

'Rupert, you are a nice guy. A straight shooter, if you know what I mean. But, you don't dig it. I'm going to have to wipe them. Probably both of them.'

There was a silence between them. Then, the shorter, older man got up and poured another coffee for himself. 'Like I said. I need someone to come and live here and help me out with things. If you want to, then come on back.'

Gerry grinned. 'Tell you what. If it breaks well, then I'll split straight away and you won't see me for a bit. Don't worry, now I know where you are, I'll find a way of getting to see you. If things don't work out, and they may not – he's got a shooter – then I'll come back and ask you for a job. I feel a bit like that anyway, Rupert. It's getting time for me to make my move before I get too old. Or too dead.'

Before he left, he cut off the ends of the chain, and borrowed a steel knife from

Rupert's kitchen. While he worked on the chain, Rupert brought him up to date on all the news there'd been in the papers and on the television about the killings in Wales and the explosion that had devastated the camp in Hertfordshire.

'Looks like there's nothing much for you to go back to, Gerry. Can't be many left of the Angels now.'

For a time, he didn't answer. The paper gave a list of dead, either by real name or by nick-name. Allowing for the usual inaccuracies and exaggerations, it had been bad news day. Riddler had bought it, as had a lot of the women. Gerry didn't know the names of most of them, and didn't even want to. The report from Wales was more cheerful.

Nearly all the dead came from the Manchester area, though two or three of the names of the Welsh brothers were familiar. It was easy for him to piece together what had happened. The threat of the attack from the Manchester Star Trekkers. Gwyn asking for help from the Last Heroes. The fight, led probably by Monk, with their violent victory. Someone, obviously one of the defeated chapter, getting back at them by blowing up their turf.

It was nearly light. Time for a move. Rupert turned off the lights in the cottage, and opened the back door. Gerry slipped through it, the knife tucked in his belt. As he reached the gate, he heard the low whisper from behind him. 'I hope you come back and ask for that job, Gerry. Take care now.'

The moon still peeped fitfully from behind the clouds, throwing shadows among the trees. A fox loped in front of Gerry, only a few feet away, but he didn't see or smell him. Remember, Gerry isn't just good. He's very good.

If a wily fox doesn't see him, then the wandering police don't have much chance. Sure enough, Gerry slips past and reaches the wall of the big house, just below the window from which he'd escaped. Silently, he clambered in, having a quick look round to make sure he hadn't been spotted. Then, out again, and round the front.

It only took a moment to force a window. Then, he was safe, inside the enemies' castle, ready to do battle and capture the papers. Wherever they were. He didn't risk a light, cat-footing across a thick carpet. The hall was a valley of shadow, and he crossed it smoothly, entering Angela's study. The door was unlocked.

Placing his feet as delicately as a cat, Gerry walked to the desk. In the top drawer, he had seen a small, pencil torch. By its light, he looked quickly round the room. The thick curtains were pulled shut, and he wondered whether to risk putting on the light. But, he decided the risk of the light being seen under the door was too great.

Using the torch, he looked through the desk drawers. Apart from paper and pencils, and the usual clips and rubbers, there was nothing of any importance or use to him. Abandoning that, he started on the bookshelves against the left-hand wall. Still nothing.

Then he remembered her smaller room, where she had occasionally gone. That was locked. But, it was an easily broken lock, on a door that opened inwards. By banging it regularly with his fist, near the lock, he was able to shift the screws in the wood.

Leaning on it, trying to muffle the crack as the screws tore loose, Gerry finally levered the heavy door open. A flash of the torch showed him what he'd come for. A neatly-stacked pile of tapes, resting on top of an equally neat heap of blue notebooks. All together in one place.

He made the instant decision to leave them till last. There was a more important chore to be executed, which was about the right word for it. He pulled the knife from his belt, holding it in front of him. Thumb pointing along the blade, ready for the upward cut of the expert. The most difficult blow to parry.

Back across the carpet, and into the silent hall, at the bottom of the rolling staircase. He hummed tunelessly between his teeth. 'To market, to market, to kill a fat pig.'

His foot was just on the bottom step, poised to take his weight, when all the lights came on. He froze for a second, and then movement was too late.

'What a surprise. Come to murder us in our beds, have you?' Standing at the top of the stairs, the Minim automatic in his hand, was Israel. Gerry noticed two things in that first flash of dazzling light. The gun carried a silencer. And, Israel had finally cracked. His eyes were wide and staring, and his left hand constantly plucked at his dressing-gown. He smiled vacantly as Gerry watched him.

'Put the knife down on the floor, Vinson. Or I'll shoot you down where you stand. A bullet in each knee, just for a start.'

There didn't seem a wide range of alternatives. At that range, he wasn't likely to miss. Mad or not. There was the faint tinkling of steel as he threw the knife down into the corner of the hall. The smile even broader, Penn walked carefully down to join him.

'In there.' Waving the gun in the direction of the sitting-room. 'Move.'

'Wait a minute. Israel, what are you doing?'

Both men glanced upwards. There, in a pale blue, very diaphanous short night-dress, was Angela Wells. In her hand, she held the twin gun to Israel, down to the same bulky silencer.

The policeman looked up at her. 'He got out. I'm going to have to deal with him.'

'Not here.'

'Yes. It has to be. We can't take the risk of having him running around or getting loose again. Don't worry, it'll look like he was trying to escape.'

Angela still didn't move, obviously worried by this new development in their plans. Oddly, she seemed unaware of Israel's mental condition, possibly because of the imminent threat that murder was going to be committed in her house within the next couple of minutes.

'Go back to bed, Angela. Out of the way. I'll come up when it's over. I think I may be able to give you something after I've got rid of this offal.' And he giggled again.

It was only then that she realised what had happened, and she began to walk down the stairs. His voice cracked out like a whip. 'Get back to bed, or you may get hurt. Now!'

Reluctantly, she turned and went out of sight. Penn again waved the gun at Gerry, its barrel looking bigger than ever. Walking carefully, Gerry sat down in a large armchair, his back to a tall, ornate standard lamp.

'This is where we have a long chat, and you snatch the opportunity to get my gun away, isn't it?'

'Maybe.'

'Maybe not. Goodbye.'

And he squeezed the trigger.

The silencer muted the sound of the explosion, making it sound like a stifled cough. The .357 bullet actually went between Gerry's arm and body, thumping into the upholstery with the force of a kick. He started to get up, when Israel dodged and fired again. The bullet scored a furrow of white wood off the top of an occasional table and hit Gerry, smashing into his chest, high up on the left-hand side.

The power of the slug hurled him violently back in the chair, sending it careering over on its side, knocking over the lamp, dislodging the bulb and holder.

He was conscious of the impact, but the pain was only numbness. There was time to look down and see the spreading darkness on the front of his colours. Strangely, he was even aware of where the bullet had gone. Entering the front of his chest, it had angled upwards and out through the back of his shoulder. Normally, the exit hole from a heavy calibre bullet would be a hunk of meat bigger than your fist. But, the ricochet from the desk had slowed it down, and the two wounds weren't instant killers. But, he was bleeding fast and heavy.

The only sound was Israel panting and giggling. A wet, obscene noise. 'I can smell a rat. I'm coming to get you. Where are you?'

Another bullet chipped the wall behind him, spraying plaster all over him. A wandering thought of a couple of lines from a western movie came to him. From the Alamo, in fact. He grinned at the recollection, halfway aware that he was going to die very soon. Two Texans are lying wounded, and the wave of Mexican attackers sweeps towards them. One says: 'Do this mean what I think it means?' and the other replies: 'It do.'

He moved slightly, to ease the discomfort, and his hand brushed against the fallen light bulb.

What happened next was so fast that you could hardly realise what it was. He closed his fingers round the light, standing up quickly. Pain almost blacked him out, but he stood there. Israel saw him at once and snapped off another shot. Yet again, it went wide, tearing the mouth out of a green-painted Eurasian lady over the mantelpiece.

Arm back, and throw. It was the last strike in a tied innings. But, it struck Israel out. The bulb hit him on the forehead, shattering on impact.

The noise was louder than the bullets had been. Tiny fragments of splintered glass shredded his skin, ripping his eyes to liquid pulp. His hands flew up to his ruined face, and the gun dropped to the blood-speckled carpet.

A scream began, low in his throat, gradually rising until it reached an unbearable pitch of agony and despair. In that second or two, Gerry had scrambled across and picked up the gun. He held it, feeling its great weight, looking dispassionately at the blinded Penn.

The air hummed close to his face, and there was a crump from across the room. A crystal vase dissolved in shards of glass. Oddly, he never heard the gun going off. He wheeled round, seeing Angela, her eyes screwed up with hatred, pointing the other gun at him for a second shot.

At that instant, like a dying stallion, Israel blundered forwards. The silenced gun spoke again. Gerry started to duck, realising the futility of the gesture as he made it. His eyes were on Penn, and he saw a remarkable sight.

It was as though a trapdoor had been abruptly lifted from the inside of his skull. A chunk of bone flapped off, and there was an eruption of pink and grey and red. The bullet from Angela's gun had hit him in the jaw, tearing upwards through his head, splashing on to the ceiling. Its impact actually lifted him off his feet, before depositing him in an ungainly and very dead heap on the carpet.

Angela stood there like one stricken by sudden paralysis. Still holding the gun, she sat down hard in an armchair, her face blank with shock.

Gerry tried to draw a deep breath, and found the pain was beginning to get to him. His trousers were now heavy with his own blood, and his boots slid greasily in the pool at his feet. He sighed, and the sound made Angela look up.

She looked straight down the barrel of Israel's gun, held steady in Gerry's hand. His finger was white on the trigger.

'No. Gerry. Please. You have to listen to me. He made me. Don't shoot me.'

She had forgotten that she too held a gun.

'Please. I'll do anything. Cover up for you. You can go where you like.' The words tripped over each other like a falling crowd on an escalator.

Gerry shook his head, genuine regret in his voice. 'Lady, I don't have the time.'

And he squeezed the trigger. Once.

Ignoring the two bodies, he went as fast as he could to the bathroom on the ground floor. He knew that he was dying, his heart pumping blood out through the holes torn in his flesh. The only chance he had was to stop those holes up. At least for the time being.

He tore up a couple of towels, and tied them in place, tightly over the double wound, pressing them in to try and check the blood. Once that was done, he walked unsteadily down the hall to the work-room. Picked up the pile of tapes and notes, and laid them together in the centre of the floor. There was a strong temptation to open the notes and read what he'd said, or slip one of the tapes on the cassette and listen to his voice telling all he knew. But, time was passing, and there was so little left.

In the kitchen, he found a bottle of turpentine, and he poured it liberally over the pile of evidence, letting it run on to the carpet, and on the drapes. He glanced round, looking for anything else that needed doing.

He lit a match to the soggy paper of the top notebook, watching the flame creep from page to page, the heat turning the books brown. Flames leaped to the curtains, striking over furniture.

Almost hypnotised by the rapid spread of the fire, Gerry broke away with a conscious effort. There was one more vital effort required from his weakening body. One that offered the only chance of getting away to a sort of safety. He had to free his hog.

The garage was a solid block, with no windows. The main doors were fold-over. Using the long blade of the kitchen knife, he slipped the catch, and rattled the doors up and over. The noise would probably bring the patrolling fuzz, but that would have to be.

Although he'd carefully closed the door of the study to contain the fire, it wouldn't take too long to break free into the rest of the house.

There it was! The monster Harley, glittering in the pale light of the single electric bulb. He limped across to it, checking the tank and ignition. A spasm of pain hit him, and he leaned on the cool leather of the saddle, waiting for it to pass.

Time to go.

He switched off the garage light, opening the doors just wide enough to pass a man and a bike. Then, he went back inside the house of death. Already he could smell the stench of scorching wood, and a pall of smoke wreathed about the ground floor. In the garage there'd been a two gallon can of petrol, and he'd struggled to carry it with him.

He splashed it liberally about, walking into the living-room with it. The bodies lay still, blood already congealing. Gerry soaked both corpses in petrol, knocking the can over in the centre of the room, and letting it slurp across the carpet.

Finally, he walked over to the closed door of the work-room. The room where he'd spent so much of the last week and rested his hand on the woodwork. It was already hot to touch.

Once that was open, the fire would rage through the house in a matter of minutes. He saw a thread of petrol worming its way from the living-room towards him. Unless he wanted to go up with the house ... in a bizarre way, the idea seemed attractive, and he hesitated. The pain would soon be over, and the idea of rest appealed to him. No more pain or killing. No more of anything.

He jerked open the door, and the flames hissed out, biting at his fingers.

'Fucking hell!' The room was an inferno, with a white-hot core of fire at its centre. Nothing remained of the furniture. The instant of opening the door fed the flames with the oxygen it craved, and it roared up, exploding out through the windows.

Clutching the towels to him, conscious of the blood that still seeped from his wounds, Gerry shied sideways, like a crab disturbed at its feeding, towards the back door. He just made it, shutting it behind him, when the petrol caught.

There was a mighty whoosh, and flames cracked out through the upstairs windows. Dimly above the noise of the fire, he heard shouts of alarm coming from the woods. Feeling weakness clawing him down, he walked slowly into the garage.

Timing was crucial. He closed his eyes, trying to concentrate on what he had to do. Standing in the shadows by the partly-opened garage door, ready for the police to come. It seemed that he stood there for an eternity, until he heard running feet crunching on the gravel of the drive.

Holding himself upright against the wall of the garage, he watched the two policemen hammer past him, their eyes fixed on the blazing house.

The moment they'd gone, he started to move. Leaning all his weight against it, he managed to get the heavy chopper rolling. He felt the wounds tugging and tearing, and a gush of fresh blood trickled down his chest and on down his legs. But, it was moving.

He risked one glance over his shoulder. The building was burning fiercely, with yellow and white flames springing through all the downstairs windows. In that moment, while he watched, slates flew off the roof, and tongues of fire licked up through into the black night air. A whirlpool of red sparks spun high above him.

There was no sign of the two policemen. He guessed they must be somewhere round the back, trying hopelessly to find some way into the inferno. Turning his back for the last time on the country home of Professor Angela Wells, Gerry pushed on down the drive.

He was helped by the slight slope towards the road, and he was soon safe among the cool shadows of the pine trees at the bottom of the front garden.

Dimly, in the distance away to his left, he could hear the first high notes of fire engines. Coming too late. There would be nothing that they or anyone else could do now.

He couldn't be sure whether he was imagining it, or whether the eastern sky really was showing the slightest signs of paling. There didn't seem to be enough breath left to get the rest of the way. A speckle of blue light showed the first engine was nearly on him. Using the last of his energy, he tugged the Harley into the side of the road, into the shadows.

Screaming like a wounded dinosaur, headlights ripping the black into tatters, the scarlet fire engine roared past him. Now was the time. While everyone was listening to that din, and people were shouting and running around. Now was the time when there might be a chance that they wouldn't notice the note of a single motor-cycle, idling away down the lane.

When he swung his leg over the saddle, the stab of pain nearly made him vomit. It felt as though there was a lot of broken bits of bone floating around inside his chest, ripping at his lungs.

One last stroke of luck came his way. The road down to the right, towards the white cottage, was almost entirely downhill. It was easy to get her rolling, and slip in the gear. Despite its week's neglect, it caught first time, and he felt the familiar vibration running up his thighs from the powerful engine.

Behind him, the noise and light faded away. It seemed to him that it had all been some kind of weird dream. As he grew weaker, the last shreds of the scopolamine fought their way back to the surface, taking over his mind. Bringing in the phantoms of the past, to ride along with him.

His lips moved: 'To market, to market, to kill the fat pig; home again, home again, home again, home again...'

It seemed as though all the old brothers were there, urging him along that half mile of deserted country road. To the left was Brenda, a tender smile on her face, her long hair blowing free in the wind. Priest, unknowable emotions in that saturnine face, with good old Kafka at his elbow.

The hog rocked from side to side, clipping the long grass at the edge of the lane. In his weariness and weakness, Gerry almost went past the gate to the house. But, he blinked open and skidded to a halt.

It was getting lighter.

Like the mist on a summer river, the ghosts of the past left him, and he was alone. The gate stood open, and he merely had to wheel the hog gently through, and lay it down on the trim front lawn.

As he laid the bike down, he toppled forward on his face, lying there in the coolness, feeling the wetness of the dew on his cheeks. He felt very tired, and there no longer seemed to be a good reason why he should ever bother to get up again.

There was the sound of a door opening.

Footsteps.

First on a path, then muffled by grass.

Although it took an enormous effort, he opened his eyes, seeing a pair of feet near his head. He felt a hand, or hands, softly turning him over. An exclamation of shock, quickly cut short.

There was a face looking down at him. A face he knew. Gerry smiled at it.

'Hello Rupert. I've come back for that job you talked about.'

Beyond him, the first light of the rising sun peered over the Shropshire hills, gleaming off the polished chrome of the Harley Davidson.

Gerry saw it.

And closed his eyes.

18. A RESTLESS FAREWELL

This poem, based on Shelley's *Adonaïs*, appeared in *The Times* newspaper in the mid-summer of 1999, signed with the initials R.C., and headed simply *For The Friends Of G.V.*

Peace, peace! He is not dead, he does not sleep.
He has awakened from the dream of life.
While we, who slowly walk our weary road
Must journey on without the hope of light.
For he is resting from this caverned world,
Alone, we travel on without him now
And deeper seems our solitary dark.
But, when he wishes, he will come again,
Rejoicing with us, while our grey again turns green.

Who mourns, who mourns for this single rider?
His last great run, alone, was for us all.
So now, a'wearied at the end of day
He lays him down and slips into his rest,
Like a young diver, into cool, green depths,
Plunges from the noisesome, sad old world.
Take care, for he will watch you where you ride
And come to join you, laughing at your side.
Above us, a free hawk bursts the chains from the sky.

CREATION BOOKS should be available from all proper bookstores.
Ask your bookseller to order titles using the above ISBN numbers.
Titles should be ordered from:
COMBINED BOOK SERVICES, 406 Vale Road, Tonbridge, Kent TN9 1XL
Tel: 0732-357755 Fax: 0732-770219.
CREATION BOOKS are represented in Europe & the UK by:
ABS, Suite 1, Royal Star Arcade, High Street, Maidstone, Kent ME14 1JL.
Tel: 0622-764555 Fax: 0622-763197.
CREATION BOOKS are distributed in the USA by:
INLAND BOOK COMPANY, 140 Commerce Street, East Haven, CT 06512.
Tel: 203-467-4257.
CREATION BOOKS are distributed in Australia & NZ by:
PERIBO PTY LTD, 26 Tepko Road, Terrey Hills, NSW 2084.
Tel: 02-486-3188 Fax: 02-486-3036
CREATION BOOKS are distributed in Canada by:
MARGINAL, Unit 103, 277 George Street, N. Peterborough, Ontario K9J 3G9
Tel/Fax: 705-745-2326.

Our full mail order catalogue is available on request.
Please enclose a large stamped, self-addressed envelope
or 2 IRCs.